TWIN WORLDS

First Contact - The Long-Held Dream

Richard Arthur

Published by: R A Walton

Email: publisher@rawalton.co.uk

The characters and events portrayed in this book are fictitious. Some individuals have been influenced by historical figures from Earth but as denizens of an alien planet their characteristics are entirely fictitious. Otherwise any similarity to real persons, living or dead, is coincidental and not intended by the author.

Published by R A Walton

Email: publisher@rawalton.co.uk

Cover design and illustration: Philip Bannister

ISBN: 978-1-9196529-0-0

To the women in my life,

Audrey, Jackie, Helen, Mary and Jackie

Table of Contents

Foreword

When I was seven I wanted to be a spaceman. Like many of my generation I was brought up on Dan Dare and the Mekon and the lost planet of Hesikos. I wanted to be a scientist and travel to Venus and meet aliens. Venus rather than Mars intrigued me, it seemed so like Earth. In the 1950s we didn't know much about Venus and it still seemed distinctly possible that there would be life there.

My disappointment when scientists discovered such facts about Venus as its rotation period and surface temperature was huge. There would be no treens, and Mars was not Barsoom.

Later in life I could become hooked on Dr Who, on Star Trek and Star Wars, and on the Foundation. But Einstein had pretty well ruined deep space travel, forcing authors to invent unlikely work-arounds to circumvent light's speed limit. Don't speed limits take the fun out of life?

These considerations drove my need to come up with worlds that would enable the meeting of alien civilisations. There were just two problems, the physics of two comfortable worlds in the Goldilocks zone remains problematic, and I hated writing.

Not the stringing together of words into sentences and paragraphs, but the physical pain of putting my scrawl on paper. I became a mathematician because at school you didn't write essays in Mathematics. I always wrote untidily and slowly and got ink everywhere. It helped my memory as a child because I was always way behind the teacher during dictation exercises. Creative writing bored me because my thoughts outran my pen. A reverse speed limit, I craved to catch up with the speed of thought. I was convinced that I would never write any story that I imagined, and my twin worlds would stay locked in my head for ever.

Then some genius invented the word processor.

Still I hesitated. Work got in the way. Then, after retirement, I found I was even busier. And anyway I had made the mistake of learning more physics. Would tidal locking or the three body problem make my worlds impossible? Would Geos strip the atmosphere from Duplos? Fitting two inhabitable planets into a small bit of space is less straight forward than it seems. I wanted my worlds to be physically possible, even if a bit unlikely. I struggled a bit. Classical applied maths was never my forte.

Covid-19's third lockdown gave me my chance. I determined to give it a go, and to my own astonishment have stuck with it. It is for you, the reader, to determine whether I was right to do so.

Do have a look at my website.

www.richardarthur.uk

I have put a fuller set of appendices there as a free download. I shall also give more background information about the worlds and their peoples from time to time, as well as news of the sequels I've already started writing. Maybe I'll even persuade Arté or one of the others to write the occasional blog.

Richard Arthur

Worcestershire UK, July 2021

Maps

1. Duplos: Isla & The Western Federation

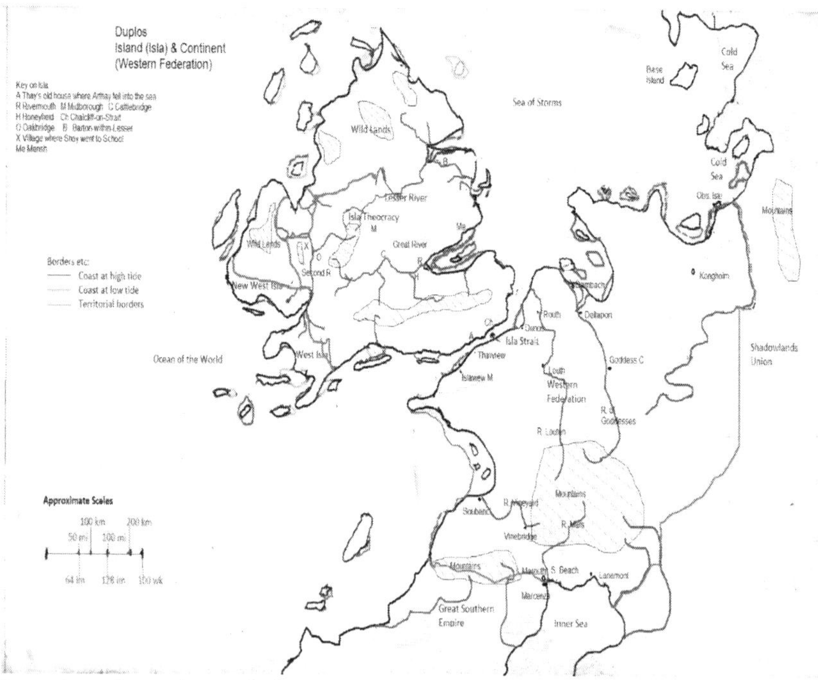

Map showing Isla and the Western Federation. The scale on the bottom left marks 50 miles, 64 imiles, 100 km, 100 miles, 128 imiles, 200 km, 100 walks. A4 versions of all three maps are available (free) from my webpage.

2: Observatory Island

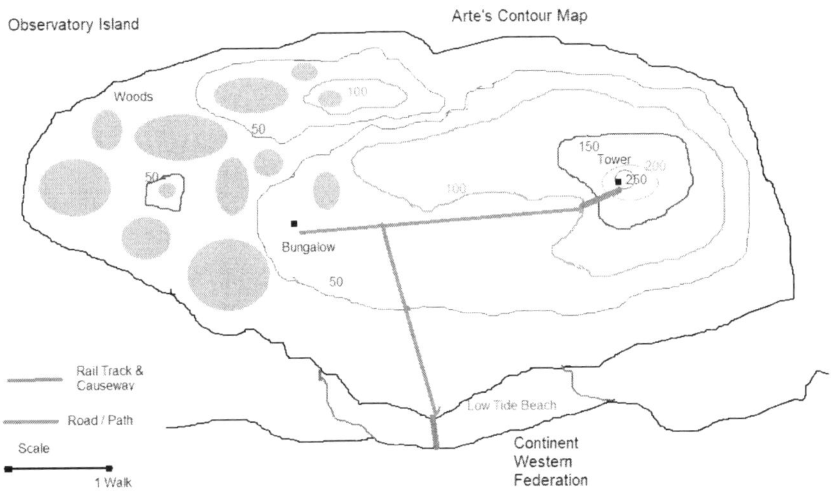

Arté's Contour Map

This is an island off the Western Federation connected via causeway over a low-tide beach. The contours are at 50 stride intervals. The map shows the roads connecting the bungalow, tower and causeway with Arté's rail track up the slope to the tower. The scale line on the bottom left of the map is 1 walk.

3: Kongholm and the NE Coast

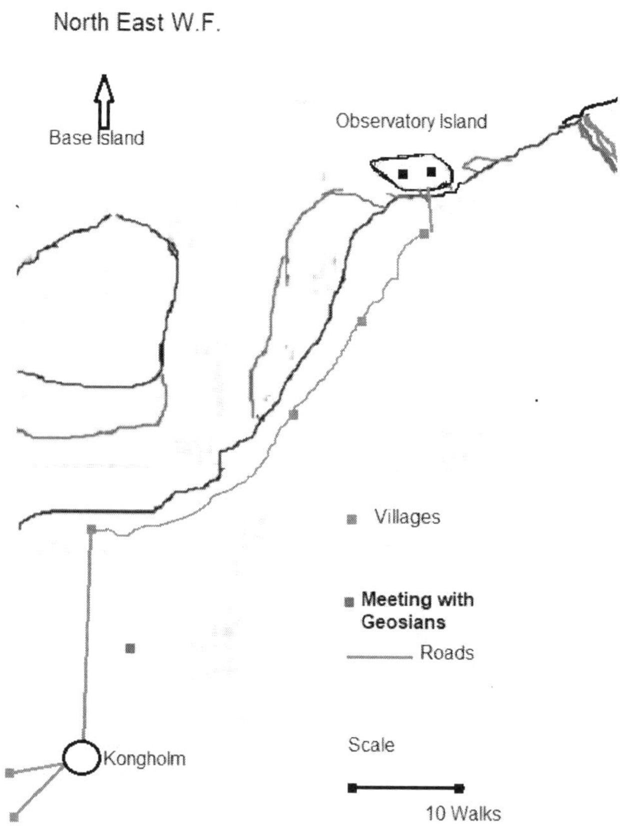

This map shows where the first meeting of Geosians and Duplosians took place. The scale (bottom right) indicates 10 walks.

Part 1

Duplos

2 First Contact

1

The beach Islaview Market, Western Federation

"So this is what it's like to be dead" was the first thought to enter Arthay's head. He was lying naked on a beach and just coming to consciousness after the ordeal that he had expected to kill him.

His second thought was "Goddess! I'm hurting." Then, as his senses de-blurred, he noticed a group of young women, aged around fifteen if he was not mistaken. They were pointing at him while chattering away amid their giggles. He wondered, "are these some of Nepa's handmaids? and will I be taken to meet her?" He couldn't understand what the girls were saying but it was sort of recognisable as speech - the language of the Goddesses?

Then, suddenly, just as his head was beginning to clear, an old man arrived on the scene, "over sixty, anyway" he thought. This man shooed the girls away, again using the strange language, but then spoke to Arthay in proper talk albeit with a funny accent that sounded a bit dated. "Hello," the man said, "you are very lucky, it is most unusual for anyone to survive what you've just been through. And your bump in unmutilated - almost unheard of on this beach. By the way, I survived the same experience 32+8 years ago, landing on Dunos beach which is why I speak Islish. I was Eshaw on Isla but here I am called Esau. Let me help you up."

"Thanks for your help, I'm called Arthay. I'm a bit disorientated. I suppose I'm not dead then and those girls are not Nepa's maidens. I thought this place was supposed to have been uninhabited since the separation. Who are they anyway and how come they seem to obey you, do men give orders to women over here?"

"Oh they are just silly schoolgirls on a skive," responded Esau, "and making somewhat lewd remarks at your expense, I'm afraid, teenage girls being what they are. But no, we don't command women here any more than on Isla. However, one of my jobs is to patrol the beach and dispose of corpses and debris washed up. Currents in the strait deposit all sorts of stuff from Isla here. Those girls knew that I was within my responsibilities and their mothers and mistresses would back me up. They would end up in trouble if there was a fuss. Generally, women remain very much our superiors and get to control much of our lives but they don't own us in quite the same way as on Isla. We enjoy some rights, so in many ways we men are much freer here. But don't over-estimate our position. For example, we have a basic legal right to refuse sex, but it takes a brave, or foolhardy, man to push his luck when faced with an insistent mistress. Not that I get bothered that much any more. In your case I suspect you might have to keep that particular 'right' to yourself, and just lie back and enjoy it, as we used to say on Isla."

"I can see that I have a lot to learn about life here. I like the idea of not belonging to anyone, but I guess it's a bit more complicated than that. What happens to me now? I've got no clothes and I don't speak the language. I don't even really know where 'here' is. I'm going to need a lot of help." Arthay was somewhat bemused, realising that his life experience to date was going to be of little value in guiding his future.

"That's OK, part of my job is to give you that help," said Esau. "The village here is Islaview Market, named thus because of the view over the strait and, that the village holds a periodic market for a cluster of several smaller villages, because the nearest towns are some distance away. Additional to the immediate cliff top area above the beach, the main part of the village is about two hundred strides[1] inland sorry 128 and then another 64 - about 128 short of 1024 people live in the village which makes it nearly as big as some towns. As for the rest, you'll come and live with me for a bit while we see to your basic needs and education until you've learned enough of the language and customs to integrate into our life here."

"That's very kind of you, I don't suppose you get very many people washed up here. Do you have books written in Islish that I can study?"

"It's very rare to get anyone alive this far down the strait, and the few I've heard of have been sacrificial victims, even the corpses. You're most unusual being still in tact. My cottage is not far from the beach, we'll be more comfortable there."

As they walked to Esau's cottage, they continued the conversation. "Do I gather you can read and write?" said Esau, that is quite unusual for a man on Isla and could make quite a difference to your value and hence your future prospects. There are no books written in Islish. Perhaps you being here will help change that."

"There are three beaches on this coast where flotsam from Isla might end up. Islaview is the middle one. Non-sacrificial survivors like me normally only turn up on Dunos beach about 128 Isla miles up-current, or 64 walks as we say on the continent, near the start of the strait and before the extreme race of the narrows. Usually these are fishermen whose vessels have been swept out of the Great River estuary and lasted long enough for a lucky sailor to cling on to enough wreckage to keep him afloat until thrown on to the shore at a tide that is sufficiently low to expose enough beach to land on. That's what happened to me

1 Details of the various measures used on the planets in this book, including conversions between them and the Earth's metric and British imperial units can be found in Appendix 3.

forty years ago. Then there's Cape Beach North, which is a very long beach covering about 32 walks downstream from around the next headland. I've never heard of anyone getting that far alive."

When they reached the cottage, Esau made sure that Arthay was comfortable, before outlining the plans for his stay. "First things first, I see that you need a bit of patching up from the abrasions you have suffered while in the strait. As well as getting you fed, clothed and rested, while you are with me you will sleep and eat here. Looking after you in these early days is my job and I will be paid enough to buy your food and clothing. The latter will be a little difficult. You're much too big to fit into anything of mine or indeed any off-the-peg male outfits. I'll get a tailor to adapt some women's clothing patterns to provide something suitable for you. Don't worry, I see your frown, you won't be dressed like a woman, that would cause a rumpus. By the way, how tall are you? I've never seen a man as big as you, nor that many women come to think of it!"

Arthay answered, "just under half a smidge over two strides, and I too have not yet met a man as tall as me. Thay and her twin sister Shay were my height and they were also considered tall even for women."

"That'll be Isla strides of course, the continental stride is a bit longer by about three quarters of a thumb, so over here you are about 1.95 strides, sorry a bit under two. I'll definitely need to get a specialist tailor. As to your education, the first imperative is to learn the language and then a bit about the way of life. The expectation is that it should take five or six periods for you to acquire a sufficient knowledge of the language to work as a general labourer and the governing council would then sell your contract for such work to recover the outlay on your education. However if you show such promise that you could undertake more valuable work, which since you are already literate, I suspect might be the case, your education could be extended to include more advanced material. They might well continue to fund you for up to a couple of selenths as your contract would then be that much more valuable to them. I was illiterate when I arrived here and it took me ten years before I could read and write our language - which we rather arrogantly call Contish as if we spoke the only language on the continent. This territory is part of what is termed the Western Federation which is a loose alliance of territories with fairly common values and culture. To the South and East of the Federation lie the territories of the Great Southern Empire and The Shadowlands Union[2] but they are far away and I have never visited either, nor have I met a Southerner or a Shadowlander."

After they'd eaten, Esau showed Arthay around his cottage, it had been built about two hundred years earlier. Its construction was timber frame with wattle and daub walls and was a little larger than might be usual for a single person of modest means.

"Nice house," commented Arthay. "A lot of accommodation for a man on his own."

"Well some years ago I earned a substantial bonus, I'll tell you about it sometime later. It's quite a long story. Anyway, it enabled me to semi-retire and buy this place. When I moved in, the council were keen for me to take on my present job, beachwarden they call it, and agreed to pay for an extension of an extra bedroom and study/schoolroom to the original two up two down cottage. The ceilings are a bit low by modern standards, especially upstairs. I have no problems as I have few visitors, let alone tall women in my bedroom. But you'd have to stoop in the upstairs rooms. However I'll put you in the bedroom in the extension, which is single story and has 8.6 length ceilings

2 The territories are often abbreviated to WF, GSE and SU respectively.

which will leave you with eight divisions of headroom. Oh, I forgot, our length is slightly longer than Isla's, still a quarter of a stride, and we divide it into ten divisions rather than thumbs and smidges."

True to his word, Esau managed to source some suitable clothes for Arthay, who after a long sleep and rest for the remainder of the period, found himself ready to begin his lessons. Esau arranged a timetable for each period with the first and third phases devoted to Contish with short breaks for exercise during which the pair discussed all manner of things, with Arthay bringing Esau up to date with events on Isla and Esau telling his life history to Arthay. Then the second and fourth phases were devoted to other areas of study to include continental history, natural philosophy and culture.

"There are are several languages spoken in the Federation but Contish is the dominant one, being understood in most places and spoken throughout almost all the western half of the federation. Further East other languages become more common, but educated people all speak and understand sufficient Contish to conduct business affairs and partake of cultural activities, so Contish will be enough for you."

"Right, I've mastered the different variants of Islish spoken in West Isla and Marches which are sufficiently different to almost count as new languages."

As he got into his studies Arté progressed quickly.

"If you look at it the right way there seem to be several common grammatical roots with Islish and some subtle phonetic shifts that give clues to the meanings and pronunciation of new words, I find this quite intriguing," he remarked to Esau once they had begun to look at the written language. "I can often work out new words from these clues. Writing in the Contish alphabet is both more flexible and, in a different sense simplified and much shorter, compared to Islish."

"Well, I never learned to read and write Islish so I don't know anything about that."

"Oh, letters in Islish have very linear forms, suited to scratching on bark or stones whereas this alphabet contains more rounded shapes better designed for pen and paper. Also several sounds can be represented by letter sequences. In Islish we have many more consonants for such sounds as sh, th and pr. Similarly, you represent vowel sounds more easily in the Contish writing which I guess explains some of the more nuanced expression in Contish."

"What you say about the vowel sounds is true but Contish speakers have difficulty with some Islish consonants like sh and th, and will stumble over your name. They use 'th' in writing but don't pronounce it, for example the cities Routh and Louth are pronounced Root and Loot. Hence my name change to Esau. You might consider something similar."

"Yes, that's easy. After all if I no longer belong to Thay a change makes perfect sense, I shall become Arté."

Arté's education proceeded apace and shortly Esau took him to meet the local council to determine his immediate future. After an interview and some tests they were ushered in to the mayor's office.

"Esau, you have done well with Arté's initial education into our ways and we agree your recommendation that it is worth continuing further before looking for a contract. Come back at the end of the selenth and we'll look again." Addressing herself to Arté she continued. "We have been most impressed by your progress. You have passed the oral Contish exam with flying colours and grasped the essential legalities and cultural facets much more thoroughly than expected. As I'm sure Esau has explained we don't get many survivors this far south and all cases I know of have been sacrificial victims who have suffered a bumpdectomy and we need to understand your status. I hope you were not too embarrassed by the physical examination, and I apologise for some of my colleagues. I'm sure you understand we women can get a bit over-excited at the sight of a good bump and I must say yours is the most impressive I've ever seen. If I were twenty years younger...."

Arté was conditioned to know his place as a slave to female requirements and had no expectation of consideration in such matters, "I'm sure there is no need for an apology for a woman's natural feelings, I am most grateful for the opportunity you are giving me."

"Back to the main point. These exams you've taken are generally used as citizen's tests for emigrants from the GSE, most of whom are escaped slaves. As someone from Isla you automatically qualify for citizenship by the strange quirk that the Western Federation claims sovereignty over Isla. You've even passed the literacy exam which we only set you as an indicator of progress. It's possible we'll want to extend for a further selenth with a tutor from the district college to cover additional mathematics and natural philosophy. Esau tells me you call the latter natural theology on Isla but what it has to do with a parcel of mythological Goddesses is beyond me."

2

Esau's story as told to Arté: The Great River, Isla & Dunos - Islaview

"I was born Efray. My mother Frayna farmed a smallholding on a cliff overlooking the northern shore of the Great River estuary about an imile from the village of Mensh. One of the local worthies there was a woman called Shawna whose interests included a small fishing fleet, actually four boats that worked the lower river and Estuary waters. I was not seen as having a very promising future. My short stature, while not all that far below average, was such that I would be unlikely to be attractive to a well-to-do farmer either sexually or as a worker. Accordingly the only land-based owner I might find would likely be dirt-poor and the best I might have hoped for was as a slave-of-all-work eking out a bare subsistence. As Mum told me bluntly on my sixteenth birthday: 'Your bump wouldn't satisfy a sex-starved spinster on drugs, let alone a respectable woman with a decent holding, nor are you much use as a worker.' However on shipboard my stature was a help rather than a hindrance and Shawna had no need for additional sexual dalliance, being well supplied in that department. Accordingly I was sold to Shawna in a deal that satisfied Mum on both our accounts. Two periods after my sixteenth birthday I left to become Shawna's slave, Eshaw, an apprentice fisherman in the Great River Estuary.

For the first few selenths I learnt my craft on the Great River itself. I did well and, as well as fishing, I undertook transport between the towns of Rivermouth and Cattlebridge, and for a selenth even ran a ferry service between the banks just where the estuary begins to widen to the East of Rivermouth. After that, Shawna decided I should start to learn the craft of negotiating the waters of the Estuary with its treacherous sandbanks and difficult currents.

Shawna was ambitious and wanted to expand her business to include transport of goods across the estuary and decided to attempt a crossing from the North bank to the South right at the mouth. Well, those of us with experience know that is crazy and the captains tried as they might to dissuade her. Not that she would have been in any personal danger of course. As I'm sure you know women rarely risk themselves on salt water."

"No," agreed Arté. "That's why the Goddess gave them men to be their slaves and do their bidding. We men, after all are pretty expendable. We are not needed to carry and care for the future generation. Our part in new life is quickly over, fun of course, but not really needed afterwards. There's plenty of fish in the sea as the priestesses in Oakbridge used to put it during my childhood. That's why it is only right and proper that women should send men to take the physical risks, while the women looked after the political, economic and religious life of the theocracy. And that's additional to the general theological concern about sending women to Nepa."

"Right, although at the time I didn't know about the theology bit, apart from actual sacrifices of women to Nepa being forbidden. Anyway the upshot was that, at the age of twenty-three I went as first mate to a somewhat third rate captain. Shawna briefed me carefully and made it clear that her trust was in me. I was promised that on return I would replace the captain who would be transferred to less arduous duties.

Perhaps if that transfer had happened before the voyage, things might have turned out differently, but probably not. Captain Urshaw's incompetence certainly contributed, but the freak wave, just as the ship was about to turn in at the South cape of the estuary, would almost certainly have defeated anyone including me. Be that as it may, the ship was swept out to sea and, spinning out of control, was dragged towards the funnel that is the opening of the strait.

Several hands were lost overboard in those first few imins. Urshaw went into a blue funk and headed down to his cabin. I gave the order for all remaining hands to lash themselves to something solid and pray for Nepa's mercy. I then managed to tie the wheel to prevent it moving and secured myself to the foremast.

It seemed like an eternity, but I think it was actually only about an ihor before the ship began to break up. Urshaw certainly drowned in his cabin. I was swept clear of the sinking ship and somehow held on to life until eventually I and the remains of my mast were tossed on to Dunos beach. Two of my shipmates also ended up on the beach. But when, eventually, I was able to stagger to my feet and go to examine them I found I was too late. One had certainly drowned before hitting the beach. The other was still alive when I reached him but was badly injured with a gash in his head and a broken leg in addition to being half-drowned. I remember holding his hand to comfort him while he coughed out his last breath about a quarter of an ihor[3] after I reached him.

At first I just sat there for a while, numb with grief, loneliness, fear and despair. All we had been taught told me that this land was uninhabited. Certainly there was plant-life and there were birds. Perhaps there were animals. But surely when Nepa tore Isla from Lana, thousands of years ago, she also destroyed Lana's people. That's what Frayna had taught me. That's what the priestesses taught me in school. They hadn't taught me to read and write, that was not seen as necessary for the son of a poor

3 See Appendix 3 on measurements: an ihor (Isla hour) is about 1.125 Earth hours

farmer, but they had drilled me carefully in basic theology. And had I not now experienced first hand the rage of Nepa!

However I was confused. Why had Nepa spared my life? What could I do here on my own. I couldn't repopulate the land. I'd need a woman for that, probably several. I could see no point in remaining alive. Did Nepa expect me to throw myself into her arms back in the sea? Well, I wasn't going to do that. Bugger Nepa, "d'you hear that, Nepa?" I shouted to the sea. "Bugger you! You've murdered my friends and my Captain. Even though he was an incompetent idiot, he was still my captain and I was going to inherit his ship when he returned to gentler duties on the river."

My zest for life had won. I decided I was going to live. I was going to fight for life, even if I had to bugger every Goddess in creation. I remember thinking "Hey, Blasphemy is fun, it makes you feel good. No wonder the poxy priestesses rile against it so much." Despite the death and despair, I was alive! I had never felt more alive. I felt the sun came out from behind a cloud. I was going on an adventure.

That accounts for my life on Isla and how I got here."

"It must have been a shock to you," responded Arté. "I look forward to you telling me more about what happened to you here, since that might teach me a lot about what to expect."

The next phase Esau continued his history.

"I explored the beach looking for a way off it into the interior, which I needed to do p.d.q. as I was sure the beach was growing narrower. I moved quickly towards the towering cliffs of Dunos. I didn't know they were the cliffs of Dunos but moved towards them anyway. I spotted a rill crossing the sands and pebbles that made up the beach. It emerged through a narrow gap in the cliff face. It was a bit of a scramble but after about half an ihor I was standing on top of the cliff. I could make out the white cliffs of Isla between twenty and twenty-five imiles distant across the strait. So short a distance, on land I could walk it in about two to three ihors. But over that inhospitable strait it was worse than 1024[4] miles. When I turned inland, to my utter amazement I saw houses. I stopped, closed my eyes, took three deep breaths, then opened them again. Yes, those were definitely dwellings. I reasoned they couldn't be relics from before the separation. Anything built and abandoned that long ago would have decayed into ruin before now. So there must be inhabitants after all. Bloody Nepa did not succeed in destroying the world. Isla is not alone, just cut off.

I strode into the village and encountered a woman who started to question me in an incomprehensible tongue. I was not educated, but not stupid either. I knew that the Islish in the Marches, while not completely incomprehensible, was not quite the same as in the Theocracy. I realised that people with no contact with Isla wouldn't speak or understand my language. So I set upon trying to explain with signs that I had come from Isla, been taken by the Sea Goddess and deposited on the beach over the cliff edge. The woman seemed to understand. After all, the people of Dunos were used to occasional corpses ending up on their beach and even that, every so often, one turns up alive. She seemed pleased and slightly surprised that I appeared to be in such good shape. But what she did next caught me completely off guard."

"What did she do?"

"She grabbed my trousers and pulled them down. She then carefully examined me, even rubbed my bump a bit. Satisfied,

4 His actual islish word literally translates as 'the tenth double' but I shall use 1024 in figures as that's easier to read.

she smiled, pulled my trousers back up and beckoned me to follow her.

The truth is that while nearly all the accidental victims of the strait landing on the Federation's beaches finish up on Dunos, they are still heavily outnumbered by the sacrificial victims. And, as you know, victims properly sacrificed are first mutilated by bumpdectomy. Cara, as was her name, had examined me to see if I was in tact. The discovery that I was delighted her. For, that being the case, I was more valuable - despite me being on the small side. In consequence her bounty for retrieving me would be enhanced."

"Yeah, the girls do like a bump, as I know only too well."

"But size definitely matters, and unlike yours, mine is quite small and I've never been in much demand, either on Isla or here. By the way they have an official posh philosophical name for the bump over here, a protopenis. You must be much more experienced in the ways of girls than I am."

"Oh yes, I was pretty big even as a teenager and the younger priestesses in the order that owned me could be quite crude at times. Although we do get some enhanced pleasure from the loose skin on the bump being rubbed during sex it really seems to be all about female pleasure. Thay told me that it touches absolutely the right spot on them and multiplies the power of their orgasm considerably, which is why they crave it so much."

"Yes I've heard that some girls try to keep on even after your real penis has completely given up, sometimes with disastrous consequences for the man, not that I've ever had such an experience."

"That's true, and I have sometimes been made a bit sore, but I have been threatened with worse. At least I escaped the bumpdectomy before I went into the strait. That is said to be painful in the extreme."

"Yes it is, I have met one or two victims here among the castaways and learnt of their experience. You'll be glad to know the operation is illegal in the Western Federation but until about a hundred years ago it was used as a mode of torture or punishment for serious crimes, like treason, prior to execution."

"Lets just be glad that neither of us have suffered this fate. Please continue with your account. I want to know how you ended up as beachwarden in Islaview Market."

"After the Dunos council had examined me and paid Cara her bounty, I was sent to stay with an Islish speaker where I was taught enough Contish to get by and changed my name to Esau. The council then contracted me to work on a road-building project. After three years the contract ended and I was free to seek my own destiny. In reality all this meant was that I could negotiate the sale of my own contract."

"I guess your life must have been quite hard at first."

"Yes it was, but my command of Contish improved and my knowledge of continental culture grew. I worked diligently and it paid off. After about ten years I managed to learn to read and write and understand basic arithmetic with the continental system. This enabled me to get better contracts which gave me more money and, more importantly, opportunity to undertake other activities. The Dunos council gave me occasional employment when a castaway appeared, both as interpreter and educator.

Every now and then I was sought out by an academic as part of her studies into ancient history or philology or some such. There are some academics that are interested in Islish and what they can learn of Island culture. There is even talk that some remote college in the middle of the Federation wants to offer a course in Islish studies."

"How extraordinary, I find that quite amusing."

"Actually, I have become well known in some academic circles and also, I believe, well-liked. I even had a sexual relationship with one academic, admittedly somewhat past her youth, and unusually short. This lasted on - and - off for a couple of years before she returned to her native district in the central part of the Federation. When she left, she thought she might be pregnant, so, somewhere, I might have a son or daughter. Not that I was ever informed of the birth, which is perfectly normal on the Continent just as on Isla."

"Isn't it strange how it is assumed that we men have no concerns regarding children other than the act of procreation itself. I suspect I may have fathered some children at Thay's bidding but I have never been told. However she did tell me that she herself was hoping to get pregnant from our last encounter."

"Now let me tell you about my biggest coup while at Dunos, the source of my wealth. Ten years ago I retrieved a female castaway. Such a thing has never happened before. Not even a female corpse. We've already chatted about the reluctance of women to go to sea and not just because of safety. While it's not actually forbidden, it is strongly discouraged by most priestesses.

Anyway in this case a young and rather wild woman called Crayza had a mighty ding-dong with her older sister, Craya. Their mother took the sister's side and threw Crayza out of the house. Having nowhere to live and not wanting to leave Rivermouth where rents are sky-high she acquired the lease of a boat. I think she got the money by seducing a well-bumped young man and then offering him up to a few wealthy acquaintances in return for cash, or something along those lines. I told you she was wild.

Indeed the dispute with her sister was on account of her seduction of a young man their mother had bought as a coming-of-age present for the sister! Anyway at a later time she spirited the same young man on to her boat for a steamy session and to get more revenge on said sister. When mother and sister appeared with the law in tow she cast off and carried the youth out to sea with her."

"The name Craya sort of rings a bell with me, she's related to Thay but I don't really remember much about her."

"Crayza sailed along the estuary's south bank which is easier for going out to sea than the north and managed to round the cape where I had come to grief. All this time the youth was terrified and only refrained from jumping overboard in the estuary because (a) he couldn't swim, (b) he was scared of Crayza and (c) he was even more scared of her sister, his legal owner, and especially their mother. In this last he undoubtedly had a sufficient reason to take his chances on board. Cray, the mother, was a prominent figure in Rivermouth society, and, as you know, Rivermouth is the largest and most important town in the Theocracy. Cray could and probably would have ensured that the young Orcray would feature as Nepa's next sacrifice.

Orcray didn't jump. He hunched on the deck, moaning to himself until they reached the open sea when he started to be sick. To be fair Crayza did pretty well even for a seasoned sailor, let alone a complete novice. But her plan to turn to port and sail up the coast to the Lesser River was doomed from the start. The currents in the stormy sea won't let you do that. You might just get away with going in the other direction North-South, Lesser - Great, but I don't know of any experienced sailor who would risk it. The attempt to drive to port probably avoided the immediate hazard of the South cape and I reckon she must have got a lot further into the funnel of the strait than I had done before her boat fell apart. Crayza remained in possession of her faculties and battled hard to steady the boat. When she realised all was lost she managed to secure herself to something that would float well and went overboard clear of the wreckage. Cray was carried off by a passing wave and drowned. But the tide was low and Crayza was actually quite close to Dunos beach. She came ashore, dusted herself down and set off down the beach where she ran in to me.

I was awarded a massive bounty for Crayza. She now lives in Louth, the chief city in the Western Federation and about fifty walks from Dunos. We still keep in touch, mainly by letter.

After completing Crayza's education I decided it was time to settle down on my own account. I was then fifty-three years old. I had just one selenth left on my contract and I decided not to renew but bought this cottage in Islaview, and the local governing council were pleased to welcome me. And that's about it."

"I can't imagine that coping with Crayza was easy," chuckled Arté. "Young women can be quite a handful especially among the Islish upper classes, brought up to consider men her slaves as they are."

"Too right, to say that spending a selenth guiding such a headstrong eighteen year old is gruelling, is one of the world's great understatements. At least Crayza had no desire to seduce me but at first she led me a merry dance. But she's a very bright girl and came to realise that I was actually her passport to a glittering future. Then she knuckled down to hard work and, we became great friends. Indeed she has become like a daughter to me.

I am now completely at ease with myself and my life, and my fishing is limited to low tide from the beach or some local trout streams that I know.

As far as I am concerned my accident was the best thing that ever happened to me and I am prepared to go on saying 'Bugger You' to any Goddess that crosses my path."

3
Arté 's progress: Islaview Market to Routh

By all historical precedents, Arté's progress was impressive. The revelation of the decimal place number system caught his imagination like nothing before. Back on Isla he had been pretty competent at calculation. He had even privately discovered ways of multiplying numbers other than by repeated doubling and drew up some tables to aid him. However he lacked the vocabulary and notation to take his ideas further. Nevertheless it was quite a feat, as anyone who has attempted multiplication or division in Roman numerals could attest.

When he had spoken to Thay about his methods, she had grown quite angry and positively forbad him to pursue such matters. She had reason, there were orders of priestesses who learnt and applied such methods, but strict secrecy was observed and such knowledge was forbidden to men.

Thay herself was a member of an extremely exclusive and elite order at the heart of the theocracy who had arithmetical methods streets ahead of the common culture. While this did not extend to a full place number system it was basically a base eight system of arithmetic, yielding both nomenclature and calculation algorithms for base eight arithmetic. Of the symbols used in the everyday Islish number system, a set of eight were chosen to represent the numbers one to eight. Dots were used to increase values by powers of eight. This way they could easily represent the numbers they wanted and perform the basic operations of addition, subtraction, multiplication and integer division. They didn't have a concept or symbol for zero as a number, nor did they accept the idea of negative numbers. Fractions as we understand them were not part of their system but they did understand the concept of a remainder when a division sum was inexact and some fractional representation by repeated halving. A few of their adepts even took this further and were groping towards a notation for fractions.[5]

All this, Thay knew. She also knew that such secrets were to be closely guarded. Indeed one of the roles of members of her elite order, herself included, was to keep a careful watch over the lesser orders to determine whether any individuals were in danger of uncovering the greater secrets.

When such an individual was identified, she was carefully investigated and if the results of the investigation were seen as positive she was invited[6] to receive promotion to the elite order. Such a promotion would result in wealth and power and was greatly to be desired by any ambitious woman. Those, and there were some, who were not deemed suitable for promotion were not so lucky. At best they might find themselves in a closed religious community with no opportunity for external contact. At worst they would be silenced by other means. For, although sacrifice to Nepa was not an option, the theocracy was quite prepared to deal with female dissension by other lethal means.

Such was the general opinion of the male intellect that Thay did not believe that Arthay could have come up with his ideas unaided. She suspected that an indiscreet girl in one of the lesser orders had revealed things she shouldn't. Thay, herself, wasn't that bothered that Arthay, who was her favourite, knew these things. Also she was tolerant of a certain amount of 'infidelity' on his part as inevitable. Just as long as he kept to the long-established customs in such matters. However, she would be considerably put out if his forbidden knowledge or the fact that

5 Details are unnecessary to follow the narrative, but for the benefit of a reader interested in such abstruse matters there are further details in the free download from the author's website.

6 in the sense of an invitation that cannot be refused.

he possessed such arithmetical capabilities ever became public knowledge - or reached the ears of her peers. Hence her determination to stamp it out there and then.

She also made enquiries to try and find the identity of the supposed transgressor. The fact was, however, that Arthay appeared to be extremely discreet and she drew a complete blank. As a matter of fact, Arthay was pretty good at warding off the attentions of most females, relying quite heavily on Thay's reputation in so doing. Sort of along the lines; "You might be able to give me grief if I don't submit to to you - but nothing like what Thay might do to you if she gets a fit of jealousy."

The practical outcome, was that Thay let the matter drop, but she retained her suspicions and when later events turned the way they did, these suspicions undoubtedly resurfaced and helped seal Arthay's fate.

I see I've indulged in a bit of a digression, a weakness of mine, I confess. This account is complex and we are not yet at the juncture where it is appropriate to describe the events in Arté's history, but need to concentrate on his induction into continental society and journey to his later place in the scientific community. For that, his mathematical progress is indeed important and no digression.

At first Arté had been unsure about the place-value. He had quickly come to see the power of a base system and ten was as good a base as any as far as he could see, but he was used to not having to worry about the order in which symbols were written and it took him a while to instinctively accept that 12 and 21 were totally different numbers, let alone not being the same as 3!

However when considering multiplication he saw the advantage of the place value algorithms. With practice and determination the system soon became second nature to him and thereafter his numerical facility grew by leaps and bounds. What a wonder these continentals had unlocked.

Before long his grasp of arithmetic and geometry exceeded the level achieved by the merely generally educated girl school-leaver. (In other words his maths was better than anyone who hadn't specialised at University - which meant pretty well every one). And he was a man! Moreover, a castaway from Isla. What's more, many councillors thought, he looks like every woman's dream of a bed-mate - not that any continental woman had actually had the experience. Arté had been much too absorbed in his studies for that. True, his Geometry tutor had tried it on but Arté had succeeded in convincing her that a sexual relationship would impede his progress so, please, if she didn't mind too much... Well, she was a kind-hearted woman and not at all unreasonable. She had accepted his rejection with good grace and a wistful smile.

Arté was washed ashore in late Summer and his early education with Esau occupied the Autumn selenth of that year, followed by the later more advanced education with the tutor. Thus it was in early Spring that he had another meeting with the mayor following a council meeting about his future.

"Have a seat Arté," she said. "It's good to see you again. You really are doing well, it's quite unheard of for a man to show such academic promise. The council believe It would benefit us all for you to receive a university education and propose to open negotiations with Routh University on your behalf, if that is agreeable to you."

"I don't know what to say, we don't have universities on Isla so I'm not sure what to expect, but I would really love to continue to study mathematics and natural philosophy. There is so much that you know here on the continent that is new to me.

I find it wonderful that you are giving me such opportunities. I don't know much about Routh either but if you think that is the right place for me I'm sure that is indeed so."

"Universities work on an academic year starting in the first period of the Autumn selenth. The first term finishes one period before the new year which is at mid-winter. There is then a two period break for a new year holiday and then the second term begins, ending at the end of the Spring selenth. If you were female you'd spend three years getting a Bachelor of Arts degree which involves studying a whole range of subjects. Naturally the universities do not accept male undergraduates, let alone award them degrees. But they do run short vocational courses which admit a few male students and they also (for a fee) will provide more tailored tuition for a man with a well-placed woman as sponsor. I anticipate no difficulty in being able to negotiate a suitable package for you for the next academic year."

"That's some way off, what will I be doing in the meantime and what happens to the universities during the Summer selenth?"

"The Summer selenth is taken as a long vacation by students, and staff also take their holidays during that time, as well as pursuing their own research projects. Before you go up we'll employ you here in Islaview on a mixture of clerical and menial work. You can continue to lodge with Esau during this time and keep up some studies with your tutor. Meanwhile, we'll be finalising negotiations with Routh."

The mayor then gave Arté some background about Routh which she said was the chief city in the region. She explained that over the last two centuries Routh had grown from an ancient market town to a modern city, and forty-two years previously had been dignified by the establishment of the University. Routh was situated on the banks of the Louten river, which also flowed through the chief city of Louth. Fifty walks downstream from Routh the Louten emptied into the Isla strait, due north of Dunos. The distance by the road, which Esau had helped to build in his first labouring contract, between Islaview and Routh was about 100 walks (90 walks as the crow flies - "if you could find a crow strong enough to carry you!" She joked). Islaview's academic loyalties are split between Routh and the more prestigious Louth University.

She then added, despite herself being a graduate of Louth, she and the whole council agreed that Routh was the most suitable in his case.

The negotiations went according to plan and Arté was accepted for private tuition with special emphasis on Mathematics and Natural Philosophy. While he was at the University, in addition to helping out with various menial duties, as is normal for scholarship students, Arté would also give some seminars in the Department of Ancient History and Theology to assist one of the professors whose current research interests included Island culture. Arté was pleased to learn that he would receive board and lodging in the University together with a small allowance, similar to that available to undergraduate scholars from poor mothers. It was also made clear to him that at the end of the Spring term, his next contract would still belong to the Islaview council, but they would remit 20% of its value to the University. Arté was assured that this was a highly satisfactory outcome for all concerned and he had no reason to demur. He was very excited about embarking on this next stage of his life.

Arté inspected his rooms at college. He thought they were simple but adequate, he had a bedroom, study, small kitchenette and washroom. The lavatories were in a separate block next to the residence. All-in-all much more comfortable than he felt he had any right to expect. After all, he mused, the residence was designed as appropriate for young women of around twenty years of age, and he was a man in his early thirty's. There wasn't any real regard for his privacy but that was only to be expected. He realised he was better accommodated than was the norm for most men on Isla, or indeed in any of the continental territories. More mature women might have been wary about having a lone man running tame about the place, but young Duplosian women have no such inhibitions, and the general opinion among the undergraduate and postgraduate students was that if he was embarrassed, that was his problem and they didn't care.

Fortunately, Arté was well able to look after himself, and took the teenage banter in his stride. He refused to be intimidated when accosted by groups of tipsy girls urging him "show us your bump" or "come in for quickie" or when a girl points at his middle and says out loud to her companions something like "Whoar I bet his could make you tingle." After a while, he found that his fellow students moderated their behaviour as they became used to his presence among them and learned that such crudities had no effect.

His classes were generally held in small groups, where advanced concepts were introduced and explained. These were then amplified in a more intimate tutorial with his Director of studies, Professor Fermos, with just one other student who introduced herself as Aimée Rastu, and held out her hand to him. He was somewhat taken aback at this and his mouth gaped rather obviously, but he quickly recovered himself and shook the proffered hand while mouthing something like "Pleased to meet you Aimée, I'm called Arté."

Fermos took a deep breath and turned to the girl saying. "Rastu, it is not good etiquette to announce your private appellation, on first acquaintance with a stranger, or indeed to anyone outside your most intimate circle!"

"Oh!" exclaimed Rastu, "but I was told that my tutorial partner should be treated as close family and that we would become like sisters - so I thought...," her words tailed off as she blushed and looked at her toes with embarrassment.

"Well, you thought wrong. Firstly you should have noticed that, tall as he is, Arté is male, and secondly he must be nearly twice your age so there can be no question of you becoming like sisters. Introduce yourself properly."

Rastu sniffed a bit, then recovering her dignity, turned to Arté, bobbed her head in his direction and said "Good Phase, my name is Rastu and I am to be your tutorial partner. I hope we will become friendly towards each other. I apologise for my earlier gaff, I hail from a small remote mountain community near the border with the GSE where almost everyone is family and my manner can be a bit rustic."

Arté found he liked her and felt sorry for her, embarrassed on her behalf even, an entirely novel feeling. He resolved to keep his burning question about her male name until they had a private moment. He smiled and said in what he hoped was a friendly tone. "Good Phase to you Rastu, my name is Arté and I, too am a stranger in these parts. I used to live across the strait on Isla until a freak accident cast me on to a beach just over a year ago and I have a lot to learn about continental etiquette. I very much look forward to working with you and I'm sure we will be on much friendlier terms than any sisters I have ever encountered."

"Well, sit down, the two of you," invited the Professor, motioning them to two chairs on either side of a table which stood in front of a blackboard. She took the seat at the head of the table closest to the board. "As you both know I am Professor Fermos, you will both call me Professor when in this room. On social occasions Rastu you will call me Professor Fermos, while in deference to your age and unique social status, Arté you may call me Fermos. Before we start the proceedings I suppose I ought to give Arté some further explanation. As the population has grown and become more mobile, and some communities have grown large, our supply of names has become too small for useful identification purposes. It is now common for individuals to have two names for better identification. However, while it is obligatory to reveal both names for certain official records, it is customary to reserve knowledge of the full name only to your most intimate circle. And for a woman, that does not include men, apart from a son, a brother or a partner in a long-term and mostly exclusive relationship. While even in those cases, it is the exception rather than the rule. I suppose Rastu that in your community girls are on such terms with full brothers?" Rastu nodded and whispered "and half-brothers and close cousins." Fermos moved her head from side to side and muttered "most improper."

"But then I am a city girl," she continued. "Arté, you have probably been perplexed that Rastu's given name is male, for as I understand it, on Isla all male names begin with a vowel and all female names with a consonant, is that right? Well, here in the Western Federation we mostly follow that convention but not exclusively, so from time to time you might meet a woman with what to you is a male name and, more rarely, a man with a female name, although that is discouraged." Arté nodded and said "yes" in a soft voice. "With private names there is no such convention and a male name is actually quite usual. Most sensible women not only know the identity of their child's father but try to avoid pregnancy from casual encounters, reserving the honour for a man for whom they feel genuine warmth and respect. Sometimes a child's private name reflects that of such a father. However that is enough of this unplanned digression, we have work to get on with."

Professor Fermos got up, turned to the backboard, and began to elucidate the very novel subject of Algebra. "As you will have heard in my lecture just a horum ago, algebra is about abstraction: that is, we abstract and generalise the properties of arithmetic to enable us us to formulate mathematical versions of a problem and thus to develop solutions and algorithms that work in a more general setting, rather than reinventing the method for every particular instance of the values of the numbers in each case, do you understand?"

This was rhetorical she didn't wait for her students to respond but launched into the use of letters to stand for the values of numbers, the conventions of using x and y for unknown values to be discovered and a, b, c etc. for values that would be constant for any given instance of a problem and rules for manipulating expressions. The pace of it all was quite fast and Arté found that he had lots of questions and insights to impart as he engaged fully in discussion with the Professor. Rastu was more timid, unusual for a girl, thought Arté, but she seemed to keep up with the topics under discussion and let Arté take the lead.

Fermos seemed unperturbed by Arté's forward behaviour, indeed she encouraged it and was pleased at his responsiveness. Arté chuckled to himself as he made a comparison between Fermos and Thay. Even though Thay had allowed him some liberties, she would certainly have drawn the line at such precociousness as he had shown with Fermos and, as for taking the lead over a female, that was unforgivable. He should have known his place!

Actually, to be fair, Fermos, troubled by her conscience, took him aside a few periods later to let him know that while in the rarefied academic circles of a University his unmale engagement was right, proper and to be encouraged. As far as she was concerned the sexist[7] attitudes of society in general were archaic. Nevertheless the way of the world was that the man's place was subordinate and Arté should be careful elsewhere. This came as no surprise to Arté. Female superiority was as natural to him as to any other Duplosian. Casting false modesty aside, he did regard himself as superior to most men, all men he had ever met, if truth be said. When feeling boastful he would think 'I'm almost as good as many women'. But he recognised such a thought as totally inappropriate. He was grateful for Fermos' tactful reminder because, while it accorded with his beliefs, he was aware of his foreignness and could easily have been misled by Fermos' treatment of him.

After that first tutorial Arté and Rastu were walking side by side when Arté suddenly recalled his place and his manners and took half a pace backwards. Rastu had been lost in thought while hoping her partner would suggest some social activity like a coffee when Arté's backward movement reminded her that by long-hallowed custom he could not invite her to anything. She was of average height, she - no - he was taller than her, and appeared to her as their natural leader. He also reminded her of her dear late brother Mikos Urdo. She stopped in her tracks, turned and stammered out "w-we are nearly at the café, would you like to stop for a coffee?"

"I would like nothing better," answered Arté. He very much wanted to get to know her better, outside class, if they were to work together successfully.

The coffee meeting was a great success. Rastu told him a great deal about her secluded life in her mountain home, legally

---

7 Naturally she didn't use the exact word sexist. Such a concept would be quite alien to a Duplosian. Nor would Arte have understood it. As far as both of them were concerned Female superiority was just the natural order.

a village, but only just. The total population was only fifty-eight and Rastu knew them all by name, and many by both names. As well as her mother, two aunts and her grandmother lived in the community. Her father lived with her mother and other men in the village included one of the aunts' exes. She had had an older brother by almost six years. As a child she had followed him everywhere and loved him dearly. He was a kind brother who would protect her from some of the older girls when they were being mean and thus she found the whole female superiority thing, while obviously natural, also rather perplexing. Mikos (for she always used his private name to herself) had loved the mountains and the outdoor life. When he reached eighteen he accepted a contract for a company that provided guides for walkers in the mountains, and, it was said, engaged in some smuggling across the border with the GSE Then the winter before last at the age of just twenty-four he was caught in an avalanche while guiding a traveller through the passes into the GSE and died, his frozen body was found when the snows melted in the Spring. Rastu was inconsolable and lost herself in her schoolwork, which she loved, and became more detached from her former girlfriends. The latter had always teased her for being a bit of a swat and preferring her brother's company to chasing more available boys. "Why do you spend so much time with Urdo," they would say, "you can't go rub-dub-dub with him, that would be most improper - but there's a new farmhand contracted to a farm across the valley and we're off to try our luck with him" - or some such nonsense. Rastu would sigh, go home and concentrate on her geometry. She did so well in her exams that she won a scholarship and finished up here in Routh, the first from her village ever to go to University. She was a proper girl, she would occasionally indulge herself with a likeable lad but she wasn't as sex-crazed as so many of her contemporaries. She wouldn't dream of troubling Arté even though he was excessively handsome and she knew girls who would go wild for him. She didn't want any distraction of that sort when studying. What she had hoped for was a study partner who would be a close friend and confidante, who would understand and share her love of mathematics and eagerness to learn, the sister she had never had. "I know you are a male, Arté, but do you think you could be such a friend, more like a brother, not to replace Mikos, nobody could do that, but that friend and confidante." She smiled and then added "not like, but better than a sister. A sister would want me to go out on the razzle with her, and share the odd boyfriend for the night, and I don't really want to do that. You would be much safer."

Actually, this didn't all come out just like that, in that first coffee together, but over several such meetings over coffee, or one of the meals taken together, or just companionable chats over assignments. In all events it was music to Arté's ears. He, too, needed a friend and was wary of mixing sexual dalliance with his work. Also, while he knew that young women could be fun in small doses, they were also very tiring as well as tiresome and, to be honest, plain hard work. He much preferred a woman his own age or older and with a serious side. One who had a good intellect and was prepared to treat him with respect and not as either a menial or a sex toy. Rastu was too young but ticked all the other boxes. He would be delighted for their relationship to grow to that of younger sister or daughter.

Thus the friendship developed as they both wanted, and at the same time they helped each other to come to grips with the novel ideas right at the forefront of mathematical research on Duplos. In Professor Fermos they were indeed fortunate. She was getting on a bit now, sixty if a day, but had been a major contributor to the development of algebraic methods and had made substantial advances in the theory of numbers.

While not having been involved in the development of the subject, Fermos also had a thorough grasp of the brand new theory of co-ordinate geometry, which applied algebraic methods to geometric problems. Rastu really excelled at classical geometry while Arté had less natural geometric intuition. He had after all grown up believing the World was flat and the fact that it was actually a sphere in the sky was astounding. His forte was algebra and when they started linking the geometric shapes to equations he was in his element. They made a good team and marvelled together at the theory of conic sections and the beautiful equations that governed their behaviour. Arté was especially intrigued by the Hyperbola. A curve with two distinct parts, forever separate, a metaphor for Isla and The Continent he mused. He was also puzzled and excited by the concept of infinity. Wow he thought, again hardly surprising for a man whose arithmetic horizons had been bounded by 1024. The ideas of asymptotes and asymptotic behaviour that the hyperbola presaged were just amazing and opened up such realms of possibility. Arté had never been happier.

You shouldn't get the impression that everything went without hitch. One night, just as Arté was considering turning in for a rest, there was a hammering on his door. He opened it to be greeted by a gaggle of not entirely sober girls. They dragged him out saying "come on we're all having a post exam celebration, all students are expected, and that includes you, no excuses accepted; do you have Rastu in there?" Two of the girls dashed into his rooms to search for her, but of course without success. As you are aware, and contrary to undergraduate scuttlebutt, Rastu was not shacked up with Arté. Neither Rastu nor Arté had taken any steps either to confirm or deny the suspicions. It did them no harm to be thought to be in such a relationship and actually provided each of them with a degree of protection from unwanted attentions. However, on this occasion no such consideration would have protected either of them from the drunken mob, who thwarted in plan A were equally prepared to enjoy plan B. Arté was dragged off to the party and plied with drink, probably spiked, and as the night drew on found himself inveigled into more intimate activity.

Somehow he did get back to his own bed, without company, but feeling very sore. When daylight returned he thought he was dying. He had never experienced such a hangover, nor had he previously experienced the demands of so many females. Various forms of group sex were common enough back on Isla, but, possibly because of her high status, Thay had generally preferred a certain amount of privacy and decorum; mostly opting for solo performances and with very few exceptions she would only invite additional participation for good reasons, carefully calculated. In truth Arté could not recall ever having had to deal with more than three women at one time. Indeed when he looked back on his previous existence he came to realise that by Isla standards he had enjoyed a privileged lifestyle as the favourite slave of one of the most powerful women in the Theocracy. Furthermore his relationship with Thay was unique. During their last physical encounter, when she punishment raped him four times in succession with her heart breaking and his whole being giving her his consent and denying the rape required by the law, it struck him that he actually loved her. How could that be he puzzled, the idea of love being even possible between a male and female was totally alien on Isla, and possibly everywhere on the planet. Yet he had no doubt. He, Arthay loved Thay, his owner.

Deep in his heart he still mourned the loss.

Being set upon by Goddess knows how many oversexed young women was completely new to him and he felt and indeed, was, literally shagged out.

It is a matter of fact that Duplosians had evolved to cope with a certain amount of sexual athleticism but not to the extent of Arté's latest experience. It could have been worse, but nevertheless he was very sore and not up to doing much.

When Arté didn't show up for his next tutorial, both Fermos and Rastu were concerned. Rastu had heard the noise of the rumpus going on on Arté's staircase and expressed a view that something untoward might have gone on.

"Right then," said Fermos, "we shall go and investigate."

They entered the apartment and found Arté in his distressed condition, "I'm terribly sorry, he said, I should have taken better care of myself. They were just girls, being a bit over enthusiastic as at that age, they will."

"I know very well that you are not to blame, we should call the watch and have the whole fucking staircase arrested for rape. Their behaviour is illegal and intolerable. I am furious."

Rastu was shocked to hear such language from am elderly lady of high class and education. "I know what those girls have done is illegal and they ought to be punished, but my chief concern is for Arté. Arresting them won't help him and the resulting fuss can so easily do more harm than good. I'm just as horrified as you but please don't do anything that might make matters worse for him. I'll nurse him back to health and I promise to look out for him in future."

The victim was somewhat bemused. "I expected rebuke from you for missing your class and for letting myself be treated as I was. I should have known better and taken better care. I know my legal rights here in the WF but these girls are only young. They had only wanted a bit of fun, girls being girls, and at that age for ever testing the limits. It's true they were a bit rough but after all my primary role as a man is to serve womankind, and if that means a bit more sex than is comfortable, well that is just how it is. Please Fermos I don't want a fuss, or for the girls to have their prospects ruined by a criminal record."

"That's all very well, and I don't want to add to your distress. But I've seen what this sort of behaviour can lead to. Before I retired here to Routh I served twenty years as a magistrate in Louth. I've seen first hand where excessive licentiousness can lead. Women who don't know when to stop can cause much worse than the soreness you feel. They go on getting pleasure from the rub of the bump not only causing serious pain but eventually they can wear through the thin skin covering it thereby doing permanent damage, and assaults of this kind can even lead to death. Worse, I have even presided over two cases where a man had turned on one of his tormentors and killed her. I have to say that much to my own astonishment my sympathies were with the accused man. The fact that the law allows no excuse or mitigation for any man who kills a woman no matter what the provocation left me with no choice but to sentence him to the most painless and dignified death the law would allow. At least those cases didn't amount to petty treason which carries the most dreadful mediaeval punishment involving torture, and mutilation followed by burning alive."

Rastu murmured, "I didn't know that; I thought you'd always been a mathematician."

"All my mathematical work was as an amateur in my spare time from public service, I was also a deputy in the Louth governing council and for a time served as the city representative to the Federation parliament. Thirty-two years ago I played a leading role in the passage of PASOA the Protection Against Sexual Offences Act which has given men the legal right to refuse a woman's advances and criminalised violent disregard of of that right, especially by groups of three or more women. It was quite a struggle to get that act passed and I was castigated for my shockingly liberal views. I take breaches of my act personally[8]."

"That's all news to me too, why three women?"

"Well Arté, as you might know, three times is the average limit for a man before his bump begins to feels sore and his penis goes limp. I would have liked to criminalise all unwanted sexual assaults but we couldn't get any tougher measures through parliament. I must get back to work now but we'll cancel the tutorial. Rastu, you can stay and look after Arté."

Rastu was lost in recollection. She was remembering an incident involving her brother. He was nineteen at the time and guiding a party of five former schoolfriends celebrating their tenth anniversary of leaving a boarding school in Goddess City with a walking holiday in the mountains. Apart from a bit of banter and the occasional rubbing up against him and sighing, all were well-behaved until the last phase. Then the girls decided to celebrate with a few bottles of hooch, obtained via a foray over the border, and an illegal but normal smuggle back into the WF. One thing led to another and they all decided to take turns with Urdo. He was young and fit, and while five is a bit much, he could have coped. But the girls were egging each other on, fuelled by booze and the lack of inhibitions that comes naturally when old schoolfriends let their hair down together, and decided to have seconds. Two of them even went for a third helping. When they all awoke they were apologetic, but didn't really appreciate the extent of Urdo's distress. The thirteen year old Rastu found her beloved brother in tears and was herself deeply affected. She

8 Her move to Routh as a Professor (originally as a visiting Professor for two selenths and then permanently as Professor Emerita) was her retirement hobby. Her duties were entirely voluntary, being only paid expenses and a small annual retainer for administrative duties - for which she gave more than value for money.

recalled the advice from the adults - both female and male, that nothing could or should be done. Indeed Urdo's contract owner made it clear, that while the excess in this instance was unfortunate, such things came with the job, just part of the rough and smooth of working in the hospitality industry. Keep the customer satisfied. If Urdo couldn't accept that, perhaps he should look for a different contract. No formal complaint was made and Rastu found how to make an ointment that helped the physical injury and nursed Urdo until he was healed. That was the end of it, except she never forgot. Her own sexual moderation and reluctance to engage in the more boisterous activities of her fellows is undoubtedly a direct consequence of that experience.

Which is why the recollection, and my digression, is relevant now.

You will have gathered that Rastu believed in offering practical help. She was not one to sit about sympathetically bemoaning fate while actually doing nothing to improve the situation. After ensuring that Arté had something to eat and drink and was as comfortable as the circumstances allowed she bustled off to the apothecary, obtained various ingredients, and then returned to Arté's rooms to make up the ointment.

"I'll use your kitchenette if you don't mind," she called out on her return. "My own room is just a standard undergraduate study-bedroom and I don't want to use the communal kitchen. You've been given one of the few apartments normally allocated to mature students, or to postgraduates or younger lecturers who act as moral tutors. I expect the university authorities thought that in your unusual circumstances, being mature and undertaking academic duties in the D of AH & Th, it was right to afford you extra luxury and privacy. Obviously you wouldn't be able to act as a moral tutor to a parcel of undergraduate females!"

Rastu did her alchemy in the kitchenette, mixing her ointment and then took it into Arté where he was resting in bed.

"Now," she said "don't make a fuss, this is nothing I haven't seen or done before, man up and do as your told." At that she pulled away his bedclothes and examined him. "Well," she said "you do look sore but it's nothing that can't be mended, I'll soon have you back to normal. I can see why those tarts down the corridor got so excited, but they should have had more self-control. Just remember to stick to a maximum of three girts in a session in future you great lummox. Lie still and let me put this ointment on you, it will help, believe me, I have experience of such matters."

Arté did as he was told while wondering how in the world this timid chit of a girl could have gained such experience, but on second thoughts she was perhaps not as timid as their acquaintance to date had suggested. Rastu massaged the ointment onto his bump and a bit on his penis, and he found he quite liked it. Swiftly banishing inappropriate thoughts, he smiled at her and said: "thank you, Rastu, that feels much better." He then closed his eyes and enjoyed the moment. As he lay there he examined his feelings towards Rastu. He was pleased to realise that he did not feel for her as a lover, despite enjoying her touch, but that his feelings were indeed as he imagined they might be for a younger sister or even a daughter, Goddess forfend, he was not that old yet. Rastu must be some thirteen years younger than him and no respectable female would have allowed herself to get pregnant by a twelve year old, notwithstanding his height and physique. Right then, he decided, younger sister it is!

With this pleasant thought he fell asleep. Rastu finished her work, noticed he was asleep, pulled his covers over him, kissed him lightly on the forehead and whispered, "Rest well dear brother, I will return in two hora."

True to her word, she returned exactly two hora later and woke him, saying "it's time for the next application." She again applied the ointment, but this time when she had finished she told him that he must henceforth do it for himself. "Every two hora for a phase except that you don't need to wake up specially to put it on when you are asleep. After that you can return to normal life but you must apply the ointment regularly six times a phase for two periods. And no sex while you are healing. That's an order!" She tried to look fierce, but ended up smiling before collapsing into a fit of giggles.

It did Arté's heart good to see this evidence of her youth, and he resolved to keep her commandments. He smiled inwardly as he recalled that these words that came into his head were a direct quote from the ownership ceremony back on Isla.

In due course, Arté returned to good health and his studies picked up where they had left off. There was just one coda to the above events. Rastu had an encounter in the corridor with one of the more mouthy girls from Arté's staircase.

"Sorry if our little escapade has spoiled your fun, but it was some party!" She jibed, nudging Rastu in the ribs. At this Rastu saw red and crashed her fist into the girls jaw with a mighty blow. Teeth flew and the girl slumped to the ground while Rastu stomped away without a word.

Well, that wasn't quite the end of it. The girl in question came from a well-to-do family and at one time there looked to be quite a storm brewing. The University senate received a complaint from the girl's mother, calling for Rastu to be rusticated or worse. However, Professor Fermos leaped to Rastu's defence and without much difficulty persuaded her Senate colleagues that the boot was very much on the other foot. Fermos then visited the mother (polite words for the way she stormed into her office) and left her with no doubt that if she, Fermos, had had her way her daughter would now be serving a long prison sentence with hard labour. The mother, somewhat shaken, and though well-connected, not in Fermos' league, reluctantly agreed to let the matter drop and to give her daughter a serious talking-to about her duties and obligations to respect the law and her fellow students. Otherwise, the incident enhanced Rastu's street cred with her peers. For the victim was seen as toffee-nosed and somewhat of a bully, and thus secretly unpopular. As one student put it: "I must say, that Rastu may seem like a mouse but she must have had some tits on her to send Toffee-Nose to the dentist like that." Rastu's approval rating went for zero to hero within a period!

The student body as a whole had also been forced to endure a lecture from Professor Fermos during which they were reminded of their legal obligations as well as the standards expected of members of an august institution like the University of Routh.

That really is the end of the matter.

The rest of Arté's time at Routh passed without major incident. Midway through the Spring term they had a meeting with Fermos to discuss their futures.

"Arté, I'm really sorry that you are going to have to leave us. Although you've been taking a specialist course and haven't been studying the other subjects required for a BA degree, you could certainly satisfy the requirements for an MM (Mistress of Mathematics) though in your case I guess we'd have to call it Master of Mathematics. The department of ancient history and theology are very appreciative of your work with them and I think your paper of Island arithmetic would earn a distinction as an MM dissertation, and you would have no difficulty with the exam, which I'd like you to sit in any case. However you understand that as a male you can't be given a degree."

"I understand that perfectly, I feel privileged just to have been allowed to study both maths and natural philosophy at this level."

"Hmm, well it's probably best that you feel that way, but you have definitely opened my eyes and maybe one day we'll see the sense of freeing men to meet their potential in the same way as women. What concerns me is what to do with you next. The work you have done so far on infinitesimals and the infinite is very promising. Your ideas on the analysis of infinite sequences are truly original. With just a small amount of polish it would be worth a Ph.D. to any woman. Before you leave you must write it up as an interim paper and I hope you will be able to pursue your ideas further."[9]

"Well, my immediate future is up to the Islaview council, they have been very generous to me and I hope that I get a contract that recompenses them properly."

"As to that, a specialist contract auctioneer in Louth has been engaged. She was dubious about acting for a man but has been persuaded by the university's reference. You'll need to go to Louth to see her before the end of term."

"Rastu, you're also special. Your natural ability combined with the pace of working with Arté has put you way ahead of what is usual for a first year undergraduate. Your last exam was actually an old finals paper, you achieved first class honours easily. However you are only a girl still and need to concentrate more

9 In this work Arté was groping towards theorems which on Earth came from the likes of Cauchy in the early nineteenth century. Details are available as part of the free download on my web site.

on the other subjects for your BA over the next two years. The university has agreed that you should also keep up with advanced mathematics and natural philosophy under my personal direction. We should plan for you to take your MM at the same time as your BA."

"Wow, I'd love that, but how can I get a postgraduate degree at the same time as my BA. Is that allowed?"

"There's no rule against it. Occasionally a woman without a BA comes to specialist studies later in life and has been awarded an MM or even a PhD. But it is unusual to say the least. You might be making a bit of history. Do you know what you want to do when you have graduated?"

"I would like to return to the borders area where I grew up, but to continue with mathematics. Perhaps I could get a teaching contract somewhere like Marouth which is not too far away from my home."

"Apart from Marouth or Marcenza I guess the borders region is a bit of a rural backwater, without much call for academics. But there are good schools and colleges in Marouth and Marcenza and maybe Soubanc isn't too distant for you. I expect you'll find something suitable. Any school should be delighted to find someone like you."

4
Astra and Zorro: Louth

"Mummy, you are impossible!" The words rang through Astra's spacious apartment in the university district of Louth. "This should be an elegant drawing room, but every surface is littered with scraps of paper, and books are scattered all over the floor. It's a Goddess-awful mess. Even though you've got far more book cases than is decent in polite society. And those shelves are crammed to overflowing with heavy treatises and notebooks of scrawled manuscript."

"Then I am not one of your elegant society ladies, even if you and your grandmother would prefer me to be. I am a Professor of Natural Philosophy at the University, and this is my home for the two selenths each year when I have commitments in Louth, and not a showroom for idle fashionistas."

The shouty voice belonged to Astra's only daughter, Zorro. Today the casus belli happened to be the state of the apartment but in reality the issue was much more complex. The exchange was typical of their rows.

"Mummy, how can I be expected to have a friend over for some entertainment, only to be confronted by this tip."

"But, my dear, you are not expected to have anyone over. Especially as all your society seems to consist of is a procession of male hulks with no brains and a ramshackle set of over-sexed women who disport themselves about town with no thought to the sensibilities of decent people. Whom do you want to invite?"

"I've not got anyone in particular in mind. But that's not the point. I tidied this very room not two phases ago and now look at it."

"Looks OK to me. What's your real problem? Anyway if my lifestyle bothers you, why do you stay? If you got a job and were less extravagant you could afford to rent a small flat of your own."

"It isn't OK, and I don't want a small flat or a miserable eighty hora per period job and no time or money for the fun things in life. I'm an actress and an artist. But money isn't the only reason I live with you. Despite everything, I care very much about you. Frankly, I can't trust you to look after yourself properly. Left to your own devices you would forget to eat or wash. Lost in your astronomical reveries you would wear yourself out and then crash on the floor in an exhausted heap instead of retiring to your bed at a reasonable horum."

"Artist Fartist, you're a failed actress at best - what have you achieved in the last seven years since leaving drama school? I'll tell you - a part in a never-ending soap opera playing an over-entitled tart. And if I am so incapable of looking after myself how come I have reached the grand age of forty-five with a grown up daughter - tell me that young lady!"

"I'm not going to heed such strictures from you. Your own celibacy is unhealthy at best and probably downright dangerous. It clearly colours your opinions. Goddess knows when you last had any sex. Did you have a real fling with that porter in the university a couple of years back or were you just making up to him for some ulterior motive? As for my upbringing, it wasn't down to you, remember. It was Grandma and Auntie who looked after me as a child in South Beach, followed by boarding school and college in Marouth. As a small child, I scarcely ever saw you, and when you were home from completing your interrupted education your nose was always firmly in some extremely boring philosophy tome. Then brief visits in the school holidays whenever you deigned to come home. Auntie even had to look after my sex education. Otherwise It would have been limited to the dormitory gossip of prepubescent schoolgirls. All you ever said on the subject was that I should be careful around boys."

"I apologise, I should also have said to take anything your Aunt told you with a pinch of salt. I had no option but to leave you with Grandma while I finished my education. I could hardly have smuggled you into my study bedroom at the university. You were much better off in South Beach than in cramped accommodation here with me in Louth. And regarding my sex life. It's none of you business or anybody else's if I choose not to join you and my sister in your nymphomania."

"So what if I have a stronger libido than average. It's well known that frequent sex is essential to keep a woman in good health. You are the exception. You have sublimated your sex drive with astronomy and in turn this has led you to a lifestyle quite out of keeping with your age and station in life."

"I'm not telling you to be celibate but I do wish you would settle down to a worthwhile job and moderate your excesses. You are now supposedly adult and need to keep to the norms of decent behaviour."

"Coming from you that's rich. You were the teenage mother. I didn't ask for one. What in the world were you thinking of to get pregnant and give birth at seventeen? That's far more indecent than anything I have ever done."

"You know full well your conception was an accident. Neither I nor the foolish boy concerned knew what we were doing. Then and now I stand opposed to the use of abortion as a means of contraception. Actions can have consequences and it is one's duty to accept them. It was a hard lesson for a teenager but I made the most of it, with due thanks to your Grandma. I like to think that I have learned the lesson of my experience and reset my moral compass. In my opinion relationships should be founded on mutual respect and not on shared appetites. That is as true for sexual relationships as it is for personal friendships. As for your Aunt, her 'sex education' was the major contributor to my pregnancy. Perhaps, I should have told you this many years ago. She had decided that I was too serious by half and needed to be helped out of my shell. It was she who persuaded your progenitor to 'give me one' and ably assisted in the whole process. "You need to learn how to have a good time with a boy," she had said, " and there's nothing better than a practical lesson. You can watch me do it and then have a go yourself." Afterwards, when my pregnancy was suspected she told me than he had been supposed to pull out before ejaculating, but being as inexperienced as me, he was too late. I see a lot of my sister in you. It worries me."

"I guess I didn't know all that, Mummy, but it really is beside the point. I am of the opinion that what you need is an assistant to tidy up after you and generally keep house for you. Then I wouldn't worry so much. That way I could spend less time on Observatory island, and when I did come, he could help alleviate the boredom. I don't think I can cope with another winter like last year. I was crawling up the walls with frustration and I must have worn out a dozen dildos."

"Don't be so crude, you know it upsets me. Ah, but now we get to the real point of your complaint. You don't really want help for me but a toy-boy for yourself, presumably at my expense. Let's make it clear, I am not going to engage a gigolo for you and I don't want a man about the place invading my privacy. It's nice to go about without clothes in warm weather, and a strange man would make me uncomfortable. However, you're right and I do need an assistant. But she needs to be a competent mathematician who can help with my calculations. As you can see I struggle with that side of things." She let her eyes move about the room and swept her hand over some scattered sheets of paper full of scrawled numbers and crossings out.

"Where," she continued, "am I going to find someone who meets my needs. A young graduate looking for her first contract would not be suitable. I can't cope with the histrionics of a near-teenager, I can only manage with you because you are my daughter and I'm used to you. I want a serious woman who doesn't chase after every well-built male in range like a bitch on heat. On the other hand a more mature woman will either have children or will want to pursue a career with better prospects than I can offer, and a retired academic will probably want to stay where she is and not face the privations of the island. No, I'm convinced that the only viable option is someone who shares my passion for astronomy, and until I find her I'll have to make do on my own. And no extracurricular activities for your one-track mind. And that's my final word on the subject."

"Oh Goddess, not a second you! I couldn't survive it. Please think on what I've said. After all, if someone else is looking after the domestic side of things, while being at your beck and call, you can spend your time stargazing and mathematizing to your heart's content. All this arguing has made me thirsty. I'm off to Gigi's. I don't know when I'll be home, depends who I meet."

"There's no such word as mathematizing," Astra frowned, "and isn't Gigi's a brothel? I hoped that you were at least above buying it."

"No mummy, Gigi's is not a brothel. You know they are illegal now. I'm sure I know a lot more than you about brothels. Remember I was educated in Marouth, and Marcenza is full of them since they are perfectly legal in the GSE. Don't look so shocked. We were kept pretty well under control at school, but once you get to college you know what students are like, always seeking new experiences and going a bit over the top. Of course we would have the odd wild time and that included visits to a brothel, but I didn't make a habit of it and soon found it was unsatisfactory to, as you put it, 'pay for it' and not just because of the money. It's much less fun, and I haven't visited a brothel since I was twenty. Gigi's is a private members' club. Members may bring male guests from time to time and are not above sharing the bounty with their close friends. No male guest is made to do anything they don't want; and if the odd one of the hospitality staff, the bunnyboys, is occasionally willing to go above and beyond to please a member, that's up to him. There are strict rules of behaviour and Gigi is scrupulous about hygiene. Even some senior watch officers and politicians are members. It's very respectable!" She didn't add that she had hoped to encounter the Islander, Crazy or Créezy - as she now calls herself, having been amused by the similarity of the contish word for 'a bit mad' in a playful sense and her islander name of Crayza. Astra did not approve of her daughter's friendship with Créezy.

"Humph," was all she said as Zorro left the apartment with too loud a bang of the door behind her.

Despite her final words to Zorro, Astra did think on what was said. She knew that it was important to keep her papers tidy and had often chided herself for her inability to keep her resolutions to do so. She also knew that Zorro, and indeed most people, finds life at her observatory uncomfortable, isolated and tedious. She, herself, is poor company when engrossed in astronomy.

In her mind Astra ran through the privations of her winter lifestyle. Five years previously she had bought Observatory island in the Cold Sea. It is otherwise uninhabited except for a few snow hares, and seals on the rocky coast[10]. Access is via a narrow causeway from the mainland in the remote North-East of the Western Federation, to the west of the river that forms the northern part of the border with the Shadowlands Union. This causeway and the beach from which it emanates is only dry at low tide. Astra had caused the observatory to be built and spent every winter selenth there.

The nearest city is Kongholm some fifty walks South South East of the Island. Some of the roads are not good and the actual path has to skirt the coast making the distance more like sixty walks.

There are a few tiny settlements on the way but nothing as large as a town or even a village the size of Islaview or Dunos. The island is particularly well-suited for observations of Geos which is what makes it such an excellent location for an observatory. The observatory itself is built on a hill, actually an extinct volcano, about two hundred and sixty strides above high tide sea level while Astra's dwelling is a modest bungalow on the Western side of the island.

When all's said and done it's in a cold, remote, desolate and thoroughly miserable place where no-one apart from a dedicated, if not fanatical, astronomer would consider spending any time.

---

10 Of course these are not the same animals as hares and seals on Earth, any more than the tall long legged Duplosian people are the same as Earth men and women. But the Duplosian animals concerned occupy much the same place in the local ecology as their counterparts on Earth. Rather than digress into precise descriptive details of creatures that the reader will never encounter in the flesh, I have adopted the convention of naming Duplosian (or, later Geosian) flora and fauna after an 'equivalent' Earth species. The only general remark I will make is that for the most part, because of the reduced gravity, the Duplosian species tend to be larger, faster and longer limbed than their Earthly namesakes.

Ruminating on the above Astra saw no realistic chance of finding a suitable assistant. She ticked off the options in her head: not a man as suggested by Zorro, not to be countenanced, she meant what she said to her daughter about that. Oh how I would love to have a true collaborator, she dreamed. Preferably a woman in her late thirties or early forties to whom I could be a mentor and teacher, while the assistant could perform the necessary calculations to enable me to unravel the secrets of the motion of the heavenly bodies. But enough dreaming, life is real.

More out of form than expectation she studied the résumé's of recent graduates from the better universities. By itself a BA, even with a first, is no use to me she mused. A suitable assistant must have at least a part three in mathematics or natural philosophy. She disdainfully dismissed all first degrees as shallow, suited to producing the chattering classes, with a core curriculum giving a smattering of general knowledge and appreciation of continental culture to produce a broadly educated young woman able to hold their own in what passes for educated circles. A slightly more educated version of Zorro, she thought. The minority, however, graduating with additional mention in a specialised area of studies (part 3) just might have enough between their pretty ears to be of some use. Better still would be those with postgraduate degrees or even diplomas for relevant short courses. An MM or MNP would be ideal, a PhD would be asking too much.

Astra went mechanically through the resumes. As she feared most were too young and looking to teach in a city. The few mature graduates tended to have children, or had been on leave from a regular contract to which they would return. As I thought, this is a waste of time, she concluded.

Then suddenly, "What's this?" She sat up with renewed attention, her excitement increasing as she read on, commenting aloud to her empty room. "Most unusual. No bioblurb here, but she looks interesting. She's not on the graduating list but she is in her thirties so probably a non-graduate who has developed later specialist interests and can do without the arty-farty stuff needed for a BA. More of a woman after my own heart. I wonder how she got her male name? Distinction in a specially tailored short course in Mathematics exceeding the usual requirements for MM, unusual! Advanced papers in both Mathematics, working under Professor Fermos, and on Island Arithmetic as part of the Department of Ancient History and Theology's Isla project. After concluding studies at Routh, Arté would be seeking employment and was likely to be subject to a contract auction, probably to be held in Louth." Astra was intrigued.

"I've met Fermos. Anyone recommended by her must be worth a second look." She resolved to visit Routh. She hoped to get to see some of these papers and to meet the author herself to see if the auction could pre-empted.

5

Sisters on Duplos, Thay and Shay: Isla

When it comes to children boys don't count at all on Isla, and not for much on the continent. The Western Federation is a bit of an exception as the most liberal Duplosian society where males are concerned and mother-son and even brother-sister bonds develop there.

On the other hand girls matter a great deal. Normally inheritance passes to the eldest daughter. On Isla it is almost always a case of winner takes all with any younger daughters having to make their own way in the world, or become a dependent of their sister. It is true that in some cases a wealthier woman will be in a position to make separate provision for a younger daughter, but there is a general reluctance to break up estates or enterprises, often built up over generations, that provide the basis for a family's influence and power. The situation is less severe in the Western Federation where most women of means will do what they can for all their daughters (usually two), but even there, the major share will pass to the principal heiress. On the other hand both in the Southern Empire and the Shadowlands Union, the general rule is for estates to be kept in tact when passing to a new generation, but with an obligation on the inheritrix to provide for her sisters, usually through employment to manage part of the family enterprise, whatever that may be.

"Which one are you going to keep, or haven't you made your mind up yet?"

"What do you mean, 'which one am I going to keep', are you suggesting that I should kill one of my daughters. I'm shocked. Surely that barbaric practice has been consigned to ancient history." Chay hugged her two bundles more closely to her chest.

Her cousin shook her head, "No, no that is not what I meant. I agree that would be barbaric, although even today not totally unheard of. I assume you will give one up for adoption. That is the normal practice."

"Certainly not, I intend to bring them both up." She peeked into each bundle, "aren't they lovely, mummy's going to look after you both, isn't she?"

"That's all very well, playing the yummy mummy, but think of your responsibilities. You are mistress of a substantial business and a major power in the Theocracy. Your twins could well cause a civil war through their inevitable rivalry. You know very well that female twins are unlucky and you know why."

"I have thought about it, we're agreed that I won't kill one of them, which leaves the choice between adoption or keeping them. It is out of the question that one of my daughters should be placed in a family below her station, which means she would have to be adopted as heiress to a similarly powerful woman to myself, and thus a rival. Anything less would just not do. The potential downstream consequences are just too uncertain and too dangerous."

"There's always a religious order. That is considered a perfectly respectable option."

"While, like you, I am outwardly conformist in religious matters, you and I both know that most theology is just so much mumbo jumbo. Helps to keeps the social status quo and provides some useful services but I'm not prepared to have one of my daughters indoctrinated with a load of rubbish. Keeping them both is the only acceptable option for me. If I'd had two boys I would have separated them before they reached school age, or if one of each it would be easy as the boy could be sent away, but with two girls, either one might become my heiress."

"That's the problem. Once they start to be aware of the way of the world their rivalry could quickly get out of control. It's always bad when sisters are close in age but with twins it's totally impossible. Neither ever accepts the right of the other to be first-born."

"I'll just have to do my best then. Thay is the first-born by half an ihor. She gets a head start. But in the end it will be for the stronger girl to prove her right to inherit. Fortunately with three good estates I can provide for them both."

"Well I'm going to make sure I have a decent gap between daughters," riposted Cray. "A five or six year gap is ideal. That way the younger will know her place and the older can form a proper sisterly bond with her and nurture her. They could be friends rather than rivals. Like you and me. I'm still everlastingly grateful for the way you introduced me to my first sex." She smiled at the recollection.

Chay also smiled, "yes, you were just fifteen and eager and scared at the same time. I remember choosing a boy I knew to be reasonably well-bumped but also nicely submissive. Careful of the babies!"

"Sorry I just needed to give you a hug, I don't think I squashed them. Oh look one of them's trying to grab one of my tits, sorry darling I don't have any milk yet."

"That's Shay, you'll have to stand Goddess for her. I think they should each have a different Goddess. Obviously Shay has chosen you. I'll ask an old schoolfriend for Thay. As for your remark about a gap between them, I didn't get much choice with these two. But on the other hand, whoever is to succeed me will have to be well up to snuff. My holdings are already substantial, but I fully intend to expand even more, especially the Great River trade route where I see tremendous opportunities with enormous potential for profits."

"Yes you'll be offering quite an incentive for your heiress. Both girls should be kept on their toes and I'm sure they'll be hard-working and diligent in the desire to impress you. We do have a winner takes all culture, but I feel sorry for the loser."

"Well as Goddess to the loser-apparent that is a reasonable sentiment. But I'll keep an open mind. Thay gets first shot but that's all. And the loser won't be cut off with a groat. Of course I hope they will get on together and enhance the family prestige, but if necessary, I'll leave the minor daughter with a good estate and enough other wealth that would be the envy of most girls."

"Well, whatever you decide will be law and there's nothing either girl will be able to do about it. Posthumous wrangling over an estate is the worst of nightmares. It's a good thing that our law forbids the contesting of a will. But I still worry about the effect on their relationship. Too many sisters are drawn into a love-hate relationship that scars them for life. We're lucky we're both only daughters and we've been able to enjoy a personal friendship based on shared childhood memories without having to compete with each other."

"As long as a will isn't seen to threaten the status quo of the most powerful interests in the Theocracy, that is. But you shouldn't refine to much on our own experience. I've seen cousins fall out too. As for our childhood, I remember how you used to dog my footsteps when one of us was staying over with the other during the holidays. When I was an early teenager I found you quite annoying. And once I'd started wanting to play rub-a-dub-dub with the boys a ten-year-old camp follower was the last thing I needed."

"True, I definitely got the better of the deal then. A six year age difference is ideal for idolatry. You were my idea of the height of sophistication. And for me, and I think any mid-teenager, a twenty-one year old willing to invite you to sex sessions is beyond wonderful. Oh dear, I'm soaking wet, these recollections are giving me the most incredible itch."

"That's inevitable but I'm sorry I can't help this time. These two would be in the way. We'll just have to store a nostalgia romp for another time." Chay laughed as she spoke.

"Don't worry Chay I'm OK really, but one thing I did want to ask you is if you knew of any suitable studs out there. I'd really like to try for a daughter myself."

"I'll let you know if I come across any or get a good recommendation. Have you asked your mother?"

"Well, no. I'm certainly not going to do the old traditional thing of asking her to come and supervise the occasion and I don't need her to help me with my rhythm calculations. She has offered to buy me a man for my twenty-fourth next year but I'm not sure that I want her doing the choosing."

"I don't know, but actually most of my girlfriends whose mother's have bought them someone seem pleased. It took me ages to find this pair's sire. I wish I'd had a mother to help. That's the downside of inheriting at such a young age. I never had a proper twenty-fourth."

"Oh I don't know about that last, I recall the most fantastic party I had ever attended. And then when you, the birthday girl herself, sought me out to join in with you for the celebratory sex session I thought I was the luckiest girl in the world. I think I had thirds and was tingling for a whole phase afterwards.

"I'm surprised you recall any of it. You drank enough to sink a fishing fleet and I had to carry you to bed, but the sex was fun and I loved the way you enjoyed it. Cray, it is good to reminisce like this, now I've got an itch. You go and have one for me too. I'll just have to have a cold bath. If I can get these two to enjoy men together, their relationship should take care of itself."

"While I won't have Mum in on the act, if you want to come and supervise me getting pregnant you will always be welcome. I think maybe I'll stick to the cold bath myself this time, this itch is definitely one for sharing. Solo sex is all very well but sometimes you need that deeper pleasure you get with someone you really respect and care about. Someone you can truly bond with."

"You're right there's nothing as good as sex for strengthening a relationship. Perhaps if we could have such a relationship with a man solo sex would more satisfactory not just a good scratch. After all masturbation sort of does that."

"Well only sort of, at least I've never found an artificial substitute for a good bump. I mean a good dildo can be as good as a man's penis but that's only half the job. I think we tend to underestimate the value of the brain as a sex organ and for that we need another woman."

"Yes, it's a pity that Goddesses made men so inferior, but perhaps they feared that if we could bond with men at a mental level we would fail to nurture our relationships with each other. But then, who knows what the Goddesses think. We can be sure the priestesses don't! Come into the washroom with me. You're not the only one with a damp gown, Shay has decided it's time to be changed, and while I'm at it I'll do the same for Thay. Here hold them for me please while I get up."

As the twins grew up Chay came to realise that her hopes for them were going to be dashed. Both Thay and Shay were strong characters and were each driven to seek the lead in all their ventures.

When the time came for the girls to start school, Chay made use of a freak chance, which, despite her best intentions, and with the benefit of hindsight, was probably the worst decision she ever made. By happenstance, the twins had been born at the time of a new selenth, and on Isla the selenths are marked by the actual motion of Selenos, rather than by the strict seven and a half period cycle as on the continent. Despite the gap between the twins being a mere half ihor, Thay and Shay had been born in different selenths.

Somewhat late in the day she decided to abandon the plan for them to start school together, and insisted that Shay's entry to school be delayed to the selenth following that of Thay.

On their fifth birthday she informed them of her decision. Things did not go well. The twins had been fighting over something trivial. She caught them and separated them saying.

"That's enough, stop it at once."

"But she.." they squeaked in unison.

"I said that's enough. It's clear you can't deal properly together so I can't trust either of you to behave properly in the same classroom in school. You can't go to boarding schools at your age so you'll just have be go into separate classes in the local school. Fortunately that can be achieved. Thay, you have to go this coming selenth; but Shay, you count as young enough to start a selenth later. This has lots of advantages for you both. It means you won't have to keep looking over your shoulder at each other and can forge you own independent friendships. Shay, for you it also means you get a whole selenth extra of freedom at home to play while Thay has to go to do schoolwork."

"Good," said Thay "I don't want Shay in my class. I want her to be a proper younger sister and learn her place."

Shay screamed, "It's not fair, I can read and write better than her and I know all my figures and doubling. You're always helping her. I hate you both." She then started a considerable rumpus as only an out of control child can.

Chay was not used to this sort of behaviour and not prepared to tolerate it. When Shay wouldn't calm down or stop when told to she turned to Thay saying. "Thay, go and fetch me the horse crop. "Shay, if you don't pull yourself together this instant, I'll give you a severe thrashing and send you bed without meals for the rest of the phase. Now stop your noise, now."

Shay went on with her screaming fit. She was beyond herself with rage and couldn't help herself if she wanted to.

Thay brought her mother the horse crop. Chay grabbed Shay by the scruff and bent her over a chair. She then pulled up her dress and struck her hard on her bare bottom many times.

When the thrashing stopped she was sent to her bed still screaming her head off with pain. She missed two meals and her own fifth birthday party. She never forgot, nor forgave.

As she gained mastery of her screams and her pain she promised herself. "I'll get my own back. I don't need you and I don't need priestesses to teach me. I'm a big girl now. You've made me big. I used to have a mummy who I loved. No longer. Now I have a mother who I don't care for. I used to have a twin sister who I could play with and compete with while staying friends. Now I have an enemy sister that I must beat. I'll show them. I'll be stronger. From today I'll look after myself and control my own destiny."

For the rest of her childhood she showed restraint in the face of both mother and sister, awarding them both outward respect, and to her mother due deference. But her emotions were detached. She never showed her true feelings and, until Arthay came into the picture, never lost her temper. This last was not difficult. It is easy to keep your temper with those you don't love and for whom you have no care.

Chay was delighted with the change in Shay's demeanour, but remained blissfully unaware of the true nature of the change. Thay was less easily fooled. She found that she missed her companion, however irritating she could be. She, too, suffered loss and emotional damage. It was as if someone had amputated part of her soul. None-the-less, she kept her feelings to herself. Thay was already a political creature, even as a young child and kept her own counsels. She might be wary of her sister's intentions but she wouldn't snitch on her.

Both girls were naturally intelligent and Thay learnt quickly and pleased her teachers, but none of her classmates offered much of a challenge and her work lacked that extra edge that competition could bring. Shay, on the other hand, was equally bright, and needed no spur from her peers. She had only one rival and that was more than enough. She had arrived at school having already made up her lost selenth from looking through her sister's books when no-one was watching and learning how to teach herself. Fortunately for her, Chay had taught both girls the rudiments of reading and writing as four year olds. In school, Shay found she was easily able to persuade the priestesses to give her more advanced work than the rest of her class, and without her mother realising it she even surpassed her sister in scholastic achievement. When the girls reached ten years of age Chay was asked to see the head priestess who informed her that both girls had outgrown what the school could offer and suggested that they should continue their education elsewhere.

Chay had always intended that the girls would attend a boarding school and she chose different ones for the two of them, each situated in a centre close to one of her estates. Estates which she had in mind each girl would first come to manage and later to inherit. In Thay's case this was in a town with a population of three thousand on the South coast overlooking the strait and for Shay she plumped for a school in a large village of about eight hundred and fifty in a delightful setting among hills overlooking the Second River.

Both girls excelled in their respective schools, but in the holidays Shay would sneak a look at Thay's books and then ensure that she kept ahead in the undeclared war between them. Both girls achieved distinctions in all subjects, and a secret memo from the head of Shay's school to the high religious order that controlled such matters to inform them that Shay had the potential to discover secret matters for herself and to consider whether she might be inducted into the order. As an existing member Chay was consulted. She was impressed and would certainly not attempt to block Shay's induction but counselled that it would be better if both twins received the same invitation. At this the secretary of the order made discreet enquiries at Thay's school and read her examination papers in number work and natural theology, which in islander culture includes what we call science. Her findings were, that while a little premature, it was highly likely that Thay would meet the order's standards in due course, and given her family background would undoubtedly be accepted into membership. She concluded that it would do no harm to pre-empt the inevitable by a couple of years and, the fact that the girls were twins, who might be expected to share everything, Chay's recommendation should be accepted. Indeed, the secretary told the President she was sure that Chay had this latter consideration in mind and her intervention was undoubtedly occasioned by the need to protect the order's secrets.

In this opinion the secretary was greatly mistaken, Shay would have withstood any amount of torture rather than reveal a secret to her twin, and her mother's motives would have had nothing to do with protecting secrets. Fortunately for all concerned, Shay knew nothing about this exchange. She and Thay would each receive that 'tap on the shoulder' that would presage their respective inductions into the Theocracy's elite.

There is no concept of a university or its equivalent on Isla and the girls returned to the family home in Rivermouth and were put to work by their mother to learn the family business.

Thay had a normal sex life for an islander girl. She was introduced to her first boy by a friend at school while still seventeen and they had a pleasant if rather fumbling time of it, all three being inexperienced. Thay and Shay had received that 'sex talk' from their mother when they reached fifteen, and had been taught by her how to minimise the possibility of pregnancy. This was reinforced by the school not much later. Thay took it all very seriously, including her mother's advice not to rush matters just because her tits had grown and her fanny begun to itch. She asked intelligent questions, and took appropriate notes. She also tried to follow the advice to have a more experienced friend with her, and was it her fault that her friend turned out to have been more talk than action and as inexperienced as she was! Both Thay and Shay ignored their mother's comment that it would be lovely if the two of them could find a nice boy who could give them both a good time together.

Shay heard her mother out without batting an eyelid. She took in the comments about a friend, but otherwise learnt nothing she didn't already know. She had already jumped the gun, partly to make sure that Thay didn't beat her to it. She wasn't stupid and hadn't relied on dormitory gossip but had researched the matter fully.

She (and Thay) had been young when they matured physically and she understood her rhythms well. Her habits from home had rendered her good at acting clandestinely and her reputation as a scholar had blinded the priestesses to her wilder side. She had tried out masturbation under the bedclothes in the dorm, and found it pleasant but not fully satisfying. She also had made the acquaintance of some of the older boys whose owners had paid for them have tuition in the school, as happened, for example, when a less educated boy had shown some promise and his mistress thought it worth her while to have him learn to read and write and do basic number work. Consequently, shortly before her fourteenth birthday she inveigled a young man of nineteen to meet her in the hills after dark where she spent a good time losing her virginity. Throughout, she remained sufficiently in control that she was able to grab his penis and pull it out at the critical moment. She was surprised at just how much he spurted out over her hand.

After that she, applied herself diligently to her work, with only very rare excursions out of school to scratch her itch. In the holidays, things were different and she made a habit of slipping out secretly at least twice if not three times a period, and had no difficulty in finding an obliging male to help her out. As for the males, they knew it was no more than their duty to respond to a female's demands, and at least this one was young and attractive, if over-bold for one so young.

What Shay hadn't done was to share the experience with another female, and until her mother's talk, she hadn't given it a thought. All her escapades had been solo, and secretive. She didn't have any really close friends, but she passed her classmates through her mind and mentally selected a couple of them as potential sex-mates. She made that term up herself. On return to school she set about cultivating these two friendships. The school sex-eduction talk was a catalyst to her broaching the subject in general terms. In any case it was hot gossip for girls her age. She was now sixteen and instead of the larger dormitories they had occupied hitherto, the girls were accommodated in threes. The girls were given some choice in the matter and Shay and her two chosen friends ended up together. The situation was ideal for her plans. Both her friends, like her, had an academic bent. Shay didn't suffer fools! They were both obviously virgins and relatively shy, and as teenagers go, pretty conformist. Shay didn't admit her experience, both because she was careful of her own reputation, and also she didn't want to frighten them off; but she was a natural leader and the others expected her to take the lead and entirely trusted her where their joint ventures were concerned. In the fullness of time, they agreed that all three would break their ducks together. Shay had offered a two at a time system, but both the others needed her and didn't want to be left until last. Shay identified a target, a twenty year old that she had tried before. She cautioned him not to admit their (i.e. her) previous experience and arranged a suitable liaison. Her friends clearly enjoyed the experience. Shay found that their joy enhanced her own pleasure. At least in this matter her appalling mother had been right. Later in her life she also had cause to be grateful for this time, as she made two life-long friends with a common bond that could not be broken.

The stage was now set for the fates of Thay, Shay and the future Arté to converge.

6
Arté's History: Routh and Isla

Over a series of interviews Arté gave the department of Ancient History and Theology a full account of life on the island as he understood it and of his life story culminating in his arrival on the Islaview beach. These interviews were interspersed with seminars where we was able to discuss detailed aspects of island culture, theology and government.

"You must understand," Arté began, "all men in the Isla Theocracy and its allied territories are slaves. That is, they have an owner. Either an individual woman or an institution like a religious order. At birth your mother is your owner and legally you are her slave as well as her son. Slavery on Isla is not quite the same as I understand it is in those parts of the continent that practise it. All females born in these territories on Isla are born free and cannot be taken into slavery except on sentence by a court following conviction for a serious criminal offence. Even then slavery is not permanent but for a term determined by the court. Usually such enslavement is to an institution rather than a private individual. Additionally slaves are sometimes taken on raids of the wild lands outside the Theocracy. Most of those taken will be men but some prisoners might be women. These women will also be enslaved but any female children they bear when in the Theocracy will be free and also the women themselves may also be freed for one reason or another, though not to return to the wild.

As a man and a mere slave, I played no part in the machinations of the Theocracy, but nevertheless I was well placed to observe several major players in action. My owner, Thay, was a prominent business woman and her mother was one of the leading citizens in the chief town, Rivermouth. My position was one of great privilege for a man, not with a seat at the table of the great and the good, but rather with a place behind the seat held by one one of the most powerful, as her most trusted slave."

In addition to being able to describe details of life on Isla. He was also highly intelligent and able to offer useful opinions on Islish internal politics.

The majority of Isla is under the sway of a Theocracy which covers over half the land area and two thirds of the population. Just under half the rest of the population live in three smaller territories that maintain close links with the Theocracy, share the religion and while not formally linked, and a bit more primitive in their culture, are more-or-less under its hegemony. There are no communities of a size that continentals would consider to be cities but there are towns dotted around, often located on important rivers. The remainder of the island - perhaps as much as a third of the land area - is only sparsely inhabited, mainly by wandering tribes with only a few settled villages. These wild lands consist of two separate contiguous territories, one in the North of the island and the other in the West. There are several smaller islands mainly off the west coast but as far as Arté knows they are all uninhabited apart from the odd one or two that can be reached on foot at low tide.

Arté knows little about the wild lands although he had accompanied his owner on raiding parties for slaves and, once, on a punitive expedition to the North following an incursion by a cattle raiding tribe during a particularly dry summer. He had also spoken to one or two slaves who had been taken on raids.

The society in the wild lands is much more primitive than in the Theocracy, being still basically stone age. Arté knows there are copper and iron deposits in parts of the wild both West and North but these have not been exploited in any way and the inhabitants appear ignorant of metal technology. Their only knowledge of metal goods is through contact with the rest of Isla. As the Theocracy has imposed a strict ban on trade of such objects, the only metal available in the wild comes from raids into the Theocracy. Arté's opinion is that the lifestyle of these primitive people has probably changed little from the time before the separation from the continent. His observations here, though scant, were deemed of considerable value by the ancient history scholars.

The languages on Isla appear to come from the same roots as Contish. Arté gave several examples of grammatical construction and of words that appeared to be related, based on his observations of phonetic shifts and subtle variations of meaning. He illustrated his ideas with examples of Contish terms whose meanings he had been able to infer, while he was learning the language. Some of Arté's insights were genuinely original and broke new ground in linguistics. The philology specialists present were both impressed and excited at the possibilities for their own research on continental language development. Nevertheless Islish and Contish have diverged so far that they are mutually unintelligible. The allied territories of the Marches and West Isla have dialects of their own, with West Islish being almost worthy of being termed a separate language with a common core to Islish. There is sufficient similarity between these languages or dialects to enable mutually shared communication. In New West Isla they speak the same language as in West Isla, although there are are minor differences of accent and vocabulary emerging as time since the colonisation grows. There are examples of imports from both Islish and tribal languages in the Western Wild Lands.

There are several seemingly different languages spoken in the Wild Lands, some of which have imported words from Islish. Those that Arté knows anything about are partly comprehensible by an Islish speaker, and they all appear to be linked to a common root. In the north, the further north and east you travel, the less comprehensible the languages become. In the Western Wild Lands the native languages appear to be less diverse than in the north and also appear to be closer to the dialects of West Isla and the Marches than to the Islish of the Theocracy.

Islish is a written language, but Arté suspects that writing is of quite recent origin. The written versions of the allied territories dialects were entirely imported from Islish and the languages of the wild have no known written tradition. The alphabet is quite different from Contish and any apparent relationships seem to be coincidental. But Arté is the first to admit that he is totally ignorant of the science of orthography. Compared to Contish, Islish orthography appears to avoid curves.

This topic led to quite heated debate. One of the ancient history professors thought Arté might be mistaken about the recent origin of the writing.

"Various ancient objects have been discovered, often buried close to rivers with some form of unintelligible writing on them. This writing is generally characterised by being very linear in form and we believe predates the invention of paper, pens and ink, let alone printing. Straight lines are much easier to scratch on to bark or clay tablets than curves. We've not made any headway in deciphering any of these scripts. It's possible that the Island writing is related and thus not of recent origin at all. Maybe it was kept as a religious secret that was released more widely in recent times."

"That's certainly possible," opined Arté, "The temples do maintain such secrets, for example in arithmetic as I'm covering in other seminars."

Arté's seminars on the topic of Islish numbering were highly regarded and resulted in an academic paper.[11]

Naturally religion plays a central role in the theocracy, but the same base beliefs are current throughout the island. The pantheon is closely related to the mythology of the continent. The two differences being the prominent role of Isla, who barely gets a mention on the continent, and the fact that it is all taken very seriously.[12]

All society on Isla is strongly matriarchal. As already noted, in the Theocracy all men belong to either an individual woman, a female-led family or a collective of women (such as a religious order). A change of owner for a man involves a change of name. The convention that all male names commence with a vowel sound and all female names with a consonant is strictly adhered to. The only part of his name that a man retains is the initial vowel group, in his case Ar. The remainder of his name derives from his owner. Matters are not very different in the subordinate territories. Arté was uncertain about the practice in the wild lands. They were definitely matriarchal with men having a subordinate role but, he thought, not actually individually owned as such. In some sense each community owned its men and would, for example, trade with other communities to maintain diversity and avoid inbreeding.

The separation story is a powerful driver for religious observance. Islanders believe (with certainty) in the rift between the sister Goddesses, Lana and Nepa and that Lana's daughter Isla had been forcibly separated from her mother by the jealousy and malice of Nepa. Islanders were the direct followers of Isla and the priestesses teach that Lana's people on the continent had been destroyed. Naturally they know the continent is there

11 This paper can be found in the free download on my website.

12 See appendix 5 for details of the Duplosian Pantheon.

as it can be seen clearly across the strait, but the official religion teaches that it is now uninhabited except by animals and birds. Indeed some religious orders go so far as to limit life on the continent to vegetation and birds. Arté knows of no recorded case of a person or land animal arriving on Isla from the continent, alive or dead.

As well as the veneration of Isla, Nepa is considered a very present threat. As continentals are well aware, the seas around Isla are extremely dangerous and currents in the strait, in particular, are such that navigating even the shortest stretch is impossible, and that any flotsam is only deposited from Island to Continent and never in the opposite direction. Elsewhere around the coast, the Great River, Lesser River and in the west, Second River have navigable estuaries. These are still very dangerous but they are fished. Indeed both the Great and Lesser estuaries are sources of wrecks that find their way to continental beaches. The rare occurrence of survivors of such wrecks being washed up alive is limited to those emanating from the Great River[13]. Limited sea-going navigation is also possible close to the land off the South West coast. There are some fishing communities in West Isla and New West Isla, that have grown quite rich on the trade to the Theocracy. Indeed fishing was one of the drivers for the colonisation of NWI a hundred years previously. The other motive was encouragement by the Theocracy in a bid to contain the wild tribes and keep them away from the rich cattle pastures in the Theocracy bordering the second river. As a rule, although they owned the boats and the fishermen, women did not themselves go to sea, which is why Crayza's arrival was unique in history.

13 Essentially all rivers on Isla are called just 'The River' with a further descriptor used only when needed to distinguish one from another.

There is a huge variety of religious orders. Some live in communities, others are more like clubs with members from all over the territory, while yet others or more like cults. Purposes are varied, some are of value to the community such as teaching or healing orders, some are devotional usually claiming to serve the Goddess Isla or appease Nepa, or some such. Others are concerned with more secular matters governing the Theocracy. The Theocracy may be officially dedicated entirely to the service of Isla and keeping the malice of Nepa at bay, but it is amazing how often the needs of the Goddesses coincide with the political and business interests of the ruling classes.

The chief town on Isla is Rivermouth which has a population of about six thousand[14] and is situated mainly on the North bank of the Great River just upstream from where the river widens into the estuary. When tides are right there are ferry services that operate across the river and the inner estuary. There is also Rivermouth bridge which is seen as a great feat of engineering. A small community has grown up at the southern end of the bridge and smaller communities near the ferry terminals on both sides. All these communities have been officially incorporated into the town. Rivermouth is also an important administrative and religious centre and all the most prominent citizens maintain a residence there, even if they hail from estates deep into the countryside. Thay was no exception and Arté had spent most of the past twelve years divided between her Rivermouth home and her estates on the South coast, just across the strait about a dozen walks up-current from Islaview.

14 Most islanders could only say more than 1024 which is the same as 'It's a town' and Thay would not have mentioned anything that might reveal secret numbers, but Arté was sure that he knew the official estimate was quadruple 1024 + double 1024, for although 1024 was the largest number symbol and number words, there were words for double and quadruple, half and quarter, but not triple and not other fractions.

When asked to give his personal history, Arté said he had been born to a reasonably prosperous farmer who owned three male slaves to do most of the labouring work about the farm. She also had two daughters as well as Arté. Arté proved to be a strong and intelligent lad. His mother thought she could do well from him and, when the priestess in charge of the village school said she thought he might be taught to read and write, his mother agreed to sell him to a religious teaching order about twenty imiles away on the outskirts of the town of Oakbridge, which was at the confluence of the Second River and a tributary emanating from the hills to the East, which constituted the watershed between the East and West flowing drainage systems.

Arté was able to illustrate his talks with a reasonably accurate map of Isla, based partly on his knowledge from experience and partly on his excellent memory of maps that he had seen in temples and in Chay's house in Rivermouth. These were by no means perfect as knowledge on the north and west wild lands and their coastlines was scant, but he was able to be quite accurate about the Theocracy. This information was seen as extremely valuable by the academics as they had never before had any real visibility of the geography of Isla. Other castaways had only been able to give a very little local knowledge and nobody had thought of asking Crayza. Indeed when Arté told them what he knew about her they were surprised that they had never heard of a female castaway.

"We've missed out on a gold mine," was the expressed view. At that point Arté had not met Crayza and only knew the little that Esau had told him.

He continued with his history.

The priestesses were kindly as priestesses go, and Arté was a diligent pupil, eager to learn. He also grew, and grew and grew. He towered over all the other pupils and even the priestesses, which was without precedent. In the end the order was sore put to know what to do with him. He had been told that if he had been female it would have been easy, they would have recruited her and marked her out as a potential leader of the order. Such a future was not for males. He worked on the home farm and was given responsibility for teaching some of the younger boys. The head priestess sighed and wished he were female. One young priestess with a bit of a wicked sense of humour suggested that he could be passed off as a girl and given a role more appropriate to his talents. After all, who would suspect someone who was two strides tall of being male. This shocked her superiors and the unfortunate young woman was lucky to have got away with a whipping and a selenth on bread and water as a punishment for her heretical thoughts. Arté recalled that he had been very upset about that. He liked her and felt some affinity with her. Also she had never importuned him despite her showing her friendship to him in many little ways. Later in life when he learnt about such things he had wondered if she was one of those very rare Duplosian women who didn't enjoy sex with men but only with other women.

Not all the priestesses wanted Arté to be female! One hot phase when he was just over 18 years of age he went down to one of the rivers for a swim to cool off. He was spotted by a couple of the younger priestesses whose lust grew as they watched him in the water, and squealed with delight when he turned on to his back. When he emerged from the water they accosted him and dragged him off for an ihor of quite different exercise. In this way he was introduced to the pleasures of the flesh.

Naturally word of this and similar later escapades reached the senior priestesses and it was agreed that the time had come to settle his future. It was clear that his presence would be too disruptive in any religious order, even though they were never celibate, either in theory or in practice. The occasion presented itself when they had a visit from a party, led by Chay, bound on an official punitive raid into the Western Wild Lands. The party stayed in the order's hospitality suites before crossing the Second River on their way to the border. Chay, was impressed by Arté's report as well as his physique and agreed to pay a handsome price for him. She thought he might make a nice coming of age present for one of her twin daughters. She only had to decide which one and she thought that his inclusion in the expedition would give her the opportunity to come to a decision.

Much to the disappointment of the younger priestesses, the future Arté briefly became Archay and left Oakbridge behind for wider horizons. As he learnt later, Archay impressed Chay in many ways and she even wished she were twenty years younger, when she would have tried him out herself. But while she was still not averse to a bit on the side, she drew the line at a mere stripling, however big, and besides, she had strict enough morals to know it was unseemly to seduce a man destined as a present for one of her daughters. That would be akin to offering a regurgitated meal. In the end her choice was easily made for her. Archay was a real find, well worth the money she had paid, and it was only right and proper that he should go to the elder twin, Thay. Shay would kick up a fuss but it was time that girl accepted her station in life. Thay was the elder, even if by only half an ihor. Thay was her principal heiress. Archay must go to Thay and become Arthay.

For the next twelve years Arthay served Thay faithfully, and proved to be a most valuable slave. He led a privileged existence for a man and accompanied Thay on most of her trips around the island. Thay was a serious business woman and Arthay undertook a variety of roles in her establishment that would normally have been thought beyond male capabilities and thus be the province of paid female employees. Indeed, in terms of the normal intersex relationships on Duplos, Thay's dealings with Arthay were unique. As a result Arthay was able to to give the university academics considerable insight into the functioning of the highest levels of Isla society.

The events leading to his current exile were complex and Arthay was not prepared to expose the details to public view. For his account to the D of AH and Th, he merely said that he had been caught up in the cross-fire between his owner Thay and her twin sister Shay, following their mother's death. He had found himself cornered at the top of a cliff near his mistress' home on the strait coast. He had fallen into the sea at high tide, where as luck would have it, he was able to hang on to part of an uprooted tree and was carried to the beach at Islaview Market. The rest, as they say, is history.

The assembled academics were happy to leave the details of the dispute unsaid. Problems between sisters were well-understood throughout Duplos, and with twins there were only extremes. They were either so inseparable that they couldn't even have sex without their twin present, or they would stab each other in the back at every opportunity.

7
Thay, Shay and Arthay: Isla

Chay arrived home in Rivermouth after purchasing Arthay. They were met formally by Thay.

"Thay, I have a present for you to mark your twenty-fourth in the traditional manner. This is Arthay, as you see he is a fine specimen of a man and almost as tall as you, a veritable giant. I've inspected him fully and I declare you should find him extremely satisfactory. As a bonus he appears to be very intelligent for a man and is literate. The head of the order where I bought him gave him a glowing reference. But I didn't have take her word for it. I was allowed to take him, on appro as it were, on my expedition into the wild. I was impressed. You are a lucky girl."

Thay showed all the gratitude that was proper to her mother, but was quite circumspect in her initial dealings with Arthay. When she had him in her quarters she was quite candid about it.

"I know it's traditional in our class," she said, "but frankly I'm not at all sure that I want my mother to choose my men for me. In all honesty I prefer to make my own choice. However, you're not to blame for that and you are physically very attractive. We must take our time getting to know each other and see how things develop."

Things did develop and half a selenth later she took him into her bed for the first time.

Shay turned on her mother, "It's always fucking Thay isn't it? It's my fucking twenty-fourth too, or is it traditional to piss on your younger daughter on such an occasion. I really don't know why you didn't drown me at birth like they did in the olden days with an unwanted second daughter. It's not as if Thay is appreciative. She wasn't exactly enthusiastic about the gift. If you'd given him to me I'd be shagging away like there is no tomorrow, whereas I see Thay has gone out on her own, probably to her club or some such place. Well fuck you, I'm going out to find someone to fuck my brains out. I think I'll go and find Crayza to help. She could do with a proper introduction to the finer things in life and her wimpish sister will never help her out."

She stormed out of the house giving the door an exceptionally hard slam breaking one of the lights as she went. She did indeed meet up with Crayza, but this had been preplanned for a while. Crayza had received the customary sex talk from Cray with the suggestion that maybe Craya could take her along with her for initiation. But much to Cray's disappointment, despite the ideal age gap, her two daughters didn't get on with each other. From early childhood they had taken different sides in the war of the twins and maybe that contributed to the problem. Cray was fond of Shay, her own goddess-child, but acknowledged she could be a bit wild. The inevitable result, she thought, of twins.

Well, that aside, Shay was fond of Crayza and was delighted when the latter had asked her help in losing her virginity and this was to be the occasion.

When she returned from this pleasant task she was met by her mother. "Shay your behaviour today was totally unacceptable and I won't stand for it. Furthermore, if you have caused any upset to Cray with your temper tantrum I shall cast you off with a groat." She waved the afore-mentioned groat in the air between them.

"Mother I apologise for losing my temper, I know I should maintain better control. I'm afraid that I felt that you had given me a final message that I wasn't and never would be good enough for you. Of the two of us, Thay may be the better politician and diplomat, but I have the sharper intellect and have the better head for business. Before this clear demonstration of your preference, I still had hopes. I'm afraid I let my hurt and disappointment get the better of me. However, you may rest easy over my dealings with Crayza. Her sister having rejected Cray's request to help her out in this way, Crayza had asked me to step in. As you are aware she always followed me around as a child when we stayed there, and unlike some others, always preferred me to Thay. I was pleased and honoured to be asked and the arrangement had been made a period ago."

"Well I am glad of that at least, Cray followed me as a child just as Crayza followed you. You got my first choice of Goddess, not Thay. I knew it would be difficult with twins. You are both natural leaders, it is inevitable that one of you must be disappointed. I had hoped you would both come to value each other and heal the rift. Arthay was not meant to be taken as an irrevocable announcement of my intentions, but like it or not, Thay is the elder, and she has not shown me any signs that she is unfit. I hadn't planned it this way but I recognised in Arthay an exceptional man. She had to be given preference. If I had pre-planned it I would have looked for two men, but I didn't. I would have loved it if Thay could have turned to you and offered to share a session with you. But I realise now that that dream is dashed and I don't think you would have shared with her either."

"No, you're right I don't think I would. Too much has been done and said in the last twenty-four years to be undone in a romp. What is to be done, I don't think I can stay under the same roof as Thay and Arthay."

"We all need a break from each other. I have an estate outside Barton-within-Lesser. My mother bought it on a whim and I have never visited. There's some sort of cousin living there, supposedly looking after it, but I doubt she is much more than a caretaker living at my expense. She's about forty so should be able to introduce you to the local life. I want you to go there and shake the place up a bit. I think two years should do it. Take a boat to Cattlebridge and then a coach to the Lesser River where you can get a boat all the way to Barton. I have tickets here for you."

"Barton-within-Lesser, that's ghastly, you can't go further into the boondocks without leaving the Theocracy. Nobody can possibly live there"

"Not true, Barton is a small town. About 1024 + 256 people live there. It's on the south bank of the Lesser River estuary. Two major rivers flow into the estuary. One from the Northern Wild Lands, and the Lesser River, from the centre of Isla. The Lesser is important. For the greater part of its length it forms the informal border with the Wild Lands, but the river itself and the traffic thereon is firmly under Theocracy control."

"Yes I know my Geography. Barton is situated on an island of low lying fen between the estuary, the sea and two arms of the river delta, one of which is diverted quite a distance to flow into the sea a lot further south. It's the back of beyond. And the indigent cousin in residence makes things even worse. I'm twenty-four and lively. How can I possibly survive with the company of a forty year old who's almost certainly of 'moderate habits'. We'll both go mad."

"Nevertheless, that's where you'll go. Unless, of course, you would prefer this groat."

With Shay out of the way, Thay began to enjoy her life. She worked hard and was rewarded with the management of the south coast estate. She took up residence in a fine house near the cliff edge about thirty-five imiles west of the town of Chalcliff-on-Strait where she had been at school. This was another sign of Chay's favour as this estate included the family's ancestral home, and the house that Thay now occupied had been built by her great great grandmother. However that house was now some fifty strides closer to the cliff edge than it had been in the days when it was built and Thay soon realised that a new one should be built further inland. She obtained her mother's permission to commission a new and much grander house. It took a year before the design of the new house was finalised and work begun on the construction.

Thay was astonished to find that Arthay made himself useful in all sorts of ways, and she gradually got into the habit of trusting his judgement on small matters and cutting him more slack than was customary for a male slave.

Arthay made himself especially useful around the building site. He noticed when corners were cut, or workers were slack, and he reported his observations to Thay to enable her to make necessary decisions and take action. Soon she found that she was accepting his recommendations as a matter of course, and the only thing that prevented her handing over to him as her project manager was that he couldn't give instructions to women.

Eventually she hit on the plan of inviting the contractor's site manager to join her for a threesome with Arthay. This was a signal honour for the manager, given Thay's high status. The session went well and, in the afterglow, Thay was able to persuade the site manager that Arthay's suggestions would come with her express authority and backing and perhaps time and trouble could be saved all round if she followed up on his suggestions, which were no more than that, not instructions from a male slave to a woman of authority, certainly not!

Thereafter Arthay was able to act pretty well as Thay's agent on the spot. The project went more smoothly, quality was assured and the house was completed within time and below budget. The total saving to Thay was several hundred marks.

While the work was in progress the sex sessions were maintained as advised to Thay by Arthay. The site manager was able to report to her employer that the reason for the slightly lower than expected profit was on account of the eagle-eyed attention of their very demanding client. On the other hand the success of this prestigious project for such a well-connected client was a strong advertisement for them that would surely bring in a great deal of future lucrative business. She was right, it did.

Thay emerged from this with valuable business experience, a grand new house, her mother's genuine appreciation, an important discovery of what she termed sexual diplomacy, and respect for Arthay's talents.

Over time Arthay's usefulness continued to grow. Thay's art of sexual diplomacy continued to develop as her status grew alongside her wealth and influence in the affairs of the Theocracy. Arthay accompanied her on several delicate missions on her own behalf and on the affairs of her mother or of state. She never had the sexual appetite of her sister but she enjoyed the occasional solo romp with Arthay. When she had other men, either with a business contact in reciprocity for one of her sexual diplomacy sessions, or when a friend invited her, she never found them as satisfying as Arthay.

Arthay enjoyed his sex with Thay, whether designed for business or pleasure and didn't really feel the need for anyone else. Occasionally he responded to the demands of other women, or granted his favours on Thay's instructions to a woman she sought to reward in this way. More often than not he was able to use Thay's imagined jealousy as an excuse to avoid unwelcome attention[15].

As for Shay, when she returned from exile her mother had her spend some time learning the river trade business. For both their sakes, Shay was allowed to occupy one of Chay's apartments in a smart area of Rivermouth and not have to live with Chay in the family mansion. There was also a flat for her use in Cattlebridge. Chay was pleased with Shay's work, for which she showed quite a flare, uncovering various scams being perpetrated by dishonest employees who found it easy to hoodwink the incompetent distant relative who was nominally in charge of the operation. Under Shay's rule the scams were ended, crooked employees sacked, with the most senior, the erstwhile deputy manager, prosecuted and the incompetent cousin retired on a modest pension.

"It wasn't her fault, Mother, she was just too trusting, and not sufficiently competent to understand. After all she is not exactly numerate."

Shortly after this Chay was having tea with Cray. She spent a lot of time now with Cray who was feeling very fragile still, following the tragic loss of her younger daughter.

"It's not that Shay makes the wrong decisions. They're almost exactly how I would have handled the issues myself. But I feel irritated that she doesn't consult me, but just informs me when all is done and dusted. It's so unlike Thay, who would have involved me in the decision making and called me Mummy. You

---

15 Female jealousy over a man's sexual encounter is virtually unheard of on Duplos, even in the WF, but ownership is a different matter. Possessions (including male slaves), status and power are causes of jealousy to be taken seriously. Perhaps Duplosian sex would be easier to understand if you think of a man as a semi-intelligent vibrator that obeys oral instructions.

know, it strikes me that Shay has not called me Mummy or Mum since she first went to school. She's always coldly formal in her address and, apart from that blow-up when I gave Arthay to Thay, she's always polite as if to a stranger. Why haven't I noticed it before?"

"You know, Chay, Shay's a bloody good business woman. She had a difficult childhood. When they were with me as children, Thay and Craya would always gang up on Shay. I tried to intervene once but Shay told me not to. She said she could look after herself. Crayza worshipped her. Reminded me of myself with you. I regret that Crayza learnt some of her antipathy to Craya from those experiences. Chay, if I'd been less hard on Crayza, she would still be here with us. I blame myself. Learn from my tragedy. Be more indulgent with Shay."

"There are limits, Cray. I feel for you about little Crayza, she was so young. It wasn't your fault. How were you to guess that she would be so headstrong as to go to sea. I am impressed by Shay's business acumen especially with the River trade, but Rivermouth is bad for her. Her lifestyle and the company she keeps worries me. She throws herself into licentiousness with a zeal that equals the energy she puts into her work. I need to get her away to one of my other estates, I'm just trying to decide which one."

"Well, Chay, I know she would prefer the Second River, but from what I hear your Barton estate needs some serious attention."

"Yes that's where I really need her, and it's further from Thay, but I worry about disappointing her again."

Chay continued, "I'll give you an example: a tale reached me that after a heavy drinking session one night, Shay and a rather disreputable friend of hers wagered a thousand Marks on who could exhaust more men. According to the rumour the two of them rounded up a group of male building workers and proceeded to ravish them in pairs until the men cried out in pain. It was said that the other girl gave up on the third man after the third time, her third man being stoically prepared to continue,"

"Some man," interjected Cray, "most men are gasping about their sore bump after the third."

"Yes, but apparently Shay who was on her fourth, didn't stop when she'd won the bet but continued to ride the man a total of five times, and it took him several periods to recover."

"Well Shay's a passionate girl, as my Crayza would tell me. You know Shay looked after her for her first time and was very kind to her, even though I now know that it was when she had become so distressed about Arthay. She didn't let her own troubles prevent her from keeping her promise to my Crayza." Cray wiped some tears from her eyes.

"Yes I know Shay was good with Crayza. Just as I gather Thay is with Craya. It's funny how Thay and Craya are similar in this way as were Shay and Crayza. Anyway earlier this phase I challenged Shay about this story and can you guess her response?"

"No, tell me."

"I quote. 'Mother, you really shouldn't listen to gossip, I am a grown woman and don't need your strictures except regarding my work on family business. I assure you the story is exaggerated in a number of details. I can hold my drink and the wager was for a hundred marks, I don't risk what I don't have. As for the rest, no woman worth her salt discusses her sex life with her mother unless it concerns them both, and I don't believe that either you or I are ready for a Mother/Daughter orgy. Now, if there is no business to discuss, I'm sure a woman of your importance has better things to do than engage in idle chatter.' At that she turned and left. I tell, you my jaw dropped with astonishment and I had go to my bedroom for a lie down to recover my composure, before coming to you."

"Phew, I can see why you're flustered. You're right, you do need to send her away. I guess it'll have to be Barton. Will it help if you settle it on her. You've already made the old family estate over to Thay, and let her build what Craya tells me is a very grand house, to replace the perfectly respectable manor house that our grandmother inhabited."

"That's helpful advice, I don't know what I'd do without you, and talking of grandmothers, I want to be one."

"There's time, your girls are still making their way in the world."

"But Arthay's an ideal choice."

"Yes he is and I'm sure Thay will get him to give her a daughter in due course, she's still only thirty-one, and they do things a bit later nowadays."

"I suppose so but I had them at twenty-nine, and you had Craya at twenty-five."

Shortly after that, Shay received a letter from her mother informing her that since she had conveyed one of the family estates to Thay, she felt it was only right to do the same for Shay. The family lawyers would be instructed to draw up the necessary papers for both estates at the same time as an advance on your respective inheritances. She admitted sorrow at splitting the family holdings, but she was persuaded that it is better for both of them to be mistresses of their own establishment. Shay was to receive the estate in Barton-within-Lesser. Chay also conveyed ownership of the Rivermouth apartment that Shay had been occupying.

Shay bore it well but was disappointed. She knew she would not be the principal heiress. She was glad she had not been cut off with a groat, but had rather hoped to get the estate near the Second River, which was much more to her liking and close to her old school where she still had friends. Indeed she had reason to believe that was her mother's plan when she chose the school. (It was). She regretted some of her behaviour while she was bored before in Barton and she knew she would need to repair her reputation. On the other hand this kick in the teeth was better than many. Despite appearances to the contrary, she had studied the estate in the two years she was there and she knew what needed to be done. She had some money of her own put by, her outward profligacy had indeed been exaggerated, and she had made some shrewd investments. She hoped she could persuade her mother to fork out for a new house on the Barton estate, on the grounds that she couldn't supplant the current occupant, and she needed all the money she could lay her hands on for the investment she intended to make, without recourse to help from the family coffers.

Chay reluctantly agreed to the new house. She tried it on with the option of buying a cottage or apartment in the town for the current occupant of the fairly modest farm house that went with the estate. Shay stood her ground, assuring her that she wasn't asking for anything half as grand as the palace Thay had erected. This did prod Chay's conscience a bit and she acceded to Shay's demands. Both labour and materials were much cheaper in Barton, than anywhere in the South East. Shay was every bit as capable as Thay, even when assisted by Arthay. Chay had neglected the Barton property, which her mother had acquired on a whim and Chay had never visited. As a result Shay did finish up with a substantial manor house, if not quite as grand as Thay's. More importantly Shay capitalised on her experience on the Great River by establishing a similar operation of her own on the Lesser River, which was the investment mentioned above. She then complemented that with a fishing business in the Lesser Estuary, which she started by buying out an existing owner and re-employing her workforce. Unlike that previous owner, she took an active interest in the business and studied to understand it, to the extend of experiencing a trip on the Estuary itself. She drove down costs, marketed the catch all down the River settlements and even opened a trading post on the bank of the un-named river flowing into the North bank of the estuary from the Wild Lands. From this post she traded with people from the Wild Lands themselves, even employing one or two to help in the shop with a promise that she would ensure they were never taken as slaves. In all these ventures she started to become a very rich woman and her status in the North East of the Theocracy grew to pre-eminence.

At a political level she was recognised as the local chief and joined the Council of the Theocracy as lay representative for the Lesser Coast Region. She managed this some two years before Thay reached the same status as lay representative for Chalcliff and the Strait.

A few years later when the twins were thirty-six years old and Arthay was thirty, Chay died. In her will, the bulk of her fortune went to Thay which included most of the property in Rivermouth and Cattlebridge as well as the business interests in the capital. Shay received a larger house in Rivermouth, more suited to her current status, than her old apartment and, much to her surprise, the estate on the Second River. This last was a late change in Chay's will. As she told her cousin, she had been hoping for a grand-daughter and was getting cross that Thay had not provided one. After all who could possibly be more suitable as a sire than Arthay - the man she, Chay, had chosen, and who in every other respect had proved most reliable as a male companion for Thay. Why, she thought, he is almost as intelligent as a woman! The will stated in bold terms if either of her daughters had given birth to a female child before her death, the Western estates should be held by the mother of her eldest grand-daughter in trust until said grand-daughter came of age at twenty-four years. If there were no such female children the property should pass to the younger of her daughters. This being the conventional lawyer-speak that translates loosely as "I want a fucking grand-daughter you no good daughters." The choice of younger (or youngest) daughter being the one with most child-bearing years left in her. In the case of the twins this is a kick in the crutch for Thay.

That clause made Shay smile inwardly at her mother, for the first time in thirty-one years. Outwardly she punched the air and shouted "Thank-you Mum." When writing that clause Chay was mentally, three different women: The Grandmother was saying "Please...," the Mother," I'm sorry for all the hurt...," and the Business woman, "I'm impressed by your Lesser River businesses, now take over the Second and do likewise." The last of these was precisely what Shay was planning.

But first there was unfinished business. Her heel had a face to grind into the dirt, and she now knew what she was going to do.

At the funeral the twins were paragons of politeness to each other, completely stiff and formal. Thay was in shock about the Western Estate. She didn't really care about the loss of the property, but she had respected and had wanted to please her mother, and she was truly grateful for Arthay. She had wanted a daughter, and had fully intended to have one. She knew Arthay was capable of impregnating a woman. She had tested that out with one of her friends who was desperate for a daughter but had found no man to her satisfaction. She had approached Thay who had gladly offered her very own Arthay. She remembered asking him as a special favour to go to cheer up her friend after carefully checking her friend's rhythms and calculating the optimum timing. Then when the girl was born she stood as Goddess to the child. Arthay wasn't with her on that occasion. He wasn't to know he was a father. That knowledge for him must be exclusively for her daughters. But she'd been so busy what with one thing or another. Why didn't Mummy say something? If she had, Thay would have set about the business that very moment. She'd have even been prepared to go through the rhythm calculations with her mother and then let her come and watch to make sure she could see what a dutiful daughter she had! "Oh, Mummy, why didn't you say? and why did you die? You were only sixty-five and in rude health." Her cries were not answered any more than Shay's had been thirty-one years earlier.

Poor Chay, one daughter was pleased with her for selfish reasons, the other grieved for her and was angry with her and herself for what had not happened.

The timing of the funeral couldn't have been more perfect for Shay. She, Thay and Arthay were all in town and the time was right. Shay's disreputable past worked in her favour. She had spent part of the previous phase in a bar where she had once been well known. She met a few contacts, strong women with a penchant for shady dealings. She bought drinks and showed the colour of money, mentioning a large sum to be available for which the women might even have to do no more that watch her having a good time.

"Understand me, if all works to my plan, you keep clear and leave quietly with your money as soon as you see I've had my fill. Otherwise, you are plan B, I'll give a signal and you will enter and pin him down. Remember he's as big as any of you and probably as strong as any woman you're likely to meet. Do not underestimate him just because he's a man, and you mustn't hurt his bits. I need to have him in tact. Do you understand me? "

The leader of the gang of four tough looking women nodded, "we understand, tell me under plan B, can we have a go when you're finished?"

"Only if I say so, I may have to threaten him with that, and may have to promise I won't let you?"

"What I can't understand is, all this fuss. Surely he's a man. If a woman like you wants a man, surely he just has to do as he's told, and anyway any man I've ever heard of would think the Goddess had made his day if you gave him half the money you've offered us. If he's that stupid, what happens if he won't come to the room of his own accord?"

"For the first, I have my reasons and that's all there is to it, as to his coming here, I think he will, otherwise it's plan C," Shay said grimly.

"What's plan C?"

"Kidnap." On that word Shay left the room.

When the time came, kidnap was unnecessary. Arthay entered the bar warily. The boy with the message hadn't said whom he was to meet but an inner voice told him it might be Shay. The boy had just said "a lady Mister, a posh-talking one, and a bit of a looker. Thought she might be after a bit of rough, but you're not a bit of rough, praps she just likes the look of your size, never seen 'un as big as you Mister, bigger than women are you? Said you'd give me a groat."

Arthay glanced at the note and handed the boy a groat. The boy just stared at the groat, then the note, then Arthay. "You can read, Mister, wow!" He then ran off and ducked down a narrow alley that led down to the river.

Arthay read the note again, and shook his head. Unusually he didn't know what to do. He wanted to take it to Thay, that would be best but he didn't know where she was, only that she had important business to attend to and didn't require his services. She would be back quite late.

Arthay never learnt whether Shay had had anything to do with Thay's absence but he wouldn't have put it past her. The note didn't say much, it asked him to go to a bar in a part of Rivermouth he had never visited before, but the directions were clear. He was to tell the barman that he has an appointment with Nemo. He could have a drink on the house if he wanted and either bring it with him or sit and drink it first before coming to a private room upstairs. He was to give the messenger a groat which he would be repaid. There was nothing else but vague hints that it was in the interests of Thay's family for him to do as asked.

Alarm bells were ringing but he was worried that Thay might have been hurt. He couldn't contact her and had to act on his own initiative. He couldn't really see what harm he could do. If Thay was in danger he had to try to help her. If there was a threat to her business interests he had to find out what he could and then act to the best of his ability. If he was in personal danger, so what, he would give a good account of himself and if the worst happened, Thay might shed a tear, but he is only a slave, and she is an important woman, especially now with her mother gone. He would go. What could possibly go wrong?

Arthay found the bar easily. It was a bit down-at-heel but that was to be expected in this neighbourhood. Inside it was quiet. A couple of elderly women gossiping over a drink in one corner and a solitary youth in his early 20's at the bar. The barman was indeed a man. Nothing unusual about that. He went to the bar and asked for Nemo. Obviously, a false name. Names beginning

Ne just don't feature in the Theocracy, too close to Nepa! He was offered a drink, but declined, saying he was there on business. "Suit yourself, " responded the barman, "the drink's been paid for and you can take it with you if you like."

The barman then showed him upstairs, "first door on the left," he called out.

Arthay entered the room and saw that it was indeed Shay. "Thanks for coming Arthay, have seat," she said. Arthay sat down, and for a while neither said anything.

Shay was debating with herself as to the best, approach. One plan was to admit she was trying to get pregnant by him. It was her and his duty to Chay's memory. Chay had wanted a grand-daughter. Obviously for the last twelve years she had wanted Arthay to be the father. That why she bought him and gave him to Thay. She wanted that grand-daughter to inherit the estate that was now hers. Yes, Shay accepted that ideally Chay had wanted Thay as the mother, but that hadn't happened, and it was also clear from the will that she would have also been content with Shay's daughter. The best way to grant Chay's dying wish was for her to have that daughter by Arthay. She now owned the estate and it would be her daughter that inherited. It would be second best for there to be a different father.

But how would Arthay take it. Would he try to convince her to let him impregnate Thay and then for her to leave the estate to her niece. Surely that's the ideal solution to the question as posed. What does Arthay know about the twins' relationship? Will he take fright at the thought of Thay's response to Shay having a child by Arthay. Should she just say she has the hots for him and must have him. What to do, she didn't really know.

Arthay too had thoughts fighting their way through. What does Shay want? Does she want to sound me out about prospects for a reconciliation? I was at the funeral in a far corner at the back of the temple. I observed the body language between the two sisters. They didn't sit together but at opposite sides of the central aisle. They walked behind the coffin over a stride apart and Shay refused to keep the customary stride behind her sister. And I've overheard Thay in tears. "Fucking Shay, Oh Mummy, what have you done? Why didn't you say? I didn't mean to fail you!"

What else could Shay want? To be honest, Arthay would have loved it if there were a reconciliation between the sisters. He fantasized about it coming about through his own sex-diplomacy. Beneath his trousers his penis stood to attention to indicate its wholehearted agreement with his fantasy, and his bump began to sweat. But in the real world he couldn't bring himself to believe in the possibility.

Shay noticed. She made her decision.

Shay stood up and announced peremptorily. "Arthay, I have a serious itch that has to be scratched. (Common Duplosian euphemism for I need a fuck, NOW). Ever since seeing you after the funeral, I can't get you out of my mind, there's a bed here, let's get on with it," at which she let her gown drop to the floor, revealing her almost perfect body, just like Thay's but somehow much sexier.

Arthay's penis stood up, speaking to him in no uncertain terms, "Goodee, " it said, "you heard the lady, let's get to it."

Arthay stood up and turned to the door. "I'm sorry but Thay wouldn't like it, and my first duty is to obey her wishes."

"The door's locked from the outside, " announced Shay. Arthay tested the handle, it was. "Come on," she continued, "you know you want to, your prick doesn't lie." She pointed at it, "Thay won't give a shit, what woman really minds who borrows her slave in a crisis of randiness. Minor irritation at the bad manners of the use of her property without asking, no worse than borrowing a favourite saucepan. Anyway, what Thay doesn't know won't hurt her, and I won't tell if you don't." She lied. If she got pregnant she certainly would tell. The whole point was to hurt Thay - really hurt her where it hurt most.

Arthay still hesitated.

"Look, if it weren't for a silly spat, the three of us would be at it together. That's what sisters do in times of family crisis. You were our mother's gift, I'm sure her intention was for shared intimacy to bring us closer together. If she'd had the sense to give you to me instead of Thay. We would have dealt together, Shay, Thay and Arshay." Her shot about her mother's intention was not that far from the truth. The rest was a lie. Shay would no more have shared with Thay than the other way round.

Arthay remained unmoved. "But Thay isn't here, If she were, and wished it, I would joyfully play my part in a reconciliation. It is my dearest dream to reconcile the two of you."

Shay thought to herself, she too wished Thay were there, restrained by Shay's thugs and forced to watch her sister impregnated by her own chosen slave. Should she have arranged a kidnap? No, the fallout-out would be too great, the war had to be fought through proxies.

She was fast losing her patience. She gave it one last try, "You know how things are between us, accede to my wish now and together we can work out a strategy to bring Thay round to a reconciliation, now that we no longer have the destructive force of the inheritance to come between us. Together we would become the most powerful political force in the land."

Arthay could see that this was a strong argument and made serious business sense. Thay was rational. It might just be possible to patch up the relationship on the back of common business interests and the prospect of political power, but it would be a long process to be taken a step at a time, and his jumping into bed with Shay would not help. His response was: "There is much in what you say, but very careful consideration must be given as to the means to bring it about. It will be a long haul. I'm prepared to work with you to that end but I will not begin the process in the way you wish. Reconciliation first, sex after."

Shay moved quickly, she caught him off guard, spun him round, grabbed him and threw him on to the bed. Arthay is big and strong for a man. Shay and Thay are also strong women and his equal in size.

"Listen, Thay has let you get above yourself, I said I was going to fuck you, and that's what I'm going to do. I was just being polite when I acted as though you had a choice in the matter. If you can't respond to normal good manners, we'll just have to do it the hard way. Don't think you will be rescued. Thay doesn't know you are here. The door is locked and guarded by four strong and lustful women, who will obey my commands without question. If you do not submit I only have to signal and they will hold you down until I have finished. After that, I will leave, and they will enjoy themselves until satisfied. All four of them. They won't squabble over you but take turns in an orderly fashion. They each like to get it multiple times. When they've finished you won't be any use to Thay for a selenth and you won't be able to hide it from her."

With this threat, Arthay knew he has beaten, and Shay knew he knew. She allowed him to get undressed and fold his clothes neatly into a pile by the bed. He then lay down on his back. "If rape is inevitable," he thought, " but I refuse to enjoy it." If only his penis would behave itself and hang down its head in the dejection he felt. He tried closing his eyes and thinking of Thay but his penis took the wrong message and his bump lubricated enough to sink a ship. He opened his eyes again but the body above him was Thay's and his was responding to its mistress.

Shay's technique was good. Objectively speaking, much better than Thay's. He ordered his brain to suppress such treacherous thoughts. It failed to heed its master. Where Thay was cool and calculating, looking beyond the purely physical, Shay was passionate, revelling in the physical pleasure of it all. Thay was measured in her approach, moderate in her demands. Shay was hedonism personified, sensual in every way. Loving the here and now of it all. Thay delighted the brain, Shay the body. Of the two, Arthay loyally pronounced the brain to be the more satisfactory sex organ. In this he was right, unique among Islish males in knowing it, or even experiencing it. But to the flesh its due, and Shay was surely the supreme mistress of the flesh.

Shay had uttered squeals of pleasure at intervals throughout the proceedings but now her pressure on his bump increased substantially and the intensity of her rubbing accelerated. Suddenly she cried out Arshay in a loud scream of delight and collapsed on to him with her tits burrowing into his face, and his third ejaculation exploded inside her.

Shay had never felt so good after solo sex, nor indeed with even the closest friends involved. The truth was that the frisson of the hidden presence of her sister was a far more powerful aphrodisiac than even the closest physical presence of an outsider. There was only Shay and Thay, Lana and Nepa. Thay didn't have to have a corporeal presence. Shay had body enough to act for them both. Thay's mind was always there, a mirror image of Shay's own. Lana to Nepa and back again. She knew that she would have a daughter. Was Nepa Isla's other parent? It was possible, with Goddesses things are possible that are impossible for people. How come there are no Gods, except the wayward Ech, and he scarcely counts. Perhaps she should write a theological paper on the subject of Goddessly procreation. With these thoughts, she collapsed into sleep, dreaming of her victory. She now had Arshay inside her head.

Arthay's ardour drained from his body as his penis fell out of Shay's. She had called him Arshay. Who's was he? What was he? Under the weight of her throbbing body he too fell asleep.

They were awakened by a loud clamouring at the door, and the sound of the key turning. The barman who opened the door was frantically apologising to Shay for the intrusion. He was followed by two burly women of the watch and bringing up the rear, was Thay.

Shay sprang to her feet, shooed away the barman, who retreated back downstairs to his proper domain. Shay realised she was naked and grabbed her gown from the floor where it still lay.

"Is that your slave, Ma'am?," asked one of the officers, Thay nodded.

Thay felt rage, as she had never done before. "Throw them both into jail to answer for their crimes," she ordered.

The officers were none too keen on this duty. Interfering in domestic affairs was not their business. Kidnapping a slave, could be, but within a family? They had no option but to assist such a prominent citizen. But this was clearly a domestic between two sisters. The twins were two peas in a pod. The law could not intervene without direct evidence of bloodletting. "We're sorry Ma'am, but the other lady is obviously your sister and there are absolutely no grounds for us to hold her, even if the law allowed us to intervene in private disputes of this nature." She really did not want to be caught up in a feud among the powerful.

Thay knew the officers were acting correctly and that she had to let Shay go. On the other hand, "take him away and lock him up until new period when I'll come and collect him," she ordered. "And while you've got him, any of you good officers can help yourselves to a bit, if you get an itch." Thereby granting the watch blanket permission to rape Arthay should they wish. She regretted that later, but not for Arthay's sake. She was in a rage.

"But you don't have my permission to rape Arshay, " Shay countered, thereby muddying the waters and further enraging Thay.

"Arthay is mine, and you know it, and it can be proved, I can order his disposal as I see fit." She yelled.

"You," shouted the officer nearest to Arthay, what is your recognised name. Arthay told her. "Right you must come with us." Arthay grabbed his clothes from the floor as the watch officers bundled him out of the door, still naked.

"You will both answer for this," were Thay's final words as she slammed the door behind her and returned to her empty home.

Shay smiled, she knew that as far as she was concerned Thay's was an empty threat. Pity about Arshay but you can't make an omelette without breaking eggs. There would never be a reconciliation now, but then there never would have been.

Still, Shay hatched a plan.

Thay cooled down, but Arthay's betrayal had shaken her to the core. Somewhere deep down some tender part of her whispered that Shay was the only one at fault. Arthay had been tricked, forced. His loyalty to Thay was absolute. Thay refused to listen to this inner voice. Her eyes had seen the betrayal in his body and in Shay's triumph as she called him Arshay. And her naked body gleaming with confidence, steaming with his juices.

Neither sister had seen the other naked since they were quite small children. On Shay's part this was incidental. She has never been embarrassed by her nudity, whether in private or public. She simply avoided Thay's presence whenever possible. Thay was the opposite, not ashamed, but intensely private about her body. As teenagers they had unusually been given separate bedrooms and kept themselves apart in the large house. They never swam together and they never used the washroom at the same time. In a sense, of course, they saw each other's bodies every day perfectly reflected in the mirror that showed Shay to Thay and Thay to Shay, only their hair styles would distinguish them.

Shay was untouchable, Arthay would have to pay for them both. If any part of him was Arshay, that part must be destroyed, and if Arthay suffered for Arshay's sake then so be it. Her decision was made and her decision was final.

The emergency that had called her away that fatal phase had been the long-anticipated crash of the old family farmhouse into the sea. She had to deal with the messenger, write some orders, and conduct various rituals in the temple. Meanwhile Shay had been seducing her Arthay. Thay was not religious, just conformist to the religious laws, a cultural follower of the pantheon, just like her mother before her, and her sister. However here was a message from on high with clear instructions on how she should proceed.

Nepa had claimed her family home, she had to be appeased with a major sacrifice. That sacrifice had to touch her where it hurt and Isla had pointed the solution to her together with a small hurt now to alleviate the greater hurt to come. The Goddesses had ordained that Arthay was to be the sacrificial victim. Only Arthay was acceptable to Nepa. He was the foremost man on Isla. His betrayal was Isla's acquiescence to her aunt's demand and her comfort to Thay to help her take the painful but essential decision of parting with her Mother's gift and destroying her most dear possession.

Thay first went to the temple to conduct the pre-sacrificial rites. The justification for the sacrifice, the identification of the victim and the location and timing of the immersion were all clearly preordained. Thay had some calculations to do to obtain the correct time. This done, she completed the temple ceremonies without a hitch and she received all the authorities and paperwork that was necessary.

She thought through the next steps. The gang rape of the victim until his bump bleeds. Then excision of his bump, causing as much pain as possible. Finally dragging him to the appointed site of immersion to be thrown into the sea. Obviously that site would be the ruins of her old house. But somehow she must ensure that the true victim is Arshay. Her Arthay, the man before the betrayal must be preserved in her memory.

Thay checked the rules carefully, there's no requirement for these rites to be performed in public even though they usually are and there's no definition of a gang. "Right," she decided, "definitely no public spectacle. I'll separate the farewell to which I'm entitled as his owner from the rape. I've ensured the timing is right to maximise my chances of pregnancy with a daughter. Then after the permitted ihor's delay I'll hand him over as Arshay for the sacrifice. Should I appoint a role for Shay? She'd hate it, but then so would I. If I never see her again, that will be too soon. I'll get my priestess to find a surgeon for the operation, who I can bribe to certify the pain was maximised while using her skill to ensure the opposite. After all I own the priestess's living. I'll then rape Arshay myself until I can't stand any more and retire to my bed to grieve. The surgeon can then come in, I don't want to meet her. She can make up the rest of the 'gang' by raping him just once before doing her grisly work. I'll then hire a crew of men to drag him to the cliff edge and throw him in. I'll then prepare the paperwork to gift him to Shay timed to coincide with the start of the sacrifice."

Sacrifices to Nepa had to be announced publicly. Thus Shay learnt of Arthay's fate, but not of the near posthumous change of ownership. She took her own steps and with her substantial fortune was easily able to bribe the surgeon to allow her to take her place.

When the time came, Arthay did not resist. He was Thay's to dispose of as she saw fit and he was not going to make things any harder for her than they already were. He appreciated her kindness in the farewell and prayed that she would be granted her daughter. After the ihor passed before the rape she told him she wasn't going to rape her dear Arthay. She would be raping Arshay.

Thay managed four times before collapsing with grief, Arshay did not accept his renaming inside, his heart went out to his Thay, it couldn't be rape if it was her, she had his lifelong consent, and the soreness after her was only slight. Thay then left to let in the surgeon.

Shay took her single go with Arthay, in case they were being watched, she said, keeping her cloak on all the while. She was naked underneath. She then released Arthay from his bonds, urging him to be silent, spattered some animal blood about the place, deliberately ruining some of Thay's furnishings in the process and led him quietly out of the house.

The six men waiting with their female supervisor to drag the victim to the cliff edge were wondering what was taking so long when the priestess came running up to the door with the surgeon in tow. The whole party didn't wait to rouse Thay, who they knew had retired to her bed, but set off after the fugitives.

Shay was not far ahead and moving with stealth rather than speed. Her transport was some imiles distant, hidden in some woods. Her intention was to smuggle Arthay to Barton where she could ensure his safety. It would be easier to accomplish if the hue and cry could be delayed as long as possible, because she knew that every priestess on Isla would be alerted to apprehend an escaped sacrifice. She was ignorant of the pursuit at their heels.

The long and the short of it was that the pursuers caught up with them and pulled them apart. Shay was in no danger, except of accident. Arthay was the target. He was separated from her and dragged towards the cliff edge. He broke away from his escort but was eventually cornered on the edge with his back to the sea. It was a temporary stalemate. A woman would not dare to fight so close to the edge, and he could throw any of the men over the cliff, and they knew it.

At least, he decided, they would not mutilate him. For that he was grateful to Shay. Even though the alternative was certain death, he was still in two minds about the rescue plan. Shay would treat him well. Sexually she was wonderful, and he didn't even have to close his eyes to see Thay during intimacy. His body had just been officially raped four times by Thay and once by Shay. His brain had had five sexual encounters with Thay. Sexual perfection was both of them in harmony. His first choice would always be Thay, regardless of the opinions of his stupid penis. If he went to his death now, his honour, like his body would be in tact. If he went with Shay, whatever the law now said, in his heart he would be a traitor. In the only eyes that mattered, he would be a traitor. He knew his duty to himself. He turned and jumped, as he did so he shouted, forgive me Thay, I love you.

That was the last he saw of the land of his birth.

In the distance under the restraint of the priestess and surgeon, Shay screamed, No!

When Arthay hit the water his arm brushed against something alongside him. It was a tree that had somehow been uprooted from the cliff face where it had been growing precariously. Instinctively Arthay grabbed at it and hauled himself aboard. In the ensuing ihors he was tossed about, ducked under the waves and generally battered but he hung on. Half-drowned, he eventually fell unconscious, but by then he was close to the shore on which a wave deposited him before retreating to the falling tide.

Chay would get her grand-daughters, two strong girls from the man she had chosen. Each one would be brought up to revere their unique father, but regard their aunt as his murderer.

8
Arté's Contract

Astra wrote a nice formal letter to Professor Fermos, recalling their previous encounters, saying a little about her current astronomical research, and mentioning her need for some assistance with calculations. She then expressed her interest in Arté and wondered if she might be a suitable candidate for the job. She asked if Fermos might allow her to visit and discuss the matter.

Fermos' reply came sooner than anticipated. She would be delighted to receive a visit. Her student, Arté was a gifted mathematician but had an unusual background, so came late to mathematical studies and would be very suited to the work and lifestyle that Astra had described. She also suggested some suitable times for the visit, or offered to travel to see Astra in Louth. Without once lying, what she didn't say was anything to disabuse Astra of her belief that Arté was female.

Astra was delighted with this reply and readily accepted the earliest period offered for the visit, and thus it was arranged. Fermos welcomed Astra to Routh, showed her round a bit and discussed her work. She was interested in some ideas Astra had about logarithms and promised to introduce the topic to Arté, who regrettably had been called away to Islaview Market at the last dumin, for sponsorship discussions with their council, regarding the up-coming contract. However, Fermos showed Astra Arté's work and discussed it with her. She was also able to assure Astra on four important points. Arté was very interested in the proposed job, would have no objection to some light domestic chores, was likely to cope with the lifestyle and certainly would not be chasing everything in trousers. Astra could rest assured on that last point!

Astra returned to Louth disappointed not to have met with Arté but otherwise highly satisfied. She told Zorro, that the prospects of a suitable assistant were good, and she hoped all she needed to do was come up with a suitable package for the contract.

Zorro was pleased but secretly did not quite trust her mother not to mess things up. In the ensuing discussion Zorro persuaded Astra to let her help with drawing up the contract and then to front the negotiation to pre-empt the auction. Actual contract auctions with public bidding rarely take place.

"Don't worry, Mummy, these auctions rarely come to actual public bidding. Leave it to me I know how these things are done and can negotiate a suitable package with the auctioneer. After a bit of toing and froing we'll come up with a winning formula agreeable to all parties. It's not just a question of the most money winning. I've got to go to an important meeting now. But I'm on the case."

She didn't say that the meeting was with Créezy, nor that it had anything to do with Astra's plans. For it so happened that Zorro had already had a hand in the matter. In reality there was much more to Créezy than her carefully crafted public image might suggest. She remained in regular correspondence with Esau, whom she had genuinely valued, and hence she had learnt about Arté when Esau told her about the unique circumstance of this Isla castaway attending a university. Créezy was intrigued, she had never met Arthay on Isla, Esau had mentioned the Islish name, but she did know Thay and Shay. Her own mother, Cray, was a cousin of Chay's so they were related. She was only sixteen when Chay presented Arthay to Thay, but she remembered it well because of her dealings with Shay. She recalled how Thay and Craya tended to gang up on Shay in a way that the much younger Crayza thought unfair. Shay's banishment to Barton had been what gave Crayza her idea for the voyage that ended with her exile to the continent.

Créezy happened to mention the story to her friend Zorro when they met at Gigi's. When her mother told her of her plan to write to Professor Fermos about her student, the name rang a bell with Zorro who then sprang into action.

After getting more details from Créezy, she high-tailed it off to Routh and called in on Fermos, uninvited. After her apologies were accepted, she and the Professor had a long and very productive discussion. Fermos was very concerned about Arté's future employment and thought that Astra's requirements were the ideal solution. Zorro in her turn was concerned that her mother would immediately lose interest once she discovered that Arté was male. In Zorro's view Astra's prejudice was irrational, and her objections were not to men as such. It was the stereotype of man as sex object that she held in such aversion.

Regardless that neither had any authority in the matter, they cooked it up between them. Fermos would be encouraging to both parties. She correctly surmised that Arté would be perfectly content with this arrangement. Zorro went home with a draft of a draft contract.

In the meantime Créezy wrote to Arté, introducing herself and explaining that Esau had mentioned him to her. She said she felt impelled to write because of her family connection to Chay, and invited him to visit any time he might happen to be in Louth.

Despite everything good about his new life, Arté still missed Thay and longed to be able to talk about her to someone who also knew her. "I can kill two birds with one stone," he told Rastu. "I've got to go to Louth to meet with the contract auctioneer. Meeting Créezy gives me something to look forward to on a phase I was rather dreading."

Arté was awestruck by the big city which was beyond anything he had ever imagined. The business with the auctioneer went well. She had already had a secret non-meeting with Zorro and was herself feeling much more positive about the whole rum process. Her partnership had never before acted for a male client and had never expected to do so.

Arté was in a light and sunny mood when he arrived at the café that Créezy had suggested for their meeting. Créezy in her turn was on her best behaviour and the two of them spent a thoroughly enjoyable couple of hora reminiscing about Isla, both of its iniquities and of the little things they missed about their former lives. Créezy told one or two anecdotes from her childhood holidays when her twin cousins visited, and, taking her cue from Arté's body language she was careful to show no partisan feelings where the twins were concerned and never to diss Thay. All in all, she recalled later, she had never enjoyed oral intercourse[16] with a man so much in all her life. She asked him to dinner where she would like him to meet a friend of hers, and offered him a bed for the night should he wish to stay. Arté readily accepted. Given his history, he did suspect her motives, and assumed he was in for a threesome. But that was OK as far as he was concerned. She surely deserved her reward for such a pleasant prelude, and anyway, despite the better manners and greater finesse over here, girls were still girls and he knew his duty and his place.

Actually he was both right and wrong. Wrong in that no threesome was planned, nor would one take place. Créezy's wild reputation was carefully cultivated and did not reflect her true nature. Her intentions here were and always had been to keep control of her desires on this occasion, which she did not expect

16 She giggled to herself when this unconventional turn of phrase came into her head, because it might have been interpreted in a very different way!

to be in any way difficult. Her feelings in this instance took her completely by surprise and off-guard. Arté was gorgeous, he was different. She imagined that solo sex with him would be as good as having her best friend with her. She had the most Goddess-awful itch, the hottest of the hots for him. "Control yourself!" she mentally told her genitals, "you're not going to bugger this up, it's too important, shut up or its a horum's soak in freezing water for you!" They didn't shut up.

In an attempt to calm her recalcitrant body down she suggested a walk in the park. It was a fine, fresh spring day with not a cloud in the sky, and they both enjoyed the stroll and further talk. Arté was able to bring her up to date, well, two years previously, with news of happenings on Isla including Chay's unexpected demise. He skipped over the subsequent trouble between Thay and Shay and the details of his own disgrace. He merely said that shortly after the funeral, Thay's old family farm house on the coast had finally fallen into the strait, and in the aftermath, he too had fallen over the cliff edge, and had been fortunate that the tide was so high that he hit deep water and the lucky happenstance of the tree enabling his survival.

It almost felt like she had been out with an old schoolfriend. Perhaps that's why, when they returned to her apartment her resolve broke and she confessed her little problem. As indeed she would have done with a real old schoolfriend. That would have been a case of: "I've got a bit of an itch, do you fancy picking up a man for a bit of fun together." A real friend would then respond along the lines of "me too," even if that were not the case, and they would go out find some hunk with a big bump and have a session, possibly even a couple of goes each. She sighed at the memory. It's different here, actually better in many ways. You have to show more consideration for the man here, which she found met with her approval, blushing as she thought of her treatment of Orcray. That was really all about putting one over on her snooty sister and rebelling against her overbearing mother. It wasn't as if she had ever needed to steal her sister's wet boyfriend. But here on the continent there were no old schoolfriends, nobody who knew her as a child, no shared secrets from the dorm, no giggles over long-past fumbling sex sessions, the failures being as much fun to remember as the mindblowing successes. Her mind was drawn to Shay and her first time. Most of all she realised, she wanted Shay. She missed her past!

When the two of them got through the door and she had hung up their coats and shown Arté to a comfortable chair in her parlour, she couldn't stop herself from blurting out.

"I've got the most Goddess-awful itch, and you are more than any red-blooded girl can stand. - Oh I'm sorry I didn't mean to say that. Look, we're not on Isla now. You have every right, if not duty, to say no, and I will respect that and I will respect you. Just excuse me for half a horum while I go and stick my nether regions into a bucket of water to cool off. I've prepared a separate bedroom for you, I won't importune you after Zorro has left us after dinner. You are safe. - Oh I have made a wretched mess of it." She sank to her knees.

Arté was bemused. He had not expected that. He had expected to be seduced, had been already been if truth be told. He didn't exactly want to have sex with Créezy, but he was quite ready to indulge her, and she was very attractive. Apart from the incident at university recounted earlier, he hadn't had sex since leaving Isla. He quite liked the freedom of not being at some woman's beck and call whenever she needed a scratch. But he wasn't really a celibate. On examination of his feelings, he was still betraying Thay. He knew that was rubbish. He knew he would never see Thay again. He knew that if they had been both back on Isla, there might well be occasions when Thay invited Créezy to join them. Now he thought about it, her sister Craya had done so on two or three occasions, admittedly forgettable as he had just proved. Physically Craya wasn't a patch on Thay, "and way below Shay," his prick added. When it comes to the 'other' women in these multi-somes it's only the physical that matters for the man. For mental or emotional connection, he needs to be properly involved in the choice, he thought. His stupid prick butted in again, "I bet Créezy's a damn sight more fun than her sister, stop your grieving for Thay."

He acted. He put his arms around Créezy, lifted her to her feet and kissed her forehead, her head being still bent forwards intent on examining the floor. This, alone, was a totally new experience for her, the first time she had encountered a man who was taller and probably stronger than her. Gently he said: "Of course I won't refuse you. I've had a wonderful time with you and that would be churlish in the extreme. You, we deserve our reward." He surprised himself by omitting 'I know my place' or 'I am yours to command'. The same omission delighted her more than she could have imagined.

As she led them, to the bedroom she had prepared for him alone, he whispered the one thought that was bothering him. "Please forgive me if I cry out Thay's name, inside I am still her slave."

She responded, "I understand completely, it is only to be expected, I would feel honoured rather than insulted. In my turn I too have something to ask, please don't ever tell Zorro about this, not when you meet her for dinner or ever." Arté had no difficulty promising this. He had no idea who Zorro was, although he realised he would soon.

The sex was magic, the first time voluntarily for two years for Arté, and physically Créezy was every bit as good as he had imagined, far better than Thay and on a par with Shay. Emotionally it was OK, but somehow Arté knew that Créezy would only ever be a casual bed-mate. A friend with benefits perhaps (not that he had that concept) if they happened to encounter each other with inclination, but nothing semi-permanent.

It was much the same for Créezy. As she expected, given his physique, that side of things was indeed the best. More surprisingly there was a level of emotional engagement that exceeded anything she had or was likely to experience from solo sex. Perhaps because probably this was the first time she had experienced genuinely consensual sex. However, solo sex was there to assuage a physical need. Scratch that bloody itch! True deep sex needed a female partner, a really good friend, a soul-sister, not like her own bloody useless sibling, her brain added. Arté was good, but he was not for sharing. Perhaps on Isla, definitely with Shay, but not here. Here she had to make her own memories, to build up that shared past with that imagined soul-sister. Isla and Shay would be in the way, Arté would be in the way.

"Come on Gorgeous, we've got a guest coming soon." At that they rose and tidied themselves up and were ready just in time for Zorro's arrival.

The dinner party went well, Arté learnt that Zorro was the daughter of his prospective employer and had been keeping knowledge of his sex from her. He understood more about his prospective role and he realised it was ideal for him. There was even a little bonus that he kept to himself. He agreed to co-operate fully with Zorro in the management of that first meeting he would have to have with Astra.

Zorro was impressed with Arté, he was right for her mother. Naturally she fancied him sexually. But resolved to keep that side under firm control, until, if ever, her mother came round to accepting it. They all had a laugh over the one clause in the contract her mother had insisted on: that Arté was not to introduce any man into one of Astra's residences for sexual purposes without Astra's explicit approval, to be obtained in advance. Naturally there were no clauses requiring any sexual services from him, nor forbidding his sexual congress with a woman.

Arté went to his bed happy, and slept better than he'd done for a long time. Shortly before dawn, Créezy crept in beside him for a cuddle. He was content to let one thing lead to another and they enjoyed a gentle quickie, and chatted about their sexual future. Their minds were in accord on the matter and both were pleased with the resolution that they would allow themselves a casual bit of fun from time to time but with no commitment to anything more permanent. Arté's interpretation was that he would make himself available if at all possible, should she ask, and would never withhold his consent. Créezy's understanding was a bit less one-sided. They also both agreed that with each other sex would remain solo. When he quietly enquired whether on their earlier session he had called her Thay, she said that indeed he had and it pleased her to be so honoured. What she kept to herself was that at the very height of release the name he had called was Shay's. That and that Shay's ghost had been present for her too.

Shortly afterwards, Arté moved in to Astra's apartment in Louth. Fermos had given him a crash course in the basics of Astronomy of the Solar System and an introduction to logarithms. The former didn't take long, because not a lot was actually known, the latter was straightforward for him because he found it gelled with some of the ideas he had been pursuing privately. He made his farewells to all his acquaintances, thanked Fermos for all she had done for him and promised to keep in touch on mathematical matters. The hardest farewell of all was to Rastu. They both cried and she spent his last night in his bed, but as a younger sister seeking emotional comfort. They each wore night clothes to avoid what they both saw as inappropriate contact. Just before he had to leave for the transport to Louth he was able to reveal his bonus. Rastu would be returning to her borders home for the Summer break in just a short time and had always announced her intention of returning to that vicinity after she graduated.

"With my contract, I'll be spending most of every Summer selenth in a village called South Beach on the Inner Sea Coast. Astra's family estate is there. Zorro tells me that you can even swim in the sea or take a boat out on to it, safely, which I find hard to believe. It all sounds idyllic. I mean, obviously I'll have some work to do, but Astra and Zorro consider this very much as holiday time and I'm sure I'll be allowed to pay you a visit from time to time. This is not Goodbye dear," he hesitated before taking the plunge, "Aimée, it is merely, 'See you Soon'."

She threw her arms around him as he fumbled to give her the address and her eyes filled with tears of joy. "That's wonderful, I promise I'll write to you with a plan. Maybe we can spend a few phases in Marouth. I'd love to show you what a fantastic city it is. We could stay in Marcenza where hotels are cheaper."

It has to be said that things did not go completely smoothly at first. Astra was not amused when she first discovered Arté's sex. She didn't blame Arté, but he had to stand there while she accused Zorro of all all sorts of crimes, labelling her a sex-obsessed tramp, having the morals of a stray dog and Goddess knows what. Zorro, for once relatively innocent of the accusations, stood her ground and gave as good as she got.

One thing was clear to Astra, however, Arté's mathematical credentials were impeccable. He would make a damned good assistant and when she had calmed down, Zorro was able to point out all the advantages for Astra. On sober reflection Astra could see that she was right and after a while she would get used to Arté and not think of him as some strange man running tame in her house. But she needed to set clear rules from the off.

"Zorro, don't you think you can lounge about the place making cow eyes at Arté distracting him from his duties and you can damn-well keep your hands out of his pants."

"Arté, let's be clear about this, Zorro has no authority to give you orders and if she makes so much as the tiniest gesture of an unwanted sexual nature, you have my permission, nay instruction, to slap her face good and hard. I don't want that over-sexed tart that I seem to have given life to, to go abusing you."

Afterwards, Zorro told him not to worry about the things her mother had said. Such ding-dongs between Mother and Daughter were commonplace and neither meant half of what they said on these occasions.

"It could have been much trickier. To be honest, I had expected to have a harder time bringing Mummy round. I am ever so grateful for what you are doing."

Shortly after, she left Mother and Assistant in peace while she went to stay with friends for a few periods saying she would join them in South Beach later. Then all began to settle down and Astra spent the remainder of their time in Louth showing Arté the ropes, and, enjoying instructing him in her research.

The move to South Beach was uneventful and Astra got used to having Arté with her.

A couple of periods in, they were relaxing in warmer weather and Astra turned to him.

"Having someone I can talk to about my work is such a relief and you are no bother to me at all. But it is hot this phase and I confess that in such weather I don't usually bother with clothes unless I'm going out somewhere. If it's OK with you I'd like to keep to my customary habit. It makes me more relaxed and saves the washing."

"Of course you must do whatever makes you comfortable. I would hate to interfere in any way with your lifestyle. Would you like me also to shed my clothes, I will do whatever makes you feel most comfortable?"

"Arté, you are my assistant and companion, not my slave. Slavery is illegal here, we are not in the GSE or the SU. You must do as you please in such matters." After a pause she added an afterthought. "But I would prefer it if you don't over-excite Zorro when she comes down because the tart can't be trusted. You must also take extra care around my sister because she is definitely not to be trusted. I suppose you shouldn't slap her face for her but, any trouble, and you should tell me and I'll teach her a much needed lesson." Astra looked fierce as she spoke.

Arté knew about sisters and sighed to himself. He resolved he would wear a pair of shorts about the house on Astra's nude days only taking them off for the beach or a swim.

Part 2

Geos

9
Geos: New Norland

Wild Cat Waters was ambitious. Xe always had been since that **meal**, twentwy-four years ago[17] when as an eight year old child xe had learnt about that strange world in the sky that loomed over the land. You weren't supposed to be ambitious. If good things happened to you, that was your good luck, but that same luck might have fallen on someone else, all men were equally deserving. In seeking your own good fortune somehow you were setting yourself up against your fellows, claiming superiority. That was not only selfish it was rather immoral, xer birthparent had said to xim when xe came home for the mid-selenth holidays. Xe looked as if xe were going to cry.

Xer seedparent just shook xer head and taking xer child on to xer knee said, "My child you must learn the ways of the world or your life will be unhappy. We both love you and Mum didn't want to upset you, come let's have a cuddle and we can go feed the ducks, while you tell me about school."

"You do mollycoddle that child, Roaring" was the birthparent's comment, "No wonder xe thinks xe's special."

---

17 The word 'meal' as used here is a measure of time equal to four Earth hours, so named because it is a sort of standard interval between meals. To help avoid confusion I shall embolden it when used in this sense. Similarly the words 'work' and 'life' are also time measures, corresponding to 1/6 of a year and 72 years respectively and will also be emboldened as will other terms used as measures that might otherwise be confusing.

Geosians use a base 12 number system, I use the words twentwy, thirtwy etc. for two and three times the base and tween instead of teen, twecade instead of decade etc. When I use figures in what follows I use ***A*** and ***B*** for ten and eleven, and use the convention of writing numbers in ***bold italic*** to remind the reader to interpret them as base 12. See Appendix 2.

"Xe is special to me. Every child deserves to be special to xer co-parents." Xe hugged little Wild to xim. "That's not belittling the worth of others. It is strengthening the relationship bonds within the family and helping to prepare the child for when xe in turn becomes a co-parent."

Roaring Deer Waters, was the more soft-hearted of Wild Cat's parents. Perhaps that was why, before starting at boarding school Wild Cat announced that xe would take xer seedparent's surname, which was less usual than average for xer class at school. Of the eightween children that had started with xim that selenth, twelve had chosen their birthparent's surname. Perhaps xer birthparent was secretly unhappy with with xer choice. Wild Cat suspected that Mum would prefer such matters to be decided by the toss of a coin, a stratagem that Wild Cat had observed that parent often used when xe had a binary decision to make.

Xe had gone off that **meal** with xer Dad and chattered away telling xim all about xer friend Flying Eagle Forest who occupied the neighbouring bed in the dormitory and desk in the classroom. "Flying Eagle is my spe... no, good friend even though we are of different types."

"What do you mean, different types?" Roaring Deer had not been to boarding school.

"There are two different types among us children. Some have got willies and some haven't. It's usually easier to be friends with your own type, but with me and Flying Eagle it's different. We are both excited by the possibilities of life on Duplos. Me and Flying Eagle make up stories about it and we're both going to go there when we grow up. We often get into trouble for talking in the dormitory."

Roaring Deer understood, and who knows, if the present political madness ends, voyage to Duplos might just be possible in Wild Cat's lifetime. So much had been the changes in technology over the past mem. Xe smiled at xer child and whispered to xim, "You are allowed a special friend, it's not selfish, it's normal."

"Do you have a special friend, Dad?"

"Your Mum is my special friend, didn't you know that. That's why we live together and why we had you as our very own child."

"Mum always complains about that, goes on about having a fat belly for a **work** and then another two selenths to look after me all by ximself; the best part of a year away from xer job, why did xe have to do that? I would much rather have been with you."

Roaring shook xer head and sighed, xe was sure xe'd been through all that before. Nevertheless, xe answered xer child. "Before you are born you grow inside the body of your birthparent, that's where the name comes from, for it takes about four and a half **works**, and for the last **work** you are big enough to show and xe looks fat, a big bulgy tummy sticking out. It marks a man out amongst all those who aren't going to have a baby. You know your Mum feels uncomfortable if xe stands out from the crowd. Xe likes to be anonymous. So xe was rather grumpy at the time, I recall. Also, xe needed more rest and had to stop working for that time. Then, when you were new born you needed xim to feed you with the special milk xer body produced, that all new birthparents' bodies produce. I couldn't have done that. Despite popular myth there are real differences between the different types, as you put it just now, those of us that can become seedparents and those who can become birthparents. When that was no longer needed I hired somebody to look after the business while I took time off to look after you. When you were a year old, you were old enough to come with me and I went back to the shop, which was much easier for me to do because I am my own boss in my furniture shop. Your mum has a high-powered job in a bank, and makes a lot more money than me."

"Do you mind about that, doesn't it mean xe counts as better than you?"

"No it wouldn't even cross my mind. We are a strong family unit and everything is shared. We are equal in our marriage."

"That's not quite how it sounded when you were deciding about my school."

"Well I would have liked you to delay boarding school for two more years, if not all four remaining years of primary school, but we made the rational decision together. Mum hadn't really insisted, xe had merely articulated the arguments for and against that led to the logical conclusion."

"It seems to me that Mum is bit more equal in your marriage."

"Well, perhaps xe is. That's OK by me, I love Bunny Rabbit very much, and still can't really believe that xe accepted me. I want xim to have everything xe wants."

In another part of the city, Flying Eagle Forest's parent's were also equal, but in xer case it was the seedparent that was more equal and the tender-hearted Basking Shark Forest to whom xe ran and poured out xer hopes and fears as Basking Shark hugged xer baby that had returned.

In xer turn Flying Eagle told xer Mum about xer friend Wild Cat.

"Mum, why are we of different types?"

"Well dear, it's all about your sex or gender which are the proper words for type; whether you can be a seedparent, who has a willy, or a birthparent like me, who doesn't."

"I didn't know that."

"I suppose I should have told you more before you went to school. I forgot that at boarding school you'd be bound to notice. You see, we are quite private about these things. Back in olden days people sometimes made more of a thing about the differences. Old Norse even had different words for man and for pronouns like xe depending on which type you are[18]. Although our modern language derives from old Norse we have only retained the words birthparent and seedparent and the diminutives Mum and Dad. Having unnecessary distinctions in language can lead to treating people differently. Which can lead to unfairness, as well as inefficiency."

"How do you mean?"

"If you distinguish between people unnecessarily you can discriminate against them. Perhaps only letting one sex do some jobs for example or paying them unequally. As well as obviously being unfair this means people's talents might not be used properly which is inefficient. When you see people with their clothes on you can't tell which sex they are. There are no outward differences. This is unlike some animals that show what we call gender dimorphism, with the two genders being of different sizes or with different markings in some way. We don't show that and while some individuals are better at some things than others, all talents seem to be equally distributed between the two sexes. If you don't know about someone's sex you can't make decisions based on prejudice. For us the only difference is the obvious one about willies and a slight bulge in the

18 As your will have observed, I translate as xe = he/she, xer = his/her, xim =him/her, xers = his/hers.

birthparent's chest where xe feeds xer babies. In our society we adhere to strict equality between the sexes and it's considered rude to ask anyone. So it's not at all unusual to have no idea about the sex of your friends unless you happen to see then without clothes, as I suppose you must do when sharing a dormitory."

"That's right, we see each other that way all the time. But how do you find out if you can't ask and you want to co-parent a child."

"There are ways, you'll learn when you get older. For example, swimming is very popular with tweenagers and people in their twentwies."

"I guess nobody would be stupid enough to wear clothes when swimming."

"No indeed, I can't imagine anything worse than having some clammy wet cloth against my skin. Your Dad and I met at a swimming party when we were at university. I'm afraid I laughed when xer willy got a bit too excited. Xe went red with embarrassment and avoided me for a selenth, but we became friends when we encountered each other a couple of years later."

The years passed and Flying Eagle Forest and Wild Cat Waters sailed through prep school and secondary school together. They competed fiercely against each other, but kept that secret from outsiders. They each had other friends of course and were a little shy of each other in their early tweens but soon got over that. They worked together, played together, swam together in the river, examined each other's bodies more closely than their parents would have approved, discussed first the dormitory rumours and later the formal life education lessons together. They became inseparable.

Flying Eagle and Wild Cat each won a place at the same prestigious university to study Aeronautic and Space Engineering. It was inevitable, each alone knew of the other's determination to travel to Duplos. Ambition was still a bit of an ugly word in their society, and theirs was kept secret between themselves. When they went to university, as they had agreed a year earlier, they moved into a flat together, with two bedrooms, each with a double bed. They didn't tell either set of parents that they only used one of them at a time.

After graduating they spent three years working for the same company, but career prospects were such that Flying Eagle felt the need to move to another part of the country. They remained in touch with each other but it proved impossible, as they had both known it would, to sustain an exclusive relationship at a distance of some ***A50*** twilomen[19].

They each had other relationships, but of short duration, neither settled down.[20] Each set of parents had despaired of ever having grandchildren. That didn't seem to bother Bunny Rabbit, but it saddened Roaring Deer's heart.

The two best friends met at professional events over the years, had the odd holiday together, even had the occasional one-nighter, one of which caused the final break-up of one of the 'failed other relationships'. Now twentwy-four years after they first met, at the age of thirtwy, half a lifetime, they were both

---

19 See Appendix 3 for Geosian measures, A twilowman is their equivalent of a mile or kilometre, and is a bit over 1.6 miles or 2.6 km. (A **man** is their base unit = 1.53 m ~ 5', the average height of a Geosian. twilo is their prefix for $\boldsymbol{10^3}$ = 1728 in decimal)

20 Monogamy is the norm on Geos. The ideal is a whole-life partnership, with perhaps one or two false starts on the way, 'Playing away' when already in a relationship is rare and frowned upon.

after the same job and each was desperate to win it for themselves.

10
Interlude 1: Space the frontier on Geos

At a technological level Geos is much like late 20th or early 21st century Earth. Like every planet inhabited by intelligent life, when you translate its language it comes out that it's a planet called Earth going round a star called The Sun. The same is true with Duplos, I can't go calling every planet Earth and every star The Sun, that would be far too confusing. I'm prepared to go along with 'The Sun' but the only planet I'm going to call Earth is my own. I've taken the names from the Duplos pantheon, because that is how they name the various planets and moons in their Solar System and being closer to their prehistory than the Geosians, they are more romantic. The only exception is Duplos itself. Which is based on the Geosian name which basically means twin or duplicate because it is so similar in size to Geos itself.

So Geos it is and its people are Geosians. Just like on Duplos and on Earth and on all the Earths, the people have evolved to suit their planet. And this planet has a slightly higher gravity than our Earth. So the people are shorter and stockier than we are. They don't all look the same, but you could be forgiven for thinking they do. Although all the usual measurements follow the same sort of normal distribution on Geos as elsewhere, the variances are particularly low, and neither mean nor variance of any of the measurements that people usually take differ in the slightest between the male and female populations. Men and Women are so equal that they are all just known as men.

Geos contains more than one country, there is no such thing there as a world Government. I can't even say that there is world peace or some sort of global unity of purpose. They have had times in their history when one country or another has experimented with various forms of division of roles, but they were never satisfactory and, while there are minor cultural variations in different regions of the planet, this successful egalitarian model for inter-gender relationships is universal.

There are several smaller, and undoubtedly very pleasant countries on Geos, but only three great powers. New Norland is the leading superpower. It is the wealthiest and most advanced technically, and the locus of the action.

Ever since people had first begun to realise that the moon that stood over so much of the sky was in fact another planet just like theirs, Geosians dreamed of the period when men might travel there. It was several lifetimes before technology looked like it might catch up with the dream and in the year ***1560*** by their reckoning a young (twentwy-eight years old) charismatic presidential candidate electrified xer country with a campaign promise to inaugurate a programme to plant the New Norland flag on Duplos. Xer enthusiasm was catching and xe won the election (New Norland is a parliamentary democracy. For readers from Earth, it's constitution is somewhat like a cross between the UK and the USA).

When it came to it, it was much more easily said than done. The new President was no fool. Xe was passionate about the goal, and accepted that the electorate would turn on xim once they realised the true magnitude of the challenge, and the timescales that would be involved.

In the popular imagination, of all the planets and moons in the Solar system, Duplos would be by far the easiest to reach, as well as offering the greatest prize. It is by a long way the closest heavenly body to Geos. The distance between the two worlds is ***64,500*** twilomen. The distance to the next nearest body, Selenos, varies between ***159,000*** and ***194,000*** twilomen. And Selenos is a barren moon with no life, water, or air[21].

In reality, the distances are the least of the problems to be overcome. The complications of the Geos-Duplos orbits about their common barycentre and the gravity on Duplos makes the technical challenge of landing there, and returning, much harder than for a less complicated destination like Selenos from Geos (or the Moon from Earth). President Racing Horse Wheatfield knew this, and knew that Duplos could not be the first destination. Xe was a little disappointed, but not surprised, when the scientists mapped out their estimated timetable that extended beyond xer own expected lifetime. If the plan survived the inevitable policy changes, and the technical obstacles were overcome as planned Xe would be eightwy-ten years old when the landing took place and life expectancy on Geos was sixtwy-four. Some men did live into their ninetwies, but it was rare.

In xer second year in office, the president launched the fiftwy-ten year programme leading to the first man to walk on Duplos in the year ***1600***. There were some exciting targets on the way, that xe hoped would help sustain the momentum as the years passed. Xe knew the chance of the programme surviving such a timescale was small, but if the first steps were not taken, the goal would never be reached and the great Geosian dream would never be realised. As the best achievable target available, xe announced the initial goal of a landing on Selenos within the twecade.

Many of the scientists were less happy about this, which they saw as a diversion of effort. They all agreed that a landing on Selenos was an essential precursor, but their calculations were

---

21 These distances are approximately 350,000, 973,000 and 1,170,000 km respectively, for comparison the distance from the Earth to the Moon is about 384,000 km.

that the optimum programme would delay that for a few years, perhaps to the mid ***1570***s. The President over-ruled them, xer political instincts told xim that an early landing somewhere was essential, and the space station, orbiting both planets, which the scientists wanted first, would not be enough. Selenos first, space-station second. Politics trumps Science every time.

The programme was launched. The roadmap described, explained and debated by various pundits on television, and the early stages proceeded according to plan. The population was disappointed. There are and always will be those who do not share the dream. Such people came out with an "I told you so" attitude and argued against this incredible waste of resources. "Just how many twilotwegs with it cost the taxpayer," they would complain, and then receive the unhelpful retort from enthusiasts, "Oh more like twegatwegs but worth every penny"[22].

Of those who supported the dream, the oldest and the youngest generations were the most steadfast in their support. The old never had expected to see the fulfilment and thus the **life** length of the programme did not dint their enthusiasm, they dreamed that their own great grandchildren would witness the events. The very young, with the optimism of youth, held on. But the middle generations who had voted that theirs would be the generation to realise the dream felt they'd been kicked in the teeth.

The more realistic and educated of these middle generations overcame their disappointment, realising that the intermediate steps were essential, and accepting the broad thrust of

---

22 'twilo' and 'twega' is like our 'kilo' and 'mega', on Geos meaning a factor of 12^3 and 12^6, thus 'twilotwegs' is most easily translated as 'billions' and 'twegatwegs' is mostly used in the sense of 'zillions', the implicit 'pounds' is left unsaid.

Programme Duplos. The less educated grumbled. They didn't see why it should take so long. Even if we did have to go to Selenos first, which they weren't at all sure was really necessary. Surely six to sixtween years after should be more than sufficient. 'Sixtween not Sixtwy' became a slogan for this cohort.

With a much reduced majority, the President won a second term of office in the ***1566*** election. This saved the programme in the short term. One of xer opponent's campaign promises was to cancel it, substituting a much reduced programme of more useful exploitation of near space. By useful xe meant projects with a short term payoff.

The programme continued with the first satellites to orbit the binary system. Previous satellites from the earlier part of the programme, and those of the previous two twecades had all been in low Geos orbits, where the interference of Duplos' gravity was minimised and the solutions to the orbital equations were dominated by the Geos-satellite two body problem. (Even then it was necessary to employ engines to keep the satellite in its Geos orbit as it neared its periapsis with Duplos). Anything further out had to take Duplos into account in a non-trivial way. Other steps forward had been in rocketry to establish the capability to cover the distance to Selenos. This part of the programme had included fly-by probes to Selenos and Eclos which gathered data of wider interest to the scientific community and the first close-up photographs of the surfaces of both moons.

Important sub-goals achieved in the second phase of the Selenos project, were:

1566: First orbit of Selenos, three times round the moon and return to Geos. First shot to round Duplos and return to Geos:

1567: First satellite of Geos-Duplos. this was in a high orbit to avoid capture by either planet. Careful planning and calculation enabled the eventual break-up to be in the atmosphere of Geos. The first unmanned landing on Selenos, with an exploration vehicle that could conduct analysis, and send data back to Geos.

1568: Space-station established in low Geos orbit. More probes and orbiters of Selenos.

1569: Low flyby's of Duplos, transmitting data and images back to Geos.

156A: First manned orbit of Selenos. Launches from the space station of small rockets and payloads, to both Geos and Selenos.

156B: Second manned mission to Selenos orbit, landing unmanned capsule and retrieving it for return flight. Landing an unmanned craft on Eclos, which took rock samples and launched a container with the samples back to Geos.

1570: Project suspended pro. tem.

What went wrong? In the fourth work[23] of ***156A***, the President was diagnosed with an inoperable brain tumour and by the end of the year xe had died. The Vice-President was a supporter of the programme, but did not have the qualities that had enabled xer predecessor to keep up the momentum. The programme for ***156B*** went ahead pretty much as planned but then political difficulties in the election year, and an unhelpful debate between scientific experts with little political acumen brought about the decision to delay the ***1570*** programme, which had been two more manned missions to Selenos, the second of which would have been that all-important first landing.

---

23 As detailed in Appendix 3, a year on Geos is divided into ***6 works***, named because it is the usual interval between payments of salaries, it is the equivalent of two months on Earth.

The psychological impact of the missed landing undoubtedly contributed, but the opposing candidate would probably have won the election anyway. The pundits argued about the hypothetical for **works** after the election. Opinion was almost equally divided, but the balance favoured the view that if the landing had taken place and President Wheatfield had still been alive, the election would have gone the other way.

The new President was not keen on the programme. Political considerations meant xe couldn't abandon it completely, but xe cut the budget, kept kicking the Selenos landing down the track, and devoted xer energies elsewhere. Progress was made in a lot of small ways. Good use was made of the space station, and a second one was launched in ***1574***. Mini-launchers between the stations were tested, which enabled the development of a number of capabilities which would be of use in the later stages of manned exploration.

During this time, a great deal more was learned about Duplos. Chemical analysis of its atmosphere and surface established that it would support Geosian life. There were tantalising suggestions that there were animal inhabitants, possibly even intelligent beings. Attempts were made to communicate, and to listen but these drew a blank. Duplos did not appear to have radio. Robotic and computing technology also advanced apace, and the President announced that xe would support a mission to land an intelligent Robot on Selenos, xe suggested (without scientific evidence) that this might be done during xer second term of office. Xe explained that, as a life-long humanitarian, xe just was not willing to risk peoples' lives on such a venture and cautioned that we should all wait until the technology advances sufficiently to allow machines to pioneer the way for exploration of our space neighbourhood, until such time as men might follow in safety. 'Stay Home, Save Lives' was xer motto and xer message.

It didn't do xim much good. Xe lost the ***1576*** election by a small margin. However the momentum was also lost and Programme Duplos did not regain its status or impetus. Some progress did occur. A manned landing on Selenos actually took place in ***157A*** but it was not followed with another. The initial plans were for building a station and launch facilities on Selenos for the Duplos shot. The problem was not so much the journey to Duplos but the return. As things stood a journey from Geos to Duplos would be a one-way ticket. Notwithstanding the fact that the orbital modelling was still inadequate, the foremost challenge was the Gravity.

Launching from Geos requires a great deal of infrastructure. The escape velocity is ***11.34*** twilomen per tick (tpt), from Duplos ***9.91*** tpt and from Selenos only ***1.8*** tpt.[24] Even though the effort to take-off from Duplos is noticeably less than from Geos, it is still quite substantial. The infrastructure isn't there and it is a challenge to carry enough fuel for the launch. Selenos is easier by a long way. The original plan had envisaged building a station on Selenos where enough fuel could be stored to enable a two stage journey, since the escape from Selenos requires relatively little fuel, it should be possible to carry enough to enable a launch from Duplos back to Geos. Unlike surface travel, distance in space is not a heavy consumer of energy, manoeuvring and escaping gravitational wells is what takes the effort.

However the Selenos plan did not enjoy universal support among the experts. There was growing support for the alternative of building a space station in orbit about both planets outside that of Duplos. This would have the advantage of being

---

24 Naturally these are in Geos units and duodecimal numbers, quite tricky to convert. In km/s these correspond to the decimal values 12.638, 9.283 and 1.587 km/s. The equivalent figures for Earth and the Moon are 11.186 and 2.38 km/s respectively. Gravity on Geos is 1.119g. On Duplos it is 0.845 g (where g is Earth's gravity of 9.81 m/s^2).

much closer and being easier both to access and to tailor the design of facilities and orbit to match the requirements more closely. Furthermore, engineers had gained a lot of experience with the existing low Geos stations and while there were still many challenges, including getting off Duplos without the benefit of a planet side spaceport, the prospects looked less risky than the Selenos plan.

While the space engineers debated the technical issues, other groups were also beginning to ask awkward questions. Images from the Duplos probes showed a number of features that could have been man made. If there was life there, would it be a threat to our landing party? Would there be dreadful diseases that the astronauts could bring back? On the other hand would we be causing damage to a native civilisation? Could our pathogens wipe them out? Did we have the moral right to undertake such a venture? Late sixtweenth mem society was much more squeamish about such matters than their ancestors who had pioneered the spread of civilisation throughout Geos.

Then in the ***1580***s politics shifted sharply towards egalitarianism. An age of political correctness dawned, and frankly, the new normal was incompatible with the drive needed to maintain the Duplos Programme. Progress in space stalled for more than thirtwy years.

11
The Egalitarian Experiment: New Norland, Geos

Throughout the ***1570***'s there had been growing disenchantment with the political parties in New Norland. The party for progress, PFP, saw itself as the natural party of Government, and had indeed dominated the political scene for the past mem. A 'mem' gets its name from memory, short for 'living memory' and is equal to two '**lifes**', a **life** being sixtwy years. Tradition being that the allotted lifespan of men was sixtwy years. There is a traditional ditty about it, which all Geosian children know. Anyway twice the traditional life span is seen as a measure of living memory, helped by the numerology that attracts people wherever they are. ***100*** years is a much better unit of time than ***108*** which is twice the actual life expectancy at birth of late sixtweenth and early seventweenth mem New Norlanders. The PFP's reputation was for sound management of the economy together with a slight tendency to social conservatism. The party was seen as business friendly, encouraging economic progress through enterprise. Its core values included personal responsibility and self-reliance. It also emphasised the role of the individual in taking responsibility for community and social enterprise. In general this stance played well in a society that had a strong pioneering tradition, with a philosophy that the world is what you make of it. Internal to the party was a permanent tension between those that emphasised individual liberty (the liberal wing) and those that emphasised individual responsibility (the conservative wing). 'You should be allowed to do what you want as long as it's what I want you to do', is how this was often caricatured.

In practical terms, the main opposition party, the Party for Consent (PFC) was not very different. They adopted a similar approach to economic policy, but on pragmatic rather than ideological grounds. They didn't really trust market mechanisms to deliver fair outcomes, and their ideological commitment was to fairness. Within their ranks was the tension between seeking consensus and telling people what was good for them. 'Surely we all agree we must be fair, and I'm telling you what fair is', was the caricature of their approach.

President Racing Horse Wheatfield, was from the PFP. Xer support for the space programme came naturally to xim as an example of technological progress that should bring economic and social benefits, but was too challenging and long-term an enterprise to be driven by anything other than the resources of the state. Opposition from within xer party mostly came from those concerned about the extent of Government spending involved. The opposition from the PFC was grounded in the fear that the programme would divert resources to already powerful technology corporations, with little benefit to smaller enterprises, and even less to ordinary people other than the very small elite that might personally benefit from such things as holidays on Duplos. It just wasn't fair!

After Wheatfield's death in ***156A*** the PFP was unable to find a candidate approaching xer stature, and the unedifying in-fighting that followed sapped the confidence of the party's supporters. The opposition were seen as a bit lacklustre, but nonetheless they scraped into power. Their performance in office lived up to expectations. They dithered where leadership was required. They saved money by cutting the space programme, and then squandered it on subsidising failed sectors of the economy. It was universally agreed that they were a complete failure. Thus in ***1576*** the PFP won the election by default, and, despite an unremarkable record and disillusioned electorate, retained power in ***1580.***

In ***1576*** an academic political philosopher advanced a critique of both political parties. Mad Dog Prairie came from the authoritarian wing of the PFC. Xer guiding value was 'fairness', but xe thoroughly distrusted individuals to do what was right. It came easily to xim to attack the PFP but xe was equally disenchanted with the PFC record, both in ***1571-1576*** and earlier PFC administrations. With some specific reservations, xe agreed that the PFC's heart was in the right place. The problem was they were just totally incompetent. They messed up the economy, failed to come up with ideas, and indulged in regular financial scandals. Most of all the PFC had shown itself incapable of providing leadership.

Prairie's big idea was to build on the one great social success of mankind (author's note - 'on Geos'). That of absolute gender equality. All historical examples of Geosian societies that had differentiated in the treatment of the two genders, had been demonstrably inferior on any measure one might care to adopt, economic, social or familial. Surely the way ahead was for mankind to evolve into a more co-operative way of working together for the greater good. This would be based on the equal value of all human endeavour, and eliminate harmful competitive behaviour that leads to waste and sub-optimal outcomes, as well as devaluing the non-winners in a way that was both disrespectful and unfair.

Prairie was able to cite mathematical studies from the ***1540's*** about a scenario in Game Theory called Prisoner's Dilemma that showed that, without external intervention to force co-operation, people's behaviour would always lead to sub-optimal outcomes against the best interests and, indeed, actual wishes, of the parties involved. The solution had to be for Government, with strong leadership, to employ both coercive and non-coercive methods to enforce a more egalitarian society that,

Prairie claimed, would lead to more co-operative behaviour and better outcomes.

In the political climate of the late ***1570***'s and early ***1580***'s Prairie's ideas attracted more than just the interest of xer fellow academics. Prairie had ximself admitted that xe personally was not the leader that was required, xer talents lay in the background, developing ideas and policies but not in implementation. Xe also made clear that neither the PFP nor the PFC were up to the job of bringing about the necessary change. The PFP would be ideologically opposed to xer ideas whereas the PFC had neither the will nor the stomach to see them through. They were just too wishy-washy and institutionally incapable of showing leadership.

Prairie's ideas were widely spread throughout New Norland; in academia, in public channels such as television and the newspapers, and via social media, where they went viral. Following the disastrous election campaigns of ***1580*** with the lowest turnout (fiftwy-ten pertwent - ***5A%*** - less than half the total)[25] since universal suffrage was introduced nearly one and a half mems previously, with the smallest vote tally recorded by a winning candidate in the past dozen elections. The clear winner was 'none of the above', while the actual winner had garnered the 'support' of just ***2A.7%*** of the electorate.

25 On Geos the equivalent of percent is out of 144, my term for this is pertwent ***% in bold italics.*** Thus 50% translates as ***60%***. The pertwentage mentioned here means 68 out of 144 voted and 34.58 out of 144 voted for the winner.

After that the PFC imploded and a new party was formed with considerable public support. They called themselves the Party of the Egalitarian Experiment (PEE)[26]. Prairie was appointed to lead a think-tank that was influential in providing the ideology for the new party, and, developing and advising on it's policies.

In the ***1586*** election the rump PFC did not field a presidential candidate, and urged its former supporters to switch to the PEE. There remained a few PFC members of parliament. The PFP put up a fight but the result was never in doubt. The politically disillusioned electorate handed the PEE a convincing victory both in the presidential election and the lower house of parliament. Some seats in the upper house had been won by PEE sympathisers in ***1583***. The upper house elections of ***1589*** and ***1593*** saw a sizeable shift in the sympathies of that house[27].

The PEE maintained their hold on power for a generation, transforming society. Anti-discriminatory laws abounded, and since there actually wasn't much in the way of discrimination around to legislate about, it entered into such areas of life as Education where discrimination included failing students who performed badly in exams, either because they weren't clever enough or because they were lazy. Workplace discrimination was blamed for some wages being lower than others. Surely it's unfair that one man is paid less than another just because xer work is seen as less valuable by the employer.

Gradually, societal attitudes changed. It became socially unacceptable to single anyone out, either for rebuke or for

26 New Norland was the first major country on Geos to introduce universal suffrage, which they often refer to as the great democratic experiment. The use of the word 'Experiment' here is an echo of past tradition that resonated with New Norland citizenry.

27 I describe the constitutional set-up in Chapter 15.

praise. Inequalities due to effort or ability were seen as suspicious, only luck was acceptable. Luck didn't discriminate, it could happen to anyone.

The outcomes did not match the expectations of the followers of Prairie's theories. Those who disagreed with the egalitarianism, kept their heads down and paid lip service to the politically correct attitudes. But they coached their children whether in sport or schoolwork. Employers found ways of rewarding their truly valuable employees to retain their services and discovered innovative ways to select for key posts.

Too many people lost incentive for that extra effort. Overall performance in the workplace and in schools dropped. Participation in sport declined. Schools emphasised the less competitive sports. Gymnastics, where individuals competed largely against themselves was encouraged. Games with clear winners and losers were discouraged.

Outcomes were precisely the opposite of what was intended.

The economy suffered as productivity fell.

Academic standards in schools dropped. In order to ensure all children passed exams, the standards were reduced and able children were discouraged from over-achievement. Universities had to run remedial classes to make up for lower standards at entry, and even then their qualifications were devalued. Of course some students were both bright and motivated. These performed as well as they'd always done. They received their devalued first class degrees and went on to prove their value to employers by other means. But too many people failed to reach their full potential.

Social mobility stalled. In this egalitarian world, home environment counted for everything. Those with supportive co-parents and an encouraging home environment more-or-less prospered. The less fortunate had no opportunity to be noticed, nobody stood out from the crowd. Family and peer group pressure dominated a person's chances in life.

Innovation and enterprise slowed. It didn't stop. Men are too resilient for that. Too many of those who might have succeeded were just sufficiently discouraged to tip a venture from success to failure, not to go the extra batwoman. Furthermore, any innovation that was not seen as immediately relevant to the population as a whole failed to gather support from Government. Had many of the great inventions of the past been first proposed in the PEE twecades they would never have got off the ground. For example things now seen as essential by the masses such as cars, television or smart-phones would never have been developed. In their earliest days all these were seen as expensive toys for the rich that would never be within the reach of ordinary people.

The space programme was an early casualty. Official PEE policy was to cancel Programme Duplos and, accordingly, that happened in the first year they took office. There were some scientific and technological advances in the years of PEE government, but nothing like the rate of progress of the previous twecades.

The other major failing of the egalitarian philosophy was that it encouraged society in general be become excessively risk-averse. Now, there is no harm in a proper degree of caution and no good in taking unnecessary risks. But failure to take any risks, or to be so imprisoned by the need for caution as to fail to brave new ventures, causes stagnation and inhibits social, economic and technical progress almost to the extent of bringing them to a standstill.

Eventually the populace rebelled. There had always remained a significant minority that hadn't fallen for the egalitarian agenda, whether for purely selfish reasons or because they had analysed the philosophy and worked out its inner contradictions. But after thirtwy years the populace in general had observed the failure to improve cooperative behaviour, noticed the slide in the economy and technological progress, despaired at the dependency culture and become thoroughly fed up with the Nanny knows best attitude of the state.

Furthermore there was now a completely new generation of PFP politicians. The egalitarian age had not been a complete waste. The PEE had presided over a number of important social reforms, not least in the management of health care, that the populace would not be willing to risk losing. However the new generation had bought into these changes and there was no further risk that the reforms would be reversed. What the PFP promised was to get away from empty slogans and micromanagement of personal relations. At the same time they would cut red tape and restore competition and incentives to kick-start enterprise and get business and society moving again.

The electorate was more than ready. The new intake in the ***15B3*** elections for the upper house was largely sceptical of the egalitarian agenda, and the PEE were wiped out in the Presidential and Parliamentary elections of ***15B6***.

You will have gathered that Bunny Rabbit Rock was a strong supporter of the PEE. Xe had voted PEE in local, parliamentary and presidential elections, and sought candidates with egalitarian views for the upper house, since xe was old enough to vote (***16*** for local elections, ***20*** for parliamentary and presidential elections and ***26*** for the upper house, where xe had votes in three constituencies, while xer partner had votes in just two). Xe kept with the PEE to the bitter end, even voting for them in ***15B6***.

Xe came from quite a wealthy family with a radical-liberal tradition. Xe had enjoyed a privileged upbringing and felt rather guilty about it. Bunny had attended a prestigious private university and left with a good degree in Economics. Xer parents had squared this with their egalitarian consciences by arguing that since they could afford the fees they should do so, to leave the places at the less expensive, state-supported, public universities to those with lesser means. Bunny had then taken up a successful career in banking. Xer partner, Roaring Deer, was a talented cabinet maker. Bunny had met xim when xe was furnishing xer first flat, shortly after starting at the bank.

For Roaring Deer it was love at first sight, but with little expectation, xe knew in xer heart that Bunny was above xer touch. Bunny was intrigued by xim. Their backgrounds were very different, which attracted xim. Bunny was also impressed by Roaring's talent as an artisan and xer strong work ethic. A couple of years after they met, Bunny helped Roaring to apply for the finance to set up xer own business, initially a shop to showcase and sell xer own work, later to expand to sell a wider range of furniture, while still accepting commissions for xer own workshop where xe now employed a journeyman and an apprentice.

Eventually they became an item and married in ***15A6*** when Roaring was twentwy-five and Bunny twentwy-four. Wild Cat came along a year later. Roaring Deer remained devoted to Bunny and would defer to xim in pretty well all matters. Only in politics, xe kept xer opinions to ximself, but xe did not share Bunny's 'champagne egalitarianism'. Like xer child after xim, Roaring had also nursed a longing for space travel. Xe also saw the many contradictions in the practicalities of the egalitarian experiment, and noted its complete failure to deliver its supposed goals. Over the years of Wild Cat's childhood xe tried to give xim encouragement to reach for xer dreams. Roaring Deer resolutely refused to withhold praise from Wild Cat for xer achievements, regardless of how politically incorrect that was.

Things started to get easier in Wild Cat's tweens, Xe had been ten years old when the New PFP won the ***15B6*** election and the cultural environment began to change. Change came slowly at first, and Roaring Deer had to tiptoe around Bunny's feelings a bit, but as time wore on xer opinions softened. Then in ***1600*** a critical event took place. No doubt with an eye to re-election, the President made a major speech, in which xe harked back to Wheatfield's Duplos Programme, with the assertion that today the New Norland flag would be flying on Duplos but for the betrayal of the Great Wheatfield's legacy and the thirtwy wasted years of the egalitarian experiment. Modestly admitting xe was not of the stature of xer idol and great predecessor, xe would, if the electorate would keep their trust in xim; revive Wheatfield's vision and press ahead with a reinvigorated programme. This time it would not take sixtwy years, but building on the greater knowledge that we now had, a landing would be achieved within twentwy years.

Wild Cat was round at Flying Eagle's house for a sleep-over, the pair of them were glued to the television watching the speech live, and sat up half the night listening to the political pundits and scientific experts. They hugged each other in excitement, and whatever else two tweenagers might have got up to, what they actually did was spend the rest of the night planning the mission, and working out how they might be in at the kill. When Basking Shark looked in on them to make sure they were not breaking the rules she found them pored over a physics book whilst beavering away on their calculators, with Flying Eagle's computer displaying various astronomical data. Xe smiled, xe knew they would get little sleep and also that neither would be tempted to indulge in dangerous behaviour, by which xe meant sex. When xe went to call them for breakfast they were crashed out over their books, snuggled up together but still dressed.

The children had calculated that by ***1620*** they would be in the right age bracket to take part. They would graduate from university in about five or six years time. That would leave them fiftween years to gain the requisite experience. Should be just about right. No time for babies though, they agreed, but we'll still be young enough, so how about it, one of them suggested. "If we both get there, let's have the first Geosian baby to be conceived on Duplos."

"It's a deal" the other responded, "even if we have to do it in public[28]."

As it happened it was ***1607*** when they left university having stayed on to obtain masters degrees in space engineering, specialising in space-stations and space vehicles. On the strength of their academic achievements, they were both hired by a major defence and aerospace engineering company to work as junior engineers on the contract to design space stations for the Geos-Duplos orbit. They were on their way!

28 Which would be a big deal! Although they have no qualms about nudity, Geosians are intensely private about their sex lives. But then they were both tweenagers and teenagers - fourtween / sixteen

12
Preparations: New Norland

Most of ***1601*** was devoted to the top-down strategy and definition of the programme plan. It was decided early on that the former plan for Selenos station was too much of a technical risk and would only be held as a low-priority fall-back option. If it did go ahead the timetable would slip by six years or so to ***1626*** at the earliest. The two existing space stations had provided valuable experience and the scientific consensus was that space stations could be constructed in orbit around the Geos/Duplos barycentre, probably beyond the orbit of both planets. Space-station design was well understood and, while there remained some engineering challenges, it was thought these would readily be overcome.

The issues that dominated the scientific community concerned the communications with the station and the ability to define and maintain an appropriate stable orbit. The difficulty here was that any calculations would involve a 3-body problem, the station, Duplos and Geos. The stability of such orbits is very hard to maintain and could cost fuel, that would then have to be supplied. It was not clear that solar power, as was used on the existing space-stations in low Geos orbit would be sufficient, a difficulty made worse by problems of shadowing by either of the two planets eclipsing the sun. The problems were exacerbated by a strong requirement that any space debris falling on Duplos should be small enough to burn up in the atmosphere before reaching the ground. The data obtained back in the ***1580***'s from satellite and fly-by imagery suggested that it was highly likely that Duplos contained intelligent life, but at a pre-industrial stage of development. Risks to that life from falling space debris were to be avoided.

A target date for the first space-station in high barycentric orbit was set at ***160B***, this would be followed by others. It would be ideal if a sufficiently stable orbit could be identified within the orbits of the two planets but as yet it was uncertain whether that could be achieved. Eventually each space station would have a capability to launch and land space vehicles to and from each other and the two planets.

Apart from the challenges just mentioned, the stations themselves would have to be much larger and more complex than the existing pair in orbit around Geos. An early project for the new programme would be to produce a requirement specification for the stations and let a contract for the work. In reality there was only one company that would have the capability, The Space Development Corporation, situated in New Camford, a city on the east coast of New Norland, and host to two of New Norland's, and the world's, top universities. One of these was the C.I.T., the Camford Institute of Technology which housed the world's number one Aeronautics and Space Engineering department where Wild Cat Waters and Flying Eagle Forest would study for their degrees. C.I.T. was the principal reason for the location of SpaceDevCo, known informally as 'Satellites R Us' by the company staff and students and academics at C.I.T. SpaceDevCo was the obvious organisation to act as prime contractor for the space station design, and indeed for the whole programme. However, formal Government procurement rules established in the egalitarian years, and retained by the New PFP government[29], required contracts of this magnitude to be competed by tender with some provisions to help smaller enterprises to participate in the process.

---

29 The party was now rebranded as New PFP, to distance itself from the disastrous ***1580***'s administration, while retaining its inheritance from President Wheatfield.

Additionally, ideas for vehicle design were still in their infancy. The type of multistage rocket carrying a capsule of limited capability as was used in the Selenos project, was totally unsuited to the task. Such technology could be used to launch directly from Geos to Duplos, but there would then be no way to retrieve the capsule from Duplos for a return to Geos. What was needed was an aeroplane that could fly in space.

One really useful development from the fiftweententies had been a small vehicle that could shuttle between the space stations. This shuttle was launched into space via a conventional rocket but then detached from its host and docked with a station. It could then fly in low orbit of Geos between the stations, where it could be stored and refuelled. The vehicles would accommodate four people including the pilot, and had been in service since ***15A7***. There were two shuttles on each station with a service life of twelve years. Every three years, the oldest one was retired back to Geos and replaced with a new one, there also being incremental improvements with every model. It had provided a satisfactory living for its inventor, Polar Bear Meadows, whose business skills matched xer prowess as an engineer, making xer company, Meadowcraft Aerospace, the front runner for the development to meet the new requirement. Xe was also a C.I.T. graduate in the class of ***1594*** but xe had established xer company in a city some ***A50*** twilomen to the South West of New Camford. In contrast to New Camford, this city, Beaver, named after an early pioneer and local hero in the settlement of New Norland, was very modern and had run a campaign to attract new high-tech industry into the region with substantial tax-breaks, that had attracted Meadows at the time xe was looking to exploit xer inventions. Meadows also named xer child Gnawing Beaver, after xer adopted city. Dr Gnawing Beaver Meadows, was also a C.I.T. Engineering graduate who went on to work for xer co-parent and took over the running of the company in **1606**, when, at the age of fiftwy, xer parent decided to step down from the business side and revert to technical work as a part-time consultant.

Actual new technical work didn't really start until late ***1602*** when the space station contract was let, as expected, to SpaceDevCo. The contract called for some of the work to be subcontracted to smaller enterprises, and to academia. Naturally C.I.T. were closely involved and when Wild Cat and Flying Eagle went up as undergraduates in ***1603*** they found opportunities to get in on the ground floor of one of the projects.

In these earliest days the centre of the technical action was with the satellite design and orbital mechanics. The latter was very much a university led subject, and good progress was made to which the C.I.T. applied mathematics department made a major contribution. This work was theoretical in its nature but it impacted on the actual engineering requirements. This was because the mathematics made it clear that regular adjustments would have to be made to maintain orbit stability. The mathematics gave answers to minimise the energy costs of such adjustments but left it to the physicists and engineers to design the sensors needed to detect just when orbital adjustments should be made and how they should be accomplished. Initial experiments were conducted throughout ***1604*** and ***1605*** on the space stations. Wild Cat actually got to go with xer tutor to one of the space stations to assist in some of the experimental work. Flying Eagle was very jealous.

Although their technical interests overlapped, Wild Cat and Flying Eagle did not follow precisely the same courses. Wild Cat very much concentrated on Satellites and Space Station Engineering. The focus of xer work for xer MEng was on maintenance of orbit stability and xer dissertation 'On the distribution of sensors and associated artificial intelligence to maintain semi-stable barycentric orbits of satellites of multi-bodied systems' was later seen as a classic in the field. Don't be fooled by the word 'satellites' in the title, the work is equally applicable to space stations and even small moons. In fact if Wild Cat had been prepared to sit around for two more years having a good time and just adding some minor polish to the dissertation, it would have earned xer a PhD. But Wild Cat had more important things to do than collect academic baubles. Xe had an appointment with destiny in ***1620*** and xe wasn't going to be late. Much to xer professor's regret, xe declined the opportunity to convert to a PhD. and accepted a job with Satellites R Us.

Flying Eagle also worked on the station project but xer interests concentrated on the inter-station traffic, the mechanisms for docking and launching the shuttles that maintained the physical connectivity of a multi-station environment and the design of the vehicles themselves. Xer dissertation 'Engineering considerations for the management of shuttle craft on space stations with implications for shuttle design', while not quite as stellar as Wild Cat's, nonetheless earned xer a distinction, and in xer case, too, xer professor was disappointed, but not surprised, when xe rejected the offer of a PhD place in favour of a job with Satellites R Us.

On the strength of their new jobs with substantial starting salaries of £***4,000*** per **work**[30] each, they were easily able to afford a nice brand new apartment into which they moved just two **works** after starting their jobs. However they didn't marry, which is unusual in New Norland, and disappointed their families. It wasn't that they had any doubts about their mutual

30 *In rough terms this would be equivalent to a salary of £41,500 in the UK on Earth in 2021. On Geos it is about 33% (**40%**)* higher than the typical top of the range salary offered to new graduates, 38% *(**54%**)* higher than average earnings in New Norland and double the adult minimum wage, which last is higher than its UK Earth equivalent.

commitment, but they agreed that they would each maintain maximum career flexibility to pursue their all-consuming goal. In their hearts they were married. Try as they might, neither could ever settle down with anyone else. In a culture where marital sexual fidelity was almost universal, any later relationships were compromised from the start, they were never free from each other.

13
Opposition: New Norland

Opponents of the NDP, as the new Duplos programme was known hadn't given up. In the immediate aftermath of the ***1600*** election the opposition was still in disarray and it took about three years for any co-ordinated campaign to emerge. There were three distinct concerns that motivated opposition to the programme which can be characterised as the sceptics, the scared and the anti-colonials.

The sceptics were a coalition of those that questioned whether the benefits were worth the costs and risk of the programme. Many of these were from within the PFP itself. There was no argument but that the programme would be expensive, and there was a significant minority that doubted that the estimated costs and timescales were credible. Historically the record of all Governments on complex projects was poor, and especially so at the bleeding edge of technology. In particular, Governments' ability to pick winners was abysmal. Too often, major programmes resulted in expensive white elephants. Public sector culture with it's emphasis on tried and tested solutions, fear of nugatory expenditure and insistence on serial rather than parallel development, is unsuited to the management of such programmes. These objections should not have and did not come as a surprise to new PFP. A healthy suspicion of public sector enterprise was in the PFP's DNA. To add to this, the further goals of the programme were unclear and unarticulated. The landing on Duplos was presented as an end in itself, the motive was not mentioned. If asked, it was to fulfil the dream. Rather like climbing a mountain, men should walk on Duplos because it was there. That was enough for the likes of Wild Cat and Flying Eagle, but away from the dreamers and enthusiasts, the question needed asking. What do we get for all the money and effort. There were answers but nobody had really set about making them clear.

Then there were the objections of the scared. Was Duplos already occupied? If so, and the scared were prepared to accept it probably was, would the natives be friendly? Would our astronauts be safe? Would there be an interplanetary war? Possibly even worse as a prospect, what about the risk of importing a deadly plague? Something endemic in the native population, whether intelligent beings like ourselves, or wild animals. Something that was relatively harmless to its host population but devastating to Geosians, and if not to people, to animals or plants back here on Geos, threatening extinctions of wild or domestic animals or plants, reducing Geos' biodiversity and food security. The risks were just too great.

The force of the anti-colonialists' objections were the obverse of those of the scared. These people were not proud of their ancestors' record on their own planet. There were too many instances of greed leading to displacement of populations, of destruction of peoples, of cultures or lifestyles, at worst of genocide, deliberately through war and land seizure, or accidentally through disease. These objectors were also sceptical of motives. Was it about eventual colonisation, looking for Lebensraum, or setting up of penal colonies to rid Geos of the least wanted in society, or perhaps about exploitation of the native population, slavery or worse, or exploitation of the land and natural resources, enforced industrialisation or despoliation of the environment and destruction of the ecology. These objectors argued strongly that there was a moral imperative to leave an inhabited world alone. Any contact could be damaging to a delicately balanced ecosystem. If what mankind had done to

Geos was wrong, and it was, then to export mankind's crimes elsewhere was simply evil.

For the anti-colonialists, exploration of lifeless worlds was morally acceptable, but surely, economically wasteful. Invasion of an inhabited world was inexcusable, even if the inhabiting life was non-sentient, even if it was just vegetation.

For the first few years of the NDP the voices of the opponents would not be silenced. New Norland was a democracy and the right to protest was enshrined in law. Protests can get out of hand, these were no exceptions. Among the protesters were some fanatics who would never be be satisfied except by total capitulation. When they claimed that Government were not listening, and not taking their objections seriously, that was not what they meant. What they meant was that Government was not doing what they wanted. In actual fact, Government, while annoyed by some of the antics of protesters, was listening. Many of the specific objections needed to be addressed and the ensuing public debate needed to be had, which resulted in a better programme with an increased probability of a satisfactory outcome.

As far as the sceptics were concerned, their opposition faded as the programme began to chalk up successes. Once the money was spent, the targets met, and technical obstacles overcome, there was less and less to be concerned about. The programme directors were as conscious of public sector failings as their detractors. The major technical risks were managed through active delegation to the lead contractors. Entities like SpaceDevCo were in a much better position to manage the technical risks. Central Government exerted political pressure but resisted the temptation to micromanage the technical strategy. They allowed the contractors the freedom to be flexible. To back more than one option without being accused of waste, and to change or cancel sub-projects without undue harassment. All this contributed to the overall success. The contractors were responsible for delivering to time and budget, and keeping Government properly informed and engaged as the risk profile changed. Those whose opposition was based on the general incompetence and wastefulness of Government were answered in the only way they could be, by the Government acting with uncharacteristic competence, and thereby confounding its detractors.

The opposing factions were instrumental in forcing the Government to articulate the desired benefits beyond the mere achievement of the landing, and assisting the necessary contingency planning. Debates were started, consensus built, transparency improved and decisions justified. In this way the objectors and protesters were indeed listened to and their concerns addressed and the programme improved. Those who would never be satisfied except by cancellation had their expectations met. They were never satisfied. Those who wanted assurance that the programme would understand the concerns and risks received some reassurance together with knowledge of how the various concerns were to be addressed and why decisions were made as they were.

The objections of the scared and anti-colonial groups were much more difficult to address because they were fundamental. Firstly the Government swiftly acknowledged the legitimacy of the objections and its intention to address them through public debate in parallel with the necessary technical developments. Men of good will were invited into the tent. The first phase of the Government's approach was to address the wider objectives of the landing on Duplos. The paragraphs below are taken from a Government pamphlet setting out the opportunities that led to the decision.

As with the voyages of discovery from past history, clearly part of the motivation is simple curiosity. Men want to go to Duplos because it is there. The happenstance of a second habitable planet in your own backyard is just too tempting to miss. Who has not looked up at the sky when it is filled with this nearby world. At an angular size of ***A3*** arc-gemin, it appears to be ***3.26*** times the size of the Sun in our sky[31]. On the other hand Selenos has an angular size of only ***8.74*** arc-gemin which makes it appear between ***1/5*** and ***1/4*** the size of the Sun. Ever since it was realised that this was a world like ours, and then more recently that it had a breathable atmosphere, surface water and vegetation it is a no-brainer that we want to go there.

Some of the benefits will be here in New Norland. We have already seen a significant boost to the economy with the creation of high quality jobs, that in themselves have beneficial knock-on effects on the wider economy. The technical innovation required has had important spin-off effects. For example in improvements to solar power generation and the fuel efficiency of ground and air transport, which directly help the green economy, by reducing carbon emissions. These benefits will continue to accrue, regardless of whether there is intelligent life on Duplos or not.

However there is more to it, some of the potential benefits do depend on that last point. If there is no intelligent life, then there is indeed opportunity for colonisation, and exploitation of the planet's resources. The former would bring much needed relief to our over population and the latter, valuable economic gain. Only this time, with greater knowledge, we can avoid the mistakes of our past and exploit the planet's resources in a

31 Geos' Sun appears very much the same size in their sky as Earth's Sun and Moon do in Earth's sky, and Duplos is about 3.18 times as big. This is slightly less than the apparent size of Earth as seen from the Moon.

sustainable manner. We will have the opportunity to work with a blank canvas.

This Government recognises that the presence of intelligent life on Duplos changes the above. We must learn from our own history and not risk repeating its mistakes. The wonderful prospect of making contact with another civilisation makes the whole experience more exciting, even as it closes off some opportunities. We accept and will enforce a primary guiding principle that Duplos belongs to the Duplosians, who evolved there. It is not ours to sequester and pillage. If Duplos is inhabited, we will treat with the inhabitants in peace, at all times respecting them and their way of life. We will not interfere, even if their practices seem barbaric to us. Colonisation will be out of the question. However, if the Duplosians are agreeable there may be prospects for an embassy or other form of diplomatic presence. It may even be possible to negotiate opportunities for tourism, if done sensitively, and to offer but not impose cultural exchanges.

By the same token, the natural resources of Duplos must remain their property and under their control. If fair opportunities arise for trade, we will negotiate deals, but we will make it a criminal offence here in New Norland to exploit any cultural or material superiority that we might have to impose an unfair trade deal. Permanent purchase of land on Duplos by a Geosian will be banned. The terms of any occupation of land on Duplos must be such as to allow for reversion to Duplosian occupation after a set period of time that must not exceed one **life**, and must be on fair rental terms, enforceable by New Norland courts, in addition to whatever arrangements might otherwise apply under the native Duplosian legal systems.

Fears have been expressed that Duplosians might be warlike and attack our mission. We take this threat seriously. However every indication is that the level of development of any putative civilisation on Duplos is pre-industrial. It is not credible that Duplosians could offer threat to Geos. It is possible that a small landing party of Geosians could be tricked or otherwise overpowered and even killed. This risk is akin to that taken by the first settlers here in New Norland. History tells us that some residual risk cannot be avoided. History also tells us that the original settlers here in New Norland were received peacefully, and it was only when the settlement began to interfere with or overwhelm the local way of life that enmity grew. We will not make the mistakes of our ancestors. We will come in peace and not retaliate if shown aggression, but merely act in self defence. To that end the landing party will carry non-lethal weapons designed to temporarily incapacitate but not to kill. Any lethal force must be used as a last resort and only in response to a lethal attack, even then it must be minimised.

In order to reduce the likelihood of a violent encounter our landing party will be of sufficient size to enable necessary defence to be arranged and there will be a military advisor to the mission commander appointed as head of security. The party will not be military in constitution, it will contain both military and civilian personnel. The military component will be there to provide necessary security but will not drive the mission.

There will also be a medical presence in the party. The chief medical officer will have the power to order any member of the party including the commander to remain in quarantine on the space station if illness is suspected. Xe will also carry supplies of the vaccines and medication for a range of conditions endemic in our population, and offer whatever assistance xe can in the unlikely event that a Geosian pathogen appears among our Duplosian contacts. The space stations will all have a medical capability and some isolation facilities in case of necessity.

All these measures will cost extra money and may cause some revision of our timescales but your Government sees them as an essential prerequisite to the responsible prosecution of the mission.

Other considerations are the obverse, to deal with any threat to Geos emanating from Duplos. Our intelligence services have advised that many of the concerns of this nature have been promulgated through propaganda and a disinformation campaign by New Norland's enemies. This is unsurprising as these same forces, hostile to our democratic ideals, are jealous of our technical successes and would like to cause this programme to fail, or at least be seriously delayed. We hardly need add that their motives are at best merely spiteful but more likely are driven by their strategic desire to supplant us in this effort. We will return to this later.

Despite the hostile intent behind many of the attacks the NDP has received on these grounds, the concerns are nonetheless important. We can dismiss the threat of a hostile act by Duplosians on Geos itself. However the concerns around Duplosian pathogens causing a pandemic brought in by our mission party have to be addressed. To this end we will institute a strict hygiene regime that will apply to all material that has had any contact with Duplos or with members of our landing party. The latter will endure a rigorous quarantine on return from Duplos. There will be facilities for this purpose on the space stations themselves. Also any visitor to Duplos returning to Geos will serve up to one year's quarantine in a new town that will be constructed for the purpose. Their immediate families may join them if they wish, but must then share the quarantine. This regime will continue until we build up the evidence that it is not necessary. The town will contain all necessary facilities including those for the medical research that might be needed to develop vaccines and other treatments in the event of any pathogen being discovered. The only reason for anyone subject to the quarantine to leave the quarantine town is if xe is required to return to Duplos.

After completing the studies leading to this report your Government has held a review to decide on the action to take. We have unanimously concluded that the continuation of the project with these safeguards is the best course for both Geos and Duplos. New Norland is not the only power on Geos and while we have a strong lead in the technologies for space travel we do not hold a monopoly. We are not the only Geosian people to wish to explore our twin world. While we can probably trust those who share our democratic ideals to maintain a similar degree of care, we cannot have any confidence that others would do likewise. Quite the reverse, we have every reason to believe that there are other powers here on Geos that would colonise and exploit Duplos entirely for their own profit and regardless of the wishes or interests of any Duplosians that might get in their way. You only have to see how these powers treat their own people and their own environment to visualise the threat to Duplos if they get there first. Only from our own strength can we in New Norland protect Duplos. Far from it being a moral duty to keep away from Duplos it is our moral duty to ensure the sound management of Geosian interaction with our neighbours.

We in the Government also recognise in ourselves a degree of selfishness in keeping the programme within New Norland. Just as a wealthy man willingly shares xer good fortune with a less fortunate friend, so too should we remember our close friends. Accordingly we have decided to invite our closest ally to take some part in our mission, to include two places in our mission party. An offer they have been pleased to accept. This way the first Geosian expedition to Duplos can be seen as truly international and not purely a New Norland affair.

This report had widespread approval in New Norland. Most of the population readily believed the threat from New Norland's enemies, and many who had dealt with them had affection and respect for the ally. Polling by the Government suggested that popular support for the NDP with these motives ran at well over tentwy pertwent (***A0%)***. In a (cynical) fit of democratic zeal the President announced that now xe was in a position to offer a genuine choice to the people, and there was a moral dimension, xe would seek approval of the above measures in a referendum.

Opinion polls are often wrong, but not that wrong. A population that secretly wanted to follow the dream had been provided with the authoritative answers to the naysayers. The referendum delivered the result the President knew it would. The opposition to the NDP could never recover. It also ensured a New PFP victory in the ***1610*** presidential and parliamentary elections. The one New PFP MP who lost xer seat was one of the very few that was publicly known to be opposed to the NDP and the only one to have campaigned for the No side in the referendum.

14
The technology comes together: New Norland

On joining Satellites R Us, both Wild Cat and Flying Eagle found themselves working on the design of the space-stations for the orbit around Duplos. The programme plan called for the first one to be launched in just three years time. The schedule was tight.

Work in the previous two years had finalised the orbital characteristics for the high altitude space-station, and the design of that station was also close to completion. The orbit about the barycentre was similar (in the geometric sense) to the orbits of Geos and Duplos, namely one with eccentricity ***0.0044***. They finally agreed an orbit approximately ***36,4A4*** twilomen above the Duplos orbit. This was a lot further than ideal for the expedition and physical communication with the planet-side party would be difficult. Because of these shortcomings there was a strategic rethink giving serious consideration to orbits within those of the two planets. Wild Cat was appointed to lead the review.

The first, outer-orbit, station was launched on schedule in ***160B.*** Some of the internal work had to be completed in space in order to meet the schedule. The launch of a second station, originally scheduled for the next year was postponed pending the outcome of for Wild Cat's technical review.

Flying Eagle's work on the space-station was also highly valued by the company, but was not quite in the same league as xer partner. For example xe had done some very good work on the design of the solar panel systems, which were designed to rotate to point to the sun whenever it was not obscured by either of the planets. Xe was also responsible for the design to wire the panels in parallel rather than in series, thereby maximising the output under partial shade.

After completion of the solar panel work, Flying Eagle was assigned to the team working on the shuttle support systems. To xer delight, this won xim xer first assignment off-planet. After the station was set in orbit, xe was sent out as the SpaceDevCo's engineer for installation of the shuttle support systems. Thus Flying Eagle was the first of the childhood friends to actually venture closer to Duplos than to Geos, and to see the planet close up.

Polar Bear Meadows represented Meadowcraft Aerospace during the same mission. Xer child, Gnawing Beaver, had been unhappy about this and would have preferred to have gone ximself, but xe could hardly deny xer parent's qualifications for the job, and yielded to xer argument that at xer age this might be xer last chance to really get into space, saying that in xer opinion past trips to the low-orbit stations didn't really count as proper space.

Polar Bear was highly impressed by Flying Eagle, and when xe returned home, xe persuaded xer child to travel to New Camford to meet xim. When the meeting took place, Gnawing Beaver recalled having met Flying Eagle before, on a visit to C.I.T. while the latter was working on xer Master's degree. The outcome was that Flying Eagle was invited down to Beaver and offered a very attractive package to relocate and join Meadowcraft Aerospace.

Consequently there was a long and painful discussion between Flying Eagle and xer partner.

"We've always agreed, haven't we, that our careers must come first," stated Wild Cat. "Getting to Duplos is the priority for both of us. I've just had a whacking great bonus for my work on the space station and from next period I'm getting a significant promotion. I'm sure I can afford to buy you out of your share in the apartment."

"It's true my bonus is rather more modest but I hate to leave you. I don't want you to think I don't love you and only care about my career, but this is a fantastic opportunity. The action on the vehicles is going to shift to Beaver and Meadowcraft and that really is where I am building my reputation."

"I love you too Flying Eagle. But we knew this would happen some day. Isn't that why we haven't married. Look, it'll be difficult to maintain our existing relationship at such a distance and I won't try to tie you down with demands for sexual fidelity but we can stay best friends. We're bound to meet up professionally and we can always have holidays together. If our circumstances allow we can still share a bed."

"Not having you next to me in bed will take some getting used to after seventween years," responded Flying Eagle, "I probably won't be able to sleep properly. Of course if circumstances allow we'll still be able to sleep together when we get the opportunity. But we are both still only in our twentwies, we shouldn't be celibate. You too must be free to find someone else. I'll understand and wish you and xim well. "

"Anyway," recalled the female between sobs, "if we're both single when we achieve our goal, we have a baby to co-parent, so we need to keep in practice lest we forget what to do."

"Yes," said xer partner, drying xer eyes and kissing xim on the forehead, there's always that. They chuckled over the recollection of their fourtween year old selves.

Despite the misgivings concerning the suitability of the high-orbit station for the expedition to Duplos, it was clearly superior to the back-up option of Selenos, and it was agreed to establish a second station in the same orbit, but one twundred and thirtwy degrees out of phase. This was launched in ***1611***, a year later than the original plan. The imagery from both these stations gave conclusive evidence that Duplos was inhabited. It appeared to be only sparsely populated, and that population was largely confined to one large super-continent. A second small continent and most islands appeared to be uninhabited.

There was a theory, supported by all the evidence obtained from the imagery that maritime activity was confined to rivers, lakes and inland-seas. One of these inland seas was quite large and there was evidence of settlements along it's coast that were almost certainly ports. Nevertheless even here sea-borne traffic was sparse and largely hugged the coasts. The evidence that the second continent was uninhabited was inconclusive. There was no sign of permanent structures, but there could well have been more primitive, unsettled communities, hidden in the jungles. As the scientists pointed out; "Absence of evidence, is not the same as evidence of absence."

On the other hand for many of the offshore islands, they could categorically say they were uninhabited by large land animals, let alone any intelligent species.

One particular island caught the NDP team's attention. This island was situated in a bay off the North-West coast of the main continent. The dimensions of the island were roughly thirtween by twentwy twilomen and the nearest continental coast was some thirtween twilomen distant, and very sparsely inhabited. The nearest major settlement lay some ninetwy-six twilomen due south of the island, the continental coast at that point itself being eightwy-five twilomen distant. There was also a string of smaller islands between this one and the mainland. The widest gap between these islands was estimated to be less than thirtwy twilomen.

This was seen as incredibly good news. New options were hastily drawn up. The result was that a change of plan could simplify the whole programme, reduce the complexity for the space stations, improve security and possibly bring forward the landing by up to two years.

The changed plan was duly adopted. Instead of trying to maintain all operations from a base on a space station. The team would build a base on the island. All shuttle flights would be between the space station and the island, and transport to and from continental Duplos would be by more conventional means. It would be possible to build a launch capability on the island base that would be able to support a regular shuttle service. The original plan was for microlight aircraft to be employed to island hop people between the base and the continent, but eventually the microlight plan was abandoned for something more robust. This Duplosian island did not have a name. Neither the Shadowlands Union, nor the Western Federation were aware of its existence, as it lay beyond the horizon from the coasts. However had they known of it, both territories would have undoubtedly claimed it even though neither possessed the means to reach it. Henceforth we shall refer to it as Base Island.

There were still major problems to be solved with the orbital mechanics of the space-stations. For a single planet the norm is to match a satellite's velocity to the rotation of the planet so that the satellite remains overhead at a particular region of the planet, a geosynchronous orbit. There is a simple relationship between the orbit height and the velocity for the motion to be sustained by the force of gravity. Geos rotates six times and Duplos four times during their common period of ***1/26*** of a year. If Geos or Duplos were on their own, not part of a binary system, the height of a geosynchronous circular orbit would be ***1310B*** and ***12937*** twilomen respectively.

For the case of a binary planet it is more complicated. The motion of any satellite sufficiently far from either planet would have to be treated as a three body problem involving both planets, both making the orbit less stable and the calculation more difficult. Unfortunately this is the case here and except for the lowest orbits around a single planet, or higher orbits around both planets, this is difficult to achieve. Indeed the orbital calculations for any satellites or space stations operating between the orbits of Duplos and Geos are extremely tricky.

Wild Cat made quite a name for ximself in the design of the space station orbits and in engineering the means of maintaining their stability. However, eventually even xe had to abandon xer optimism and admit that space stations placed between the two planets would not achieve sufficiently stable orbits to last long enough to be of value. They would just have to make the best of the stations beyond the orbits of both planets.

Wild Cat had frequent trips into space for various matters to do with the operation of the space-stations in preparation for the landing, including one tour in ***1612*** as senior station commander. That is, xe was in direct charge of one of the two stations and had overall responsibility for them both. On xer return to Geos xe lobbied hard for yet more stations. These, xe thought, were necessary because of the inability to find stable orbits closer in. The station's orbit was exactly twice that of the Geos/Duplos orbit, i.e. two periods, and xe wanted to ensure there was almost always a station within reach of the party on the ground. As a first step, old plans for two more stations in the outer orbit were revived. These were launched in ***1614***, to fill the slots at seventwy-six degrees to the existing pair.

When back in New Camford, xe had a brief partnership with a younger man, which was probably aided by their frequent separations for Wild Cat's ventures into space and other absences elsewhere in New Norland. Xe had upgraded from the apartment xe had bought with Flying Eagle and now had a comfortable house in a leafy suburb on the outskirts of the city.

It was a good place to bring up a family and xer new partner would have liked them to marry and have children. Wild Cat just wouldn't commit. They had a blazing row not long after xer return from xer tour as space-station commander, during which Wild Cat as good as admitted to having sex with Flying Eagle on one of xer business trips to Beaver. That was too much for the partner and xe found ximself single again.

To xer surprise, Wild Cat found xe was much relieved at the break-up of the relationship. After that xe strictly avoided anything serious. Xer work dominated xer life and the occasional meeting with Flying Eagle gave xim all the sex xe really wanted.

The last time Wild Cat had seen Flying Eagle, was when xe had a working visit to xer station. They had shared a bed, as they always did, but just for sleeping and chatting. After all, they had been sleeping next to each other since they were eight years old, why change the habits of a lifetime. There was no sex involved on account of Wild Cat's current entanglement back on Geos. The infidelity that broke the relationship had occurred some time before his tour on the station.

It hadn't happened in a moment of passion but much more prosaically. Wild Cat was in Beaver for some business with Meadowcraft Aerospace. Naturally xe stayed with Flying Eagle. They'd had a long tiring working session until dark. After a late dinner they remained chatting into the night, eventually finishing up in bed to chat and sleep. In the semi-sleep in the sixtween tocks or so before it was time to get up, a hard penis brushed against a thigh, whose body responded by adjusting its position and letting its hand guide the penis to where it belonged, the two bodies then gently rocked together until their owners were sufficiently compos mentis to join in the fun. This gentle encounter soothed both parties as they lay there feeling loved and comforted.

Afterwards both were apologetic. Flying Eagle was mortified that xe had been the instrument of Wild Cat being unfaithful to a recognised partner, however unsatisfactory. Wild Cat was horrified that xe had allowed ximself to cheat on someone, even with xer true love. They vowed that while they would not give up their few nights together, they would take other precautions to avoid a repetition.

Flying Eagle had also made quite a name for ximself in the programme. Xe was currently in a foreign country where xe was working for three **works**, a whole half year, on a project to do with the vehicle designs for the NDP. Recalling that last occasion before xer tour brought Flying Eagle's current whereabouts to mind. Wild Cat realised that though xe had been in space, xe had otherwise never left New Norland. Xe hadn't had a holiday in over two years, perhaps xe should take some leave, xe was owed enough, and travel overseas to see Flying Eagle. Xe would write to xim.

Flying Eagle wrote back with alacrity. Yes, xe would love a visit, and included a list of various goodies that were not locally available for Wild Cat to bring with xim. Xe warned however that xe was very tied up with the work but was able to suggest a time when they could have a full period's holiday together, and there would also be opportunities for shorter trips to show xim round and do touristy things.

All was arranged and one **work** later, Wild Cat flew across the ocean to visit a real foreign country for the first time. Not that it was all that foreign. This country was the one that in a sense gave birth to New Norland. Its full name was the Kingdom of Northern Nations (KNN), with history going way back. Wild Cat was looking forward to it. Many of xer ancestors had come from there, the most recent being one of Roaring Deer's grandparents. The KNN was New Norland's closest ally, and two of it's citizens would be in the party to land on Duplos. Xe didn't know the details but did know that Flying Eagle was over there as part of a technical exchange to do with the NDP. Flying Eagle had told xim to get SpaceDevCo to arrange for xer clearances to be sent over, so xe could show xim round xer project.

Flying Eagle had a bit of sorting out to do before Wild Cat arrived. Not things like cleaning and tidying the house or making the bed or suchlike, but more serious matters like xer temporary sex life. Xe hadn't been celibate. Who of xer age would, if given the opportunity, when officially single and away from home for half a year. Xe was enjoying a pleasant uncomplicated arrangement with a young engineer working at Nordic Aerospace and Defence Systems here in the KNN. They both knew it was temporary, and young Jezzie Peteschild had not actually moved in with Flying Eagle, xe just stayed from time to time. Also in Flying Eagle's opinion, xer cottage was too small to share on a long term basis with anyone other than Wild Cat. Xe liked xer own space too much. For a start it had only one bathroom, but for just half a year it was OK, and rather quaint. It had been built before New Norland had existed as an independent country.

Anyway xe had to explain things to Jezzie, who understood, or at least acted as though xe did. Xe had not been looking for a permanent relationship and had been pleased to hook up with Flying Eagle on a casual basis. A relationship going back to xer university days had broken up less than a year previously and xe was not ready for another, while still wanting some company in a strange town. Xe had only joined Nordic after xer relationship break-up and didn't yet know xer way around. Xe was flattered by the attention of such a distinguished colleague and excited by xer foreignness. As for Flying Eagle, xe too was flattered by the attention of a bright colleague six years xer junior. In any event they agreed to end their fling before Wild Cat's arrival. They would remain good friends, and then, who knows. After Wild Cat's visit, Flying Eagle would only have a short time left in the KNN, and they might finish up on a high. Jezzie would be welcome to stay when, as one day xe surely would, xe had reason to visit Meadowcraft in Beaver. But Flying Eagle warned, "what happens in KNN stays in KNN." Flying Eagle then treated Jezzie to a slap up dinner and show in the big city about ***50*** twilomen distant.

When Wild Cat arrived. Flying Eagle explained about Jezzie. Wild Cat said xe would have been horrified to learn that Flying Eagle hadn't found some such comfort when alone in a strange place, and xe would perfectly understand if Flying Eagle wanted to abstain from sexual contact with xim, and xe could always go to a hotel if Flying Eagle wanted to play with Jezzie. "Don't be silly," was the response. "I'm here for you first and foremost and always. Jezzie is fun but temporary. There is no question of xim following me to New Norland, or of me staying here with xim. Xe knows that and is content. We've officially ended the intimate part of our relationship, and will only pick it up again for the short time that I have left here, if you convince me it's OK with you."

"Darling, I don't want to think of you being lonely in a foreign country. I'm sure enough of you not to get jealous of what you do when we can't be together. As long as neither of you are going to be hurt, have your fun, but for now, it's been a long flight and I'm jet lagged so let's go to bed for a cuddle and maybe some fun of our own." They went to bed but the fun had to wait, xe fell sound asleep the moment xe wrapped ximself around xer friend and xer head touched the pillow.

The holiday went well, they relaxed on a beach, and swam in the sea, colder than Beaver but warmer than New Camford, then had some time in the local capital city (KNN has more than one) taking in some shows and generally enjoying the high life. Finally they returned to where Flying Eagle worked and xe was able to show Wild Cat round and brief xim on the project.

The plan for using microlights on Duplos had encountered stiff opposition from the military on security grounds, and some concerns from meteorologists worried about the weather conditions they were likely to encounter. The advantage of the microlights is that they are easy to carry, and the disadvantage is that they are vulnerable.

The chosen solution involved KNN technology. They had pioneered work on vertical take-off and landing aircraft (VTOL). Technically they were brilliant but had no real application outside the military and even there were now considered less useful than helicopters. But for this purpose, the technology looked ideal. The meteorologists had also expressed doubts about helicopters which, while versatile and a good deal better than microlights, might not perform so well in bad weather conditions. Fixed wing aircraft were deemed more robust.

The plan was to implement the VTOL technology in a lighter aircraft, designed to carry passengers. The heavy armour and weapon systems required in a military aeroplane were not needed for this application. Meadowcraft Aerospace had the contract to design and build the aircraft and also come up with a way to transport it to the space station and then from the space station to the ground. Flying Eagle was the project manager and chief designer, although xe did receive help, sometimes more than xe wanted, from Polar Bear and Gnawing Beaver Meadows.

Between them they came up with an outline design of a craft that would fulfil both purposes, act as a VTOL aeroplane in the lower atmosphere, and then as a shuttle in the upper atmosphere and space. The trouble was that some crucial issues still had be addressed and their earliest estimated in-service date was ***1623***.

This solution remains the best option for the longer-term, but a delay to the landing is undesirable for all sorts of reasons. Not least, thought Flying Eagle, xer personal ambition. There is no doubt that this ambition drove xim to cudgel xer brain until it produced something. In the end xe produced two craft. The VTOL passenger craft is much as had been envisaged originally. It can fly in the lower atmosphere and, indeed reach quite high into the stratosphere. It can carry a dozen people, and be operated by a pilot either on board or remotely, as a drone, or completely autonomously on a preprogrammed course. The second craft is a re-engineered shuttle. The VTOL craft can be attached to the shuttle for transport to and from space. Furthermore the on board flight systems can be linked in such a way that power from both engines can be combined. This way when undergoing flights from space to ground the space leg will be entirely managed by the shuttle systems, then after the combined craft enters the atmosphere, the VTOL can take over for the landing. In the reverse direction the VTOL will not be sufficiently powerful to carry the more massive shuttle against the gravity on Geos, but with the lower gravity of Duplos, ***90%*** of that on Geos, the VTOL will be able to lift the combined craft to a height where the shuttle can take over and complete the journey into space. It is also possible, in theory, for the craft to separate in the high atmosphere and go their separate ways, the shuttle back to the space station and the VTOL craft back to the planet.

There are a number niggles that could be better, but improvements will have to wait. Flying Eagle's timescale has the VTOL craft and Shuttle available in mid ***1616*** with trials of the combined vehicles scheduled for early ***1617***.

15
Interlude 2: New Norland & The Kingdom of Northern Nations

Before continuing with the narrative, it may be useful to give the reader a bit more insight into Geos with particular emphasis on New Norland and its history. As this chapter is primarily designed for readers from Earth I shall adopt Earth measurements and the decimal number system for all the statistics and mention comparisons with Earth where these might prove helpful.

For example the surface gravity of Geos is 10.98 m/s^2 or 1.119g (Earth:9.81 m/s^2 or 1 g). Geos has adopted a common date from which to number the passing years. The exact origin has been lost in prehistoric mythology but is believed to be a later estimate of the founding of an imperial dynasty long gone. Whatever it is, the events of this book are set in the years either side of 2600. In the duodecimal number system used on Geos this is around the turn of the nineteenth (seventweenth) mem. A mem being 144 years. The opening of chapter 9 when Wild Cat Waters is 8 years old is in the year 2584 (**15B4** in duodecimal).

The mean radius of Geos is 7275 km (*Earth: 6371 km*), giving a total surface area of 6.65 $x10^8$ sq km (Earth: 5.10 x 10^8 sq km), of this 30% is land (Earth: 29%). Geographically New Norland occupies an entire continent in the northern hemisphere *of* Geos, together with a few off shore islands with a total land area of about 38 million sq km. Because this continent was colonised by people from a continent about 7,000 km to the East, New Norland is known as the North-Western continent.

The history of New Norland begins 6,000 km away on the North-Western edge of the largest land mass on the planet, and some 1500 years in the past, around the year now known as

1000. The people there were a hardy folk living a hard life in a cold climate. They were also warlike and great sailors. The seas off that part of the continent are stormy and dangerous, and relatively shallow, being effectively a flooded part of the continental shelf. Accordingly these seas are dotted with several islands, large and small. The men of the North lands, as they called themselves raped and pillaged their way around their neighbourhood and eventually ruled a number of small communities across the region. The Northland communities covered about 7.8 million square km consisting of both continental and island territories. Gradually over the centuries these communities consolidated into a small number of kingdoms living and squabbling within a reasonably well-defined trading group, known as the league of Northland cities. By around the year 1500 when other continental powers began to emerge, the North Lands grew closer together and became a formidable trading unit and mutual defence alliance, which was undoubtedly the foremost maritime power the world had yet seen. Where others had hugged to their coasts or navigated relatively calm, sheltered seas, the North Land mariners ventured far into the ocean developing navigation by the stars and discovering the magnetic properties that led to the compass. Eventually people from the North Lands discovered and settled the North East coast of the North-Western continent, while maintaining links with their former communities. This continent was already occupied by more primitive peoples, largely nomadic tribes with a way of life not long out of the stone age. The coastal areas settled by the Northlanders, were only sparsely populated and the incomers themselves were not numerous. With no more than the usual amount of violent bickering that breaks out from time to time the peoples, indigenous and immigrant, dealt reasonably peacefully with each other. Trade was common, and some trade goods even made their way back across the ocean.

The rot started when sailors from emerging nations from South of the Kingdoms of the Northern Lands began also to venture out over the ocean, eventually discovering both the North-West and South-West continents. Unfortunately these adventurers were more interested in plunder than trade.

Partly driven by competition with those to the South of them and partly by internal dynastic struggles the Northern Nations came closer together politically until they more-or-less unified under a single supreme King by about the year 2000. At this point colonisation of the North-West continent began in earnest, and in large numbers. Over the next two centuries the Kingdom of Northern Nations or KNN, fought their way to supremacy over the whole of the North-West continent's Eastern coast to an inland depth of around 400 km. In the wars that brought this about the indigenous peoples fought mainly but not exclusively on the side of the KNN and against the other wannabe colonial powers. Then in about 2250 the western expansion slowed while the KNN consolidated its colonial gains. This was about the time that the New Norlanders, as they were now known, changed their nominative habits by adopting animal based names, a common indigenous practise, with a surname based on some other feature. The New Norlander lifestyle was that of a frontier pioneer, requiring and encouraging a high degree of self-reliance, of initiative and innovation and general toughness. Over the next fifty years their interests and outlook began to diverge from their cousins back in the KNN. Their population also began to be joined by immigrants from KNN's more southerly neighbours. Fortunately the ties of blood and trade still held.

Eventually the divergence of interest changed to dissatisfaction and the desire in an articulate minority for independence from the KNN. There were a few violent clashes between those eager for independence and those loyal to the King and it could have got quite nasty. The salvation came from an unexpected source, a general election in the KNN. The KNN wasn't very democratic by later standards, but it and its New Norland colonies were indubitably the closest thing to democracy that Geos had yet seen. The predecessors of the KNN had never adopted the serfdom of their Southern and Eastern neighbours, although its culture did maintain class distinctions. It was the first Geosian society to insist on absolute gender equality and didn't countenance slavery. At that time about five percent of the adult population (over 24) had the right to vote for the lower house of Parliament, which had by then grown to be the main seat of actual power in the land. The party in power was currently unpopular and lost the ensuing election. Many in the new Government were sympathetic to the New Norland viewpoint. Many of their MPs had lucrative trading interests or property in New Norland and did not want nationalistic politics to disrupt their profits. The upshot was that the King was persuaded to go against xer instincts for an obdurate stance and instead hold out an olive branch. The resulting settlement avoided civil war and moved New Norland closer to its present day constitution. The King appointed a Viceroy from the KNN but with extensive experience of NN to negotiate a package of quasi-independence. The settlement kept the former colony under the sovereignty of the King, but made it independent of the KNN parliament. The King would be represented by a Viceroy. At first that would be the man just appointed, but after six years, or earlier if xe recommended that New Norland was ready, xe would be replaced by a Viceroy to be appointed by the New Norland houses of parliament acting in concert, and would have to be a New Norlander by birth. New Norland's parliament would otherwise have all the powers of a fully independent state except that of making war, which would require the King's consent and must never be conducted against any of the King's dominions. Also New Norland must never give succour to the King's enemies and thus there must be a permanent alliance between the KNN and New Norland. There were also some agreements about trade and tariffs between the KNN and New Norland. Furthermore, the New Norland Government would assume control of all the King's territories now and in the future on the Northwest Continent, to include any islands on the continental shelf.

All in all, the declaration of everlasting friendship of 2304[32], as it was called, met with the general approval of most influential New Norlanders, and they set about their self government with alacrity, and the westward expansion over the whole continent.

From the start the arrangements for Parliament were more democratic than Geos had seen hitherto and other further change severed the tie with the King of KNN (Reform Bill of 2364 - actually passed in 2363 but took effect with the Presidential election of 2364), in which the serving Viceroy was elected President, and changed the constituency of the upper house, but kept its title as The House of Lords. Originally membership of the House of Lords was for life, by appointment of the Viceroy acting with advice from a committee which included the Deputy Viceroy, 3 members appointed by the House of Representatives and 4 members appointed by the House of Lords. The present system was brought in gradually over 86 years culminating in the great reform bill of 2390.

The current constitutional arrangements are:

Presidential elections are held every six years in years whose duodecimal numbers end in zero or six. An election for the

32 Numerology rules, as so often, the year was chosen to start the new chapter of history ***1400*** *in* duodecimal.

(lower) house of representatives is held at the same time. Constituencies are geographical areas returning a single member with election by a first past the post system. All citizens, and certain resident foreigners, over the age of twenty-four (twentwy) on election day may vote. There are two ballots, one for an MP, the other for a delegate to an electoral college. Individuals may be candidates for either or both. It is common for voters to vote differently in the two ballots. The electoral college has the sole function of electing the President.

The Vice-President is not elected in the ballot. The President-elect selects potential candidates and submits them to the House of Lords for approval, three names (in the President-elect's preference order) are sent to the House of Representatives for endorsement, if all three are rejected by the HoR, the HoL will choose one of the candidates, bearing in mind the nature of the objections and the President-elect's preference.

The President has the power to dismiss the lower house of Parliament and call a new parliamentary election at any time except in election year, or within one year of the previous election.

The House of Lords has four styles of members: Lords Permanent, Lords Political, Lords Official and Lords Ordinary. Around 80% of the members must be Lords Ordinary[33].

Lords Permanent: these are retired former Presidents who are entitled to claim lifetime membership. Having done so, they may not stand for President again. Any sufficiently distinguished individual citizen may also be offered this honour. It has occurred twice in history. It requires approval of the President and Vice-

---

33 Actually, at least ninetwy-six pertwent (114/144) which is just over 79%.

President, all the past Presidents and 80% support (again actually ***96%***) in both houses of parliament.

Lords Political: the parties represented in the lower house may nominate Lords Political in proportion to their representation in the lower house. These would include the Government spokesman in the Lords.

Lords Official: certain official appointments come with a seat in the Lords. Examples include the Vice-President and certain Senior Judges.

Lords Ordinary: These are elected for a twelve year term. Elections are in years ending in a three or nine (duodecimal), with half the seats being up for election on each occasion. Constituencies are geographical or non-geographical representing some other group. Examples include Universities (in the old days each university had a member, now the universities are grouped for this purpose), Employers organisations, Trades Union organisations, and various other 'modern barons'. Citizens over the age of thirty (twentwy-six) may vote for the Lords. An individual citizen may have up to three votes in different constituencies. For example Bunny Rabbit Rock is entitled to vote for xer geographical constituency, xer university and a bankers association. Roaring Deer Waters has only two votes, geographical and the worshipful company of cabinet and furniture makers. Voting is by approval voting. There is no requirement to vote for only one candidate. If you want to vote for everyone, that has the same effect as voting for nobody. Similarly, voting for everybody except one candidate is saying anyone except xim, essentially equivalent to casting a single negative vote.

One other quirk is that no candidate for Lords Ordinary may have sat in the house of representatives at any time during the past twelve years, nor may xe hold office or have held office in the past six years in any of the parties represented in the lower house, nor may xer candidacy be supported financially or otherwise by any such party. Similarly nobody may be a candidate for the lower house if they have served as a Lord Ordinary in the past twelve years.

These provisions help ensure the independence of the HoL to allow it do do its duty of holding the lower house to account, and in particular reducing the influence of the political parties on the HoL.

The roles of the two houses and the President are clearly defined. The day to day executive is the President working with a Prime Minister who commands a majority in the lower house. Bills may be started in either house or with the President but normally require approval by all three. However the HoL may not turn down the annual finance bill. In most matters they act as a revising chamber and their main power is to delay a bill, and send amendments back to the lower house. They also have a duty to advise on matters of strategic importance. They have to agree to a declaration of war, various constitutional matters, and certain semi-archaic matters concerning the special relationship between New Norland and the KNN. Under the strategic importance clause they can make trouble for a Government that is too profligate with borrowed money. Thus they can't prevent the Government from raising taxes, but can act to defend the pound from excessive profligacy.

There are special provisions to resolve stalemate stand-offs between President, HoR and HoL.

There are also various tiers of local government, a continent wide country like New Norland is vast and much smaller units are needed for efficient democratic government. Many important services are devolved to local level, regions, cities and counties. For all these local bodies the voting age was lowered in the year

2538 from the original twenty-four, as for parliament and president, to eighteen.

16
The choice of Captain: New Norland

The vehicle trials in ***1617*** went well. Both of Flying Eagle's vehicles performed according to specification. The only thing that couldn't be trialled was the lift off from Duplos. VTOL craft were transferred from Geos to the space station currently linked to the Geos spaceport, using the conventional launch system for shuttles. Transfers were made mid-orbit to one of the adjacent stations (recall that by now there were four space stations in the orbit). The vehicles were then transferred back to the first station and finally a landing was made back on Geos.

Yes, some minor issues emerged, and improvements made to hardware, software and procedures, but nothing major was identified. Reruns of the tests confirmed earlier success. Wild Cat found ximself having to make adjustments in the stations, there was a minor crisis when one of them wobbled too much in its orbit and major corrections were required to bring it back to stability. It was a nervous time for all concerned but by the end of the year all the boxes were ticked. The technical challenges were solved. They were ready to go ahead just as soon as the mission personnel were identified and the go button was pressed.

Early in the new year of ***1618***. The formal decision was taken to bring forward the mission date to ***161A***. The next task was to assign the crew.

Throughout the past year, while the scientists and engineers had been slogging their guts out to eradicate glitches, double and triple check calculations, run simulations and all the myriad activities required to ensure that all would be right on the night, the military had been plotting and lobbying.

There was deep unease in the Hexagon, defense headquarters, at the decision that this should be a civilian mission. Even worse they were convinced that the Government wanted to impose a civilian Captain. "How can a bunch of useless civvies be trusted with such a mission, surely anyone can see that managing contact with savages is a job for the army. You can just imagine what will happen with a load of over-eager boffins in charge, no discipline, and as likely as not walk into a trap. It's unthinkable."

These sort of views held widely in the upper echelons of the forces. A relentless campaign was waged throughout ***1617***. They even got the KNN military attaché to chip in xer tuppence worth. This the latter did, trying to balance xer genuine desire to assist xer friends in the New Norland MoD with xer Ambassador's strict orders not to get involved in any way that might upset relations with New Norland, and thereby embarrass Xer Majesty's Government with their most powerful ally. "It is absolutely forbidden for you to interfere in New Norland's internal affairs, and that means taking no part in the sort of shenanigans going on here. In any case XMG's position on the matter is clear. This is a NN party to which we are privileged to have been invited, and our public actions and words must be to support whatever they decide. In fact, as well as in public statement, XMG applauds the stance on the rights of Duplosians, and is pleased (relieved) at the intention to make this a civilian mission. The last thing any of us needs is some trigger-happy clown in uniform in charge of a contact meeting with aliens."

What was xe to do? Well, xe didn't disobey orders. After all xe was a soldier and a diplomat. Xe didn't even mention the subject of personnel for the mission. All xe did was complement the Secretary of State on the quality of xer Generals, first-rate soldiers, men of integrity with the interests of NN and xer allies at heart. Xe couldn't wish for better men to work with for the mutual defence of our nations. "And no names no pack-drill, but I sometimes wish we had Generals who were half as good."

Did the Secretary of State smell a rat? Xe was an experienced and consummate politician, rat-smelling was xer speciality. You could say xe had a PhD in the subject.

The call for applications went out. By now both Wild Cat and Flying Eagle were well qualified for the mission. They had each earned fearsome reputations within the programme and had caught the notice of the great and the good. Each of them applied to be Captain of the mission.

So here we are, back where we finished chapter 9. Each of the friends prayed that if xe were unsuccessful, that xer friend would get the job. Each resolved that if the other other got the job, that xe would be happy for xer, would swallow xer personal disappointment and celebrate like there was no tomorrow, and each resolved that if successful xe would not punch the air and celebrate, but would devote all xer energies to comforting xer friend.

"I don't think they'll let us have a job-share," was all Wild Cat could think of saying.

"No I don't suppose they will," was the reply.

There were five candidates short-listed, and all were called to an assessment centre for a period long grilling. "Probably seeing how we stand up to torture," thought Wild Cat, for torture it most certainly was. There were briefings and group sessions, psychological assessment tests and physical training exercises. You name it, everything and anything that could be thrown at them was thrown at them. Crisis handling, where everything that could go wrong did go wrong. Put out one fire and another went out of control behind your back. They were watched all the time.

Earnest psychologists with clipboards, watching and ticking boxes, making notes and nodding or shaking their heads. "I bet even the bogs are bugged," mused Flying Eagle.

They did sleep next to each other, but there was a wall between them, each could hear the other through that thin hotel wall. "Not a good place for a honeymoon," thought Wild Cat.

Of the five candidates, three were civilian and two military. The other civilian was a psychologist and multi-linguist called Stripy Tiger Svensdot. Xer seed-parent, Peter Svensdot, had emigrated from the KNN and Stripy Tiger had decided to take xer surname just to be different from the usual New Norland pattern, xe liked that it must have come from a long way back as it's derived from Sven's Daughter, which harks back to an ancient time when male and female children were differentiated. The two military candidates were Captain Brock Badger Woodlands (NNN) who had a distinguished naval career, having recently commanded an aircraft carrier, and now holding a desk job in Defense procurement, and Colonel Mountain Lion Mountain, formerly of the Military Police, now assigned to the Ministry of Defense Security team.

Capt Woodlands' strength was xer experience in command. Running an aircraft carrier requires a high level of leadership and management skills. Of all the candidates xe was clearly the strongest in this regard. On the other hand, the team would necessarily be a small one and wouldn't require quite the same set of leadership qualities that are required for a command of over a twousand personnel. Otherwise Woodlands didn't have any specific technical skill to contribute to the mission, and given the small size of the team it was desirable that every member could contribute something to the party.

The other four candidates met this criterion. As we have seen, Wild Cat Waters, combines a deep understanding of Space Engineering, with experience as a Space-Station Commander. The conundrum for the selection panel was not whether to employ xim on the mission, but where. Xe would be a shoe-in for the job of commanding the Space-Stations, a job of at least equal status and importance as that of commanding the landing party. Flying Eagle Forest was less well qualified on the management side, xe had solid relevant experience with a good track record, so that was not thought to be a real problem. Xer real strength was xer expertise with the vehicles. Someone with those skills was essential for the landing party. If xe were not appointed then xe was still needed on the mission. There were very few others who could fill that role adequately, Waters could contribute or maybe one of the Kingdom people might be suitable, they had made a contribution to the systems involved. Svensdot also had skills that were needed on the ground. Xe would be expected to play a leading role in the contact with the Duplosians, there was definitely a place for xim, but perhaps not in overall command.

For the selection panel the most difficult candidate was Col. Mountain. The MoD was pushing xer candidature hard, definitely their commander of choice. The mission did need a security officer, that was clear and written into the mission requirements from period one. However xer leadership style left much to be desired. Xer old-fashioned approach might have been acceptable in the military police but did not go down well with civilians. With a small team of professional experts, a man like Mountain could cause a riot. Xe led by giving orders and was not good at dealing with expert advisors. The reports from the assessors for the various exercises had confirmed this opinion. Meetings chaired by Mountain were a disaster. Xe was a poor listener and tended to be dismissive of others. Xe was decisive, but too often the decisions were based on prejudice and xe fell into traps that were carefully hidden within the exercises. Psychological tests indicated a degree of inflexibility. The panel saw it as their role to come up with a solid justification for a decision not to appoint xim to either the Captain's or Deputy's job. The justification being necessary to convince the military authorities. They wished that Woodlands were better qualified for the security role, but xe wasn't.

Wild Cat and Flying Eagle had actually enjoyed many of the exercises. They were both impressed by the care that had gone into the design and the subtle way they brought out the leadership skills that might be needed on Duplos. Each thought xe had learnt quite a lot from the experience.

Generally they appreciated their fellow candidates. They weren't sure that Capt Woodlands had anything to offer the mission but xe was easy to get on with and knew how to handle people. Their only problem was with Col Mountain, xe was much too full of ximself and thought xe knew it all, which xe certainly didn't. They were also rather disturbed by the outcomes of some of the exercises xe led, particularly one involving a protest by a primitive tribe in part of a rainforest being cleared to make way for development. Mountain's handling of the event was heavy handed and resulted in things getting out of control and several protesters being killed.

All that was now behind them, they had enjoyed an end-of-assessment banquet at the end of the **watch**, and all that remained were the formal interviews that would start after breakfast. The interviews were to be in alphabetical order so Flying Eagle would be up first, and Wild Cat fourth: Forest, Mountain, Svensdot, Waters, Woodlands. Then there would be a feedback session before departure. Wild Cat and Flying Eagle then planned a short break together in the mountains, before returning to their respective homes. They were given no information regarding when to expect to hear the results.

Neither of them slept well, each could hear the other tossing and turning, if only they could be together they might be calmer. Eventually the night passed, as nights do, Wild Cat had a hearty breakfast but Flying Eagle rather picked at xer food and had little more than a couple of mugs of strong coffee. Xe was getting very nervous about the interview due immediately after, just a few tocks away. When xe came out all xe would say was xe thought the questions were fair but gave no indication as to how xe thought it had gone. Xe then took ximself off for a rest and a long walk.

Each interview took about sixtween tocks (a quarter of a **meal**). There was a gap between interviews and a scheduled break for lunch between the third and fourth. It was Wild Cat's turn to lose xer appetite. To make matters worse, Col Mountain's interview went on rather longer than scheduled, and as a result Wild Cat's was delayed by eight tocks. It didn't help Wild Cat's nerves that Col Mountain ate heartily and looked pleased with ximself.

After the interview Wild Cat went back to xer room to finish packing and have a short nap. They could have stayed one extra night, but Wild Cat and Flying Forest had agreed to leave immediately after the Feedback session, skipping dinner at the centre and heading for the hills, where they had booked into a bijou hotel for their R&R.

The Feedback was to be given individually. The chosen order was Woodlands, Waters, Forest, Svensdot, and lastly, Mountain. Captain Woodlands was shown straight back into the interview room that xe had just left a few tocks ago. Wild Cat was shown into a waiting room next door and the others were given times to present themselves in the waiting room.

The sessions weren't scheduled to take very long. Captain Woodlands poked xer head into the waiting room to say Goodbye to Wild Cat and Flying Eagle who had just arrived. Xe was going straight home so wouldn't be seeing them at dinner.

A couple of tocks later the panel Chairman came in and asked them to both to come in together. Much to their surprise, when they got through the door they found themselves face to face with none other than the Vice-President of New Norland. Xe stood and greeted them and invited them to be seated.

After a few words in which the VP stated xer admiration for all that they had achieved for the mission and how grateful the nation was, xe went on to say: "I'm afraid we do have just a couple more questions for you both, the first is actually illegal for an interview panel to ask, but as I'm not formally on the panel I'm going to ask it anyway. Is either of you pregnant?" This came as a shock, it was not only illegal under the fair employment rules, it was also quite against the rules of polite etiquette. However, both Wild Cat and Flying Eagle understood why it was being asked. The Government would not wish to risk a birth-parent and unborn child travelling to Duplos while so much was unknown about the safety of the planet. Happily, each was able to reply "No my Lord[34]."

"Good, that's got the difficult one out of the way, I also need to ask each of you, if you were to be appointed to lead the mission to Duplos, would you be prepared to accept the other one as a member of the team?" No difficulty here, each was able to respond affirmatively. "Finally, if the situation were reversed and your colleague were appointed, would you be prepared to serve under xim?" Again each was able to respond in the affirmative.

---

34 Recall that the VP is ex officio a member of the House of Lords.

"So, all that is left for me to to tell you the panel's decision. The problem is that they have failed to make one. Their recommendation is that either of you is suitable for the role, but they cannot decide between you, and have left it to me to decide. Well I have decided," a long pause, "to borrow from the book of the late-but-not-lamented Party of the Egalitarian Experiment and trust to luck." At this xe took out a coin. "The panel chairman has two envelopes, one white and one brown, Forest please call heads or tails for the brown envelope."

Wild Cat smiled, this was what xer birth-parent would have done. Flying Eagle was nonplussed, but managed to call out "Heads."

The VP tossed his coin, looked at it and said: "Heads it is, Chairman please pass me the brown envelope." The chairman did so, the VP then handed it to Wild Cat saying, "one of you is to be is be in charge of the mission with honorary naval rank of Captain, the other to be second in command with the same honorary rank. This way Colonel Mountain will not outrank either of you in military terms. Your salaries will also be the same. You will find which of you is mission commander and which is 2 - i - c when you open the envelope, Congratulations, Captains, it's been an honour to meet you both." He bowed to them and shook hands.

The panel chairman then took over. They would be called to meetings shortly to help pick the team, arrange training and team bonding exercises etcetera. Xe then looked serious and said: "There is a lot to be done in the two years leading up to the actual landing, and you will both find yourselves very busy. You will have a certain amount of freedom to select your team but there are some constraints. Obviously we will leave the KNN to fill their two places, and we have decided to appoint Svensdot as team psychologist with special responsibility for first contact and alien communications, I hope that meets with your approval, we would have appointed xim as 2-i-c if either of you had declined. The other appointment to be made is less easy for me to say. The Ministry of Defense insists we appoint Colonel Mountain as head of security. I regret this very much and just hope xe won't sabotage the mission. Formally xe will be third in command, let's hope xe never has to command anything. We will do what we can to support you and will organise special training for you both in handling people of xer disposition."

They left off opening the envelope until they were safely tucked into their bijou hotel. They couldn't both have won the top job, and after all, their dream had only been to be in the landing party. This result represented the best of all possible outcomes, it hadn't even handed superiority to either of them, merely superior luck. They are equal, it's just that one is a little bit more equal than the other! Perhaps the PEE was not all wrong!

Part 3

Duplos meets Geos

17
Astronomy on Duplos

Arté was quite busy down at South Beach, he made himself generally useful about the place as Zorro had hoped he would. This was a time of semi-holiday for Astra but she also liked to spend some time on her astronomical tasks.

"Now we've settled in, and you've been able to find your way around, I'd like to bring you up to date with my observations from last winter." She began. "As I understand it, on Isla you still believe that Geos, Selenos, the Sun and all the planets orbit around Duplos. Well lot's of the less educated people on the continent believe the same, but there is a much simpler explanation for what we observe, which most experts think is how the heavens really work. We now think that the so-called fixed stars are suns just like our own, and the reason they look so small is that they are huge distances away. What's more, they aren't really fixed at all but all the universe is in motion.

Our sun is just the closest star to us, which is why it looks so big. It is a fiery ball in the sky, and by some unknown mechanism it keeps us and the other planets revolving around it. Apart from us and Geos, we can see three other planets which revolve around the sun, Thermos, Zuvos and Sépanos. Thermos is the closest to the sun and takes a bit less than eleven periods to complete its orbit. If you lived on Thermos, which you couldn't because it is much too hot, that's how long you would think a year was. Next in order round the sun comes us and Geos, Selenos and Eclos. Our planet and Geos form a binary planet system, that is we are two planets that go around each other. Selenos and Eclos go round us both, and all four of us then circle the sun. Further away from the sun but still orbiting it are Zuvos and Sépanos. Since I started watching it properly, six years ago,

Zuvos has moved right across to the far side of the sun so I think its orbit will take it about twelve years. Much of my work has been to observe Zuvos, and last winter I think I have discovered it has three moons in orbit around it. One of the things I want us to do before next winter is to try and work out their orbits and see if we can predict where to find them when we go to the observatory. Finally there's Sépanos, I don't know much about it, but it seems to have moved about six dudegs around its orbit in four years which implies about forty years to complete one orbit."[35]

Arté knew some of the above from his studies at Routh with Fermos, but the bit about the moons of Zuvos and the time for the orbits of the two outer planets were new to him. Astra wasn't yet ready to publicise her work. She needed another observation season first, and some more accurate calculations than her rather rough and ready ones.

"This is very interesting, if we and Zuvos have moons, shouldn't the other two planets also have them, and what about moons of moons?" Queried Arté.

"I'm pretty sure that Thermos doesn't have a moon. It is much closer to us than the other two planets, and although there is some difficulty in observing it because of the sun, I'm sure I would have spotted if there was a moon of any size. I have examined it pretty closely looking for one. As for Sépanos, I think it is most likely that it does have moons, but it is so far away that my telescope isn't powerful enough to spot one."

Arté didn't really have any idea about what a telescope was. Optics hadn't been in his study programme. He knew it was a tool used in astronomy and that Astra had one in her observatory. Rather than have a digression now he thought he

35 This just represents what was known on Duplos at the time. Fuller details of the Solar System as known on Geos are to be found in Appendix 1.

might easily wait until they went North. "And what about shooting stars, do you know where they fit in to the scheme of things?"

"That's a hard question, Arté. The simple answer is I don't know. However my best guess is that they are very small bodies that travel in very strange paths from much further out from the sun beyond Sépanos and we only get to see them when they come close enough. I would need a much more powerful telescope to be able to study them properly. I think Eclos might be a shooting star that somehow got stuck in orbit about us, it certainly has a weird orbit as far as I can tell. Indeed our own little system has enough mysteries all of its own. Duplos and Geos are in orbit about each other but I don't know exactly how. Viewed from here on Duplos it appears that Geos goes round as in a circular orbit, but I think it's more complicated than that. We each complete our orbit in one period which is one thirtieth of a year. Both of us are also spinning on a North-South axis which is slightly tilted. The tilt towards or away from the sun is responsible for the seasons and the spin is why different parts of the planet face the sun. Night comes when we are facing away from the sun or when Geos comes between us and the sun, blocking out the light. Here on Duplos we spin four times every period, while on Geos they spin six times. I guess that on Geos they have six phases every period. Then there's Selenos. It orbits both planets in a strange orbit that looks very loopy when viewed from here[36] and takes nearly a quarter of a year. Close enough that here on the continent we stick to a strict quarter year selenth and just don't worry about the alignment of the calendar with the true position of Selenos."

"Isla differs there," said Arté, "selenths are strictly defined by Selenos, which means that the seasons slip by about half a phase

36 See the end of Appendix 1.

a year. This means that the solar new year occurs later in the selenth each year until every fifty years or so, there are five new selenths between new years, and the temple decrees a Holy Selenth between Autumn and Winter."

As the periods passed, Astra and Arté grew more comfortable together. Arté made a start on producing the logarithm tables to enable calculations to proceed more quickly and accurately. It was painstaking and tiring work, and everything needed to be double and triple checked because mistakes are all too easy to make.

In between sessions on the logs, he looked at Astra's notes on her observations, to see if he could get anywhere with the orbit calculations. It would help if we knew how far away these wretched things are or how big. He realised that it helped being by the sea, and he spent some time trying to estimate distances to the horizon, which then enabled him, with a bit of elementary geometry, to produce estimates of the radius of the planet. Then by guessing that Geos was about the same size he could come up with an estimate of their separation.

He came up with the following ranges: Horizon: 1.9 to 2.2 walks; Radius of Duplos 1805 - 2420 walks; Distance to Geos 82735 - 118847 walks.[37]

When Arté presented his calculations to Astra and explained his methods she was most impressed. When he then broached the subject of going to Marouth to meet his friend Rastu, she laughed like a drain, "I've told you before, you're not a slave, Arté. You are fully entitled to holidays, and this is the right time of year to take them. Please go and enjoy yourself, I'm glad you

37 This compares with the true values of approximately 2.04, 2080.8 and 139600 walks respectively. The main source of error is that Geos is larger than Duplos. Later when Arté and Rastu make orbit calculations they are able to improve the estimate considerably.

have friends, I know it must be difficult for you away from all the people you knew on Isla and never being able to go back."

Arté met Rastu for a pleasant break in Marouth. He was most impressed by the city. It had a liveliness and vibrancy about it that he had never before experienced. As well as Contish he heard languages from the GSE being spoken and was awed by the variety of fashions and building styles on display. He and Rastu stayed in an inexpensive pension on the Marcenza side of the border, since neither were flush with funds. They shared a twin-bedded room and sat up late talking about everything and nothing.

"So this is the GSE," said Arté, "it feels like we're in the same city. The walls go round both. Do I have to pretend to be your slave when I'm here?"

"My slave! Whatever gave you that idea?"

"Something Astra said about me not being her slave, because slavery is illegal in the Western Federation, not like in the GSE or the SU."

"Well, you don't have to worry about that. They do have slaves in parts of the GSE, but further South and East. Slavery is not approved of in the regions nearer the border and is actually against the city laws in Marcenza. And anyway even in the slave regions you'd be safe. It's not like on Isla, slavery doesn't apply to men automatically. It's complicated and I don't pretend to understand it; but some men and women are born slaves or can be enslaved after being taken prisoner in a war, or because they are criminal."

"How is it that Marcenza and Marouth are in different territories?"

"It all goes back to history. The WF and GSE were always having fights over just which bits belonged to which territory. Marouth/Marcenza are situated just where the border meets the inner sea, it really is one city and was called Marouth when in the WF and Marcenza when in the GSE. Eventually, a hundred and twenty years ago the two sides agreed that their continuing border wars were exhausting them both and signed the "Treaty of the Mountains and Sea" which has settled the border in perpetuity. The final stumbling block was this city. Eventually it was agreed that the northern half, which includes the mouth of the River Mars, would belong to the WF and be called Marouth; and the southern half would be belong to the GSE and be Marcenza."

"That seems weird to me, how does administration work."

Rastu explained. "Although the inter-territory border runs through the middle. It is really one city and enjoys unique privileges. For example, customs posts are situated on the city boundaries and the city itself has status as a free trade entity. Citizens and visitors from both sides can roam freely within the city walls and in many ways the city functions as a single entity with two administrative districts."

"But isn't it easy for criminals, can't they just commit crimes in one half and then escape across the border, out of the reach of the watch?"

"It's true that usually there are all sorts of difficult legal formalities in extraditing wanted criminals from one territory to another, but between Marouth and Marcenza things are different. The watches on either side at least claim to co-operate fully to keep crime under control. If Marcenza wants you to answer for a crime, the Marouth watch will hand you over without question and it is the same the other way."

"Still I'm dubious. It seems to me like somewhere good for slightly shady characters to take advantage to play off both territories against each other."

"There may be something about that, it's supposed to be part of the charm, but actually the city authorities keep matters reasonably under control. Not just anyone can live here. To own or rent property in the city you have to have a formal citizen's permit, but when you have one you are permitted to buy or live on either side."

The time to leave came all too soon, but he had to get back and Rastu's mother was also waiting for her daughter to come home for the Summer. Before they parted, Rastu offered to come to South Beach and help with the log tables and some of his other mathematical work, if Astra allowed it.

The phase after he returned to South Beach, Arté broached the subject of Rastu with Astra. As he had feared, Astra was dubious. There were only the three bedrooms said Astra, and one had to be reserved for Zorro, who was expected any time now.

Arté told her that he realised that, but he and Rastu could share. She could have his bed and he could sleep on a camp bed or even the floor. Astra looked even more dubious. Recalling her blow-up with Zorro, Arté was quick to reassure her that he wasn't attempting to abuse her hospitality by using her house for sexual play. He explained carefully that his relationship with Rastu was like brother and sister and there was no question of any improper behaviour. Honestly, as well as the pleasure he would undoubtedly have in Rastu's company, she really would be helpful with the work. Rastu's geometric intuition was much superior to his own and he was sure that she would contribute some valuable insights to the orbit problems.

Although she didn't like to admit it, Astra was mollified by Arté's assurances about his sex life. She felt guilty about that. She knew she had no right to impose celibacy on Arté just because she had chosen it for herself and was a bit squeamish on the subject of sex. "All down to my bloody sister," is what she thought to herself, "I really ought to be over all that by now." She resolved to be nice to Arté's friend, even if he was fool enough to think of her as a sister.

When Rastu did come to stay for a full period, Astra was true to her resolve. She took to Rastu quite quickly and caught herself wishing her own daughter took a leaf out of her book. Watching them together, she soon recognised how close they were and also how productively they worked together. Each phase, they adhered to a strict timetable. Of the eighty hora in the phase, twenty-six were reserved for sleep, twenty-eight for work and twenty-six for eating and play.

They worked on the log tables in three hora sessions. For two hora each of them would work independently on calculating table entries. Then they would swap papers and check each other's work for a further horum. They would have three or four such sessions every phase. The remaining time of their self-imposed work schedule they would pore over Astra's observation notes and engage in various algebraic and geometric doodles, sketching out potential orbits and trying to make future predictions that might be tested in the winter observation season.

As well as eating and resting, they would go for long walks along the beach and have regular swims. When, as was her wont, Astra shed her clothes on a warm day, Rastu followed her lead. She told Arté that while his decision to keeps his shorts on in the house was sensible, given the threat of attention from the sister, notwithstanding that said sister had not yet shown herself;

that consideration doesn't apply in Rastu's case and it was only polite for her to follow her hostesses example.

Astra happened to overhear that exchange taking place and was impressed both by Rastu's good manners and the thoughtful motive for Arté's dress choice. What a good thing she had allowed Arté to overcome her reluctance to invite Rastu.

In the last phase before Rastu was due to leave, Zorro at last showed up. As was only to be expected, she misconstrued Arté's relationship with Rastu. She managed to behave with reasonable politeness, after all Rastu was a guest in her mother's house, but she did flounce about a bit in a grumpy mood. Her intention had been to work on her mother to allow her some fun with Arté. She reasoned it would be easier to talk her round in the holiday atmosphere of South Beach, especially as she had left it late enough in the Summer to counter her mother's inevitable accusations of ulterior motives in Arté's recruitment. It wasn't that she couldn't cope with abstinence in what was left of the Summer. But she just had to ensure that they had a sexual relationship before they were all locked up together at the observatory.

Later, while Arté was walking Rastu to where she would catch a stage coach to Marouth, Zorro had a row with her mother.

"What were you thinking, letting Arté bring his fancy-girl here, after all you've said on the subject. And all the time refusing to let me, your own daughter, have fun with him! Not to mention that she's far too young, it's indecent."

"Rastu is not a fancy-girl, Arté's or anyone else's. She may be young but she's a damn sight better mannered than you are. You could do a lot worse than take a lesson from her. She's exactly the sort of girl that any mother would be proud of. She was Arté's study partner at university and is a very competent mathematician. Arté quite properly asked that she be invited here to help him out with some of the work. I am so pleased I agreed. They have worked so diligently and made tremendous progress. In addition, they have both been extremely helpful about the house, and shown me every consideration. If you so much as lay a finger on Arté against his wishes I shall disown you. If Rastu didn't have a perfectly respectable mother of her own, I would adopt her myself."

To say that Zorro was taken aback, was an understatement. This was not the response she had expected. Obviously her mother would go on the attack, but she had expected that to take the form of defending her action by saying something like it not being reasonable to ask Arté to share her celibacy, and that he had to be allowed a certain amount of indulgence especially in the holiday season. That was the response she had been seeking, an opening for herself, if not immediately, at least in the future. She needed to change tack and work out a new strategy.

When Arté got back, Zorro suggested a walk on the beach. He agreed, as he would. She launched into an apology for her rather off-hand reception of his friend. She had been tired after her journey and had a bit of a headache. She didn't mean to be rude and was sure she would get along fine with his friend next time they meet.

The rest of the Summer passed without major incident. Zorro would regularly take Arté for walks or a swim. Sometimes Astra joined them, and Zorro was happy to include her mother on such occasions. Just once, a couple of phases before they left she tried it on, a bit half-heartedly, after she and Arté had been for a selenth-light swim together. Arté was polite but firm.

"You are very attractive Zorro and I'm sure I would enjoy a bit of fun with you and, indeed, I am very grateful to you for all you did to get me this job. However your mother is my mistress, and I am very happy working for her and fully intend to keep it that way. I can't pretend to be ignorant of her views on the subject. Without her explicit consent, I am not prepared to indulge in sex play with you. It would feel like a betrayal. I'm sorry but that really is all I can say on the matter. Can't we just be friends, I have enjoyed our walks and swims together."

"Mummy has grown used to you, indeed is very attached to you. It's not at all like it was when she first discovered you were a man. I'm sure that you could talk her round. She'd give in after a couple of goes, three max, I assure you. I know her."

"I'm sorry, Zorro, I'm not going to upset her by raising the subject. I will not harass her, not for anyone. The more she comes to depend on my help and to value me, the more seriously I will take my obligations to her. If you want her talked round, you are going to have to do the talking. I will not act unless she gives me permission herself, or gives you permission in my hearing."

Zorro knew she was beaten, and decided to accept with good grace. "Of course we can stay good friends," she said, "and continue to enjoy our walks, talks and swims together. After all we appear to have Mummy in common, and for all our fights I do care for her a great deal." At that she gave him a hug and kissed his cheek. If she held her naked body a bit too tightly to his for a tad too long, he was too much of a gentleman to complain.

When the time came to return to Louth for the new university term, the three of them seemed to be in harmony. Arté packed up all the papers carefully, neatly arranged for when later unpacking and keeping tidy in the Louth apartment. He and Zorro also sorted out all the many other chores that have to be done when packing up a summer residence. Astra had never experienced such an efficient and hassle-free move.

The Autumn selenth also passed without fracas. Zorro remained on her best behaviour. Astra found it quite remarkable and thought that Arté was obviously a good influence on them both. Astra found that with Arté keeping her papers so tidy, and having just the right ones available for her when she needed them, she was less harassed and less prone to outbursts at her daughter than hitherto, and better prepared for the winter at the observatory. She even became more tolerant of Zorro's friendship with Créezy. This she realised was in part on account of Arté. She completely understood that as Arté and Créezy had their Isla origin in common, and had even known some of the same people, it was only natural that he should visit her from time to time. She was also much touched that he was sufficiently mindful of her feelings as to ask her permission, not only to visit Créezy, but to accept an offer of sex should it be made. She told him that she had no right to object, and her only concern was that he should not be coerced into anything he didn't want for himself. She knew what some women were like, she said. "Like Zorro," she didn't say, just thought. She also thought that had she raised even the slightest objection, he wouldn't have argued, but obeyed without question. This fidelity touched her, but also worried her on his account.

Arté completed the log tables (up to seven figures of decimals) ready for the winter. Professor Fermos invited him to Routh to give a seminar on the subject. Arté used the opportunity to publicly acknowledge and thank Rastu for her contribution. She blushed, which is of itself unusual for a Duplosian woman, but then she is an unusual Duplosian woman. He wasn't able to take her for a nice cosy dinner for two, because he had to attend a Natural Philosophy Department dinner given to honour his visit, as is normal when they have a visiting speaker. Fermos had ensured that Rastu was also invited to the dinner, which was also quite rare for an undergraduate. Fermos was pleased to see Arté, and the pleasure was mutual. They had a long talk before the seminar, with Fermos asking about his work. After dinner he was able to have a bit of time with Rastu, but there was no question of them spending the night together. Arté caught the overnight boat back to Louth along the river Louten.

18
Winter at the Observatory

The journey to Observatory island was a long one and Arté was looking forward to seeing more of the countryside and two more cities. The first leg, that would take about six hora, was by stage coach to Goddess City. Astra planned to stop there for a couple of phases to show Arté the sights. Goddess City is situated mainly on the east bank of the River of the Goddesses. For much of its length this river used to form the boundary between rival territories, and some cultural differences persist. Although not the longest river in the WF, it is the widest and wider than any Arté had seen before. Goddess City boasted an impressive ancient temple. In the secular culture of the Western Federation, it is no longer operated as such, but is open as a museum and also used for public lectures, plays and concerts. Astra took Arté to a concert of modern music which he found amazing in the richness of its sounds and complexity of the orchestration, so much more sophisticated than anything they had on Isla.

Louth and Goddess City both consider themselves to be the true capital of the WF, and there is fierce rivalry between them. Patriotically, Arté came down in favour of Louth, with its vibrant social scene, rather than the more austere feel of Goddess City, despite the latter being the larger city and the main financial centre in the WF.

Apart from sight-seeing there was nothing to keep them in Goddess City. They would be stocking up with supplies in their next city stop, Kongholm, just over twenty walks inland from the cold sea coast. Kongholm is a hundred and ten walks from Goddess City as the crow flies, longer by road. The journey would take at least eleven hora by coach, depending on the state of the roads. They would do the journey in two stages, with an eight hora sleep-over in a coaching inn, around half way. For the first fifty walks the road was good and wide, and they bowled along at a fair lick. Then as they entered a less populated region, the road deteriorated and they slowed considerably. Astra was well-used to the journey and had planned accordingly. The inn was unremarkable but adequate. Arté rather liked the beer, which Astra told him was a speciality of the region. It was lighter and a bit more fizzy than he had been used to on Isla, but tasty all the same. Arté thought, a good deal better than stuff they serve in the parts of the continent he had known so far. Decent beer was one of the things he missed about Isla. The inn was small and they had to share a bedroom. There were two beds and neither Astra nor Arté were bothered. All his life Arté had been at the beck and call of women. He was accepting of the circumstances, whatever they had to be. On the other hand Astra was more protective of her own privacy than was the norm on Duplos, even in the WF She would have been uncomfortable sharing a bedroom with a stranger, but Arté was no longer a stranger to her. He had become family, and she didn't mind having him around.

Once they were within ten walks of Kongholm the state of the roads improved again, and they arrived about twenty hora after their departure from Goddess City. They stayed there for the best part of a phase, stocking up with various items they would need at the observatory, including enough food to keep them going for a period. It was Astra's wont to leave her island for resupply from a local village no more than once a period, and to go as far as Kongholm only once during the season. When Zorro was there, Astra preferred not to leave the island at all but to rely on Zorro to shop for provisions, which the latter was happy to do to relieve her boredom.

Zorro was not with them this time. Taking advantage of Arté's presence, she had told her mother she would stay in in Louth for a bit longer, and then join them later. Astra was quite relieved. She and Arté had work to do, and Zorro would be a distraction for them both.

There were still sixty walks remaining from Kongholm to the island. For the first twenty or so there was a good coach service to the coast. After that transport was more irregular but they were able to find rides as far as a small village about five walks away. The last stage had to be completed on foot, with the final crossing to the island being over a causeway that emerged at low tide. Astra had a hand cart that she kept in the village and into which they loaded all their luggage and provisions. Arté towed it behind him.

There were two buildings on the island. A small bungalow on the flat western half, where they would live. Here they had two bedrooms, a living room, a kitchen and a wash room, with a privy outside. The island was about seven walks long and three walks wide at the extremes, The eastern half was an extinct volcano rising to two hundred and sixty strides above sea level. At the top of this was Astra's observatory, which was a square tower of side four strides and was some twenty strides high, with a small dome on the roof that could be opened out to aid observation. There were three floors between the ground and the roof. The highest of these was also suitable for observation as the tower narrowed for the final stage to the roof. There were also primitive living facilities in the tower as sometimes Astra became so absorbed in her work that she didn't return to the bungalow for meals and sleep.

It was winter, the island, at some nine dudegs North of the equator, was pretty northerly, and set in the cold sea which lived up to its name. Weather was unpredictable, but generally there were many good clear nights for observing the heavens. Invariably these nights were cold. Basically, it was not very comfortable. Astra didn't seem to mind. There were trees on the western side, which provided firewood, and they were able to have fires in both the bungalow and the tower, and also wrap up warmly. This was no place for Astra's Summer habit of going without clothes. Perhaps that is why she indulged in nudity so much when in South Beach. They even had to wrap up warmly when in bed. In warmer climes most Duplosians sleep naked, even on Isla which is generally cooler than most of the Western Federation. Arté took some getting used to wearing a sleeping suit, but he was nevertheless grateful for it, and for the trick of a warming pan to heat the bed before he got into it. That was a luxury he had never seen before.

They threw themselves into the work and Arté was totally entranced by the telescope. Astra actually had two telescopes. Her first one was acquired from an optician in Dambach. She made eyeglasses to improve the sight of wealthy people with short sight. Astra didn't have short sight but was intrigued when a friend told her about the magic of these eyeglasses. Thinking they might also help her see further into the sky she spent part on one Autumn in Dambach learning from the optician, and between, them they produced this early telescope with a magnification power of about ten.

Astra then took it to Kongholm, where she was accustomed to go for part of the winter, because of the clear northern skies. Her initial success that winter caused her to look for a permanent base when she happened to hear of the island, which had been occupied by a recluse a couple of generations ago, but was now abandoned. She managed to buy the island (from the Kongholm authorities since it was uninhabited and didn't really belong to anyone). She slightly extended and refurbished the recluse's bungalow and had the observatory tower built on the volcano. Using local labour, she didn't personally do the building work, but did draw up the plans and instruct a young architect to supervise the works while she was away in Louth. That summer she had not gone to South Beach but instead had returned to the observatory to see to the completion of the building. After a couple of seasons with the old telescope she returned to Dambach with plans for an even better one. This one has a magnification power of thirty and is the one installed on the roof. She had collected it on her way to the observatory the previous winter, and all the hustle over the past year was on account of the observations with the new telescope.

Working together they were definitely able to confirm the existence of the three moons of Zuvos, and take measurements to help determine their orbits. Arté also was able to identify features on Zuvos, that enabled him to demonstrate that it was spinning and to estimate the rate of spin. Since Zuvos was named after the Goddess Zu, they named the moons after others associated with Zu in the ancient pantheon. Arté summarised his findings in the Table below:

Name	Orbit period	Relative orbit size	Relative Size	Rotation period
Zuvos	12.4 years	N/A	1	11 hora
Proxis	0.165 period	3.2	unknown	
Mexia	0.66 period	8	unknown	
Maxos	1.35 period	13	0.075	

All the relative sizes in the table are based on the diameter of Zuvos.

What Arté actually reported was ranges of values, the table above gives numerically convenient choices from the middle of his ranges. That winter, they also took observations of the other bodies in the solar system. When they got back to Louth in the spring, they co-authored an academic paper which grabbed a lot of attention because of the announcement of the moons. One difficulty was that no other natural philosopher had been using telescopes. However, Arté had persuaded Astra to take the smaller telescope back to Louth with them, and knowing where in the sky to look, they were able back up Astra's discovery. First by showing that Zuvos itself looked as large as Eclos at apogee, when viewed trough the telescope, and then pointing out the three moons, with Maxos in the telescope looking nearly as large as Zuvos does with the naked eye. This in itself was a marvel. When Astra added that with her bigger telescope, Zuvos looked two thirds as large as the sun does with the naked eye her audience was truly amazed.

Eventually Zorro turned up, arriving just in time for New Year. She brought presents for Astra and Arté, and set about making herself agreeable to her mother. Astra was worrying about sleeping arrangements. There were only two bedrooms in the bungalow. She knew she would never persuade Zorro to sleep in the observatory, and was reluctant to ask Arté to do so, or, she found, to do so herself. She surprised herself by the thought that she would prefer for Arté to move in with her over the other possible arrangements. She didn't want to share with Zorro, and she didn't trust Zorro to behave herself with Arté. Then, when her mind started telling her what an attractive young man Arté was, she decided she couldn't trust herself either.

Arté went into the kitchen to wash up the dinner things and Zorro decided to take the plunge. "Mummy, I know you don't like discussing it, but you are bit unreasonable when it comes to your attitude to sex. You know perfectly well that most women have a strong sex drive and both their physical and mental health suffers from too much abstinence. Men may have less sexual stamina than women, but honestly, they do enjoy it too. Especially if the woman is considerate. You must know by now that Arté won't do anything to offend you, but are you being fair to him, let alone me? Could you please reconsider your objections and let us have the occasional romp together. I won't abuse him, and it would be easier domestically, if he and I share the spare room, which I confess would be difficult if I have to remain celibate. Right now, I think he's preparing to go and sleep in the observatory, is that fair on him?"

Astra didn't really know how to react. She understood some of the force of her daughter's argument. She certainly wanted to ensure Arté was well-treated. She had found over the year that she was starting to have opinions on gender relations. Being with Arté had taught her that men were worthy of respect, and she felt disgusted with the way so many women just treated them as sex objects, or worse as sex toys. It's true she'd never been happy with that lifestyle, which was why she'd generally avoided sexual encounters. But, she thought that had been a matter of personal distaste, rather than consideration of the respect due to men. Arté, without knowing he was doing so, was causing her to question the assumption of female superiority that was the basis on which Duplosian society and culture was built. An appalling thought came uninvited into her mind: "Why don't you abandon your celibacy and have Arté for yourself. You're not too old. Tell Zorro to "fuck off, he's yours."

"I am too old for him," she thought back, "he must be over thirteen years younger than me." She couldn't put up with her mind nagging her like this. She'd just have to let Zorro have her chance.

"Alright Zorro, but I really won't have you mistreating him. I need to be convinced that he is consenting, and not tonight. You can share his room but I'm not having you jump all over him like a bitch on heat. Now go and take over the washing up and ask him to come in here."

When Arté came in she sat him down next to her for what to her was a difficult conversation. "Arté, this is a bit embarrassing but now that Zorro's here, I have to have this conversation. You must be aware that Zorro has a strong sexual appetite, and that she finds you desirable. It may even be that you reciprocate."

"I assure you I will never do anything to displease you, and I have said as much to Zorro," Arté quickly butted in.

"No, I'm sure you wouldn't but this isn't about pleasing me or about pleasing Zorro, it must be about your comfort and your wishes. You don't only have the legal right to refuse importunate women, we women have the moral duty to treat you with respect and consideration. Initially I was concerned that I might get an assistant who allowed herself to be distracted from her work by her sexual appetites. Of course at that time I hadn't considered that my assistant might be a man, although the concern applies equally. However, our time together has reassured me that you are no such flighty person, and I no longer have fears on that score. What I need to know is your views on sharing a bedroom with Zorro, with the probability that it would lead to sexual relations."

"I will willingly share a room with Zorro, I realise we have only two bedrooms here, so either two must share or I could sleep in the observatory. I can behave myself, and would refrain from all sexual activity if that were your wish."

"It's not about my wishes, it's about yours. Zorro will not be able to keep herself to herself if you are sharing a room for any length of time. You have my blessing to indulge but I need to know more about your feelings for Zorro."

Arté thought hard about how to reply. "I like Zorro, she is very attractive and I'm sure she's a lot of fun in bed, so I would enjoy it. I am not a celibate but I have found the freedom not to be generally available to women to be one of the good things about my life here. I was actually pretty privileged on Isla, and my lot was far better than most men. My owner treated me well and I grew to love her, and being available to her was no hardship. But she did have control over my life in a way that I'm glad has gone. She never mistreated me sexually but I was expected on occasion to also be available for her friends or associates if it suited her. Since I've been here, there was an unfortunate incident in Routh which is best forgotten, but otherwise I have only had sex with Créezy, and by mutual agreement that is only occasional and with no strong commitment on either side. It helps us both to be able to share some moments of nostalgia for our past life. Whoops, I forgot, Zorro is not supposed to know about that, although perhaps that's not so important now, but please don't tell her. In terms of my feelings, I don't feel for Zorro as I did for Thay, my owner on Isla, or indeed for Rastu or for you. So while

I'm happy to have sexual fun with her, I wouldn't want it to imply a closer relationship. Perhaps similar to what I have with Créezy. Do you understand what I'm trying to say - I wouldn't be on private name terms with her like with Rastu?"

"Yes, I think I do, 'not on private name terms' is a good way of putting it; have some fun together when it suits you both, but no commitment to exclusivity. That seems reasonable to me, and I think is how Zorro is likely to feel. OK, you two will share the bedroom, but take it slowly and first ensure you understand one another's expectations, because disappointment can lead to soured relations that will be difficult for us all. We'd better get her in and give her the good news."

Thus all was arranged. Arté was right and Zorro was fun in bed. She didn't get sex quite as often as she would have liked but otherwise she was well-satisfied with the arrangement. They settled that while they would be sharing a room on observatory island, they would not do so in Louth or South Beach, although they would probably have occasional sex if they were both at a loose end. As with Créezy, the relationship would be 'friends with benefits'.

*Although Duplos does not have a system for dating their years, it would be helpful to us to adopt one. To that end I will start to use the Geos timeline. The events in this chapter occurred in what on Geos was the Winter of 2608/09 (**1614/15**) when Wild Cat Waters was working on the possibility of inner orbit Space Stations.*

This will help to explain the strange happenings that Astra and Arté had noticed while studying the skies around Geos, and their own planet. The previous year Astra had spotted what looked like new stars that were occasionally visible in the sky, often close to Geos. She hadn't been able to make it out at all. Her best guess was that she had discovered two extra moons that were orbiting both planets, well inside the orbit of Selenos and apparently at almost exactly opposite ends of a common orbit. Of course she could never see them both at once but no sooner had one disappeared than the other appeared, the two moon theory seemed to provide the simplest explanation. This year with Arté also working on the conundrum he was able to confirm her previous observations and also they spotted two more. There was now one at each of the four cardinal points of the compass, in other words at fifteen dudeg intervals around the orbit. Astra decided they didn't know enough about the phenomenon to publish anything about it. After all they didn't want to get a reputation as nutcases who see strange lights in the sky.

19
Astronomical Calculations

The entire Spring selenth was given over to calculations based on the Winter's observations. In addition to completing the paper on Zuvos' moons and the other observations, Arté wanted to get a better idea of the astronomical distances and sizes involved. He had his estimate of the size of Duplos itself from his horizon experiments the previous Summer, but could only guess at other astronomical dimensions.

Using similar methods to his calculation of the radius of Duplos and the relative radii of the orbits of the Zuvian moons, he was able to estimate the radii of the orbits of Thermos and the Geos-Duplos system, and the diameter of Thermos as compared to the diameter of the Sun. He was also able to compare the orbit radii, of Selenos and Geos. All he needed was just one actual dimension and he could sort out a great deal. He had also plotted the orbits of Geos and Selenos as seen from Duplos, i.e. assuming Duplos was stationary. The orbit of Geos could be approximated by a circle, but that of Selenos could not. Based on the apparent size of Selenos, he was able to estimate that the ratio between its distance at periapsis to that at apoapsis was approximately 1.6:1 and the orbit was very loopy.

He decided that it was worth consulting Rastu, as she always seemed to have geometric insights that eluded him. Naturally he asked Astra's permission to go, and also to make a trip to the coast at Dunos where he wanted to do an experiment of his own. For this purpose he asked to take the small telescope with him. Astra had no problem with this and told him he didn't need her permission to visit Rastu, only to take the telescope!

He found Rastu revising for her second year exams, and felt a bit guilty about disturbing her. On her part, she was actually quite glad of a break from her non-mathematical subjects, and felt she could afford a short time away from them. They spent a phase looking over the sketches of the orbits, with just breaks for meals and a short sleep. Arté kipped down on Rastu's floor, the bed being far too narrow for the two of them to sleep. When they woke she told him off for snoring. He was most apologetic, which then made her feel guilty for complaining. As he had hoped, she came up with the required insight. The simplest model that fits the observations is for all three bodies to be moving in approximate circles about a common fixed point. This point lying on an axis connecting Duplos to Geos, at about 72% of the separation between Duplos and Geos. The radius of the Duplos orbit being 72% of the separation, while that of Geos is 28%. The radius of the Selenos orbit is then about 3.07 times the separation of Geos and Duplos. Arté was also able to estimate the relative diameters of Selenos, Geos and The Sun. Tying in the data from Zuvos would need observations from further round its orbit of the Sun, which since it takes about twelve years to orbit means they just have to be patient.

Rastu told Arté she would think about what might be done to get at the true measurements. She was sure that she could come up with some appropriate geometry, then it would just be a question of trying to get the right observations. She wondered if it might be possible to do something with eclipses, or making observations when Selenos, Duplos and Geos are collinear. "I'll see you in the Summer, speaking of which, it's been on my mind to warn you. You need to take care around Zorro, it's obvious she's got the hots for you."

"Well I'm afraid it's too late for your concern," he confessed, "Astra wouldn't let her near me for quite a while, but eventually after New Year Zorro talked her round. We shared a room at the observatory, but since then we've only had the occasional liaison, we're on a 'good friends' basis, but not on private name terms. Actually she's pretty good at sex, so it's not all one way."

"Hmm, just as long as she doesn't hurt you, I can still pack a punch. Please promise you will look after yourself."

"Don't worry, she won't hurt me. Astra's every bit as protective of me as you are. We have a 'no threesomes' agreement, and casual sex only, which suits us both. I can have fun with her, but I can't feel for her like I do for you, or indeed for Astra."

"Don't tell me you're at it with Mother and Daughter, that would shock me I think!" The expression on her face certainly suggested shock.

"No, Astra is celibate, which Zorro thinks is unhealthy, they seem more like sisters than mother and daughter, and not the sort of sisters that would share a man. Nothing like as bad as Thay and Shay, or indeed Astra and her real sister. The thing is that Astra was only seventeen when Zorro was born, and then she went off to university leaving Zorro with her own mother, so you see it is not the usual Mother-Daughter relationship." He paused before continuing. "At the risk of shocking you, if Astra wanted to have sex with me, I don't think I could refuse her, despite Zorro. You see, while Zorro is a bit of fun, and almost certainly much better at sex, I deeply respect Astra and am comfortable with her, like I am with you, and if it came to a choice between them I would choose Astra over Zorro. But how about you? My experience suggests that total abstinence isn't good for younger women, on that I do sort of agree with Zorro."

"Maybe, but we're not all as randy as Zorro or those girls on your former staircase. I am much more moderate in my appetites. I don't like random pick-ups or booze-fuelled group sex. I don't indulge while in Routh, I find my work sufficiently stimulating. I like to know a man a bit and be able to respect him before using him for sex. There are one or two lads at home, that I'm happy to go to when my itch needs scratching. I'm not completely celibate like Astra, but perhaps I'll grow that way when I get to her age. I don't know. Please don't worry about me. I think I'm a bit like my Mum. She doesn't go overboard for it. She no longer seeks out new men, but I think she has a quiet fling with my father every now and again."

Rastu grew thoughtful and mused that the age gap between Astra and Arté was about the same as between Arté and herself. Well, she didn't want sex to spoil their relationship. She really did think of Arté as a brother. Of course if Arté were female, given the sexual norms, they probably would enjoy nights of passion together with some man they both fancied. But that wouldn't work with Arté unless she were into women and they could seduce one together, but she was definitely heterosexual, just not a raving nympho like most of her age-group seemed to be. Perhaps she would end up celibate like Astra.

While he was there, Arté also showed Rastu the telescope and when it grew dark they had a look through it at Selenos. Geos was not visible from Routh at the time. Rastu was impressed and wanted to know more about how it worked. "I don't know the details," said Arté, "Astra knows more. There's a woman in Dambach who is the real expert and she and Astra made it together. Astra has a much bigger one at the observatory that makes objects appear three times larger than this one does."

"Wow, I'd love to see that, looking at Selenos through this one is amazing, it looks twice as big as the Sun in the sky and half the size of Geos. No wonder you got the measurements you did. How did you persuade Astra to let you take it away?"

"Well I told her I wanted to conduct some experiments. The observation we've just made of Selenos, will be useful, but I have something else I want to do which requires me to go to the coast."

When he left Routh, Arté headed for Dunos where he went down to the beach and took horizon measurements, both with and without the telescope. He then climbed the cliff and repeated the measurements. From the clifftop, the horizon increased to about ten walks horizontal, but he could see higher features on Isla. With the telescope he could even make out parts of taller buildings on high ground. It was much as he had expected. He would need a higher platform and a slightly more powerful telescope. Plans for next year, he thought.

From Dunos he walked to the Louten river, near its mouth. It was a longish walk which took him about six hora. At the river he boarded a boat that took him all the way back to Louth, a total journey of about fourteen hora. He reached Louth a couple of hora before dark. Astra was pleased to see him and the telescope safely back. He told her about what he'd been up to, his measurements from the beach and cliff top would enable him to improve his estimate of the diameter of Duplos, and the Selenos data would add a little to their knowledge. The most exciting news was Rastu's insights into the orbit of Geos and their implications.

"This may give us a real handle on the mechanics of the universe," she opined. "Empirically we do indeed know that smaller bodies revolve around larger ones. What we have here is that Duplos and Geos are relatively close in size and seem to be fighting over which one is boss, with Geos winning, but not overwhelmingly. This must be a pretty rare circumstance."

"Just like sisters," was Arté's response.

At the end of the academic year, all three decamped to South Beach. Astra was relieved that Zorro and Arté chose to have their own bedrooms. She noted that Zorro's sojourns in Marouth were less frequent which she thought was a good thing. This was undoubtedly a result of getting some of her sexual release here with Arté. The house at South Beach is much larger and more convenient than the bungalow at the observatory, and she wasn't disturbed by bedroom sounds, which was much more satisfactory for her. Just occasionally Astra heard the footsteps heralding a nocturnal trip between their rooms, followed by a return a horum or so later. She was glad to note that the traffic was not entirely one-way even if the norm was the anti-alphabetic Z-A. She suspected that some of the long walks Zorro and Arté took along the beach ended in more al fresco entertainment than just a swim. She also noticed that now, on her nude days, Arté no longer bothered with his shorts. All-in-all the outcome of the decision to let Zorro have her way was a lot better than she had feared.

For her part, Zorro was also satisfied with the way things were working out. Arté was fun in bed, and it was a great relief to have it on her doorstep, so to speak, rather than having to go to the trouble of making complex arrangements in Marouth. She still preferred the heightened sexual experience of sharing with a close friend to solo sex, even though with Arté the solo variety was better than with others. Having someone familiar to share sex with, makes it mean more than simply 'scratching the itch'.

Astra and Arté took the opportunity to use the telescope to make more astronomical observations from South Beach. The extra data helped confirm some of their other calculations and using Rastu's model of the Geos-Duplos system they were able to work out an orbit for Eclos and also for the strange extra moons they had noticed at the observatory. These appeared to share the same almost circular orbit about the same centre as the planets and the other moons, and were coplanar with the Geos-

Duplos orbits. On the other hand Eclos was clearly following a highly eccentric[38] elliptical orbit with the centre at one of its foci, and was also tilted at an appreciable angle to the plane of the Duplets-Geos orbits.

Using the telescope and the results of his observations from Dunos, Arté was able to refine his estimate of the true horizon, and of the diameter of Duplos, which he now calculated as lying between 4100 and 4250 walks. Then he made a leap of faith based on Rastu's model. He hypothesised that the position of the orbital centre would be governed by the relative size of the two planets, and thus the ratio between the radii of the two orbits would be the same as the ratio between the volumes of the planets. From this he could calculate bounds for the diameter of Geos, and hence bounds for all the dimensions of the Geos-Duplos System. He drew up the table below to summarise his results, omitting Eclos because the upper and lower bounds were so far apart (all distances are in walks).

38 Arté's calculations put the eccentricity somewhere between 0.8 and 0.9 and the inclination to the Geos-Duplos plane between 6.5 and 8 dudeg (39-48o). The actual figures accepted on Geos are, eccentricity 0.84 and inclination 43.17°.

Name of body min/max	Diameter	Orbit Radius (semi=major apsis)	Distance from centre of Duplos
Duplos min	4100	95900	
Duplos max	4250	101500	
Geos min	5617	37300	133000
Geos max	5823	39500	141000
Selenos min	850	408800	312900
Selenos max	910	433000	534500
Strange moons min	Small	176000	76000
Strange moons max	Small	180000	218000

He waited for Rastu to come to stay, before unveiling this to Astra, as he wanted her to check his calculations and anyway felt she deserved a lot of the credit. Astra was very pleased with the results and also delighted to see Rastu again. Why couldn't Zorro be as nice as Rastu? Arté blamed their stormy relationship on them being too close in age, more like sisters than mother-daughter. She was less sure, she blamed it on the bad influence of her real sister when Zorro was a teenager.

Anyway while Arté had gone to meet Rastu at the coach stop four walks away, she had a serious talk with her daughter.

"While Rastu is here, I want you to keep your hands off Arté, no padding off to his room in the middle of the night, or flaunting your body at him. I don't want either him or Rastu to be embarrassed by your behaviour. Rastu will be staying in his room anyway."

"What if they invite me to join them?" was Zorro's retort.

"They won't."

Zorro, was not going to give up quite so easily. She wasn't exactly jealous. She perfectly understood that Arté wanted to enjoy his girlfriend's visit, but that didn't necessarily mean they couldn't all have some fun together. Indeed if Rastu had been like almost all other girls of her age, and her relationship with Arté had been what Zorro supposed, she would probably have been right, but neither of her suppositions were correct and her conclusion was equally wrong. When she suggested to Arté that a threesome with Rastu would be nice, and surely an exception to their no threesomes agreement, he quickly put her right. "My relationship with Rastu isn't as you might suppose. We are very close, like brother and sister, which is not at all like two sisters, but much more supportive and friendly. Also Rastu is unusually moderate in her sexual preferences, and says she doesn't enjoy threesomes. So a threesome between us is not at all appropriate. If you don't mind, I think I'd prefer to pause our sex life. We can still all enjoy our beach walks and swims together. I'm sure Rastu would enjoy that, and it would make me very happy if we could all be friends."

And so it was. The time went all too quickly. Zorro behaved herself impeccably, and grew quite fond of Rastu, marvelling at the beneficial effect she seemed to have on Astra's moods. Every phase, Arté and Rastu would take breaks in their work and the three of them went for a good walk, stopping every now and again for a swim, or just a splash about in the sea. On occasion, Astra would also join them. True, Zorro got the odd itch, but despite the protestations she was wont to make to her mother, she actually was perfectly able to keep herself under control when, as now, she wasn't at all bored.

There was one occasion after a playful splash about that Rastu noticed Arté's penis was getting ideas of its own. She didn't say anything but grew thoughtful. After their next work session, she said that she had some things she needed to get done. If Arté and Zorro didn't mind, she'd drop out of the next walk and leave them to go by themselves. She also had a quiet and separate word with each of them. To Zorro, she said, "I expect you noticed that Arté is in need of some sexual release. I don't have that sort of relationship with him, but I know you do on occasion. If you could find it in you to indulge him when you're out, I would be most grateful."

To Arté she was more blunt. "You worry about my sex life, now it's my turn to worry about yours. You and Zorro have been very good while I've been here, and I am most appreciative. I wouldn't like to be on my own in bed, while you shared hers, but it's clear to me that you both need some sex. So when I'm not with you this time, please feel free to indulge yourselves, with my blessing. I'm not just making excuses I really do have some things to do on my own and I also want a chance to speak with Astra."

When they went off on their walk, Rastu sought out Astra, whose first words were. "Oh, have you let them go off without you, don't you think we ought to go with them, I'm sure we could catch them up."

"No Astra, I want to take the opportunity to speak to you about some work stuff, and also I think it best to let them off the leash for a bit. Zorro's not the only one with an itch to scratch. I couldn't help but notice on the beach earlier that Arté was developing an enormous erection, until he went back into the water to cool it down a bit; and it's obvious that Zorro is trying very hard to stay under control. I'm very appreciative of the domestic arrangements you have made for my comfort, but it would be wrong of me to expect Arté and Zorro to do without completely, just for my benefit. The occasional release for them will do them good, and me no harm."

"You are very understanding, Rastu. It does you credit. I'm much more selfish, especially where Zorro's concerned. What else did you want to talk about?"

"I've been thinking about the problem of measuring real astronomical distances. Arté's method for the diameter of Duplos is sound, but difficult to get tight bounds. His idea based on my model of the Geos-Duplos system is ingenious, but depends on a hypothesis of how the size of planets affects the orbits, which, however plausible cannot be proved. I'm sure it's not far from the truth but it would be better to find other methods to confirm his results. In any case we still only have relative sizes of the other moons and planets, and the sun."

"Yes, Rastu, you're right, have you come up with a method?"

"Well, three different ones really that show promise, one is simple to describe. Consider the triangles formed by The Sun, Duplos and either Geos or Selenos. When Geos or Selenos are at exactly half phase, the angle formed at Geos or Selenos is a rightangle. If we could also measure the angle at Duplos we would be able to tie up the relationship between the distance to the Sun with that to Geos or Selenos. A second method, which I think is the most likely to work, is to make simultaneous measurements of the apparent location of a body against the fixed stars from different places on Duplos, where we know the separation. Then using parallax and some geometry we could get a measure of the true distance. For a decent level of accuracy we would need places quite far apart on Duplos. For example, here at South Beach and the observatory, might do. My third method, which I haven't yet thought through enough is to measure shadows when one body crosses in front of another, where again

I think we'll get data from which we can work out distances by geometry."

"Very interesting," said Astra, "to take simultaneous measurements, we'd need some pretty horrendous organisation, and also one or more extra telescopes, which will take time to obtain. Do you think you and Arté can sort out the mathematical details? Oh and while we're having a private conversation, I do have something I need to say to you. I know you see your visit here as a bit of a holiday, which is nice, but you are doing an awful lot of work while you are here, far more than might be considered polite good manners from a guest. I think I ought to pay you for what you are doing."

"That's quite unnecessary, I enjoy working on these problems, especially with Arté. I get an awful lot of pleasure from my time here," was Rastu's immediate response. "There is one thing you could do though. You already treat me like family, and I feel completely at home with you. Please can you call me Aimée when we're alone together or with Arté."

"Aimée, I feel honoured to call you by your private name, a privilege which I think should not be extended to Zorro. You already call me by mine. Astra was my private name, after my grandfather. I abandoned my other name when I rebelled against the way men were treated, especially by my appalling sister. When Zorro was born, I let it be known that henceforth I would be Astra in public as well as private. It caused a bit of a fuss at the time, but was soon accepted, and is a good name for an astronomer, don't you think. However I do insist that you should be paid the same as Arté, while you are working on my problems."

And so things were settled. Rastu couldn't but agree that the money would come in useful. As Astra had known, her family wasn't wealthy and her expenses at university were a struggle even with the scholarship.

The work with Arté proceeded well. At last the time came for Rastu to return to her mother's home. At her invitation and Astra's urging, Arté went with her for a break, walking in the mountains together. Zorro travelled with them as far as Marouth where she had arranged to stay with an old friend from school and university. Her friend was eager to show off a new man, and Zorro anticipated a wild time.

After some initial awkwardness, Arté got on well with Rastu's mother, whose name was Sturdon. The latter took him aside for one of those serious talks about intentions, was satisfied that he would be considerate of her daughter and mildly disappointed that his and her daughter's intentions were a tad too honourable. She approved of her Aimée's moderate habits and smiled at the obstinate expression on her face as she made it clear that Arté would share her bedroom, but was worried that her daughter was too bookish and concerned that her behaviour was driven by an inability to get over the loss of her brother.

Arté had never seen mountains like these up close. He had been in quite mountainous country in the wild lands on Isla but compared to these, they were just hills. The visit was short, for soon it would be time for them to return to Louth and Routh respectively. While in theory they could have made the journey together as far as Louth, Arté felt he ought to get back to Astra to help with shutting up the house at South Beach, and preparing for the move back to Louth. One period before the end of the Summer selenth, Arté made his farewells to Aimée and her mother and returned to South Beach.

Astra expressed herself surprised that he hadn't gone directly to Louth, escorting Rastu, but she wasn't really. She was well aware that Arté's sense of duty would ensure that he would be on hand to help her.

20
Another Astronomy Season, Louth, Dambach, Observatory

In early autumn, Astra took Arté to Dambach to consult Hugano, the optician who had built her two telescopes. Dambach lies on the delta where the River of the Goddesses flows into a shallow gulf of the sea of storms. The land is low-lying and marshy. Over the past two centuries a number of canals had been cut through the delta to drain the marshes, and much of the local transport is by boats of one sort or another. Although it is possible to travel overland to Dambach, the easiest route is by boat on the River of the Goddesses. That was the route taken by Astra and Arté, by coach to Goddess City and then a fast boat all the way to Dambach. Hugano met them at the quayside in Dambach where they transferred to one of the narrower canals and were punted to Hugano's house.

It took a while for Hugano to get used to Arté. In her experience, to employ a man in anything but a labouring or menial capacity is most unusual, even if not totally unheard of. She knew Astra well enough to be reasonably sure that Arté was not her toy-boy, and assumed his role to be that of a general servant. Astra's introduction came as a bolt from the blue.

"Hugano, this is my assistant, Arté. We need to design and build some new telescopes which will take some time. I have to go back to Louth because of my commitments at the university. If you don't mind, Arté will stay in Dambach to work with you on the specifications. He is a much better mathematician than I am and understands the problems that we are trying to solve better than anyone. However he hasn't had any experience of optics, and I have only been able to give him some rudimentary background because of my own limitations. I would appreciate it if you could give him a few lessons."

To say that Hugano was taken aback, would be an understatement, but she managed to get over her initial shock and respond positively. After all, Astra was an important client as well as a friend. "How unusual," she said, "of course I can work with him, I suppose he could stay in a hotel, but I have a spare room he could use and I suspect it would be better for him to be close at hand." She mused that an unaccompanied man in a hotel would be bound to cause a stir. She also wondered how she'd get on with a man about the place. It had been many years since she'd had a man-servant. Would it interfere with her liaisons with one of her friends' servants? She was a creature of regular habits. Well, she'd just have to see how it panned out.

It panned out perfectly well. Arté was a quick learner of the geometrical optics at the heart of telescope design, and was even able to come up with improvements. As had been agreed with Astra, the first requirement was for a duplicate of the observatory telescope. Arté introduced a minor modification using a mirror and a second eyepiece to enable two people both to view an object. He also conducted a number of experiments, replacing the concave lens at the eyepiece with a convex lens. This enabled him to increase the power of the telescope at the cost of having the image upside down, which he reasoned wouldn't really matter for astronomy.

When he left to return to Louth, the work on the new telescope was going well. He would return to collect it from Hugano on their way to the observatory for the winter. In the meantime he wanted to work on his other ideas. This involved a visit to Routh to consult with Rastu, whose geometric intuition once again proved invaluable.

When the time came for Arté to return to Dambach, he had a design for a telescope with two convex lenses that could be used for different magnifications ranging from thirty-five to fifty. He also had a design for a smaller instrument that fitted both eyes, having magnification power ranging between ten and twenty. Hugano thought she would be able to turn these designs into reality, and would work on them over the winter. Arté could then return in Spring for the final adjustments.

He made his own way from Dambach to Kongholm, where, as agreed, he met up with Astra and they went on together to the observatory. Astra was pleased with the new telescope and decided to keep it in the observatory and take the old one back to South Beach for the simultaneous observations. The plan was that Astra and Zorro would return to South Beach with the telescope, towards the end of the winter. Then they would each take measurements of both Selenos and Geos at pre-arranged times, making careful sketches of their positions against some of the fixed stars, and noting the times of the measurements and phases of the heavenly bodies as well as their positions. At the start of Spring, Astra and Zorro would return to Louth directly while Arté would close up the observatory and travel to Louth via Dambach.

The routine at the observatory was much the same as the previous winter. They found the moons of Zuvos more-or-less where expected and confirmed their orbit calculations. The strange extra moons were still there, orbiting both Duplos and Geos, with a period of twice the Geos-Duplos period. On one occasion they observed what appeared to be a tiny shooting star travelling from Geos to one of the strange moons.

As in the previous year, Zorro stayed in Louth until New Year, she then came to join them at the observatory, moving into

Arté's bed again. Arté was pleased to find there was less bickering between mother and daughter than usual.

When Astra and Zorro left early to go to South Beach with the older telescope, Arté busied himself with some improvements. Among his other pursuits he had been thinking about cycloids, and this triggered the thought that if you turned a small wheel linked to a larger one, that when the small wheel rotated once, so would the larger, and that a point on its rim would move 3.14 times the difference in the diameters more than a point on the rim of the small wheel. He thought he might be able to use this principle to find a more efficient way of hauling loads up to the observatory.

He walked into the local village and had a long discussion with the wheel-wright and the blacksmith and their assistants, both of whom, like Arté were men. Between them all they came up with an ingenious set-up. At both the top and bottom of the incline, they rigged up a device where Arté could turn a wheel by lying on a couch raised at a slight angle to the horizontal, and with his feet use pedals to turn a wheel of about two lengths diameter. This wheel was linked to the hub of a much larger doubly-flanged wheel, the hub's diameter was just three divisions, while the larger wheel's was one and a half strides. A long rope was passed around the two large wheels (top and bottom of the incline). The ends of the rope were tied to a cart with four wheels. The idea was that from either the top or the bottom of the incline, Arté could drag the cart up to the observatory, by pedalling.

This worked, but not as well as Arté had hoped, the problem being the roughness of the ground. His solution, which he didn't have time to implement that winter, was to lay a pair of wooden rails along the ground to form a smooth track for the cart. Thinking about this had also given him another idea. He thought he could adapt the principle to allow him to pedal the cart himself while riding on it. He would consult with Aimée and see what could be done.

He dutifully took all the measurements of Selenos and Geos as required by their plan. Indeed he took several at four dumin intervals either side of their agreed schedule. He also tried another experiment. Hugano had taught him about the camera obscura, whereby an image could be thrown on to a screen in a darkened room through a tiny aperture. Arté set up such an arrangement in the observatory and used it to trace accurate drawings of the telescopic images. He also found he could point the telescope towards the Sun while looking at the image on the screen, and thus get better measurements of both Thermos and the Sun without blinding himself. When they all returned to Louth, they were able to collate the results and prepare for the triangulation calculation. The last, Rastu was going to help them with.

First, as planned, he returned via Dambach, where he and Hugano finished work on the new telescopes. The higher magnifications were slightly blurred at the edges because of chromatic aberration, although Arté and Hugano didn't know that was the cause. Experiments with the lenses showed that this could be improved by using an objective lens with a very long focal length, but that was mechanically impractical. He was especially pleased with his binoculars and he paid for these himself. His contract with Astra had initially paid him $500 a selenth, of which half was deemed to be his keep, but the other half was paid in cash. Then after his first year Astra increased the amount to $600 because it was clear that Arté was much more valuable than the average new graduate.

In reality Arté had very little to spend his money on. He would buy meals for himself and Rastu when he visited her at Routh, and had a few petty expenses, but the bulk of his earnings just accumulated. Thus he could afford the cost of the binoculars himself.

Around the middle of the Spring selenth, Créezy announced that she planned to travel to Islaview Market to visit Esau. He had written to her saying that he was feeling every one of his sixty-eight years and would like to see her again before it became too late. She asked Arté if he would like to accompany her and perhaps enjoy a little holiday together under the shadow of their old home, as she put it. After talking it over with Astra, it was agreed that he should go with Créezy and then detour via Routh on his return. "You go," is what Astra said, "and enjoy yourself, physically with Créezy and emotionally with Aimée. It will do Zorro good to remember she doesn't own you."

By now, Zorro knew about Arté's relationship with Créezy, just not when it had begun. As Créezy had feared, Zorro's initial reaction was that as they were all three of them bed-mates perhaps they should all get together for a session. She had shared other men with Créezy so it seemed quite natural to her, and an obvious exception to her no threesomes agreement with Arté. Créezy explained that it was not going to happen, giving all the reasons why it wouldn't work for any of them. "My affair with Arté is strictly solo and based on our shared Isla heritage. It wouldn't work in the same way that it wouldn't work if I were to join you when you had a reunion with a close school or university friend." Zorro could see the force of this, thinking of some of her times in Marouth, but still felt a bit grumpy about it. Astra was prepared to overlook her daughter's dishonourable intentions with Arté but not if she was also going to get possessive.

Arrangements were made and Arté and Créezy set off in a holiday mood. Esau did look older and frailer than when Arté had last seen him, but, he thought, not quite at death's door as he had feared. Esau, on his part, was pleased to see them both and chuckled when Créezy let him know that she was on good terms with Arté and they would be happy to share the bedroom in the extension while they were there. "You two are my greatest successes," Esau told them. "Between you, you have made me a lot of money. My fee for finding you, Créezy, bought me this house, and your contract, Arté was so good that I received an extra bonus. I am so happy that you are both doing so well and are friends."

Arté showed them both his binoculars and they all walked out to the cliff top just North East of the village where the distance across to Isla is about seven walks. At the height of the cliff, the horizon is quite a distance and you can see all the way to Isla, but not make out much detail with the naked eye. With the binoculars at a magnification of twenty it is possible to make out a lot of detail. For example an average cottage appears about the size of the Sun with the naked eye. Esau and Créezy were both amazed. Esau thanked Arté profusely, "I thought I would never see the land of my birth again. That is a part of the Theocracy that I had never visited, but it's still the home where I was born. Even though life here is so much better, one's roots are still one's roots."

"That's how we both feel," replied Créezy. " Even though as a well-to-do woman, my life on Isla was much more comfortable than yours. As I put it to myself, you can take the woman out of Isla, but you can't take Isla out of the woman, which is why I value my times with Arté." She smiled to herself as she recalled her first time with him. It occurred to her that he didn't call out Thay's name any more, but there was a recent occasion when in a moment of high passion he had called 'Oh Shay what are you doing to me'. Créezy locked this in her heart as a secret she would never reveal. On the other hand, she was very pleased to note that Arté had never once confused her with Zorro. There had been that occasion when they'd been drinking and relaxing after a lovely walk and chat about everything and nothing, when he had inadvertently called her Aimée. He had stammered an apology and seemed very embarrassed. She had thought no more about it and just assumed that Aimay had been an old drinking buddy, probably from Isla, some man she didn't know.

Arté asked Esau about local land prices especially along the coast between Islaview Market and Dunos. According to Esau the area was not well-populated, with only a very few villages and the odd isolated farm. There was nowhere as big as Islaview Market or Dunos, between the two. There were no accessible beaches and at one point the cliff rose to nearly eighty strides, more than twice as high as here at Islaview, and this meant no fishing. The cliff top was mainly used for grazing sheep or goats. The living was hard for the farmers, and consequently land prices were low.

The next stage of their holiday was to walk to Dunos along the cliff top. Arté had calculated the distance as about seventy-seven walks which could be managed in nineteen hora. As Arté was keen to explore the area, they planned to take it a bit more leisurely and include a couple of rest breaks on the way. Arté had brought a tent, groundsheet, and sleeping bag with him and they intended to snuggle in that together. Créezy was quite excited about it. She had never before slept on the ground under just a flimsy bit of canvass. The thought of snuggling in a bag with Arté made her feel quite randy. Come to think of it, she hadn't had al fresco sex since she left Isla. If she could persuade him, it would take her right back to her schooldays.

The first rest was after just over three hora. Arté had calculated that this was pretty well directly opposite Thay's house, where the strait was close to it's narrowest, maybe as narrow as five walks, then about a walk inland to the house. He should be able to see it, especially as the cliffs here were very high, maybe sixty strides or more. He got out the binoculars and, sure enough, he could spot the remaining ruins of the old farm house where he had jumped into the sea. Looking up slightly he saw the house he had helped to build. Indeed he had to turn down the magnification to ten to have the whole house in his field of vision. It is a large house he recalled. At the higher magnification he could make out individual people.

He passed the binoculars to Créezy. "If you look at the cliff edge straight opposite you can see some ruins, that was Thay's family home which fell into the sea, and is where I also fell in. If you then look up a bit, and a bit to the right, you will see a big house. That is Thay's and I helped her to manage the building works. Finally to the one side of the house you might spot a swing, which had a small child on it when I looked. That's probably my daughter."

"I didn't know you had a daughter, let alone that you knew about it. On Isla men are not usually told about their children."

"Well, I haven't been told, and maybe I have fathered some I don't know about, I have my suspicions. However both Thay and Shay were determined that I should get them pregnant. With Thay, of course, it was perfectly legitimate, but Shay had resorted to an underhand trick to get me to do my bit. That was the reason behind all that happened to me subsequently. Shay actually told me that she was pregnant, just a horum or so before I went into the sea. Thay had also timed things to maximise her chance of pregnancy when she bade me farewell. Which all means that there's a good chance that I have two daughters with mothers who are identical twins, and are themselves born within a period of each other. The presence of a child who has been sufficiently indulged to have a swing built next to Thay's house suggests to me that Thay did indeed get pregnant with a daughter."

"You're probably right, so that's your ulterior motive behind all this, I was wondering."

"I plead guilty, I hope you don't mind too much, me dragging you into my private nostalgia. I'll make it up to you once we get into the sleeping bag," was Arté's response, he was determined to give her as good a time in bed as possible. He thought she deserved it.

"Don't feel too to guilty. It's my nostalgia too. Although I've never been there, you know that was my great-grandmother's house too. My mother would sometimes talk about holidays she had there as a child. She was a few years younger than Chay and would follow her round when they were children. Rather like I did with the twins. It's also interesting to see Thay's new house. My sister had told me it was grand, but I hadn't realised just how grand. As for the sleeping bag, I can't wait, let's strip off and do it right here and now, we can always have seconds later when we've put the tent up and got into the bag. Mind, you're not to call me Thay, I can't imagine her having a good romp in the open air, and you must leave me my illusions. And especially don't confuse me with Craya, since I guess that her visit to that house was one of the occasions she joined in with you and Thay." At this she started undressing.

"I didn't think I'd called out Thay's name for a long time. I don't confuse you with her. You are much sexier, and I could never confuse you with Craya who isn't sexy at all. Craya was duty, you are pleasure. If you want it outside, so it will be." He joined her in removing his clothes only he folded his neatly while she threw hers off with gay abandon.

When they rose again, Arté inspected their immediate surrounds and noticed a small farm house not far away. Examining through his binoculars he was pretty sure it was empty. It looked like it had been abandoned for a couple of years or so. They had a quick snack as breakfast and then set off again about nine hora after their arrival. Créezy was in an exceptionally sunny mood. The fresh spring air was glorious. She and Arté had the world to themselves so she didn't bother to dress, put her clothes in her backpack and let the fresh air caress her body as they walked in the sunshine.

Their next break was after a further twenty-four walks, which they accomplished in a bit over the six hora that average walking pace would have taken. Here they found themselves opposite the Isla coastal town of Chalcliff-on-Strait, where Thay had gone to school. They both looked over at it through the binoculars and Créezy was able to point out some landmarks she recognised from a childhood holiday.

A further eight hora walk took them to Dunos, where they caught the coach to Routh. Arté explained that he had some business to attend to at the University, and offered to see his companion on to the boat back to Louth. For her part, Créezy was perfectly willing to amuse herself exploring the city which she had visited only once, briefly, some ten years earlier. She could wait for Arté to finish his business and they could catch a later boat together.

This made Arté feel awkward, and he embarked on a roundabout explanation that his business included consulting on some mathematical calculations with his erstwhile tutorial partner, and that she would be offended if he spent the night in Routh in an hotel.

"Ah, you pig! Now I get it, you've arranged a better offer and you want me out of the way so you can spend the time banging her." She said this teasingly, but nevertheless was less than happy.

"No," said Arté, feeling quite distressed. "It's not like that. We are close, but not in a sexual way, more like a brother and sister brought up together. The only way I would get any sex would be with you. But Rastu will want to spend some time with me, and I think it would be awkward for all three of us if we were together."

Slightly to her surprise, Créezy believed him, and also felt mollified. She certainly understood that it would be awkward, just as it always is when a third party butts in on a reunion of close friends. She still didn't want to catch the boat by herself. She negotiated, saying that she could occupy herself for however long Arté thought he needed, and they would meet on the boat. Arté knew that Aimée would be very busy, what with her finals upon her. He hadn't planned to stay long anyway. An agreement was reached, they would catch the next night boat to Routh and meet aboard. Créezy would book them a cabin.

Arté met Aimée in her room. She was indeed in the middle of her final examinations and was revising hard, although she knew deep down that she had nothing to worry about. Arté brought out all the figures from the observations, and Aimée was able to explain how the geometry worked to make the calculations. Arté soon got the hang of it and after they had worked through some of the observations, he was confident he could do the same for the others and then try to come up with a best estimate for the required distances. Each set of simultaneous observations would allow an estimate of the distances to be made. They would end up with a whole lot of estimates for the same quantity. All they had to do then was to work out what was the most likely true answer and within what error bounds. Arté was probably better able to do that himself, which he would do when back in Louth.

This meant that the work proceeded quite quickly. Arté was also able to show off his binoculars, which impressed Aimée. They had time for a good talk and some dinner. Aimée was secretly pleased that he wouldn't be staying, because she had more exams imminently. She invited him to come to her graduation and he promised to be there.

She also was able to tell him the exciting news that she had been offered a post to teach Mathematics and Natural Philosophy at the Federation Grammar School in Marouth, and also the Empire Grammar School in Marcenza. This combines having a really good job, with being relatively close to her family and near him in South Beach.

"But isn't that two jobs, one in each school?"

"No. They're not really two different schools. They were one foundation but had to separate after the treaty. They are situated on opposite sides of the street, and the border runs along the middle. I only have to cross the road to take classes on the Marcenza side."

"That is good news, congratulations Aimée, I am pleased for you, and for me of course. I expect your mother will also be glad you will be nearby. Now I come to think of it, I recall that Zorro went to school there."

"Yes, Mum will be relieved. She didn't like me going away, to come to Routh and was afraid I'd move away and she'd hardly ever see me. She would never stand in the way of my career, but we are a close family and it would break her heart to lose me, after what happened to Mikos."

They said their farewells at her door and Arté made his way to the landing quay to catch the boat to Louth. Créezy met him in the bar and asked politely about how his business had fared as they chatted over a beer and sandwich. She then led him off to their cabin to enable them to end their holiday in a fitting manner.

21
Speculation and Invention: South Beach and Observatory

Arté and Astra delayed their Summer departure from Louth to enable then both to attend Aimée's graduation with her first class honours BA and Mistress of Mathematics, where Astra met Aimée's mother for the first time. Despite their very different backgrounds and interests, they found that their politics and general attitude to life were very much in tune and Sturdon soon got over her initial awkwardness at meeting such a distinguished personage.

After the ceremony, all four of them travelled together on the boat up the Louten river to Louth, and then on another to the head of navigation, where they were able to catch a coach to Marouth, with only one change at Vinebridge, the head of navigation on Vineyard river, which flows westwards to empty into the Ocean of the World at the city of Soubanc. When they reached Marouth, Aimée and Sturdon stayed for Aimée to visit her school and make some preparations for her starting work in the upcoming school year. Astra and Arté travelled on directly to South Beach, where Zorro was already waiting for them.

Over the next two periods, in addition to finishing off the distance computations that he and Aimée had started, Arté worked on his inventions, finalising the details of his self-propelled cart, as well as working out the improvements needed for the rail cart. He realised that laying rails all the way from the house to the observatory was just not practical. He decided that the best compromise would be to lay the rails for the 320 strides of the steepest part of the route, covering the rise from about 100 to 256 strides above sea level. He would also need sheds at either end to provide shelter for the cart in bad weather. He also came up with an ingenious improvement to reduce the effort involved in moving the cart, but that would need a second set of rails parallel to the first, and would have to wait. These rails would require an awful lot of wood. Otherwise he thought that, widening and smoothing the paths from the house to the lower end of the railway, and from the house to the causeway would enable him to use his putative self-propelled cart for those routes.

When he outlined his plans to Astra, she was fully supportive. "This railway should make a tremendous difference to our lives on the island. However, I don't want you to waste your valuable time labouring to lay all those rails and dig about on the roadworks. We should hire some men from the village to do all that while you do the important design work and supervise the project."

While Arté had been working away on his road and rail project, Astra had set up the old and new telescopes to allow her to compare them and also catalogue the various heavenly bodies as seen from South Beach, to complement her observations from the observatory.

At midsummer, Aimée came for what had become her regular Summer break in South Beach. Using the new telescope with a magnifying power of forty she was able to study the strange moons more closely. She noticed what appeared to be traffic of stars flying between the strange moons and Geos. They had heated discussions about what it could all mean, even Zorro joined in.

Unbelievable though it was, their favourite speculation was that there had to be a civilisation on Geos that was so far in advance of their own, that they had discovered how to travel into space, and that the strange new moons were some kind of buildings in space. Astra decided to write an article describing their discoveries and speculations.

Serious academic journals were unwilling to publish such arrant nonsense. They limited themselves to saying that Astra has reported some interesting observations, that are as yet unexplained. Some quite fanciful suggestions have been made by the astronomer herself, which is perhaps less surprising given her eccentric reputation. After all she even goes so far as employing a man to conduct serious philosophical studies. In all probability this will turn out to be due to aberrations in the complex workings of the telescope, and nothing to do with what is actually out there in space. On the other hand one of the more sensationalist popular magazines was prepared to publish Astra's speculations.

All the fuss didn't help Astra's academic reputation, but it certainly brought all sorts of cranks and conspiracy theorists out of the woodwork. Most worrying were those who saw the putative Geosians as a threat. An invasion of 'little green men' with the evil intent of taking over the world and enslaving the population, was how some of the more lurid pamphlets put it.

When no such invasion occurred that Autumn, the public generally forgot about it. But just as flotsam is left on beaches by a retreating tide, so some factions of believers remained. Among these were those who looked forward to contact with a superior civilisation, but the majority consisted of xenophobes calling on the world to unite to resist any invasion. Neither the Western Federation nor the Great Southern Empire, paid any heed to the cranks, but in the Shadowlands Union, where people are generally more distrustful of outsiders, the xenophobic tendency was taken more seriously.

The only other item of note that Autumn concerned Arté following up on his visit to the Isla strait. With help from Esau, he discovered that the farm he had noticed was indeed for sale. It was actually quite small and wasn't really economic. The owner had inherited it from her late mother. Not wanting to share the same hard life of her ancestresses, she had put it on the market while she pursued a career as a schoolmistress in a small town further inland. There had been no interest in the sale. A neighbouring farmer was prepared to rent the grazing, but had no wish to buy the house, or pay very much for the land. Arté consulted Astra about the possibility of his buying it.

Astra was not one to stand in Arté's way but was concerned for herself. "Arté, of course you should be able to afford to buy this property and your contract with me ends at the beginning of next Summer, so you will be free to move if you wish. I had been hoping you would want to stay. We are all so comfortable together now, and with Aimée in Marouth. It is your wishes that matter in this case, but I must warn you that you won't get much of a living on a small farm of that kind."

Arté was taken aback, he had forgotten all about his contract term, and had no thought of leaving Astra. "I don't want to leave you, My wish for the farm isn't to live there permanently. My motives are complicated and to do with my past life. Please let's arrange a way for me to remain with you after this contract ends. I love the work and I love being part of your family. You and Aimée are the most important people in my life. It would break my heart to lose either of you."

"You forgot to mention Zorro or Créezy." Astra smiled as she spoke.

"They are not important like you. I like them both very much and enjoy playing with them. They are both incredibly good at sex, and as things stand I will continue be available to them for as long as they want. But if either you or Aimée become unhappy about it, I will end either or both sexual relationships. If you please, can we now agree to continue my employment after next Spring."

Astra, grew thoughtful, the future was looking bright for her, possibly less so for Zorro! "The details of our arrangement will have to be slightly different. You are now much more valuable than a new graduate employee, but we can settle that later. You don't know how relieved I am that you will stay." She stood up, put her arms round him and kissed him heartily, lingering a bit longer than she had intended and feeling incredibly flattered when she felt the evidence of his pleasure press against her middle. "Don't be embarrassed, I like it," she said, observing his reaction to the same evidence. "Now, to your original question, it's time Zorro earned her keep. She claims to be an actress, she can act for you!"

Astra's contention was that Arté would encounter all sorts of prejudice if he tried to buy the property himself. Provincial vendors and their lawyers were not noted for their progressive views. Furthermore if they detected that Arté had some emotional attachment to the property, they wouldn't hesitate to inflate the asking price. Zorro could front the purchase, perhaps posing as a disinherited daughter needing an inexpensive place of her own. "I could always oblige with the disinheritance if necessary."

Arté was a bit shocked by this last sentiment, but decided Astra was not serious about disinheriting Zorro. He readily agreed that Zorro should be asked to act for him and resolved to be extra accommodating the next time she wanted his presence in bed. By now he knew her preferences.

When asked, Zorro was delighted to help, and set off to the small town in question to make enquiries and pursue negotiations. In the end she acquired the property for just $200; negotiated with the neighbouring farmer to continue to rent the grazing rights for her sheep and found a local builder to make the house habitable. She even went to the trouble of staying there to supervise the building work.

She then suggested that she and Arté should have a short holiday in the farm house so that the neighbours would continue to believe her legend of needing it as a bolt hole and lust nest away from the prying eyes of her over-bearing mother. Arté enjoyed the holiday, despite being a bit anxious about being away from Astra when she was needing help to prepare for the winter at the observatory. He loved pottering around his own property, smiled to himself when he waited on Zorro as she politely entertained the neighbour to dinner, and looked over at Isla hoping to catch a glimpse of his daughter. Somehow, seeing Thay was no longer that important to him.

Zorro was as enthusiastic as ever, doing her best to wear him out in bed, it seemed. Arté didn't mind, a little bit too much sex was a small thing after all, and Zorro was careful not to actually overdo it. She went back to Louth feeling very satisfied, thanking Arté for giving her enough to keep her going until she came to the observatory for new year. Solo sex with Arté really was as good as most threesomes. Only with her closest friends in Marouth was it better. Novelty in partners can be fun, but for the best sex you need history.

When they reached observatory island, Astra inspected Arté's work on the rail cart with approval. She recruited a small workforce of men from the village and the work on rail and road proceeded apace. She installed the newest telescope and continued her observations of the activity around the Geos-Duplos system. She also was able to view Geos with the larger scope, as well as making good use of Arté's pinhole camera and screen to make observations closer to the Sun, as well as producing accurate plots of her observations.

The new observations allowed Arté to refine the various estimates of distance that they had calculated. Astra was disappointed that she couldn't see proper evidence of intelligent life on Geos although there were a number of regions that she thought might be interpreted as cities. The winter's new discovery came when she turned her attention back to Zuvos. Her purpose was to use the greater detail available from the extra magnification to confirm the estimates of Zuvos's rotation and the relative size of Maxos. This she did, and, using Arté's methods found that Mexia was showing enough of a disc to estimate its diameter as 1/17 times that of Zuvos. She was a little disappointed that Proxis still appeared too small to get a decent enough disc, but she managed to convince herself that maybe its diameter was between 1/30 and 1/25 times that of Zuvos.

These results, while important, didn't break any new ground. The excitement came from discovering yet another moon. Talos, as she called it, had an orbit beyond that of Maxos, orbiting Zuvos about once in every two Duplos periods. She had Arté check her observations. Once they were convinced of the results, she wrote up a further paper announcing her discovery. Perhaps this would help restore her reputation after the 'little green men' affair. At the same time she felt able to announce a calculation of the period of Sépanos' orbit about the Sun as between thirty-eight point five and thirty-nine point five years, this being based on observations over seven years.

As the winter drew to a close, Arté's railway was finished and he was able to transport goods up the hill to the observatory more easily, but it was still quite hard work and he thought they would have to put his next plan into effect the following year. This would involve a parallel track with a second cart linked to the first and acting as a counter weight, creating a one-up-one-down system with the pedalling only having to make minor adjustments due to any imbalance in the loads, and natural breaking from friction.

His self propelled cart had also gone well. At the front of the cart were two seats each equipped with pedals so a passenger could help with the motive power. There was also a single wheel at the front that could be steered. The cart was itself a two wheeler, as distinct from the four-wheeled rail cart. Arté found that he could pedal it at a fearful rate, and caused quite a stir when he first rode it into the village, cutting the journey time from one and a quarter hora to fifteen cumins[39].

After he was satisfied with the prototype, Arté set about making a second model, with a slightly lighter and more aerodynamic cart, and more robust wheels and steering gear. He also produced a spare set of wheels and driving chain. He announced that he would ride this back to Louth. The three of them travelled together as far as Kongholm, two upfront and one in the cart with the luggage. Arté took the driving seat, with Astra next to him sharing the pedalling most of the time, but occasionally Zorro and Astra swapped places, to give Astra's legs a rest. With Arté and Zorro both pedalling on the good stretch of road between the coast and Kongholm, they covered seventeen walks in under a horum, over one and a half times the speed of the fastest stage-coach. Zorro was exhilarated, and when they zipped past the stage, she whooped for joy. "Goddess, there's just the one thing I need now to make life perfect."

"Well, you can't have it," retorted Arté, "we need to press on, and anyway think of your mother."

"A girl can dream can't she? When we get to the hotel I tell you, I'm going to fuck your brains out."

---

39 This implies an average speed of about 37 km per hour.

She didn't get the chance. Astra and Arté agreed that he would drop her and Zorro at the hotel with their share of the luggage, and he would continue without them, taking his tent and sleeping by the roadside. They didn't want to risk leaving the SPC[40] in a populated area in case it got stolen. When he got to Louth, he was to rent a lock-up shed near her apartment to keep it out of harm's way. If Zorro had had her way she would have gone with him, but he was insistent that she should stay to assist her mother on the rest of the journey. He went on for about six walks beyond Kongholm and put up his tent by a small hillock not far off the road. He was able to hide the SPC from the road and also lock one of the wheels with a chain and padlock he had brought for the purpose.

He experienced a little bother when crossing the River of the Goddesses in Goddess City. He was keeping his speed down so as not to frighten people, but nevertheless a watch officer stopped him to ask what he was about. He was able to explain that he was working for Astra and his unusual cart was a recent invention that she had asked him to transport back to her home in Louth. Fortunately they had anticipated something like this happening and Arté was able to produce a formal letter from Astra attesting to his story. The watch officer took a bit of convincing but eventually let him go on his way on the grounds that she couldn't think of any law that was being broken. Arté mused that perhaps it would have been easier if Zorro had come along with him. The officer's problem had really been because he was an unaccompanied male doing something unusual. A respectable woman would have made a difference. Not that Arté would have accused Zorro of being respectable, but the officer wouldn't have known that.

---

40 Self Propelled Cart.

It took him just eight hora to ride to Goddess City. He stopped for a short sleep about a horum before his arrival there, because he wanted to be reasonably fresh for the last stage of the journey. Weaving his way slowly through the city took its time, but once on the open road west of the bridge he clocked up a good speed and took just four hora and eight dumins to reach Astra's apartment in Louth. Once there he chained the cart to some railings and took the luggage into the apartment. He then went to the letting agent that Astra had recommended and rented a suitable lock-up close to the apartment. That done, paying the rent for the whole selenth, he took the key, fetched the cart and stowed it in the lock-up. He then returned to the apartment and busied himself making it welcoming for when Astra and Zorro showed up, which they did about a phase later. His new transport was really something.

They settled down to their usual Spring routine. The academics at the university were excited about Astra's discovery of a fourth moon of Zuvos, and interested in her calculation of the orbital period of Sépanos. Arté travelled to Routh by conventional means to give a seminar on his and Rastu's calculations of astronomical distances, and spent the rest of his working time on his mathematical contemplations of the infinite and infinitesimal.

Appertaining to the latter, he had an interesting discussion with Fermos about using infinitesimals to calculate the gradient of the tangent to a curve. Fermos had developed this some decades earlier but it had been largely ignored by the mathematical community. None of them knew it, but in fact Fermos had been on the verge of discovering differential calculus. Now that Arté had so much more experience of continental ways, he came to realise that the western part of the WF was the leading centre for mathematical knowledge in the world, and Fermos' place was right at the forefront. The other universities in the WF were somewhat behind Louth and Routh in this regard, and the next two in mathematical prestige were to be found in the GSE. The Shadowlands Union was far behind the others and in many ways was still quite primitive and rife with superstition.

Apart from work, he also had two short breaks in his farmhouse. The first was with Créezy and the second with Zorro. It only took six or seven hora in the SPC. That vehicle was going to transform his life, he thought. He wanted Créezy to see the fruits of their holiday and also to show off his SPC. She was fascinated with the SPC, and like Zorro had found that speed stimulated her sexual appetite, which she found interesting. They had an enjoyable time. Créezy did not wear him out with her sexual demands, but was moderate and relaxed. The cart drew some attention but otherwise the visit didn't cause any tittle-tattle with the neighbours. It was perfectly natural that Zorro would lend her house to a friend, and if the friend also took along the same male servant, that was also normal. He would be familiar with the property and so would be able to make her more comfortable, and good friends often shared men. It helped the friendship bond.

The visit with Zorro involved rather more sex. Otherwise the main purpose for Arté, was to select a suitable builder to construct an observation tower on a small rise slightly inland from the coast. Arté remembered the fate of Thay's farmhouse and didn't want to suffer a similar loss. It was known that Zorro was the daughter of a famous, if eccentric, astronomer so the observation tower seemed logical. There was some recollection that this was supposed to be Zorro's lust nest, away from her mother, but no doubt the mother had found out and talked her daughter into allowing the tower to be constructed. Arté also wanted a cart shed to be put up next to the tower, and a good quality road between the two. There already was a suitable outbuilding at the farmhouse.

A competent builder was selected, who they felt could be trusted to get on with the work with minimal supervision. The one thing that the builder thought was strange was the way that Zorro left all the details to Arté and made it clear that he was to be treated as having her full authority on anything to do with the tower.

Back in Louth, Créezy had sought a meeting with Astra. It might not have been obvious from her flighty public image, but far from being the crazy tart everyone thought her, she was actually a very astute businesswoman. She wanted to talk to Astra about Arté's SPC. Astra listened very carefully to what she said and her opinion of Créezy was rapidly revised upwards. Her friendship with Zorro was now definitely to be encouraged, even if they bedded every eligible man in Louth together.

When Zorro and Arté returned from Thayview Farm, as it was now known, Astra announced that they had a meeting with her lawyers that it was essential they both attend. Zorro told Arté that it was bound to be about his contract renewal, but why she was expected to be there was anyone's guess.

Well it was about the contract, and much more. The contract bit was taken first and Zorro was left kicking her heels in a waiting room, being brought coffee by a well-groomed young man, who she assumed was probably the lawyer's latest toy boy. Arté was a bit taken aback by the new contract, and clearly the lawyer was also dubious. He was not to be any sort of employee, but a partner to Astra. "Most irregular, " said the lawyer. There were also clauses about this partnership being separate from other ventures that Arté might have, either on his own account or in company with others. None of this made much sense to

Arté, but he trusted Astra and was happy to go along with her wishes.

Once that was over, Zorro was called in and Créezy also joined them. The purpose of this meeting, Astra announced was to set up a company for the commercial exploitation of Arté's rail cart and self propelled cart inventions. The lawyer then took over. The company would apply for patents for the inventions and arrange to have them manufactured and marketed throughout the Western Federation. Initially, apart from nominal holdings by the others as required by law, the shares in the company would all belong to Arté in respect of his intellectual property. The others would work initially in return for shares until such time as the company produced sufficient revenue to allow them to take a salary. The board of the company would consist of those persons present. Astra would be Chairman; Arté, Technical Director; Créezy, Business Director and Zorro, Marketing Director. Arté was a bit bemused. "Hang on." He said. "I didn't do it all by myself, Rastu worked out a lot of it with me, and then there's the blacksmith and wheelwright up near the observatory."

Astra responded. "The blacksmith and wheelwright were paid for their work, the concept was all Arté's. Since I paid the various bills for the development of the prototypes, it is reasonable that I should be reimbursed in shares. However Arté has a valid point regarding Rastu. I propose that Rastu also be invited on the board as Assistant Technical Director, and be allocated a proportion of the initial shares as yet to be determined. I also propose that Arté, Créezy and myself be empowered to determine that proportion and that I should pass on the invitation to Rastu when we see her at South Beach later in the summer."

These proposals were agreed to, unanimously, Zorro and Arté just doing what they were told in matters they didn't fully understand, and thus Wheels within Wheels (or WwW as it later became known) was founded.

Afterwards, Créezy took Astra aside and said she planned to invest in some of the road building companies and also divest herself of shares in other transport companies, both road and river, because she said, they will all suffer a short term downturn, even if they then recover later. She advised Astra to do the same.

Astra and Arté diverted via Thayview on their annual journey south. This allowed them to inspect the progress on the tower, and Arté to show Astra round the property. After this, the locals surmised that Zorro had really been acting for her mother all along and that the story about a lust nest was a sham designed to mask the true purpose of the purchase to keep the price down. This did Astra's reputation no harm. She was now known as a canny lass who should be treated with respect.

22
Preparations for contact

The full story of Wheels-within-Wheels is beyond the scope of this book. Suffice it to say that the next three years saw considerable growth. Créezy proved to have exceptional business skills and together with Astra, looked after finances and organised manufacture. She began by doing a deal with an elderly coach-maker who had no heiress and was looking to retire shortly. Astra also developed a manufacturing base with the blacksmith and wheelwright who had worked with Arté on his prototypes. Once products started to arrive, Zorro proved good at the marketing. Sales were no problem as the wealthy sought them out. The first sales occurred in the Winter selenth (2611 DGY[41]) and Zorro stayed in Louth that whole winter. Meanwhile Arté and Rastu worked on new models, including a very racy design, first marketed in Summer 2613, which could reach speeds of between five and six walks[42] on good roads, or more with two pedalling.

While WwW distracted them a bit from other business, as they all grew pretty rich, pretty quickly, it didn't stop them altogether. Rastu spent most of the summers with them in South Beach, and also visited the observatory one midwinter for the holidays. Otherwise she continued at the Grammar School where she became popular with staff and girls alike, but failed in her efforts to persuade the school to also take boys.

Arté visited his farm for short breaks during Spring and Autumn. The journey from Louth being so fast on his SPC. Sometimes Zorro or Créezy would accompany him for what they

41 Decimal Geosian Year as distinct from GY for the duodecimal version.

42 As a speed a walk is 4 walks per horum (10 km per 54 mins), so 6 walks is speed of nearly 67 kph or 42 mph.

called a dirty break. Zorro was particularly keen to travel in separate SPCs so they could race. All part of marketing, she said. In reality she just loved the speed. Sometimes Astra went with him and they travelled more sedately in a slower, coach model, and spent time observing from his tower.

Astra and Arté were still following the strange moons and their shooting star companions. Following the earlier rumpus, they kept quiet about this except among their close circle, but they were becoming more convinced that they were observing preparations for a visit to Duplos from Geosians, and the moons were way-stations of some sort. The closest point of these way-stations to Duplos appeared to be slightly to the North of the observatory and they assumed the landing would be in the vicinity. They could keep watch from any of their three telescopes, whether in the observatory, South Beach, or Thayview. Even in Louth, Arté could watch through his binoculars. Arté extended his Winter stay by a period or so either side of the Winter selenth from 2612 onwards. Astra would stay for part of that time, depending on her commitments at the university.

Although they never caught a way-station being manoeuvred into position, they saw their number grow steadily until by the winter of 2613-14 there were a total of twelve stations, evenly spaced at five dudeg intervals around the orbit. As these slots began to fill, Astra was sure that a landing attempt would happen imminently, and plans were laid accordingly.

In the first period of Spring 2614, Astra and Arté were still at the observatory when they noticed, activity just over the horizon to the North of them. "This may be it," said Astra as they looked into the skies and saw lights ascending and descending down to about a height of 2500 strides before disappearing below the horizon. Arté did some quick calculations and announced. "That seems to be coming down about ninety walks away on a bearing of about three dudeg West of due North. It's too far West and South for the continent, if our maps are anything like accurate. There could well be an island there in the Sea of Storms that can't be seen from the coast."

"Right," said Astra, "that suggests they are just establishing a base out of the way, to observe us. They are bound to have noticed that there is life on Duplos, and surely wouldn't come all this way if they didn't intend to make contact. The nearest bit of the continent to them is in the Shadowlands Union, but that region is virtually uninhabited, just a few nomadic people and the odd hunter or fur trapper. My guess is that they will head for Kongholm. Obviously if they can fly, the sea won't be a problem. Of course, they could be sea creatures, but we'll guess not."

Arté then pedalled off to the local village and put their pre-agreed plans into operation. He sent messages to Zorro and Créezy in Louth and to Rastu in Marouth. These would get to them pretty quickly. They had already recruited a messenger in the village, paid with a fast SPC, making her the envy of all her friends. She would take the letters as far as Kongholm, where they would continue via the new ultra-fast courier service that had been established between the major cities, using WwW vehicles. The fastest express service, at a huge cost, went by the sporty carts, and it was this service that was now employed. The letters would go first to Louth via Goddess City, and then Rastu's would be taken on to Marouth. They would be delivered to their recipients directly. It should take at most thirteen hora to get to Zorro and Créezy, and twenty to get to Rastu.

The next steps had been carefully preplanned. Terms of absence (unpaid) had been agreed for Astra at the university and for Rastu at her school. The former had been straightforward and Zorro would just inform them that Astra would be unavailable for the Spring term. The latter had been more difficult, but when the school received a cart that would carry six, with two pedalling, and the headmistress, her very own sports model, as well as the endowment of the Wheels-within-Wheels Prizes for Mathematics, and Natural Philosophy, they saw that it was only reasonable that Rastu should be released for the anticipated emergency, especially as a recently retired teacher had been persuaded to step in as locum for her.

Zorro and Créezy travelled together in one of the two seater sports models, taking turns for the front seat. A speed of 7.5 walks (over 50 mph) could be sustained, enabling them to reach Kongholm in under six hora and observatory island in a further two. A rest break would be unnecessary. Rastu would take longer. She would leave after school and stop for rest at South Beach, where she would also collect some extra gear they might need. Her route would then continue along the coast to Lanamont and then on to Kongholm, resting half way. Her journey time to Kongholm would take her sixteen hora pedalling and eight hora resting. She had travelled the route before and knew her way and timing.

23
Geos: The Home Straight

Following their appointments to lead the expedition to Duplos, Flying Eagle and Wild Cat found they had a great deal of work to do in addition to the 'day jobs', which for Flying Eagle was about perfecting the shuttle and VTOL craft. For Wild Cat it was continued involvement with the launch of more space stations.

The politics of the extra stations was quite heated. After all, they are expensive. Eventually it was agreed to launch eight more to bring the total to twelve and fill the orbit slots at twentwy-six degree separation. This was very much a compromise between those that thought eight was sufficient and those wanting thirtween or sixtween. Wild Cat's intervention was crucial in achieving the compromise. Xe was able to argue strongly against such a long gap as thirtwy-nine degrees, which xe felt would endanger the mission through delayed support. Xe would have liked a higher number but agreed that twelve would be acceptable. Flying Eagle would have preferred sixtween but was persuaded that wasn't politically tenable. The stations were launched in ***1618*** and ***1619***, four in each year. Wild Cat went up to inspect each one as it was settled down, while Flying Eagle also went up to supervise the installation of the facilities for the shuttles and aircraft.

Fitting around all this was the task of selecting the crew and undergoing training. It was decided that the landing party would consist of twelve personnel. Four had already been chosen and two would be selected by the Kingdom of Northern Nations, which left six places to be filled.

A boot camp was held for the selection, both for the landing party, and for crew for several support roles in the space stations. Reserves, if needed, would be taken from these support crew. The KNN sent four candidates for their two places and also some others for the support crew, which included Flying Eagle's ex, Jezzie Peteschild.

The boot camp consisted of interviews, team exercises, psychological tests and a host of other activities, not so much to select individuals, as to select a team. For example everyone would have to be capable of covering a variety of roles and all should be team players. Col. Mountain had already received specialist training from the mission psychologists in an attempt to improve xer attitudes, and that certainly helped, but didn't completely overcome the misgivings about xer suitability. Thus there was some relief when the KNN's first selection was also an army Colonel who came with all the right qualifications and excellent people skills. Colonel Jacky Jackson was formally appointed as deputy chief security officer. However the hierarchy was to be flat and as a foreign officer of the same rank as Mountain was to all intents and purposes xer equal. Of the others, the KNN selected Professor Jan Martskind, a distinguished geologist who also held qualifications in the life sciences, xer initial degree being in Zoology, switching to Geology during xer postgraduate studies. Although young (***28***), xe held a personal chair at one the most prestigious universities in the KNN, and indeed, the world.

Of the New Norlanders, the selection panel, which included Flying Eagle, Wild Cat and Stripy Tiger Svensdot, selected five for the party: Dr Dancing Bear Grasslands, Dr Great Whale Ocean and Nurse Red Robin Garden would form the medical team, Major Bald Eagle Sky of the New Norland Air Force was a distinguished test-pilot and general all-rounder and Professor Wise Owl Cornfield, a specialist in Astrophysics.

For the last place Flying Eagle made a strong pitch that xe needed back-up as engineer for the shuttle and VTOL craft, as their lifeline was entirely dependent on them. The panel readily accepted this but the difficulty was who. None of the candidates for the ground mission fitted the bill. It might be possible to appoint an engineer and then give xim some intensive training, but that was riskier than the panel would like. Flying Eagle then suggested Jezzie. The initial reaction of the panel Chairman was that it would be politically impossible to ask the KNN to change their selection.

"No," said Flying Eagle, "that's not what I'm suggesting. Could we not allow a third person from the KNN, I'm sure they would not object to that, and Peteschild really is the best qualified person from either country." Wild Cat and Svensdot both nodded in approval. The chairman then adjourned the session, while xe made some phone calls to a number of stakeholders, culminating in the Vice-President.

When xe reconvened the meeting, xe announced that the V-P had given xer approval and the twelfth place would be offered to Jezzie Peteschild. The panel then went on to select the station support crew, assign them to the various stations, and decide on their understudy roles, should they be needed to replace one of the ground party.

Jezzie had been hoping for a place on one of the stations. Xe knew xe was well-qualified but concerned that xer nationality might tell against xim. Xe needn't have worried, xe was a shoe-in as one of the leading engineers on shuttles. Xe was overjoyed when told xe had actually been selected for the ground mission. Xe was sure xe had Flying Eagle to thank for that, because otherwise how would xer name have come to the selection panel's attention.

Xe had the opportunity to thank Flying Eagle in person when later xe joined xim and Wild Cat at the post-selection banquet. Xe also was able to give xim the news that when the mission was over xe was going back to the KNN to get married and xe hoped that Flying Eagle and Wild Cat would come to the ceremony. That clearly called for more celebrations, and Wild Cat ordered champagne all round to toast the bride to be[43]. Xe didn't add that xe and Flying Eagle would also get married after the mission, and certainly not that they hoped it would be a shotgun wedding!

When xe got back to Beaver, Jezzie had an urgent message to fly to the capital and see the KNN ambassador to New Norland. The ambassador congratulated xim on xer appointment. Then xe received the inevitable lecture on being a representative of xer country and conducting ximself accordingly, of striking the delicate balance between upholding Xer Majesty's dignity by not kowtowing to New Norland, while respecting the fact that KNN was the junior partner in the alliance. The ambassador reminded xer that Col. Jackson was the senior KNN representative on the mission and xe should refer to xim if xe found ximself in any difficulties.

After the selection there were several team exercises that involved Wild Cat and Flying Eagle. They received expert training from psychologists and management gurus on how to deal with all kinds of issues. This included specialist sessions on managing military personnel in general and awkward ones like Colonel Mountain in particular, which included some tricky exercises with scenarios so bizarre that surely nobody could be quite as difficult as their protagonist in the scenario. In some of these one of them had to lead the other in tasks, both where the leader was

43 There is no gender-import to this statement. Geosians have only one word for 'person to be married' I have chosen to translate it as bride.

instructed to behave unreasonably and where the led was instructed to be as bloody-minded as possible.

Another set of exercises were designed to get them working under Duplos gravity, which is a bit over three quarters that on Geos. Thus the average Geosian who weighs one **man** on Geos would only weigh nine rocks on Duplos[44]. You might be forgiven for thinking that moving in the lower gravity would be easier, and in a way it is. You are lighter but with the same muscles, so you will tire less easily, run faster and lift bigger masses. On the other hand, mass doesn't change so inertia will be unchanged but feel different. You will be more likely to stumble, miss steps and misjudge movements. All the things that your body does unconsciously, expecting a higher gravity, will be more difficult. Physical training in a low gravity simulator became a regular feature of all of their lives.

Then there were bonding sessions, some including both the ground party and the station crew, others (most of them) with just the ground party, and yet others confined to the rest of the senior team: Colonels Mountain and Jackson and Dr Svensdot.

Among the most interesting exercises were those simulating first contact. New Norlanders of native descent would play the Duplosians and refuse to speak or understand Norse while conversing in one of the ancient languages spoken by their ancestors. It had been quite tricky finding a suitable tribe of 'Duplosians', partly because very few were still fluent in their ancient tongues, and partly because Stripy Tiger had a smattering of quite a number of them. An important goal of these exercises was to ensure that the military members of the party learnt that 'shoot first and ask questions later' was not an acceptable policy.

---

44 Confusingly, Geosians use **man** as a unit of weight as well as of length, relying on context to distinguish. There are **10** (twelve) rocks in a **man.**

Eventually the time came in early ***161A*** when six of them boarded a shuttle to the space station currently at perigee while the rest waited for the station twentwy-six degrees behind. Flying Eagle and Wild Cat tossed a coin for who went with which. Wild Cat went on the first shuttle, with xim were Col. Mountain, Maj. Sky, Dr. Grasslands, Prof. Martskind and Mz. Peteschild[45].

The full orbit of the space stations takes two periods, twice that of the planets. This makes the journey between perigee and peridu at half that (one period or six **watches**) and the intervals between the arrivals of successive stations at one **watch**. A station is considered to be within reach of a planet (Duplos or Geos) if it is within twentwy-six degrees of its closest approach, in other words there are normally two stations within reach.

When the station containing Wild Cat's party approaches peridu, they will make the journey to Duplos, if possible. If circumstances are such that they can't make the journey, they will have to go round the orbit again until they next approach peridu. Similarly for Flying Eagle's party in the station behind them in orbit. Thus while Wild Cat has a **watch** lead, there is no guarantee that xe will get there first. In the event, xe did, but not by as much as a whole **watch**. As it turned out, a storm on Duplos delayed xer departure until xer station had gone two degrees past peridu, while Flying Eagle's party was able to follow quite quickly and the gap between their landings was a mere fiftwy tocks.

That first period on Duplos was spent constructing their base on the island in the Sea of Storms. This included four visits back to a space station, piloted by Major Sky accompanied by either Flying Eagle or Jezzie, to fetch additional material needed for their camp that couldn't be carried with them on the original

45 Naturally on Geos they don't have a separate Mr and Ms but just use the abbreviation Mz for Mizzer.

landing. Among the most important being the components for their electrical generators.

Although they had solar panels, these were of limited use this far North in early Spring. More productive were a couple of wind turbines and some specially developed generators using wave and tidal power, which the scientists claimed would be particularly good in the environment on the island. Together, these gave them considerable generating power, more than enough for their anticipated needs, even for the local transport with the VTOL craft which were capable of a range of three twundred twilomen on electric power alone. The three microlights that they also had with them had a range of two twundred.

24
First Contact

Once they had completed the construction of the camp and Colonels Mountain and Jackson had satisfied themselves there were no dangerous predators in the vicinity, the landing party settled down for a rest. The patterns of light and dark needed some getting used to as Duplos rotated at only two thirds of the rate of Geos and the Geosians' bodies had evolved to follow their planet's rhythms. Before patrolling more widely the medics had recommended that they all should be well-rested. The mission commander readily agreed to this.

"We should all take the Doc's advice and get some sleep and I declare a three **meal** break. We need to set a guard in case of unknown threats. Major Sky and Nurse Garden, please take first duty. Colonel Mountain and Professor Martskind, please relieve them for the second **meal**, then Colonel Jackson and Professor Cornfield for the third. I need to have a discussion with the 2-i-c about the next stage of our mission. Mz Peteschild please make sure nobody disturbs us for the next twentwy tocks."

When they went into their tent, Wild Cat gave Jezzie a sly wink. Xe smiled and winked back. "Good luck," xe whispered. On the way out in the space station Wild Cat had had a quiet word with Jezzie explaining the secret plan to conceive the first Geosian on Duplos. Jezzie was delighted to be brought in on the secret and entranced that it had been first proposed when Wild Cat and Flying Eagle were only fourtween years old. Xe assured xim that xe would do what xe could to ensure they had the necessary privacy.

They didn't actually need to have any discussion about the operation, they had worked out all the details already. Relying on Jezzie to guard their privacy, and knowing that they were at a point of maximum fertility, they set to with a zeal to ensure the desired conception. A whole range of factors combined to make this one of their best encounters ever. There was the fact that it had been a while since they last had sex, that the female was at her most receptive part of xer cycle, which they had always avoided as an extra insurance on top of contraception, the mechanical advantage of low gravity, the added frisson of the possibility of being disturbed, despite Jezzie, and the final realisation of their dream. Afterwards they each felt on top of the world. When Flying Eagle poked xer head out to let Jezzie off guard, the latter grinned and said "well, that ought to work. I don't recall you ever being so noisy with me, or having such a self-satisfied look on your face afterwards." Xe then skipped off before Flying Eagle could respond.

The next period was devoted to flights over the neighbourhood. As expected from their satellite surveys, the closest land was very sparsely inhabited with only the tiniest of settlements. Their best bet would be to choose a spot due south of their island. There was a sizeable city about tentwy twilomen due south of their base, some seventween twilomen inland from the coast, then there were a few villages along the coast. Finally they noticed a high tide island about seventwy twilomen slightly to the east of due south which contained a single dwelling and a tower atop an extinct volcano. It was a safe bet that this could be a primitive observatory. If there were an observatory, reasoned Wild Cat, there would probably be an astronomer and that could be a good sign.

The overall civilisation appeared to be pre-industrial. Much of the population seemed to be engaged in agriculture but within settled communities. The city looked like it contained around thirtwy-nine twundred dwellings, suggesting a population of around eleven twousand. There was a reasonably good road linking the city to the coast, and a coast road though a number of smaller communities as far as the observatory island. Traffic on the roads was steady but light. Mostly people travelled on foot but there were a few riders of a horse-like animal and a very few coaches or carriages on the road. They didn't see any shipping on the sea, which Flying Eagle thought was not too surprising given the weather, the size of waves, and the tides.

The inhabitants were tall and thin, that is they were slightly thinner than a Geosian and more than one and a half times as tall. There was no sign of military activity and Stripy Tiger opined that there was unlikely to be a serious threat from the locals. The mission commander ordered that only non-lethal weapons should be carried. They had dart guns that could fire fast-acting tranquilliser darts and these should be used if violence was absolutely necessary to counter a threat to their own lives. There were some sizeable herbivores on base island. Some of these had been captured and studied by the doctors and Professor Martskind. From these studies they had been able to determine that the animals were safe to eat and work out the dosage of tranquilliser likely to be appropriate if they had to use it on a Duplosian. They had also been able to give some assurances about pathogens.

A site for the first landing was selected about halfway between the coast and the city, and about three twilomen east from the road. They would breakfast at daybreak and leave base island shortly after. They would take nine people, a ground vehicle and two microlights. Dr Grasslands, Nurse Garden and Mz Peteschild would remain behind on base island. "Sorry Jezzie, but if all goes tits up, you will be needed to to take the others back to a space station, and we can't risk our entire medical team on first contact," Flying Eagle said. Jezzie wasn't going to grumble, naturally xe was slightly disappointed, but told ximself xe was damned lucky to be there at all.

The mission commander then briefed the contact party. "When we land, I want Dr Ocean and Professor Martskind to remain by the VTOL. Colonel," addressing Mountain, "you, Colonel Jackson and Major Sky will form a guard around the aircraft. We don't want curious locals getting too close and either getting hurt or inadvertently causing a problem, but no rough stuff. The remaining four will go to meet the locals. Professor, bring something to help us communicate with an astronomer, maybe to indicate where we've come from, you know the sort of thing. The 2-i-c and I will attempt to open the proceedings. Dr Svensdot, I need you to observe closely and be ready to intervene if you notice anything untoward."

Having observed some of the comings and goings between the space station and base island, Astra's party had plenty of time to get themselves organised. As already described, Zorro and Créezy had got to the observatory pretty quickly after receiving Arté's letter, before anything noticeable had happened. Rastu was that bit later and quite by chance she was on the road from Kongholm to the coast when she saw the Geosian aircraft flying high overhead. She stopped and watched as it circled Kongholm before flying off to the North at a great height. She wished she had Arté's binoculars with her.

When she got to the observatory she reported this to Astra. "As I thought," she said. "They are surveying the area around Kongholm. They're not going to land that thing in the middle of the city but I bet it won't be too far away, or, for that matter, too long now." It was decided that the four women would camp out in the vicinity of Kongholm, just off the road between the coast and city, Astra thought, near where Rastu had seen the aircart. The road would give them the fastest route if the Geosians were to land to the South of the city, but Astra's bet was they would stay to the North. Arté would remain at the observatory to observe using the large telescope. Rastu would borrow his binoculars and Astra would take the small telescope. Arté would keep a sporty SPC on the continent side of the causeway, in case he needed to move at high tide. He would then employ his latest toy to cross the submerged beach. This was what on Earth would be called a kayak. He called it a boatskin, because it wrapped round his lower body like a skin. It consisted of a light wooden frame covered in sealskin, with a hole in the top just big enough for him to climb into, leaving his top half outside. Another seal skin tight around his waist fastened to the boat so that water could not get in. He then used a double-headed paddle to propel the boat The boat skin was shaped like a double-pointed needle, and he had become adept at crossing from the island to the mainland.

Thus it was that Astra's party was in good shape to intercept the landing.

However, they were not alone, just well in advance with their preparations. Once the Geosians had started their surveying of the continent, they began to be noticed by others. The authorities were perplexed, and, as with authorities everywhere, slow to react, preferring the option of denial. However the conspiracy theorists and assorted nutcases were having a field day. Naturally, they were totally disorganised. Some held to the 'little green men' theory, others to something dastardly from the Shadowlands Union, yet others saw it as heralding an apocalypse, vengeance from the Goddesses following centuries of religious decline. Opinion was divided between hostile and friendly intent, but clearly the hostiles were in the majority. Accordingly various ragbag 'armies' started assembling in fields around Kongholm intent on welcoming the Goddesses or little green men or fighting the invaders. This did cause the authorities to act, calling out the militia; not to attack the invaders, but in an attempt to control the various mobs.

Both the GSE and the SU kept spies in Kongholm, and the spies duly reported back to their masters. For the GSE it was a matter of too late and far away. The conclusion of their Government, such as it was, was that they would need to keep abreast of developments in both the WF and SU, and especially to look out for troubles between them, and thus opportunities for the GSE. For the SU, unrest around Kongholm was closer to home and in the unlikely event that there were contact with aliens, they wanted part of the action. Accordingly steps were taken to assemble an army for 'exercises' close to the north-west border with the Western Federation.

Arté followed a couple more survey flights, one actually passing over the observatory. Then when a third took off he thought, "this is it," and set off to join the others. In fact he was premature. What he had observed was the start of the very last flight before the main mission. When he reached the campsite, they were all still there; but clearly packing up all but the one tent, where Rastu would have been waiting for him. This last flight had been to the east of them and had dipped right down almost to ground level before setting off again. Astra was sure, and as it happened, right, that this was finally confirming the chosen landing ground.

They had had a good look at the aircart, both with binoculars and telescope. "It is pretty big and appears to be made of metal. It has wings like a bird but they don't flap. I can't imagine how it is powered." Said Rastu. "My guess is that it has a wingspan of between ten and twenty strides and a length of about the same. It might hold anything from six to fifteen people, but they would have to be sitting down. The inside height can't be more than six lengths."

"I don't know about that," replied Arté, "perhaps 'little green men really are little." This brought a smile to their faces.

`"Anyway," went on Rastu, "now you're here, I don't have to wait for you and can pack up our tent. We're moving camp to nearer the landing spot. We have a good place in mind, just the other side of a rise in the ground, a couple of hundred strides away from the spot. We don't think they'll land on top of us there because a flatter space would be more suitable for them."

Between them they had three SPCs. Astra and Rastu had travelled in a coach model, in which they had been able to stow all the gear while they both sat up front doing the pedalling. Créezy and Zorro were in a two seater sports model, the seats were one behind the other, and with both pedalling they could, and did, reach incredible speeds on a good road. Zorro had wanted them to come in separate carts so they could race, but Astra had vetoed her plan on account that the high speed of the two seater might be needed. Arté had arrived in a single seater. Since they were now off-road, they made their way gently to their new camp ground, set up their tents and, as it was growing dark, went to bed, but taking turns to watch. Astra had a tent on her own, Rastu and Arté shared another, while Créezy and Zorro shared a third. "Seems a waste, Rastu having Arté, when she doesn't even want the benefit," mumbled Zorro.

Créezy laughed, "You're incorrigible, Zorro, you know we can't share him, and he wouldn't be prepared to choose between us. Much as I enjoy him, I actually would like it if he got together with either Rastu or Astra. He loves them both, you know, but between the two of them they've got so many sexual hang-ups you could write a book about them. And Arté is too much a gentleman and too besotted to do anything without direct invitation."

Zorro was puzzled, "Rastu, yes, after all, time will cure her youth, but Mummy, surely not. Arté just sees her as his employer."

"No, Zorro, I know about Arté's background in a way you never can. It's much more complicated than you imagine. He would willingly give his life for Astra. You and I are a sideshow for him. He enjoys his sex with each of us. But, however regretfully, would drop us in an instant if Astra or Rastu were to ask. Rastu won't of course, unless she overcomes her own hang-ups, her brother nonsense. But Astra is another matter."

Zorro became very thoughtful, "Créezy, if you're right I've really fucked things up, haven't I? I mean, Mother-Daughter really is a bit much to ask. I'll go mad if I have to listen to him and Mum shagging away in the next room at the observatory, while I have to play hunt the dildo, but I do want her to be happy. If she'd had the sense to bed him from the start, we wouldn't be in this mess. Créezy, when this is over can we go into Kongholm and pick up a hunk and fuck all of our brains out together!"

"It's a date. But since we don't have a hunk here, we might as well get some sleep," at this Créezy turned over and pulled her sleeping bag over her head.

As expected, nothing happened during the night. Astra had taken the last watch and woke them all for breakfast. About two hora later Arté called "here they come." It was his turn at look-out and he was standing on top of the rise with his binoculars trained on the sky to the North.

Sure enough, shortly afterwards the aircart was visible to the naked eye as it came down, hovered over the ground for a while and landed. Astra assembled her party and waited behind the rise. Soon a number of short, squat people descended from the aircart. Three of them took station about the cart, as on guard, two stayed by the cart and the other four walked a bit further off.

There was the sound of a bit of a kerfuffle in the distance, towards Kongholm. Clearly one or other of the nutcase groups was heading this way. Astra acted. She stepped out from behind the rise, motioning the others to follow her. She was carrying the telescope visibly in front of her. She walked steadily towards the visitors. "Well, they are little, if not green," whispered Zorro in an aside to nobody in particular.

Colonel Mountain feared Astra's telescope was a weapon and pulled out his dart-gun. Jacky Jackson saw the movement out of the corner of his eye and said. "Hold your horses Mountain Lion, I don't think that's any threat, we're all pretty sure they don't have firearms here."

"It could be one of those blow-pipes with poison darts, used by some of the primitive tribes in the rainforests," responded Mountain Lion.

"Just keep a watch on them, but don't fire, unless they fire first or I order differently. We shall be careful," ordered the mission commander. The four in the greeting party moved forward, Flying Eagle and Wild Cat in the centre and half a pace in the lead. They all held their hands out in front of them to show they were unarmed.

Astra put her telescope in her pocket and also held her hands out, the others did likewise and the two parties advanced towards each other. When they were close enough Astra stopped, bowed to them, and took a hand of each of Flying Eagle and Wild Cat. From a vantage point atop the aircraft Dr Ocean took a photograph using a telephoto lens.

Letting go of their hands Astra pointed to herself and clearly annunciated "Astra."

She then introduced the others. "Arté, Créezy, Zorro, Rastu." Each of them turned to the Geosians and bowed when their name was called. Stripy Tiger Svensdot, returned each bow, repeating the names and committing them to memory. It was then the Geosians' turn to introduce themselves. They had decided on informality. Each introduced themselves along the line, the mission commander pointing to each one in turn; "Wise Owl, Wild Cat, Flying Eagle, Stripy Tiger." Xe then called to the others in the party to bow from a distance, but asking Jan Martskind to come and join them. Astra then turned to point to a table she had set up behind them and in sign language invited them to come and sit down. The table seated six and Astra flanked herself with Créezy and Arté, while Rastu and Zorro stood to one side. Flying Eagle, Wild Cat and Stripy Tiger sat down opposite them. Astra then put her hand to her ear and pointed away to the South towards Kongholm, where the commotion was growing louder. She tried to convey the message that there were some idiots around who would be intent on spoiling the party. The visitors would need to take care. Stripy Tiger got the gist of the message and passed it on to the mission commander, who dispatched xer 2-i-c to convey the warning to Mountain Lion. When this was done xe came back and resumed xer seat.

Interestingly, as they were the subordinate culture, Astra seemed to take charge. Stripy Tiger was fascinated by this and thought he saw an interesting article in 'The Journal of Alien Psychology' emerging. Astra put her telescope on the table and asked Arté to do the same, she then invited the Geosians to inspect them. Wise Owl picked them up, inspected them and looked through them. "The telescope is clearly an early model," he told the others. "The binoculars are more advanced." Arté pointed to the rise and took his chair put it down there and invited Wise Owl to stand on it. He then handed him the binoculars and pointed at where the observatory was. It was just possible to see the top of the tower over the horizon. Wise Owl got the message. He reported. "These people have been observing us from the observatory we saw on the summit of the volcano on the high tide island. I gather that Astra is a distinguished astronomer over here."

Rastu had scurried off behind the rise and returned with a jug of coffee and some biscuits. These were offered and accepted. They were getting on famously. Then Zorro incurred her mother's displeasure, by 'embarrassing us all with your grossly inappropriate behaviour'.

As you know too well by now, Duplos is obsessed by gender differentiation, and Zorro really wanted to know if these visitors were male or female. They all looked pretty much alike, in terms of height and build. She thought they were probably male as there was no obvious chest bulge, but she really wanted to know. She faced them pointed to herself and said "Woman." She then pointed to each of her companions, saying the same word for three of them and "Man" when she pointed to Arté. Then to make sure they understood which was which, Arté being so tall, she proceeded to undo the front of her clothes and made it obvious. When she then approached Arté putting her hand on his trousers, her mother slapped her wrist hard and told her to behave herself.

This exchange amused Stripy Tiger who found it difficult to contain xer mirth. Xe and Wild Cat then spent some time trying to explain that they didn't really differentiate between the sexes, and all were called men. Their party was indeed mixed but they tended to keep their gender private. They wouldn't even know the gender of many of their colleagues. While this was going on Flying Eagle got up and took Zorro aside where xe satisfied her curiosity with regard to ximself, and pointed out that Wild Cat was the opposite, while indicating that xe didn't know about any of the others.

In xer turn, Wise Owl pulled out out two charts and spread them out in front of Astra. One showed the orbits of Geos and Duplos with the relative sizes of the planets and the twelve space stations more or less as Rastu and Arté had calculated. Wise Owl then pointed to their journey to Duplos. Astra nodded in understanding. The other chart showed the solar system. Astra recognised it immediately and excitedly pointed out to Arté, a fifth small moon of Zuvos between Proxis and Mexia, two tiny moons of Maxos, a large moon of Sépanos and an extra planet beyond the orbit of Sépanos. She also noticed a belt of small planets between their own orbits and that of Zuvos. Lots of extra bodies for them to look out for, she said to Arté.

Just as they were getting on so well, they were disturbed by a loud noise from the direction of the aircraft. The mob had arrived and one of them had been shot by a tranquilliser dart. Wild Cat and Flying Eagle dashed over to the aircraft in the hope of calming the situation. Stripy Tiger had managed to convey to Astra that the tranquillised woman was not dead but sleeping and would come round eventually with nothing more than a headache. Astra ran over to the prone individual, pronounced her alive and gave her a vicious kick to prove it. Flanked by the others she faced down the crowd.

For the moment it was stalemate, when a party of militia appeared wanting to know what was going on. Créezy managed to take the commanding officer aside and explain the situation. Fortunately the woman was intelligent, and it looked like things would get under control.

Astra was explaining to the crowd. "No, these visitors are not servants of the Goddesses come to seek vengeance. Yes they were from outer space. They came from Geos. They were indeed little, but they were not green. There were more of them who would get news back to Geos if we killed these few. It would not be a good idea. If they could travel through space to reach us, they would certainly have the most fearsome weapons that could destroy us all. No I don't speak their language, but we are communicating through sign language and charades. We will learn to speak to each other if you lot give us a chance. They are here in peace, and they could teach us a great deal. That woman was hurt because she is stupid. They have a right to defend themselves against attack by a mob. She isn't dead even though she deserves to be. And if the Geosians were hostile she would be, and so would all of you. She'll wake up in another horum with no more than a headache and a bruise where I kicked her bum. She's damned lucky I didn't kick her in the fanny so hard she could never enjoy a man again, which frankly is what I should have done."

Then just as the crowd was looking to disperse and the militia get a grip on things, a detachment of shadowland troops appeared over the horizon. Arté inspected them through his binoculars. "I'd guess about two hundred of them," he said, "about four walks away and moving quite slowly. My guess is they'll be here in about two hora."

The scene was set for quite a ding-dong. Shadowlands had violated a treaty. The militia commander sent someone to go for reinforcements. Arté offered his SPC, but the militiaman declined on the grounds she didn't know about those newfangled things. The mob turned ready to fight the shadowlanders alongside the militia, apart from those among them who were actually shadowland agents, who quietly snuck away.

Astra turned to 'talk' to the Geosians. They would have to decide what to do.

"Whatever happens now, we will get through it, and we have indeed made contact," was the message that Wild Cat and Flying Eagle gave to their party, and Astra gave to hers.

Key Events Timeline

All dates below are in the Geosian calendar in duodecimal for events on Geos and in decimal for events on Duplos. This is an extract from a more complete timeline available in a free download package from my website.

Date (duo)	Events on Geos	Date (dec)	Events on Duplos
1560	President Wheatfield elected	2520	
1562	Programme Duplos started	2522	
1587	Programme Duplos cancelled	2553	
15A6		2574	Arval (later Arthay, Arté) born
15B4	Wild Cat and Flying Eagle meet	2584	
1600	Old Programme Duplos date for landing New Programme Duplos announced	2592	
1602		2594	Chay buys Arthay for Thay
1609		2601	Astra buys Observatory Island
1612	Decision to build	2606	Chay dies. Arthay

Date (duo)	Events on Geos	Date (dec)	Events on Duplos
	base on Duplos. Wild Cat commander of Space Stations		washed ashore on Islaview beach, becomes Arté
1613		2607	Arté at Routh University, meets Rastu
1614	3rd and 4th Stations launched	2608	Arté leaves Routh for contract with Astra
1616	Flying Eagle in Kingdom of Northern Nations	2610	Rastu graduates
1617	Advanced VTOL tested. Decision to bring forward mission	2611	Arté's contract ends. Astra makes him a partner. He buys Thayview Farm
			Wheels-within-Wheels is formed
1618	Wild Cat and Flying Eagle candidates to lead mission. Next 4 stations launched.	2612	
161A	Duplos mission sets out	2614	Contact

Appendix 1: The Geos-Duplos Solar System

Abbreviated form

This note is extracted from a more detailed description of the Geos-Duplos solar system available in a free A4 PDF download from my website.

The Sun is very much like Earth's. It is a type G2V star of diameter 1,408,415 km and a mass of 2.05965 x 10^{30} kg which is 34,500 Earths. Its mean angular size from Geos-Duplos is 32.22 arc-minutes. The binary planets Geos and Duplos orbit at a mean distance of 156.261 million kilometres and are the only planets in the habitable zone. The period of their orbit is 359.999 days. There are four other planets in the solar system, one rocky inner planet, Thermos, two gas giants, Zuvos and Sépanos, and one outer ice planet, Ultimos. There are also several moons.

We now come to the Geos-Duplos system, As well as the two planets in orbit around their barycentre, there are two moons. Selenos is the larger and orbits in a near-circular orbit some way out. Eclos is a captured asteroid and travels in an eccentric orbit which is highly inclined to the plane of the Geos-Duplos orbits.

The Geos-Duplos orbit is itself inclined at 2° to the ecliptic, here defined as the plane of the orbit of the Geos-Duplos barycentre about the sun. The two planets orbit about the barycentre in a 'dumb-bell' orbit in a similar manner to Pluto and Charon, as distinct from the intersecting ellipses common with binary stars. Although there is tidal locking between the planets, it is not in 1:1 ratio like the Moon with its orbit of Earth, or the Jovian and Zuvian moons. But in a simple ratio, as are Mercury and Thermos. The Geos-Duplos year is almost exactly three hundred and sixty Earth days long. The period of their rotation about their barycentre is twelve Earth days, during which time

Geos rotates six times and Duplos four times, giving local days, of two and three Earth days. Shadowing by the other planet is such that the light and darkness pattern is complicated and both Geosians and Duplosians are very flexible about their rest times. Geos and Duplos both rotate with an axial tilt of 17.61 degrees and hence have a narrower tropical band and more northerly arctic circle than Earth.

Some details of these planets and moons are given below in Earth units.

Geos:
Mass: 8.71×10^{24} kg (1.459 Earths)
Diameter: 14550 km
Average Density 5.4 gm/cm^3
Surface Gravity 1.119 g
Escape Velocity 12.64 km/s
Rotation Period 2 days
Orbit period around barycentre 12 days

Duplos:
Mass: 3.36×10^{24} kg (0.563 Earths)
Diameter: 10403 km
Average Density 5.7 gm/cm^3
Surface Gravity 0.845 g
Escape Velocity 9.28 km/s
Rotation Period 3 days
Orbit period around barycentre 12 days.

Selenos:
Mass: 2.09×10^{22} kg (0.0035 Earths)
Diameter: 2217 km
Average Density 3.67 gm/cm^3
Surface Gravity 0.116 g
Escape Velocity 1.587 km/s
Rotation Synchronous

Orbit period around barycentre 89.61 days.

Eclos:
Mass: 9.19 x 10^{18} kg
Diameter: 154 km
Average Density 4.8 gm/cm^3
Surface Gravity 0.011 g
Escape Velocity 0.126 km/s
Rotation Unknown
Orbit period around barycentre 325.11 days.
Eccentricity of orbit 0.84

One aspect that comes up in Arté's calculations is that of the angular size of various bodies in the solar system as seen from Duplos. Table A1.T1 below gives the angular size in Arc-minutes of various bodies as seen from Geos-Duplos.

Table A1.T1 Angular Size from Geos-Duplos (all in arc-min)

Angular Size	Sun	Thermos	Zuvos	Selenos	Eclos
Mean	32.22	4.97	0.16	7.18	N/A
Max	N/A	15.23	0.663	9.37	1.31
Min	N/A	N/A	N/A	5.82	0.11
with x40 telescope			26.52		

For comparison the angular size of both the Sun and Moon from Earth is around 30 arc-min. Of course Geos and Duplos each appear much larger in each other's skies, at about 143 arc-min (Geos from Duplos) and 102 arc-min (Duplos from Geos).

Much of Arté and Rastu's energies were spent on teasing out orbits. Fig A1.1 below may help the reader appreciate the issues. This shows the apparent orbits of Geos and Selenos as observed from Duplos over one full 89.61 day Selenos cycle. The Geos orbit is the inner circle which as already stated completes every twelve days.

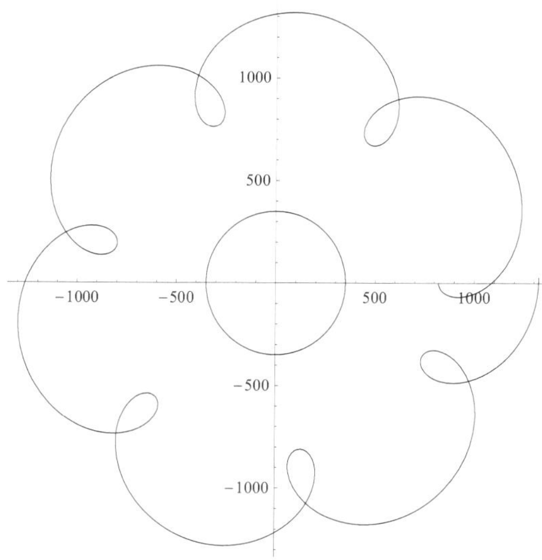

Fig A1.1 The apparent orbits of Geos and Selenos as seen from Duplos (scale in Megametres)

Appendix 2: Duodecimal numbers

On Earth we count and express our numbers using the decimal place value number system, that is we work base ten. In continental Duplos they use the same system so there is no difficulty there. On Isla, the isolated island culture on Duplos, which is more primitive than the continent, they use a system more akin to Roman Numerals. This is covered in more detail in appendix 6 in the free download of full appendices available from my web-site.

On Geos they have adopted a duodecimal system. This makes a lot of sense in many ways, but can be confusing for us. Rather than introduce twelve completely new symbols, I have decided to use the ten we are familiar with and two additional ones, A and B to denote ten and eleven respectively. In order to limit confusion I shall put a number in ***bold italics*** whenever it is to be interpreted as a duodecimal number. Thus while 10 will mean ten, ***A*** will also mean ten and ***10*** will mean twelve.

Powers of twelve are the numbers consisting of a one followed by a number of zeros. Thus ***100*** is 144, ***1000*** is 1728 etcetera. The number ***1728*** is the duodecimal for 2768. ($1 \times 12^3 + 7 \times 12^2 + 2 \times 12 + 8$). For fractions, the familiar form of numerator/denominator is the same as we are used to, it's just that the numbers have to be interpreted as duodecimals. However when we use the analogous notation to our decimals, we have to remember than now it is not a decimal point but a duodecimal point and the duodigits after the point represent twelfths, one hundred and forty-fourths and so on. Thus ***3/4*** is the same number as 3/4 but if we want to put it in the 'decimal' notation it won't be ***0.75*** but ***0.9.*** ***(***9 twelfths is the same as three quarters, ***0.75*** would be 7/12+ 5/144 = 0.618055555..). Just as with decimals all rational numbers (fractions) in the duodecimal form will either stop after a finite number of places or eventually the last part will be recurring. The fractions that give finite duodecimals will be those which in their lowest terms have only factors of powers of 2 and 3 in the denominator (just as for decimals the denominator has to only have factors of powers of 2 and 5).

One of the common usages in the main book is for dates on Geos. The events that are being described occur around the year ***1600*** in the Geos calendar, which is close to 2600 decimal. Duplos doesn't have a calendar for us to number its years, and in part three of the book as the events on both planets come together, I have expressed dates in the decimal equivalent of the Geos dates. Thus the final chapter occurs in the year ***161A*** or 2614.

Finally on language. The numbers one to twelve are as in English. However after that a different set of number words is required. Instead of the teens, we have the tweens; onetween, twoteen, thirtween to ninetween, tentween, leventween. Then we go through the twentwy's to leventwy's until we reach a twundred for ***100*** or 144. Finally a twousand for ***1,000*** $=12^3$ = 1728 and a twillion for ***1,000,000*** = 12^6.

On Earth we use micro, milli, kilo, mega as prefixes to denote powers of 10^{-3} and 10^3. On Geos they have a similar system for powers of 12^{-3} and 12^3. Thus swega, swili, twilo and twega means respectively multiply by 12^{-6}, 12^{-3}, 12^3 and 12^6. Finally we have pertwent and pertwentage for the base twelve version of percent and percentage.

Appendix 3: Weights and Measures

As with Appendix 1 this is extracted from a fuller version available from the free download on my website. The latter includes fuller conversion tables from the three cultures, whereas here I just include brief details of those measures used in the text.

People on Geos and Duplos

Just as on Earth in ancient times our systems of weights and measures owed some reference to measurements on people, the same is true on each of these planets, so by way of introduction. I will cover the basic dimensions of Geosians and Duplosians.

On Geos there is no gender dimorphism, apart from the obvious. Both males and females have an average height of 1.53 metres (a tiny bit over 5 ft) and an average mass of 75 kg (165 lb). That is, on Earth, an average Geosian would tip the scales at 75 kg, and a 75 kg Earthling would weigh the same as the average Geosian on Geos (nearly 84 kg weight).

Geosians have a thickset stocky build compared to us on Earth, and female breasts are small. Fashions of both clothing and hairstyle are unisex. So it is impossible to tell male from female when dressed. Variation in height, girth and natural weight[46] are lower than on Earth. Height is approximately normally distributed with standard deviation of just 3.5 cm (1.38"). Thus 68.3% of Geosians are between 1.495 and 1.565 metres tall and 95.44% are between 1.46 and 1.6 metres tall.

On the other hand Duplosians are tall and thin and do show gender dimorphism. Their limbs are also proportionately longer than ours. Duplosian men have an average height of 2.2 metres

---

46 Just as on Earth some Geosians (and indeed Duplosians) are fatter or thinner, lighter or heavier due to lifestyle choices.

(7' 2.6") and average mass of 72 kg (159 lb). Duplosian women have an average height of 2.3 metres (7' 6.55") and an average mass of 73 kg (161 lb). The standard deviation of height for both men and women is 10 cm (4").

Measures in general

On Geos, as on Earth, the traditional definitions of measurement have been replaced by references to physical constants in a way that preserves the old nomenclature while ensuring the exact quantities are precisely defined. Geosians also make use of prefixes for powers of 12 as we do for powers of 10. Commonly used prefixes are:

swega = $12^{-6,}$ swili = $12^{-3,}$ twilo = 12^3 and twega = 12^6.

Duplos is less advanced. On the continent they have exact standards based on standard physical objects. On Isla things are a bit more rough and ready, but there are standard rulers and weights kept in the more important temples. Those in the principal temple at Rivermouth are increasingly seen as the base standard.

Time

The **year** and **period** are common to both planets. The period is the time that Geos and Duplos complete their orbits around each other at exactly 12 Earth days, while the year is 359.999 Earth days, almost exactly 30 periods long. Most other time units are divisions or multiples of the period, influenced by binary, decimal or duodecimal divisors. The only exception is the **selenth**, based on the orbit of Selenos, at 89.614 Earth days. On Geos and continental Duplos, the selenth has been decoupled from the motion of Selenos, and refers to a quarter of the year. (90 days). On the island of Isla, they stick to the lunar calendar but adjust at New Year to maintain reasonable alignment between the seasons of the year and selenths.

Main time units are as follows:

In all three cultures the base is the period with 30 periods in a year. The selenth is also used for the quarterly seasons.

Geos:

The smallest unit is the tick which equates to 2.778 seconds.

72 ticks = 1 tock, 72 tocks = 1 meal, 12 meals = 1 watch, 6 watches = 1 period, 5 periods = 1 work.

Longer timescales are 1 life = 72 years and 1 mem = 144 years.

The terms meal and work derive from a meal being a historic 'standard' interval between mealtimes and a work being the usual time period for payment of salaries, although casual labourers are often paid per period. A watch is also the length of the Geosian day. Because of possible confusion I put the words **meal, watch and work** in bold typeface when used as a time unit. Inconveniently for us there is no obvious equivalent to an Earth hour which is 18 tocks or a quarter of a meal.

Duplos continent:

The smallest unit is the dusec which equates to 2.025 seconds. 40 dusecs = 1 dumin, 40 dumins = 1 horum, 80 hora = 1 phase, 4 phases = 1 period. As on Earth they use a century for a hundred years. A phase is also their day and a horum is exactly 54 minutes.

Isla:

The smallest unit is the isec which equates to 0.989 seconds. The phase and period are the same as on the continent.

64 isecs = 1 imin, 64 imins = 1 ihor, 64 ihors = 1 phase.

Thus an ihor is 1.125 hours or 1.25 hora.

Length and Distance

The base unit of length and distance in all three cultures was set by reference to people, in the way that such units as foot, yard and mile were established on Earth. On Geos the base standard is the 'man' which was defined by the average height of a Geosian. 1 **man** = 1.53 metres = 5' 0.236". All the other length and distance units derive from this via multiples of 12.

On Duplos the base unit is the 'stride', like the Earth yard. The value of a stride on the continent is slightly longer than on Isla. Where I need to distinguish I shall write the Isla version as 'istride'. A **stride** is 1.25 metres = 4' 1.21", an **istride** is 4' = 1.2192 metres. All other length and distance units are derived from these by simple multiples or factors. On the continent these tend to be mixed binary and decimal. On Isla, binary is the norm.

Geos:

The important units from the narrative are the man and twiloman which is 12^3 men equating to Earth's 2.644 km or 1.643 miles.

Duplos Continent:

The units mentioned in the narrative are the division, length, stride and walk.

10 divisions = 1 length, 4 lengths = 1 stride, 2000 strides = 1 walk. In Earth terms the walk is exactly 2.5 km (1.554 miles). It is also the distance covered at average Duplosian walking speed in a quarter of a horum.

Isla:

The units mentioned in the narrative are the smidge, thumb, foot, istride and imile. The foot (isla length) is exactly the same as Earth's.

8 smidges = 1 thumb, 8 thumbs = 1 foot, 4 feet = 1 istride, 1024 istrides = 1 imile. Thus an imile is about 1.248 km (0.776 miles).

Speed:

Geos: speed is measured in twilomen per meal (tpm) or races per tock (rpt). In most towns the speed limit is *60* tpm which works out as 118.31 miles in 4 hours or 29.58 mph. Converting from tpm to rpt is simple, just divide by six - very easy in base twelve. As seen in chapter 10, twilomen per tick (tpt) is also used for some astronomical velocities).

Continental Duplos uses 'walk' as a measure of speed as well as distance. Walk's actual derivation was from the typical distance covered in a quarter of a horum. As a speed, walk means four walks per horum (= 11.11 kph = 6.94 mph). Similarly Duplosians use the terms Jog and Run for eight and sixteen walks per horum respectively.

Isla doesn't have any specific terms for speed.

Volume

All these societies have adopted some volumetric measures from historic liquid measures otherwise they will use cubic, as we do, in the same way as square for areas. Volumes are not referred to in the narrative so I won't cover them in this abbreviated appendix, (although the Duplosian 'doop' = 954 mls or 1.678 pints is mentioned below).

Mass & Weight

These two quantities are linked on Geos just as on Earth. Of course on Geos their local g defines the relationship. Surface gravity on Geos is 1.119 times that on Earth or 10.98 m/s^2. This translates as 55.38 $men/tick^2$ which in the Geosian duodecimal system is ***47.47*** *men/tick*^{2}.

As with linear measurement the measurement of weight and thence mass is based on a 'standard' person at 75 kg. Confusingly, Geosians use the same term 'man' as for linear measurement, relying on context to distinguish. For smaller and larger quantities other terms are used for some duodecimal multiples/factors of the base man. The text also mentions the rock. 12 rocks = 1 man.

For astronomers, **1** Geos = 1.4588 Earths, 1 Earth = 0.685 Geos.

Continental Duplosians have not yet worked out the physics of weight and mass, their science is pre-Newtonian. However they do have the concept of weight under Duplosian gravity[47]. On the continent their standard weight is that of a doop of water (1 dupound - dp), which under Earth gravity would be 976.5625 grams or 2.152 lb. (On Duplos this weighs 1.82 lb or 0.825 kg). The average mass of Duplosians is 73 kg (Female) and 72 kg (Male) which under Duplosian gravity weighs 61.65 kg and 60.8 kg. However because the gravity factors cancel out these averages in Duplosian units are 74.752 dp and 73.728 dp respectively.

There are colloquial terms for other weights but nothing that is universally recognised.

On Isla weight is based on an arbitrary (religious based) standard object - a near spherical ball of iron, of mass 1.823 kg. Thus the average Duplosian woman weighs 40.04 balls. For more domestic convenience island Duplosians use the quarter, which as the name suggests is a quarter of a ball.

Angular Measurements

The value of π is universal and the natural radian measure of angle is used in Geosian scientific work just as on Earth. A common approximation to π on Geos is the duodecimal value π =

47 *Surface gravity on Duplos is 8.28 m/s^{-2} or 0.8445g.*

3.1848. Geos has adopted the same degree as Earth (360 = ***260*** degrees in a circle). However further subdivisions are by 72. Thus 72 gemin = 1°, 72 gesec = 1 gemin.

Educated Duplosians are aware of π as the ratio between the circumference of a circle and its diameter and of the area to the square of the radius, they have not developed the concept to include radian measurement of angles. The continentals divide the circle into 60 equal angles, Thus 1 dudeg = 6°.. There is no other universally accepted term for angular measurement other than a right angle which is 15 dudeg. Those wanting more precise measurements use various subdivisions, usually by powers of 2 or powers of 10 or a mixture of the two.

On Isla all divisions are by powers of 2. In the temples they divide a right-angle into 64 idegs. Circular measure is based on practicalities. Those that need to know about such things know that the ratio of the area of a circle to the square of its radius is greater than 3+1/8 but less than 3+3/16. Working with fractions is limited to dividing by 2 (or its powers) and they lack the mathematical notation to deal with fractions.

Temperature

Temperature on Geos is measured on a scale of ***100*** (144) divisions (div) between the freezing point (***0***) and boiling point (***100***) of water at sea level on Geos. The Earth Kelvin is 1.44 div Geosian. Geosian science is aware of Absolute Zero.

There are no standardised methods of measuring temperature on Duplos.

Currency

New Norland, the dominant country on Geos, has a three unit duodecimal currency system, for convenience I shall denote them by penny, shilling and pound[48]. As there is no trade between Geos and Earth conversion to Earth currency is pretty meaningless but in terms of wages the pounds are close to 'parity'.

Duplos is even more difficult to compare. Isla's money is issued by the temples, and much of its use is for religious purposes. Much of the economy is based on barter or exchange of obligations. Some money does also circulate, however, and some people are paid wages.

On the continent the various territories have their own currencies. I shall only give details of that of the Western Federation.

Geos: New Norland/KNN £1 (pound) = 12 s (shillings) = 144 d (pence).

In New Norland the minimum adult (24+) wage is £3,456 per work (£691 2s 5d per period), (£20,736 pa). Average adult wage is £30,096 pa. Typical salaries for school leavers and new graduates are between £13,824 and £19,008 pa and £24,096 and £31,104 pa respectively. Wild Cat and Flying Eagle started on £41,472 pa. But then they did have top qualifications from the leading technical university in the world in a very much sought after subject. My guess is that they were on six figure salaries before too long.

Duplos: In the Western Federation all money is coin. The main unit of currency is the dollar, the smallest is the farthing. 4 farthings = 1 cent, 4 cents = 1 groat, 10 cents = 1 dime, 25 cents = 1 crown, 2 crowns = 1 doubloon, 2 doubloons = 1 dollar ($1).

---

48 The KNN also uses £sd. The exchange rate fluctuates. On the **watch** of the first contact the official rate was **£1** (NN) = **£1.16** (KNN), or **£1** (KNN) = **As 8d** (NN).

Farthings, cents and groats are bronze, dimes, half-crowns, crowns and doubloons are silver. Dollars are silver or gold. $5 and $10 are gold.

There is no minimum wage. Labourers receive between a groat and a dime per horum. An educated woman might expect to earn around $2,000 per annum from her own work on which she will live quite comfortably. At first, Astra paid Arté $500 per selenth of which 50% was deducted for his keep.

On Isla the main unit of currency is the Mark and the smallest the denar, but much of the economy functions without actual money. 4 denari = 1 groat, 8 groats = 1 quarter (mark), 4 quarters = 1 mark. Where wages are paid, a male labourer might get up to 1 groat per ihor. An educated woman in a clerical or professional role might expect a salary of 20 marks per period. Of the coins, anything less than a quarter is bronze, quarters, half marks, mark, and 2 mark coins are silver. There are gold 5, 10, and 20 mark coins.

Appendix 4: Duplos Statistics and other Details

Most people on Duplos live in village communities although there are a few towns and a very few larger urban centres on the continent. For convenience I shall define:

City: An urban population centre of more than 10,000 people.

Town: A centre of population between 1,000 and 10,000 usually associated with a market or specific community activity. (On Isla a town is defined as 1024 or more people).

Village: a settled community of population between 50 and 1000, including outlying farms that consider themselves as part of the village community. (On Isla they define a village as a named community of 64 or more people).

Isolated or Unsettled: where dwellings are unsettled (e.g. nomadic) or in isolated communities of fewer than 50 (64 on Isla).

Isla

While there are no countries in the Earth sense the Island, Isla, is dominated by a theocracy within which various 'chiefs' vie for local leadership.

The population of Isla is estimated at around 150,000 (1024 x 128 +1024 x 16). It is hard to be sure. The number of people living in the wild lands is anyone's guess, where there are no real centres of population. A community of 128 is be considered large.

Even in the allied territories of West Isla, New West Isla and the Isla Marches, accurate statistics are hard to come by. In the Theocracy, the temples are supposed to maintain records of births and deaths as well as ownership of males and familial relationships of females, but in practice their performance is patchy. For administrative convenience a community of 1024 or more is designated a town, and one of 64 or more, with a name, a village.

Roughly two thirds of the population live in the Isla Theocracy, having some sort of loose common allegiance. Bordering the Theocracy are the Isla Marches and the territories of West Isla and New West Isla. These territories are in a sense allied to the Theocracy and follow a similar lifestyle. NWI was colonised/conquered by people from West Isla with help and encouragement from the Theocracy and remain politically connected despite poor communications between the two territories. From the point of view of the Theocracy, NWI and the Marches serve to contain the Western Wild Lands, while the Marches also play an important role in limiting communication between the West and North Wild Lands. The Wild Lands are sparsely populated with no towns and few communities justifying the distinction of village. They are seen as a good source of slaves by the Theocracy and its allies.

The largest town on Isla is Rivermouth, which is mainly on the north bank of the Great River, shortly before it opens in to its estuary. Some linked communities lie on the south bank close to ferries or the bridge.

Approximate populations of the towns in the Theocracy mentioned in Arthay's story are:

Rivermouth: 6,144; Midborough[49]: 4,624; Cattlebridge: 3,456; Chalcliff-on-Strait: 3,072; Honeyfield: 2,176; Oakbridge: 1,408; Barton-within-Lesser: 1,280.

---

49 Midborough isn't actually mentioned, but it is the second largest town in the Theocracy.

Continent

The continent is divided into 3 powers although the political ties within these powers are very loose and certainly do not prevent internal strife. The power with which we are mainly concerned, The Western Federation is self-contained within reasonably well-defined borders with the other two, following wars that ended around a century previously with agreed border treaties. The other two claim territories extending well beyond their respective administrative reach and generally sparsely populated by people wholly ignorant of the powers that are claiming sovereignty over them[50].

The approximate population of the cities mentioned in Arté's story are as follows:

Louth: 58,000; Routh: 15,000; Goddess City: 70,000; Marouth: 32,000; Marcenza: 16,000; Kongholm: 22,000; Dambach: 25,000; Soubanc: 12,500; Lanamont: 10,500.

Rastu and Zorro have compiled a distance/ journey time chart for the above eight cities (counting Marouth/Marcenza as one) together with the bridgeheads at Deltaport and Vinebridge, the villages of Islaview Market, Dunos and South Beach, Observatory Island and Arté's farm at Thayview. This chart shows distances in walks and journey times in hora, being Rastu's estimates for the journeys in a two seater self propelled cart with just one person pedalling and one passenger. The chart doesn't fit well with a small book format but is included in the free download package from my website.

---

50 Between them the 3 powers claim all territory on Duplos, even though they have no idea of its extent. The Western Federation claims sovereignty over Isla, even though that is an absurd claim. However, this is to the benefit of castaways like Arté who automatically qualify for WF citizenship.

Appendix 5: The Duplosian Pantheon and Associated Mythology

Gay (or Gé as she is known on the continent) is the creatrix of the universe. She is too great to be concerned with the details of life on Duplos - but her presence forever looms over all things. She delegated the oversight of her creation to her three daughters, Su, Zu, and Say assisted by her niece Saypa (Su, Zu, Sé, Sépa on the continent).

Su's special responsibility is for the world to which she brings light and warmth but her sisters are not without influence and being as contrary as human sisters bring about night, darkness and cold. Su has two daughters Lana and Nepa and their respective domains are the land and sea. Lana was ever a force for good but Nepa was jealous of her and, not being content with her own estates, ever seeks to steal her sister's domain and destroy its life. Lana has a daughter, Isla who asked her mother if she might have a part of the land for her own. Lana being a wise mother agreed to give her a peninsula with a fine temperate climate, goodly uniform rainfall and fertile ground where her people might live comfortably and serve her.

This made Nepa especially angry and she made terrible war on her sister and niece. In this war she separated Isla from her mother. The people of Isla saw that they were now alone in the world and resolved to serve their goddess with renewed zeal. However, from time to time, they must make sacrifices to the sea to appease Nepa.

Zu, Say and Saypa make their presence felt more at night and the only male in the pantheon, Ech (Ec on the continent) will cause all sorts of mischief, for he is the wayward and erratic son of Say. Zu and her daughters (Max, Mex, Prox) play little part in

Isla theology although they were more prominent in ancient continental mythology - all dating from before the destruction of the land-bridge to Isla.

This religious system that so dominates Isla is no longer followed seriously on the continent but does form part of their mythology and some rituals survive in local cultures.

Acknowledgements

My thanks to Philip Bannister for the cover design, to John Ramsbotham, Joyce Ramsbotham and Helen Walton for reading the manuscript and offering constructive criticism and to my wife Mary for putting up with me throughout the writing of this book.

R. A.
Worcestershire, UK
Earth

Author's Note

Thank-you for reading my book. I hope you enjoyed it. If so, please leave a review on Amazon. It doesn't have to be long but is really important for independent author's such as myself. This is because it is through the review system that Amazon positions books in its search listing. Please also visit my web site where I shall give news of sequels and occasional blogs by some of the characters. I also welcome any feedback or other comments via email to author@richardarthur.uk.

About The Author

Richard Arthur was born in India just before he and his soldier parents were ejected following independence in 1947. His earliest years were spent as a camp follower of the British Army, until his father retired to spend more time with his family. After Prep School in Buckinghamshire and Grammar School in South London, Richard spent six years studying mathematics at university, emerging with a PhD. Richard then spent three years as a lecturer before joining GCHQ. Since retiring from the day job he has maintained some academic links and consulted in Information Security. He still enjoys mathematical problems, but spends most of his time helping his local pub to survive and growing fruit trees in rural Worcestershire. Twin Worlds and its companion works are his first foray into writing science fiction. Richard is married and has a daughter and grand-daughter.

www.richardarthur.uk

Email: author@richardarthur.uk

Printed in Great Britain
by Amazon

67753404R00183